Praise for Gregory Bastianelli

'A creepy novel which doesn't rely on gratuitous blood and gore but rather world-building to tell. And it's very effective.'
YouTube reviewer @HorrorReads on *October*

'This is a gripping horror story from an author who deserves a wider audience.'
Booklist on *Shadow Flicker*

'It's a dark, disturbing treat.'
Publishers Weekly on *Shadow Flicker*

'From its highly original premise to its deliciously isolated setting, Gregory Bastianelli's *Shadow Flicker* hooked me and kept me squirming until the very last page. An entertaining and emotional read. I had a blast!'
Jonathan Janz

'This book grabbed me from the start! It had a creepy atmosphere that fit the storyline very well. Must read!'
Naomi Downing on *Shadow Flicker*

'Readers will be riveted by this genuinely scary holiday phantasmagoria.'
Publishers Weekly on *Snowball*

'Thank you, Mr. Bastianelli, for one heck of a sleigh ride.'
New York Journal of Books on *Snowball*

'If you want Halloween-infused Christmas terror tale … Bastianelli has got you covered … with several feet of blood-soaked snow.'

Rue Morgue on *Snowball*

'Bastianelli serves up the perfect holiday monster for every reader.'

The Nerd Daily on *Snowball*

'Gregory Bastianelli's debut is the perfect read for the depths of winter. With one foot in crime and the other in horror, Bastianelli has crafted an irresistibly schlocky thriller.'

CrimeReads on *Snowball*

GREGORY BASTIANELLI

OCTOBER

This is a **FLAME TREE PRESS** book

FLAME TREE PRESS
6 Melbray Mews, London, SW6 3NS, UK
flametreepress.com

US sales, distribution and warehouse:
Simon & Schuster
simonandschuster.biz

UK distribution and warehouse:
Hachette UK Distribution
hukdcustomerservice@hachette.co.uk

Publisher's Note: This is a work of fiction. Names, characters, places, and incidents are a product of the author's imagination. Locales and public names are sometimes used for atmospheric purposes. Any resemblance to actual people, living or dead, or to businesses, companies, events, institutions, or locales is completely coincidental.

Thanks to the Flame Tree Press team.

The cover is created by Flame Tree Studio with elements courtesy of Shutterstock.com and: Artazum, LedyX, Tuomas Aho, Thanakrit Moonkum. The font families used are Avenir and Bembo.

Flame Tree Press is an imprint of Flame Tree Publishing Ltd
flametreepublishing.com

A copy of the CIP data for this book is available from the British Library and the Library of Congress.

PB ISBN: 978-1-78758-923-0
HB ISBN: 978-1-78758-924-7
ebook ISBN: 978-1-78758-925-4

Printed and bound in Great Britain by Clays Ltd, Elcograf S.p.A.

GREGORY BASTIANELLI

OCTOBER

FLAME TREE PRESS
London & New York

To my daughter, Jenna, for all those Halloween nights

OCTOBER 1

1

The train halted atop the hill above Maplewood. It was unusual for it to stop at this small town in central New Hampshire. But it did early in the morning on the first day of October in 1970 with a shrill blow of its whistle.

A fragment of the moon, like a broken piece of communion wafer, hung low in the sky between cotton candy shreds of clouds just above the treetops on the northern horizon. To the east, the sun made its first appearance to start the new day.

A lone passenger stepped off the train onto an old rickety wooden platform. He was dressed in black with a cloak around his shoulders; a top hat rested at a crooked angle on his head. An old man with a wrinkled face and eyes sunk deep into their sockets. Lonely eyes.

In one gnarled hand, twisted by the years as if Father Time had tried to wring them dry, he held a dark leather valise. He set it down on the platform and surveyed the town. Behind him, the train hissed as it began to pull away with the loud cranking of its steel wheels. Soon it built up speed and a gust of rushing wind blew against the old man, causing the tails of his cloak to flap around the backs of his legs. He raised a hand to his hat to keep it in place until the train passed and the wind fell away.

To his right lay a stone foundation of what had once been a ticket station back in the days when the train made regular stops in the little village. Grass had now overgrown much of the cement walls, which were chipped and chiseled like neglected teeth. Downhill from the platform lay the village center, its main street running north, parallel to the railroad tracks, till it reached the Town Green. There the road split east and west running along the front of the park. To the west, the road ran underneath the railroad trestle and toward a development of poorly kept houses and tenement rows on the other side of the tracks. The road to the east led over a wooden covered bridge, crossing a lazy river along the back side of the Town Green, and disappeared into rolling pastures of farmland.

I'm back, the old man thought.

Below in the town, he spotted the country store. He pulled the cloak tighter around him to fight off the morning chill. A tear appeared from one eye. Maybe because of the cold air, but he doubted that. Something else made that tear fall, something he had left behind when he was last here. He couldn't believe it had been this long. *Where has the time gone? If only I could wave my magic wand and bring it all back.*

He reached down with a slight twinge in his spine and grasped the handle of his valise, almost afraid he wouldn't be able to straighten back up, and lifted the bag off the platform. The wind picked up a bit and he could sense something in the fall air more than the smell of dying leaves. Dramatic things were going to happen in the coming days, he thought. A little magic was in the air. He could feel it all around. With determined steps, he descended the wooden staircase built into the side of the small hill that led to the village center below.

By the time he got to the bottom of the stairs, he felt nearly out of breath. He stopped and gathered in enough air to prime his lungs, and then continued to Main Street. Lights were on in the country store. A great porch fronted the business with a cast-iron bench resting between two large windows and the front door. A chalkboard hung on the wall between the two windows and written in dusty white chalk were the specials of the day.

He ascended the four small steps to the porch and opened the door, a creak emanating from its tired hinges. Assorted smells assaulted him as he stepped through the doorway: cheese, pickles, maple syrup, and the sugary scent of candy.

He remembered buying penny candy in here a long time ago.

A quick glance around spied the object of his quest: a pile of newspapers on a shelf built into the front counter. He glanced down, passing over the Boston papers till he found the local one. He pulled out of his front pocket a small change purse and pried it open, sticking two long trembling fingers inside and extracting a couple of coins.

He set the money on the counter, smiling faintly at the man by the register, but making no attempt to engage in conversation, and picked up the newspaper. He tucked it under his arm and headed out to the porch. There he sat on the bench with his bag on the floor at his side and the newspaper on his lap.

He gazed out at the businesses along Main Street: a pharmacy, flower shop, hardware store, barber shop, bakery, bank, cinema. He smiled. The sadness marking his earlier arrival remained absent for the moment. This would be a nice town to stay in forever. It would be a nice town to live in. And a nice town to die in.

He opened the newspaper on his lap and turned to the apartment rental section of the classifieds.

2

Twelve-year-old Eddie Scruggs heard the train that morning, like he did every morning, and hated it. It wasn't the sound of the train waking him that caused his distaste. In fact, he liked the sound of the train chugging along, its horn blaring like the foghorn of a lighthouse. It was the feel of the train that he hated. The rumbling vibrations that shook the apartment house, rattling his bed and making him aware of where he lived.

As soon as his eyes opened each morning, the train reminded him that he did not live on some quaint country lot, or in one of the picturesque suburban developments near town, but instead in the two-bedroom apartment house squished among a row of tenements alongside the railroad tracks on the opposite side of the village center.

'The Box Cars' is what people in town nicknamed the narrow, flat-roofed building that housed low-income families, like hobos living in abandoned freight train cars the building's shape resembled. Eddie listened to the train every morning and felt his bed shake and remembered that his family didn't have a nice house and nice things like other kids and that his father rode a bicycle to his job as a janitor at the junior high school Eddie attended.

As he listened to that train screaming north to some unknown destination, Eddie thought how nice it would be if that train would slow down just enough for him to hop on it so he could ride away from this place to where he could be free and didn't have to be reminded of his life here.

But this morning, something different happened. The train did slow down. In fact, it even came to a stop. *Could that be right?* Eddie rolled over in bed and reached a scrawny arm out to the window shade and pulled it aside. He leaned over and stuck his freckled face to the cold glass of the window.

The train had stopped.

It chugged a little, as if the engine were catching its breath in the cold morning, and sat there. Waiting.

Is it waiting for me? After all this time, has it finally stopped for me? He felt the urge to leap from bed and jump into his clothes, pack a bag, and rush outside. *Wait for me!* he would scream at the train. *I'm coming!*

But he did not move. He could not move. He felt afraid, unsure what to do.

Then the train's horn blew, as if to say, *That was your last chance, Eddie,* and then the engine tugged the freight cars along the rails and pulled away to continue its northerly course to destinations unknown to him. Eddie sank back in bed a bit, knowing he was stuck here. Before turning his eyes away from the window, he noticed something outside.

A man stood below on the old station platform.

A man dressed in black who almost blended in with the shadows.

Eddie watched the man standing there for a while and wondered about him and what he was doing here. The man picked up his suitcase and walked down the staircase toward the town.

Eddie rolled back over onto his bed. *Strange. The freight train doesn't discharge passengers.* He remembered how his parents talked about the days of daily passenger train service to Maplewood when they were younger. Back then they told him you could ride the train south all the way to North Station in Boston, and north to Montreal. But they said the last passenger service ended back in the early 1950s, once motor vehicles became the predominant form of transportation. Now only freight trains rode the lines through town.

So how had this stranger in black managed to hitch a ride on the train and get it to stop to let him off?

It puzzled Eddie and now he couldn't wait to get up and start asking questions.

3

A classmate of Eddie Scruggs also lay awake that early morning. Ryan Woodson lay in the bottom bunk of his bedroom in a two-story house on Oak Street in a neighborhood on the other side of town. He had a habit of waking early and staring up at the bottom of the bed above that belonged to his twin brother, Curtis. Ryan listened, hoping to hear some movement from above, hoping Curtis's head would pop out over the edge of the bed, his blond hair hanging down, a big grin on his face. Then he would hop down from above, itching to get the day going.

Ryan listened and waited.

The only thing he heard was a scuffling of feet in the hallway that he knew meant his father was getting up to go to work. The light from the hall spilled under his door and Ryan heard the doorknob turn.

He closed his eyes and could feel the light spread over his face as the door opened. He sensed his father leaning in the doorway to look at him. Then the light dimmed and he opened his eyes to see that the door was closed.

Ryan continued staring at the bottom of the top bunk.

Curtis was born ten minutes before Ryan, and always reminded him of that fact. Because he was older, Curtis got first choice. That's why he got to sleep in the top bunk. When their parents let them get a dog three years ago, Curtis got to pick out what kind. He even got to name the German shepherd: Smokey.

The door opened again and his mother entered, pulling her pink bathrobe tight around her before she sat on the edge of his bed and looked down at him.

"Time to get up for school," she said in a soft voice.

Ryan rolled over on his side away from her and toward the wall.

"And it's time to feed Smokey," she added.

He rolled back quickly, meeting her face.

"He's not my dog. I shouldn't have to feed him." How dare she ask him, he thought. She knew how he felt about it. Smokey was Curtis's dog.

"We've been over this again and again," she said with a pouty frown.

"We should just get rid of the stupid dog." He rolled back toward the wall.

He felt her weight lift from the mattress.

"You can't just ignore the dog."

Ryan rolled over onto his back after hearing her leave the room and continued staring up at Curtis's bunk, listening for movement.

There was none.

4

Ryan Woodson walked up Walnut Street with his friend Lance Stanton toward the bus stop at the intersection with Elm. Barely a month into the new school year and he already missed being able to walk to elementary school instead of riding the bus to the junior high across the river that divided the town center from the rural areas north of the village.

At that thought, a maroon El Camino drove by and Ryan spotted his older brother, Dane, a sophomore in high school, in the bed of the vehicle with his friend Ben Karney. Dane flipped him the bird and laughed as the car passed. It pissed Ryan off that Dane felt he was so cool now that he had a friend with wheels. It made Ryan hate taking the bus even more.

"Are we still going to try and go to the movie?" Lance asked as they were approaching the bus stop and the group of about a dozen boys and girls already waiting there.

"But it's rated R," Ryan said. "They won't let us in."

"It's *The Vampire Lovers*. I hear there's naked women in it."

"Even more reason they won't let us in."

"I told you I've got it all figured out. Don't you want to see naked vampires?"

"Of course. Who wouldn't?" *Did he?* He'd seen naked pictures of women in some of the issues of *Playboy* magazine that Lance squirreled away from his father's collection. But to see them moving and talking on the big screen? It intimidated him a bit.

"Or would you rather just see Barnabas Collins naked?" Lance erupted in laughter.

"Funny," Ryan said and socked him in the arm.

"I'm telling you, this is going to be so much better than your show."

"Hey!" Ryan exclaimed. "*Dark Shadows* is the greatest show on television."

"It's a friggin' soap opera."

"You show me a soap opera with vampires, werewolves, witches, zombies and ghosts," Ryan said in defense.

They arrived at the bus stop and joined their friends Russell Mallek and Wesley Roark.

"But *The Vampire Lovers* is Hammer horror! And what does that mean?" He looked at the others.

"Blood and boobs!" Russell and Wesley cried out in unison.

"That's right," Lance said and turned to Ryan. "This is a grown-up vampire movie. With naked boobs. We're going to be teenagers soon. Time for us to grow up."

"I want to see it," Ryan said. "I just don't think we will be able to get in."

"You leave that to—" Lance stopped, distracted by something across the street.

A figure strode down Walnut Street and turned onto Elm, on the opposite corner from where the kids stood waiting for the bus. An old man dressed in black, with a top hat perched on his head and carrying a dark suitcase. All four boys watched the stranger walk down Elm away from them.

"Who the hell is that?" Ryan asked.

The boys watched in silence.

"It's Barnabas Collins," Lance finally shouted with a big grin. "He's on his way to the Old House at Collinwood." He laughed. "I bet he's got the head of Maggie Evans in his bag and he's going to suck out the remains of her brains for a snack later."

The old man stopped in his tracks and turned to look back at them.

The glare from his dark eyes sunken in that wrinkled, aged face silenced the laughter from Lance's throat.

He heard him, Ryan thought. Though the man was old and Lance hadn't spoken that loudly, the man in black heard him.

He sees us.

It seemed as if the old man's eyes were taking them in, drinking their images into his sockets to remember them. Ryan's heart thudded in his chest as he held his breath. Or maybe those eyes stole his breath.

The stranger's face remained rigid as granite. He turned and continued walking down the street.

5

In the third-floor bedroom of a nineteenth-century home on Elm Street, Harold Bertram Lothrop sat in a chair having a cup of tea and reading a Zane Grey western. The boardinghouse was normally quiet this time of the morning, and often he'd take his tea downstairs in the parlor, but today he didn't feel like socializing with the other guests.

Most of them were old, like himself, and you would think a group of people who had lived as many years as they all had would have more interesting things to say. But that wasn't the case. It was a shame, since Harold never ventured outside, not even to the porch on a hot summer day to sip lemonade with the others. Conversations in the parlor were the most human contact he had these days.

Of course, that was by choice. Things he experienced 'out there' in the real world had opened his eyes to a reality others wouldn't be able to comprehend.

So, Harold stayed in his room often and entertained no visitors except for the occasional times the two young boys in town stopped by to see him. As much as Harold disdained company, he enjoyed the companionship of his adolescent neighbors, even though Ryan Woodson would want him to talk about his days as a pulp horror writer with hopes of imparting some wisdom on his young creative mind. The boy hungered to be a writer of the macabre and wanted to pick his brain or share his own ghastly tales.

Harold saw a lot of himself in that young boy: the curiosity, the determination, the exploration of imagination. He could teach the boy a lot, but he would rather warn him.

Because Harold was aware of things 'out there' and that's why he ended up secluding himself at the boardinghouse.

Voices worked their way up through the ductwork of the heating system and spilled out the vents in the metal grate on the floor of his room. A new voice that caused Harold to put down his book and listen.

Only bits and pieces of chopped conversation disseminated up from below and by the time they reached the third floor, it became a jangled mess of syllables. One voice he recognized: Wilfred Downey, who ran the boardinghouse with his wife, Ruth. A nice old couple, late seventies like himself.

Harold himself had never married, though he had been engaged once to a beautiful woman who didn't mind the dark and disturbing things he wrote and, occasionally, sold to the lurid pulp magazines back in the thirties and forties. And he imagined that if he had married that woman, she would have made him very happy.

But on that fateful night many years ago that brought him here, Harold made a sacrifice, and whether it was the right thing to do or not, it changed the course of both their histories. He always wondered whatever happened to her.

Footsteps on the back stairs from the kitchen brought Harold back to the commotion below. A new arrival, it sounded like. Well, there was only one room left in the house, the one down the hall from his on the third floor that looked out onto the street. As the sound of Wilfred and the new guest, a male he could tell by the voice, reached the second-floor hallway, their steps continued to the stairs that led to the third floor.

Harold set his tea down, and got up from his chair. He tried to walk lightly toward the door but the ancient floorboards creaked with every step of his light, thin frame. He brought his right eye to the peephole and peered out.

Wilfred's voice got louder as the two men approached down the hall. Harold could hear the proprietor explaining the house rules to the new guest, the same lines he heard more than forty years ago when he arrived at the fairly young age of thirty-six. Hard to believe he only stepped outside once in all that time, and it was enough to make him regret it.

When the two men came into view of the peephole, Harold got his first glimpse at the new guest. An elderly man, maybe just a few years younger than himself. He was dressed in black, with a cloak around his shoulders and a top hat on his head.

Harold watched as the old man passed by his door and then come to a sudden stop. The man's head turned slightly and Harold saw him glaring at the peephole.

Harold pulled away. *He sees me.*

It's not possible, he thought. Of course not. But somehow the old man in black knew Harold was watching him through the peephole. A chill scurried its way through his body. He tried to stand still, but his legs felt wobbly and his hands trembled. He took a step away from the door and a floorboard cried out with an aching groan.

Something else occurred to Harold. When the old man turned toward his door and directed his cold dark eyes toward the peephole, Harold realized something.

He'd seen this man before.

6

At lunchtime at the junior high, Ryan and his friends sat at a picnic table outside the school. As Ryan finished his fluffernutter sandwich, he looked over at the tetherball poles where several eighth-graders were deep into a series of tense games. Quite a few girls watched the activity with admiration.

One of the boys playing was Kirby Tressler. Among the gang of girls watching was Becky Williams, a seventh-grader. She belonged to the only Black family in town and her father was the junior high gym teacher. Ryan thought Becky was one of the prettiest girls in school, and liked the smooth look of her cocoa-colored skin and the long, thick braid of hair that reached almost down to the curve of her rump. In elementary school, he hadn't paid much attention to her, but now he noticed how her breasts had suddenly developed and her once lanky frame had taken on rounder shapes.

"Don't let your eyeballs fall out," Lance said and jostled him in the ribs with an elbow.

"Cut it out," Ryan said and pulled his gaze away from Becky. His face reddened.

"You can see a lot more than that if we go to the movies tomorrow," Lance said.

Russell perked up.

"*The Vampire Lovers*!" he said, almost shouting.

"That's right," Lance said. "You can see all the bosoms you've ever wanted."

Ryan kept quiet while Russell and Wesley laughed.

"We're going, right?" Lance asked.

Ryan looked at him. "You really think we can get in?"

"I told you. My brother is going to meet us there and tell them it's okay for us. He's seventeen. He's practically an adult. They'll have to let us in."

"But is he going to go in with us?"

"No, stupid. He wouldn't be caught dead with us. He's just going to meet us at the ticket booth."

"Why would he even do that?" Ryan asked.

"I'm paying him, that's why. You don't think he'd do that out of the goodness of his heart, do you?"

Sitting on the hot-top, not too far from the picnic tables, Ryan noticed Eddie Scruggs and Wayne Barnes, often referred to as Eddie Spaghetti and Booger Barnes, the latter on account of him being caught picking his nose in class back in elementary school and things like that tend to stick with you.

Eddie threw some sticks onto the ground and he and Wayne seemed mesmerized. Eddie muttered something, but Ryan couldn't hear. When he realized what they were doing, he left the picnic table and approached to get a closer look.

"What are you doing?" Ryan asked Eddie, as Wayne sat with his large legs crossed and head hung down with closed eyes.

"Sssh," whispered Eddie. "Don't interrupt."

Ryan glanced at the black sticks with white markings in the middle. He wanted to laugh.

"You've got to be kidding," Ryan said. "You made your own I Ching wands from *Dark Shadows*?"

Eddie looked up, his freckled face scrunched up in the glare of the sun.

"Yes," he said. "I'm sending Wayne's mind through the door, just like they did to Barnabas."

Lance joined Ryan's side in time to hear this last bit.

"Oh, come on!" Lance said. "That's not real, you morons. It's a stupid TV show."

"It's not stupid!" Eddie yelled, spittle flying from his mouth.

Ryan turned to Lance. "It isn't stupid, even if they are."

"I've got Wayne in a trance," Eddie said. "So get lost before you ruin it." He concentrated on the big kid seated before him. "What do you see, Wayne?"

Wayne lifted his head, eyes still closed.

"I see black smoke," he said, his voice deep. "Everywhere."

"Oh my god," Lance said with a laugh. He turned to Ryan. "See, is this how you want to end up? Like these losers? We're in junior high now. We've got to better ourselves."

"Shut up!" Eddie said. "You'll break the trance."

"Don't tell me to shut up, dip wad." Lance stepped forward and kicked the sticks, sending them scattered across the hot-top.

"What did you do?" Eddie screamed.

Wayne's eyes opened.

"What happened?" the big kid asked, a dopey look on his face.

Eddie stood up and began gathering the sticks. He turned toward Lance, tears almost in his eyes.

"You screwed everything up! Just leave us alone."

"You're the one screwed up, asshole," Lance said. "Scram before I knock your buck teeth out."

Despite the threat and his small, scrawny frame, Eddie stood his ground.

"We were trying to find out about the man in black," Eddie said.

Ryan stepped forward.

"Wait, are you talking about that old guy in the top hat? Did you see him this morning?"

"You betcha," Eddie said. "He got off the train this morning before sunrise. I saw him."

"The train?"

"People don't get off the train, fart face," Lance said.

"That's the thing!" Eddie screamed. "The train stopped to let him off. A friggin' freight train."

"Weird," Ryan muttered.

"Right!" Eddie said. "And we were using the I Ching wands to find out who he is and what he's doing here, till you guys ruined it."

The recess bell rang and Eddie and Wayne stormed off.

"Losers," Lance said. "Next thing you know, they'll say they found the hidden Staircase into Time at Collinwood Manor."

"It's a fun show," Ryan said. "It's got lots of neat stuff in it."

"They can have it," Lance said. "We've got better things to do if we want to impress *them*." He pointed to the girls heading toward the school doors.

Ryan watched Becky Williams, and the way her skirt moved when she walked. But now he couldn't stop thinking about the mysterious man in black.

7

In a house of embers, on the edge of darkness and dusted in ash, a boy made his way along the shadowed corridors, always afraid a heavy step might bring the crumbling structure crashing down like a stack of cards. No light entered through gaping holes that once were windows. Nothing but blackness swirled outside.

It was always dark. As long as the boy had been in this decadent place, it'd been dark. No. Not dark. Black. As black as a sky devoid of stars. The house rested on no ground that the boy could see. It floated in the darkness like a dead ship traveling through space with its ghastly crew.

For the others were indeed abhorrent, and that's what he wanted to speak to the master about. It took a lot of courage to approach the tall, thin, angular man with hair as black as coal and eyes to match. When the boy went up the steps, one at a time to make sure they'd hold him, he saw Mr. Shreckengast looking out a ragged hole in a wall.

"Yes," the master said, lingering on the 's' like a snake's tongue. "What is it now?"

The boy stopped, his heart cold in the icebox of his chest. Shreckengast heard him approach but still stared outside, knowing who it was as if he had eyes in the back of his head.

"The others," the boy said.

"The Scamps? What about them?" Shreckengast cocked his head, as if examining something in the darkness.

"Why don't they like me?"

The master turned to face the boy. The pale flesh beneath his dark eyes gripped tight to his skull beneath, the long chin and nose pointed toward the boy.

"Come closer," Shreckengast said.

The boy felt afraid. He always did in the presence of the master. But he knew to obey and took slow steps forward till he reached the man, who towered above him. Shreckengast reached down and placed his palm on the boy's chest.

"What do you feel there?" he asked.

The boy tuned in to all the senses of his body. The blood pulsing through his vessels, the stomach churning in knots, the brain throbbing in his skull. But one stood out more than all.

"My heart beating," the boy said, looking up at Shreckengast with wariness.

The cold hand retreated from his chest and hung limp by the master's side.

"That's right," the man said. "They hate you because your heart beats, unlike their own."

The boy swallowed hard. Even that sounded loud inside his body.

"That's not my fault," the boy said. "I didn't ask to be here."

"No, you didn't." Shreckengast turned to look back out into the blackness. "But nevertheless, here you are."

"But for how long? It seems like it's been for—" *How long had he been here?* No trace of time existed in this place, like the way things feel in a dream. But he knew this wasn't a dream, even though it felt more like a nightmare. And he couldn't remember how he'd got here.

"Till we find a light that will lead us out," Shreckengast said.

"Out where?" the boy asked.

"Out of the darkness."

OCTOBER 2

1

At the Downeys' boardinghouse on Elm Street, Harold Lothrop sat down to breakfast in the dining room, curious to meet the new guest, as were the others at the table. The man in black was the last to come down and took the only empty seat left, parsing out a meager nod to the rest while Wilfred and Ruth Downey clattered in the kitchen as they prepared the morning's offerings.

When the man in black sat down, all eyes fell upon him and he lowered his head as if not wanting to initiate contact. The Stich sisters, who shared the Brown Room on the second floor, were the first to greet the stranger, well Noreen actually, as she often spoke out over her younger sister.

"Welcome to the Downey House," Noreen said, a smile putting creases in her chipmunk cheeks.

"I was just going to say that," piped in Pearl, who at seventy-three was not only two years younger than Noreen, but at under five feet tall, looked one-fourth the size of her taller, heavier sibling.

"Thank you," the old man mumbled with a nod, not looking too enthusiastic about engaging in conversation.

Harold studied him, especially the lines on his face, trying to determine the man's age. Early seventies, he surmised, several years younger than himself. As he examined the creases on the man's face and his hollow eyes, he attempted to visually de-age the man, stripping years off his face to try and figure out why he seemed familiar.

I know this face. I've seen him before.

The guest seated to the man in black's right extended a hand. "I'm Calvin Armstrong," he said with exuberance. "Glad to have you aboard." He laughed.

The man in black looked down at the hand and, with hesitance, offered his own, seeming wary of the grip that followed.

"Let me introduce you to our gang." Calvin gestured around the table.

"The lovely Stich sisters, Pearl and Noreen."

"Noreen and Pearl," the elder Stich corrected, as if to clarify the correct birth order.

"And across from them are Mr. and Mrs. Fifer, Darrin and Lydia." The youngest of the guests at sixty-eight.

"And that old curmudgeon at the opposite end of the table is Harold Lothrop, our senior resident."

Resident? More like prisoner. Harold had arrived at the boardinghouse more than forty years ago, when the Downeys were a middle-aged couple and first started receiving tenants. He came here to escape, and felt trapped all these years through no fault of his own. Things out there had driven him here. An imagination run amok, perhaps, which brought him to the brink of madness, but not quite over the edge. As long as he had this place, he felt safe, protected.

But something about this new arrival tweaked his senses and he felt he needed to keep his guard up. The old man's eyes looked like something had driven him here to this out-of-way place. Why had he come? And where had he come from? Harold needed to know.

"Mr. Lothrop is your neighbor on the third floor," Calvin continued. "The rest of us occupy the rooms on the second floor, including the Downeys."

The man in black's eyes lifted, and cast a weary gaze down the length of the dining table to Harold at the other end. *Was there recognition in them as well?*

"I didn't catch your name," Harold said, not letting those eyes divert from his grasp.

The man in black cleared his throat.

"Rigby," he uttered. "Mortimer Rigby."

Harold's eyes widened for the tiniest of moments, then narrowed.

I know that name.

Through all these years of loneliness and isolation, imbued in a haze of spirits to keep the things that frightened him away, there are some events he never forgot. His mind rifled through the years of memories, filtering them through the past ten, twenty, thirty years. The face of the man across from him aged backward, the wispy hair growing out and darkening, the rigid skin softening and smoothing, the creases disappearing.

Yes, Harold thought. *I've seen this man before.*

The magician.

2

Mortimer Rigby walked down Elm Street after breakfast, determination in his long strides, maybe even a bit of excitement as well in those steps and – dare he say it – apprehension. He held on to the brim of his top hat to keep it from blowing off in the blustery autumn breeze, which flapped his cape behind him like bat wings and stirred up orange and red leaves around his ankles as if his feet were on fire.

How long had it been? Forty years. Time melted away. He had become an old man. And what about—? No. He shivered at that thought.

Worse yet, he did not want to entertain the possibility she might not live at the house anymore. That would be disastrous. After all this time and all this planning. The search that took decades and brought him around the globe. If he came back here only to find she had moved away or died and no longer possessed his special item.

But she promised. They had made a deal and he hoped she kept her end of the bargain. It concerned him though that she hadn't answered any of his letters for a very long time, decades it had to be. Mortimer never realized it would take him this long to find the answers. His quest seemed hopeless at times as he scoured the ends of the earth for the solution. Now that he had it, he needed Rita Stone to have kept her word and return his possession.

If she still lived in the house on Washington Street. If she still lived, period.

When Mortimer reached the end of Elm, he turned left. He might not remember the house, but the number was emblazed in his memory and had been for the last forty years. He scanned the homes as he walked down the sidewalk, some brightly painted in stark colors brought out by the glow of the morning sun that cast its rays down over the maple and oak trees to shine a spotlight on the stately homes. Others seemed neglected, paint dulled and withered, cracking and peeling. Looking as old as he.

Then he stopped. Number 68. White with black shutters.

This was it.

His heart felt like ice in his chest, as if he'd sucked in a great gulp of the fall air.

How long? He had become an old man in the process. She must be in her sixties by now. Where had the time gone? Would she even remember him?

That Lothrop fellow at the boardinghouse remembered him. Oh, the old guy didn't say anything, but Mortimer could see it in his eyes when he announced his name to the breakfast table. The man's eyes lit up after a few seconds as he remembered something. Mortimer had no recollection of the man, though the name had a vague familiarity to it. He hoped Harold Lothrop would not be a problem.

Mortimer preferred no one know him, no one remember him. Not with his task finally at hand. He had come too far and too long after too many years. But he needed Rita Stone to remember him and to have kept her promise. For if all went as planned, there would be someone else who would need to remember him. If it wasn't too late. Mortimer had aged these forty years, but he hoped someone else hadn't. Not after all this time.

He walked up the brick path that led to the front steps. The wind had died down, as if an obstacle to his journey here surrendered. A frosted window in the front door blurred whatever lay on the other side. Mortimer pressed the button of the doorbell and heard a faint chime from inside. He waited, his nerves jittery.

Please be here.

Heavy footsteps sounded. Faint but getting closer. Encouraging, he thought.

A large shape filled the other side of the frosted glass. The doorknob turned and as the door opened with caution, a curious face looked back at him.

"Hello, Rita," he said, waiting for the recognition in her eyes.

The woman in the doorframe had been the largest person he had ever known, her torso ballooned, her arms and legs thick and flabby, her face a round moon. It was as if someone had stuck an air compressor hose down a normal person's throat and blew her up till her skin seemed ready to burst at the seams. She had to top off at more than four hundred pounds and that was being generous. It was the main reason she ended up working as the Fat Lady in the traveling carnival sideshow tent where he first met her.

But even as large as she remained, maybe even bigger than he last saw her forty years ago if that was possible, the biggest parts of her now were her coffee-brown eyes, which studied his face for several seconds before widening beyond comprehension as if ready to pop out of their sockets, and he realized she did remember him.

"Morty!" she cried, though the voice coming from her thick neck managed to sound strangled.

"It's been a long time," he said with a sly smile.

Rita seemed lost for words. The mouth above her triple chins opened and closed without finding words to respond.

"May I come in?" he asked.

Rita backed from the doorway and gestured him inside. Mortimer removed his top hat as she led him into the front parlor. He looked around the room, noticing the built-in bookcases flanking the fireplace held no books, only Hummel figurines. He took a seat in a cushioned wingback chair. He could tell from her expression that she'd rather he not make himself comfortable, but she gave in and took a seat herself on a Queen Anne sofa with legs so thin he found it hard to believe it supported her weight. The wood groaned as she settled into it.

"I'm stunned to see you," Rita said. "After all this time, I never expected you to find your way back here."

"My journey took me much longer than even I expected. There were many detours and complications. And somehow time…." He paused and gripped the brim of his top hat. "Slipped away."

"How'd you know I'd still be here?" She spoke as if angered he found her.

"I hoped," he said. "I wrote often, but you stopped answering my letters."

She snorted through wide nostrils.

"I had better things to do than correspond with you. Besides, your letters were postmarked from all over the world. I never knew where'd you be from one year to the next. I couldn't be expected to airmail letters every time you decided to drop me a note." She lifted her tree-stump legs and rested her feet on a tiny footstool in front of the couch. As she leaned back in a more comfortable position, the couch cried out with a creak. "Besides, I had a husband to take care of."

Mortimer looked around the room for any signs of a man's presence. Maybe a pipe, or a pair of slippers or newspaper. The room held nothing but Rita's Hummel figurines.

"And where is your husband?"

Rita's lips puckered and she shifted in her seat with agitation.

"He is no longer with us."

"I'm sorry," Mortimer said, and he genuinely was. He knew about loss. Knew as much as anyone what it was like to lose the ones you loved most. It was the reason behind his whole purpose here. "Did he pass unexpectedly?"

Rita pulled her eyes away from him and looked off toward the front entryway as if reminded of something forgotten.

"No," she said and turned her face to glare back at him. Her eyes narrowed, the thin brows above them inverting. "He left."

Mortimer nodded. "A shame," he uttered softly. "Sometimes it's truly hard to believe in people you want to trust. Children?"

Her eyes sank. "No. I couldn't give him any children. There were… complications."

He scanned the fine furnishings of the room and his mind tried putting pieces together. "And he gave you the house?"

"He left me everything."

"Odd." Mortimer wondered if her husband ran away willingly, or did she chase him away?

"He wanted me to be happy."

Mortimer met her gaze. "And are you? Happy?"

"I'm comfortable and financially secure. I have a nice home and want for nothing."

"But that didn't answer my question."

She removed her legs from the footstool and struggled to sit upright on the couch. Once she managed a defiant posture, her face grew stern.

"What do you want, Morty?"

His eyes narrowed. "You know what I want."

"You can't be serious." Her face flushed.

"I'm more than serious."

"That was 1930," Rita cried out. "It's been forty years. Do you think I ever thought I'd even hear from you again?"

"Where is it?" Mortimer asked. His nerves tightened.

"I haven't got it."

"What?" he yelled as he stood from the chair, his blood boiling in his veins. He stormed across the room toward the couch. "What have you done with it?"

"Did you really expect me to keep it all this time?"

"We had a deal." His mouth frothed with spittle. "I kept my end of the bargain. I expected you to keep yours."

As large as she was, Rita managed to push herself off the couch in one swift, limber move and stood before him.

"I was a young woman then!" she yelled right back to him. "I kept it for as long as I could. But I grew old and as time went by,

I got rid of the junky trappings of my former life. Including your stupid box."

Mortimer wanted to lash out at her. "Do you realize what you've done?"

"It's too late!"

"I've spent my life searching for the answer to what I did wrong, and I finally solved it after all these years. I need that box!" He tightened a gnarled hand and raised it, as if he would strike her.

Rita stepped forward, her large body intimidating and forcing him backward by its sheer size and the look of agitation on her face.

"Don't you try and threaten me, old man. I'll snap your skinny bones like a twig. Get the hell out of my house!"

She plowed forward and he retreated as she advanced. He thought about reaching into his top hat and retrieving the one thing he knew she feared, but her red face and lips peeled back from angry teeth frightened him and he stumbled backward to the door.

Rita flung it open.

"Get out of here!" she cried. "And never step foot on my property again or you'll regret it."

Sunken, he stepped out the door and down the front steps.

"You shouldn't have come back here," Rita said from the doorway.

Mortimer looked at her with eyes that burned with rage. He placed his top hat back on his head.

"You don't really believe he's still out there somewhere?" Rita asked, her tone condescending.

He shuddered at the implication.

3

Rita Stone watched out her front window as Mortimer Rigby walked down the street away from the house and did not leave her perch till the old man was out of sight. Satisfied, she released the curtain she had pulled back and stepped away, still a bit shocked by the sudden appearance of her long-ago traveling companion and one-time savior.

How dare he, she thought as she maneuvered her ample figure down the hall toward the basement door. After all these years, she never expected the man to show up. Just pop in out of the blue with the nerve to make demands.

A deal. Yeah, they had a deal. But there had to be some kind of statute of limitations on something like that. It had been forty years, for Christ's sakes. He couldn't expect her after all that time to hold on to something he gave her.

Sure, he had saved her. Sort of.

Rita remembered that night back in 1930 like it was yesterday. Her job as part of the sideshow tent was simple. She was the Fat Lady, and that meant she didn't really need to do much. One could say she was born to play the part, had been practicing her whole life for it.

Then she met Gordon Thurlow. The rail-thin man with the balding head and the round, black-rimmed glasses showed up in the front-row seat of her performances every single night that week. It was the fourth night of the carnival when he finally got the gumption to stay after the show and approach her. A shy boy he was. Hell, not a boy. Gordon was at least ten years older than her. A man. He had his own accounting firm in Maplewood, he told her. Loved numbers. He wore a gold-plated dollar sign belt buckle that shined under the big tent spot lights and wasn't lost on her as she sat up there on the stage.

To Rita's surprise, Gordon asked her to stay behind when the carnival left town and marry him, but she knew the carnival master wouldn't let one of his prized attractions leave.

That same night, Mortimer Rigby had his unfortunate incident, and the fates of both became entwined.

The news about the magician spread throughout the camp the next morning and Rita heard Mortimer planned to stay behind when the carnival left. She went to his trailer hoping he could help her escape the carnival. Mortimer hid Rita in his trailer and after the carnival left, Rita wed Gordon Thurlow at the Town Hall the next day and moved into his house on Washington Street. Mortimer stayed and rented a room at the local hotel in town. After a few weeks he came calling for his favor.

"I'm leaving town for a while," he told Rita on the front steps at her new house. "I'm going on a trip to search for some of the answers I'm seeking. But I need you to hold on to something for me until I get back. It's very important that you take good care of it, because I'm going to need it when I find the solution to my problem."

But Rita never expected it would take forty years for Mortimer to return. She assumed he had died or moved on and forgotten about Maplewood and the carnival...and her. She descended the basement steps trying to remember the last time she had been down here. God, it was so long ago. Not since Gordon had been gone. She never was able to provide him with any children. Once he was out of the picture, she moved most of his stuff down into the basement and began furnishing the house to her liking.

The cellar stairs groaned with each step. At the bottom she stopped to catch her breath. Refreshed, she moved through the piles of junk and stacks of boxes toward the back of the dark basement.

In one corner stood the item she'd held on to for the past forty years. But if it was that vital to Mortimer, she certainly wasn't going to part with it just yet. Maybe it was worth more than the dust it had collected all these years. It sure seemed that way to Mortimer, she thought as she stared at the old magician's cabinet.

4

Mortimer returned to the boardinghouse at a pace quicker than that on his way to Rita's house, his bony legs propelled by the heat of the blood pumping through his veins like a kettle ready to boil over. He stormed inside the front entrance with nary a glance at his housemates gathered in the front parlor and went up the stairs with clomping feet to the third floor.

Once in his room, he slammed the door shut and went to the window, his teeth together in a seething clench. He stared out the arched window that looked out the front of the house onto the street below.

That damn woman, he thought. *How dare she!* After what he did for her those many years ago, she repaid him by reneging on the simple favor he had asked of her. The nerve of her to dispose of his cabinet! He raised his arms up, uncurling knotty fingers and thinking how much he wished he could have put them around Rita's neck. If only he thought he'd be able to provide enough force in his arthritic digits to squeeze through the blubbery flesh to crimp her esophagus and drive the life out of her.

Mortimer removed his top hat and reached in, only to glance down and withdraw an empty hand.

Gone, he remembered, thinking of the only thing in the ensuing years that had brought him comfort. Like everything else. Gone, but not forgotten.

His rabbit, Daimon, had passed away many years ago, once time had seemed to run away for both of them. *God*, he thought, *forty years*. All that time spent searching for the answer. He never realized it would take this long. He'd circled the globe in search of a resolution that should have been in front of him the whole time.

He gripped the brim of the hat and sailed it across the room, where it hooked on the back post of the wooden chair at the desk along the side wall and hung there at a cocked angle. How could he really blame Rita? She had no idea he was even still alive. Sometimes he didn't feel alive himself, especially after that three-year stretch in Singapore where he'd slipped into an opium haze of depression and despair.

But that didn't stop his search. No. He allowed nothing to interfere with his quest. He plodded on from the alleys of Venice to a castle in Romania. But it wasn't until that Sherpa guide led him to an old shaman's hut near the Himalayas that he finally found the answer to where he went wrong all those years before.

Mortimer had his black leather-bound notebook, which was stuffed with his notes, contacts, diagrams and words, and he pulled it out of his pocket and removed the rubber band that kept the worn pages together. He had lost his original cabinet and he'd always assumed he needed it to be the same one. But he had no choice now.

He could get a new cabinet, but would the trick have the same effect?

Mortimer had to try. He had come all this way, through a lifetime of distress, depression and to the brink of his own sanity. But he hadn't fallen off the edge and now he had one last chance to redeem himself and make everything right.

He had to try. There was nothing else to lose. He had already lost everything.

Mortimer flipped through the pages of his black book, his eyes crawling over the scrawl written in it till he discovered the phone number for the shop in Boston. He hurried downstairs to the front foyer, where there was a telephone closet in a small alcove beneath the grand staircase.

He ignored the curious glances from the people in the parlor and opened the frosted-glass door beneath the stairs and slipped inside. The room was small and narrow and held a tiny table where a black rotary phone rested near a phone book.

Mortimer sat in the chair before the desk and placed his black book on the table, open to the page he needed. He picked up the receiver and dialed. After several rings, a man answered. Mortimer explained the exact style, size, and dimensions of the magician's cabinet he desired and the address he needed it to be delivered to.

After a few minutes on hold, the man got back to him.

"We can have it delivered on Tuesday, COD," the man said. He stated the price, including the delivery fee.

"You can't get it here any sooner?" Mortimer asked, perturbed but not wanting to sound pleading.

"Tuesday's the best I can do," the man said.

"Fine," Mortimer said before hanging up.

He had waited forty years; what was a few more days?

5

Ryan helped Lance toss newspapers onto front stoops as the two boys made their way down Walnut Street. They worked opposite sides of the street and then met on the corner of Washington and Oak so Ryan could grab some more papers.

"Which side do you want?" Lance asked, once they both reloaded.

"That side," Ryan said, pointing to the south side of Washington.

"Of course," Lance said with a nod.

"What's that mean?"

"You know," Lance prodded. "You want to avoid her."

Ryan didn't mean for it to be so obvious, but he didn't like going near Rita Stone-Thurlow's house.

"She creeps me out."

"Because you think she's a witch?" Lance laughed.

"No," Ryan said. "She's a fruitcake. You know what they say about her husband."

"That he disappeared?"

"That's right."

"Just a rumor," Lance said. "I heard he left her. Can you blame him? She must weigh like a ton or something. Hey, maybe she ate him."

Lance nearly doubled over with laughter and Ryan joined in. It made him feel a little better, but he still didn't want to deliver on her side of the street. He took his papers and crossed the road. A few houses later, he watched as Lance went up the front steps of Rita's house instead of just tossing it on her porch. He looked back at Ryan and made exaggerated faces of fright, eyes bugged out, mouth open wide.

Ryan couldn't help but laugh at his friend. Lance dropped the paper by the door. When the front door opened, Lance nearly jumped a foot in the air. Rita stood there with a scowl on her face, her body filling the frame of the door. Lance picked up the paper, handed it to her, and then ran down the steps.

Ryan finished his end of the street and the two boys headed down Elm, Ryan anxious to get to their final stop at the boardinghouse. They each had one newspaper left when they arrived at their destination and bounded up the steps to the front double doors.

Mr. Downey answered, broom in hand.

"Here's your papers," the boys said in unison. The boardinghouse always received two copies, one for the Downeys and one to be placed in the parlor for the tenants.

"Is he in his room?" Ryan asked, knowing full well Mr. Downey knew who he meant.

"Where else?" the landlord said.

The two boys bounded up the stairs all the way to the third floor. At the top level, they paused when they heard the door to the front bedroom creak as it opened just a crack.

One eyeball sunk into an old craggy face peeked out at them.

Ryan's heart jumped into his throat and his insides felt like an ice cube had slipped down his spine. He gawped at Lance with open mouth and then the two of them hurried to Mr. Lothrop's room and knocked on his door.

Back down at the end of the hall, a door closed.

"Come in," came the voice of Mr. Lothrop.

The boys hustled inside and shut the door behind them, pressing against it as if they expected something to barge in.

"Did you see him?" Ryan asked Lance. He wanted to be sure he hadn't imagined it.

"Yes," Lance confirmed. "The weird old guy from the bus stop." He spoke in a whisper, afraid to be heard.

"Boys," Mr. Lothrop said as he looked at his visitors from his seat in front of the window, "what's all the fuss?"

"You have a new neighbor," Ryan said as they removed their hands from the door and approached the old man.

"Oh yes," Lothrop said. "Moved in yesterday. I had grown accustomed to having this third floor to myself after Mr. Smith died this summer. Now I'll have to get used to sharing the bathroom again."

"Where'd he come from?" Ryan asked.

Lance leaned over and whispered, "Another time period."

Mr. Lothrop didn't hear and shrugged. "I don't know. He just showed up."

"Like magic," Lance said and winked at Ryan.

The old man's face shifted. "What makes you say that?"

Ryan and Lance took seats on the edge of Mr. Lothrop's bed.

"I heard he came on the freight train," Ryan said, as he unslung his backpack from around his shoulders and set it on the bed beside him.

"That the freight train stopped and let him off. Eddie Scruggs said it must have been magic."

"Scruggs is a moron," Lance said.

"How else could he have gotten the train to stop for him?" He looked at Mr. Lothrop. "Do you think magic could work like that?"

Mr. Lothrop diverted his eyes from the boys and gazed out the window as if lost in a thought...or a memory.

"There are different kinds of magic in this world," he said.

Ryan stared at Lance, an uneasy feeling in his stomach. He wanted to change the subject and thought of the reason for coming here. He unzipped his backpack and pulled out the notebook.

"I have a new story I wrote," Ryan said as he flipped open the cover and rifled through several pages. "It's called 'The Jack-o'-lantern Man'." When he got to the spot in the notebook, he handed it over and Mr. Lothrop took it with reluctance. "It's about an evil man who removes his face to reveal a jack-o'-lantern beneath his skin. He goes around eating people." Ryan modeled the villain after his gym teacher, Mr. Williams, who was a hard-ass on him in class.

Lothrop glanced at a few pages and then tossed the notebook back to Ryan.

"Silly," the old man said.

Ryan caught the book and looked down at the pages he had spent all that time working on. "You didn't even read the whole thing," Ryan said when he looked up.

"Horror stories are silly," Lothrop said. "A waste of time. Why don't you write something serious instead? Something real." He leaned forward. "You've got talent, my boy. I can see that. Now all you need is practice."

"But—"

"Forget all this rubbish about spooks and creatures and all that garbage." He leaned back in his chair.

"But you wrote that kind of stuff," Ryan said. "You wrote for all the big pulp magazines. "*Weird Tales*, *Macabre*, and all the others." His mind became jumbled, his feelings skewered. It stung.

"Do you realize how long ago that was?"

Ryan sensed Mr. Lothrop was getting angry. He had never seen the man like this. He had always been friendly and appreciated the boys' visits.

"When was the last time anything of mine's been in print?" He stared deep into Ryan's eyes, as if he could see into his soul. "I haven't published anything for more than forty years."

Ryan didn't know how to respond.

Lothrop pointed at the typewriter sitting on the desk against the wall opposite the bed.

"See all the dust on that?" he asked. "I haven't touched it since I got here. And that was in 1928."

Lance broke an awkward silence.

"Why was that?" he asked and Ryan cringed at the question, afraid to hear the answer and only wanting to get out of the room.

Lothrop looked out the window, as if trying to ignore the question.

Ryan followed his gaze and, noticing the streetlights had come on, breathed a sigh of relief.

"We've got to go," Ryan said as he nudged Lance's arm. "My mom will be expecting me home for dinner." He shoved the notebook into the backpack. The two boys stood up and said goodbye, but Lothrop only continued to gaze out the window. They went to the door and the old man spoke again.

"There is real magic," he said, not looking at them. "Out there." He nodded out the window. "And things worse than magic. Much worse." Now he turned and looked at the boys.

Ryan flinched at the grimace on the old man's face.

"I've seen horror. And it's why I haven't left this house in over forty years."

6

In the House of Embers, the boy looked around at the other children, the Scamps. Horrible they were. Grotesque. Faces full of scorched flesh, blisters crawling along the skin, eyes boiled in their sockets. One older boy didn't even have eyes, just two black pits. These weren't children, the boy thought. Not like him. No. Not like him.

Mr. Shreckengast entered the room. The boy didn't know the master like the Scamps did. They had more intimate knowledge of Shreckengast and the boy felt jealous.

But the master treated him as special.

"You have a purpose," Shreckengast told him many times. "You were sent here to help us. You were sent here to lead us out of the darkness. The time will come."

But when, the boy thought. When would the calling come?

"When the time is right," Shreckengast said. "And we must be prepared."

In the center of the room, the master surveyed the inhabitants.

"Grasp hands," he said with a sly smile. "A circle of hands that must remain unbroken."

The Scamps glanced at each other and then blackened hands reached out and clasped.

The boy looked around. No one reached out to him. Shreckengast stood next to him and looked down, still displaying that captive smile. The long bony fingers of his right hand reached down. The boy looked at it and took it in his own, feeling the cold as if the bones of the fingers were made of icicles.

"When the time comes," Shreckengast said, "we must all hold tight." His dark eyes surveyed the room. "We may only get one chance, and we must take advantage of it. There might not be another opportunity."

Once the chain was made, the master's smile grew even greater. He looked down upon the boy and then his gaze flowed across the disturbed faces of the Scamps.

"He is important," Shreckengast said, and gestured with his long chin and nose toward the boy. "We must not lose sight of that. He is the key."

OCTOBER 3

1

The Colonial Theater was only about a quarter full, typical for a Saturday afternoon. Lance surveyed the seats and saw the front row empty.

"There," he said and pointed.

Ryan glanced around the vacant seats near the rear of the theater. An uneasy feeling crept inside him. What if someone he knew saw him in here and told his parents? They had no idea he was at an R-rated movie and would be furious.

"Maybe we should sit in the back," he said.

Lance looked at him in disbelief.

"What? We always sit in the front row for horror movies. What the hell's wrong with you?"

"I just don't want anyone to see us."

"Don't be such a wuss," Lance said. "Come on."

He marched down the aisle with a confident strut and Ryan and the others followed. Ryan tried keeping his head down, hoping no one would recognize him. At the front, the four boys took the middle seats in the first row.

"Front and center for all the action," Lance exclaimed.

"Sssh," Ryan said. "Not so loud."

"Mellow out," Lance said.

Ryan slunk down in his seat. He couldn't wait for the lights to dim and bathe them in cinema darkness. He cranked his head around to glimpse back at the rows of seats behind them and wondered if there was anyone who might recognize him and report to his parents.

The lights dimmed and Ryan turned to get ready for the previews, grateful for the darkness that blanketed the theater and obscured his presence. Russell and Wesley shared a big bucket of popcorn and their crunching was the only sound before the previews blared to life. Ryan beamed while watching the *House of Dark Shadows* preview and couldn't wait for the film to come out at the end of the month.

When the trailers ended and the main attraction started, Ryan sank further into his seat. The movie got off to a good start with a buxom blonde vampire in a white gown getting beheaded by sword. But then the story seemed to drag with a lavish dance ball and people doing a lot of chatter.

Ryan thought Ingrid Pitt was mostly attractive, but seemed older than the other girls in the movie. When the first girl fell victim to Ingrid's vampire, it was nothing spectacular. Not scary or bloody.

About halfway through the movie, the Madeline Smith character walked into Ingrid's room while the woman was in the bathtub. Naked. Ryan's mouth dropped open. Her boobs were big and round and stuck out with such prominence.

His friends around him all fell silent. Ryan watched the actress in the tub, barely hearing the dialogue on the screen. It didn't matter. These were the first naked breasts he'd seen, except for copies of *Playboy*.

But this was different. This naked woman was moving and talking, her breasts shifting and on full display on this giant screen towering over him. She rose from the tub, water cascading along every curve of her glistening flesh.

Ryan squirmed in his seat. His mouth went dry.

The other actress, Madeline Smith, took her top off as she prepared to change clothes. Her breasts were a little smaller, but still amazed Ryan. Ingrid put a towel around her body, but left her breasts exposed as she sat down in front of a vanity to brush her hair. The two women on the screen began laughing and then Ingrid got up and chased Madeline around the room before they both fell giggling on the bed and began to embrace before the scene cut out.

"Wow," Russell said in a hushed whisper.

Ryan's nerves began tingling. Could anyone see him watching this? His hand began to tremble. He turned his head to look but could see nothing but silhouettes of people in the rows behind. *No one knows I'm here*, he told himself. He turned back to the screen, praying no one recognized him.

Later in the movie, Ingrid entered Madeline's bedroom. Madeline was in bed and Ingrid sat beside her and caressed her before removing the woman's top and, once again, Ryan got a close-up view of Madeline's breasts. The two women's lips met as they shared a passionate kiss. And then Ingrid's head moved down lower and Madeline seemed pleased.

Ryan felt himself getting erect beneath his jeans.

Oh god, he thought. *Not here. Not now.* He cast quick glances at his friends on either side of him, but their eyes were glued to the screen. *Are they experiencing the same thing?* He shook his head, not wanting to think about it. He rested his arms across his lap, wishing his erection would go away.

Later in the movie, Madeline showed her governess bite marks on her left breast. Two small puncture wounds, neither of them understanding that it came from a vampire. It never occurred to Ryan that a vampire would bite a woman on the breast. Especially a female vampire.

When the movie ended and the lights came on, Ryan hustled out of the exit to the side of the screen, hoping no one would see him. The others followed quickly out the door which dumped them in the alley beside the theater. The four of them walked to Main Street, Ryan in the lead, hoping to get as much distance as possible from the theater before the main crowd spilled out the front entrance.

"That was awesome!" Russell said.

"I can't believe that vampire bit the woman on the boob," Wesley said.

"You won't see Barnabas Collins doing that," Lance said. "Right, Ryan?"

Ryan stopped and turned, looking back at the others.

"Vampires are supposed to bite you on the neck," he said, his voice agitated.

"What's bugging you?" Lance asked.

Ryan shrugged. "It's just not how it's supposed to be, that's all."

They continued walking.

"No," Lance said. "It was better."

2

The Downeys' boardinghouse had two sitting rooms adjacent to each other. The front parlor had a couch and chairs positioned to face a television set in the corner. An aerial antenna on the roof drew in all three network stations as well as PBS.

The interior parlor room held a fireplace flanked on one side by a built-in bookcase, with a pair of wingback chairs and a cocktail table facing the brickwork. A bistro table and chairs were set by a bay window overlooking the driveway by the side yard of the house. Only the Downeys, the Fifers and Calvin Armstrong had motor vehicles.

A partial wall separated the two sitting rooms with a pair of pocket doors that could be closed if one desired separation from the other parlor. During the week, the Stich sisters occupied the front parlor watching an endless string of soap operas along with Lydia Fifer. But it being a Saturday, Pearl and Noreen Stich had gone into town to see a movie at the cinema, so the room was quiet.

Harold Lothrop sat at the bistro table in the other room, grateful for the serenity as none of the other guests were around. He stared out the window at the majestic maple trees in the side yard, their green leaves showing dabs of red and orange as the season progressed. The branches swayed from a light breeze. Soon they would be bare as the winter season approached, but for now the day was sunny and bright outside, in the mid-sixties.

Not that the weather mattered to Harold. He never went outdoors. The outside was as distant to him as the moon, able to be seen but not walked upon. It wasn't how he preferred it, but he had no control. This house had become his prison, a place of self-exile. A punishment.

The house had everything he needed. The Downeys provided food and shelter. Once a year the doctor made a house call to check on anything that might ail him. Sporadic royalty checks from reprints of ancient stories sold a lifetime ago came in the mail and provided enough income to pay his rent.

Ironic that those tales of the macabre that drove him to this exile continued to provide the income to enable him to live in his fortress. Harold felt bad about his words to young Ryan Woodson yesterday and almost regretted them. But not quite. The boy was heading down the same dark path Harold had followed those many years ago and he only wanted to prevent the young lad from experiencing the same mistakes.

Harold made a living from his stories. But at what cost? Look at him now.

All because he had seen the truth.

As Harold gazed out into the bright sunshine of the brisk autumn landscape, he knew how soon the night would come and what it would bring. He had seen the reality of his writings. And they had cursed him those many years ago.

More than forty years, he thought, since that train brought him here to Maplewood where he thought he might be safe. But looking out the window, he knew he could never be sure.

He'd been living in Salem, Massachusetts, back in 1928, eking out a living selling stories to the pulp magazines while living in a one-room apartment above a bakery on Essex Street. The stories brought him a few dollars every week, enough to pay his rent and buy food, but not much else. He decided to attempt to write a novel, for the main reason that it was the only way he knew to make a bit more money and he had a good reason for it.

Harold was in love.

Violet Sommer was her name, sounding as fresh and sweet as a spring flower. He only met her the year before when she attended one of his readings at the public library. The head librarian wasn't enamored by his story or the crowd it brought in and never invited him back, but one member of the audience made it all worthwhile.

The raven-haired beauty stayed behind after the audience filtered out and she told him how poetic she thought his flowery prose was even though it described the ghastliest events she could ever remember hearing.

Violet was a student just finishing up her final semester at the university. She was studying to be a school teacher. She came from Burlington, Vermont, and planned to return there after graduation. They courted for a couple months before he asked her for her hand in marriage the morning of her graduation. She said yes. But she had to catch the train back to Vermont the next day, so he would have to come there and ask her father's permission.

He would do that, he told Violet. He told her he needed some time to put his affairs in order, but what he really wanted was time to write a novel in order to make enough money to show her father that he wasn't just some worthless scribe, and then he would be on the next train to Vermont to join her. The day she left, he began his first novel. No, it would not be a love story. He only knew how to write one kind of tale.

The Goblins in the Shadows, he titled his manuscript, and inspiration came to him like a ferocious storm of imagination. He modeled his cast of characters after some of his fellow pulp writer friends. As he wrote, it seemed a coincidence that one of the authors fell into the path of a subway train and was killed, when only the day before Harold had typed a scene where the goblins attacked and killed a character based on that man.

Harold chalked it up to one of life's odd quirks of fate and continued with his manuscript.

But it happened again.

How could this be? Harold pondered. Mere coincidences? Is that possible?

It began to frighten him, and he wondered if he should abandon the manuscript. But that would be absurd, he thought. Besides, he needed this if he ever hoped to meet the approval of Violet's father.

Harold ventured on.

When it happened to more characters, Harold wanted to hurl his typewriter out the window.

A trip to the liquor store, a bottle of cheap whiskey and Harold holed up in his apartment trying to purge the nightmares in his brain. *What if I never finish this story?* he thought between shots. *Would the deaths stop too? Am I doomed either way? Don't finish the book and I may never get the lovely hand of Violet Sommer. Finish the book and spend a lifetime haunted by the guilt of what I've done to my friends.*

Goblins aren't real.

Of course they aren't. Can't be. He took another gulp of booze hoping to set his brain on fire. *It's just my imagination. Need to get a grip on it.*

He knew what to do and quickly began packing. A suitcase for his clothes, and the case for his typewriter. He packed the manuscript too. Harold decided he wasn't ready to let go of it yet, but until then he needed to get to Vermont, and Violet.

At the train station he bought his tickets. The train from Salem would stop in Portsmouth, New Hampshire, and from there he would switch trains to one that would cut across New Hampshire on its way to Burlington, Vermont. The train car he boarded was nearly empty, so he found a seat for himself and kept his baggage beside him. He dared not store it overhead. He wanted to keep an eye on the suitcase with his manuscript, afraid to let it out of his sight.

His hands trembled and he fought off the urge to go to the dining car and get a drink. He had already drained the contents from his flask that he kept in his inside coat pocket, but it wasn't enough. *No. Keep your head clear. Think of Violet.*

Night had fallen by the time his train reached Portsmouth. He grabbed his bags and exited. Harold knew he had a little more than a half hour before his next train would arrive, so he set his bags down by a railing and paced back and forth on the platform, never leaving sight of his bags but needing to expel the pent-up energy coursing through his body. He wished the train would hurry.

A misty fog descended on the station with swirls of white vapor curling over the platform. He noticed only a few other people waiting for the next train: an older couple who stood arm in arm near the station house, and a tall, dark figure of a man at the other end of the platform wearing a derby and holding a walking stick.

A quiet night, Harold thought, and once again wished he had some whiskey in his flask.

A skittering noise sounded past the end of the platform, just out of the corner of Harold's eyes. When he looked, nothing was there. Rats, he surmised. They could often be found scurrying along the tracks. He tried to dismiss it, but when he heard another sound, he turned his head sharply and saw an odd shape dart into the bushes beside the track beyond the platform.

Harold knew hobos often hopped the trains to catch a ride, but what he glimpsed was much smaller, almost childlike. Curiosity got the best of him and he wandered down toward the end of the platform, casting periodic glances back toward his baggage, noticing the old couple and the thin man had not moved. Feeling assured his bags were safe, he quickened his pace. When he reached the railing, he glanced out into the bushes and shrubs that lined the edges along the tracks. He heard a rustling and saw the branches of one bush bend.

Red eyes looked out at him.

A startled Harold took a step back. An animal. Maybe a raccoon or skunk. But as he peered closer, he thought he could perceive an odd hooked nose. What kind of animal could that be?

He heard a soft, childlike squeaking noise, maybe something a rat or mouse would make. But the thing he saw seemed too large for that.

The branches parted and a face peered out.

Harold gasped and jumped back. It did not look like an animal's face; in fact, despite its distorted features, it seemed human-like. *What the hell?*

A light appeared in the far distance and he felt the soft tremor of the platform as his train approached. The light seared a path through the darkness and lit up both sides of the track. That's when Harold got a good look at it. No, not *it. Them.*

There were at least three or four, maybe five. They scuttled into the brush at the appearance of the light and disappeared, but Harold could not help catch the texture of the green scaly skin and the tiny clawlike hands and feet as they dashed into the shrubs.

Goblins.

He should have attributed it to the whiskey he downed earlier or the heightened state of his nerves from the traumatic events of the past few days, because he recognized the brief glimpses he had gotten of the little creatures from his exact description of them in his manuscript.

Madness. I've finally driven myself to the brink of insanity.

He turned and hurried back to his baggage as the train pulled into the station. He dared not look down at the end of the platform for fear of seeing the little critters crawling onto the back of the train.

What if they're following me? he thought, as his hands gripped the handles of his cases till his knuckles turned white. His palms sweated as he tapped his toes, waiting for the train to glide to a stop with a screech of its brakes.

When the conductor opened the doors, Harold hurried aboard, threw himself into a seat and plastered his face to the window to look about the platform. *What if they get on board with me?* What would he do then? Would they follow him all the way to Vermont? To Violet?

Harold's heart thudded as he waited for the train to depart, not knowing if he should jump off or stay on. He couldn't move his legs, which felt stiff even though they seemed to tremble. His whole body felt detached, as if he had no control over it.

The conductor outside looked up and down the platform. *Do you see them?* Harold wondered. *Or am only I capable?* The conductor signaled the engineer with a wave of his hand and he climbed aboard and the doors closed.

They're in your head, Harold thought as the train lurched forward and he sank further into the cushion of his seat. They can't have gotten out. But, then, how did the others die? Something got them. At the exact time in his manuscript that he dispatched his characters, something got a hold of his friends and brutally killed them.

All my fault. Harold wanted to scream inside his head. He glanced at his suitcase beside him as the train picked up speed and left Portsmouth behind. He took out his manuscript and began throwing the pages out the window one by one, scattering them all along the railroad tracks where some hobos could use them to feed their fires.

He had poured his life's work into those pages. Everything he cherished was lost.

The conductor came by collecting tickets. Harold handed the man his with a shaky hand.

"Burlington," the conductor said. "You've got a long night ahead of you." He moved on to the man farther down the aisle.

Yes, Harold thought. *A long night. But not if* they *get me first.*

He wanted to sleep, but his eyes wouldn't let him. He peered out the window, half expecting to see a green leathery face and claws groping along the side of the train. Harold picked up his typewriter case and held it in his lap for security. If needed, he could bash their heads in with it. He had seen at least four. But how many couldn't he see? In his manuscript, he never gave a count of the number of goblins who stalked the writers in the story. He had no idea how many there were, only that they were out there looking for him, waiting for him.

More than an hour later, the conductor came down the aisle again.

"Maplewood," he called out, though there was only Harold and the other man in the car. "Next stop is Maplewood."

Harold looked out the window as the train pulled into the village. He saw the lights of the town below a small hill. He stood up and grabbed his suitcase and moved toward the door.

"Excuse me," the conductor said from the other end of the car. "This isn't your stop, mister."

"This is where I get off," Harold said through a tense jaw.

"Your stop is Burlington, Vermont," the conductor said. "This is Maplewood. You have a ways to go yet."

"No," Harold said and looked out the door. "I need to get off here."

"But you paid for a ticket to Burlington."

"I don't care," Harold said. "I'm getting off here."

Harold stepped off that train onto the platform in Maplewood forty-two years ago. He carried his luggage into town and rented a room at the American Hotel downtown. The next morning, he began inquiring about rooms in town and was directed to the Downeys' boardinghouse. He never heard from Violet again. And he never left the house in all those years except for one night when he dared to step out and visit a traveling carnival and watched a man perform magic.

As if on cue, Mortimer Rigby walked into the parlor room, interrupting Harold's reflection of the past. The two men stared at each other.

You, Harold thought. *You were the magician.*

3

I am the key, the boy thought in the House of Embers. *But if that is so, then what is the lock?* What was the master looking for him to do to lead them out of the darkness? He didn't understand.

He looked at a group of the Scamps, much older than he, even though he had no idea how old he was. He wore a locket around his neck, but he didn't know its meaning. A faded picture inside looked like it might be of a woman, but it had deteriorated too much to be discernable. But it must be someone important to him. That's why he kept the locket.

He remembered being a boy among a strange collection of individuals, but not as strange as the inhabitants of this place. Not as horrible.

The teen boys looked at him.

"You're lucky Mr. Shreckengast favors you," one said. "Otherwise, we'd eat you."

"And spit you back out," another said.

"I could tell him what you say," the boy said in hopes it would frighten them, but their expressions still hissed at him like snakes.

"He may protect you now," one teen said. "But it won't last forever. Not once we leave this place."

"And where would we go?" the boy asked, though he felt sure they had no answer.

"Anyplace but here," one of them said. "Someplace where we can be free."

"Free to do what?" the boy asked.

The teen's mouth spread wide and the whiteness of his teeth seemed enhanced by the blackened crispness of his face.

"Anything we want."

OCTOBER 4

1

Smokey followed Ryan down to the river's edge, no matter how much the boy tried to shoo the dog away.

Not my dog, he thought. He belonged to Curtis.

"Leave me alone!" he yelled at the dog, who tilted his head in confusion at the tone directed at him, tongue hanging out as he panted. "Can't you see I'm not him!"

I'm not, Ryan said as he picked up a stick and mustered enough strength to launch it nearly halfway across the river, where it landed with a splash, ripples spreading out in concentric circles as the piece of wood floated.

Sure, you *float*, he thought. Not like his brother.

He turned to look back at the dog and hissed through his teeth.

"Go away. You don't belong to me." He wanted to pick up another stick and throw it at the dog, but he figured the dumb animal would think he was playing games with it and fetch it and bring it back to him. "Stupid dog."

Ryan sat down on the grass by the riverbank and gazed out as the slow current tugged the stick downstream. It seemed to get caught in the branches of the trees reflected in the river, but then the current picked up and swept the stick away.

"Gone," Ryan muttered to himself.

He heard voices and turned to look over his shoulder to see who it was interrupting his solitude. He spied Lance, Russell, and Wesley heading this way.

"Whatcha doing, Ryan?" Lance asked as the boys stopped a few feet from him, as if sensing a barrier he put up around himself.

"Nothing," he said and gazed out at the river. And that was the truth. He was doing nothing.

"Your dog's eating grass," Russell said, and Ryan looked to see the German shepherd tugging at tall blades of grass with its teeth.

"Ain't my dog," Ryan said and looked away.

An awkward silence fell.

Ryan knew his friends couldn't understand. Well, maybe Russell did. Two summers ago, he lost his dad. But that wasn't the same. No.

Ryan leaned forward over the riverbank and looked down at his reflection. Russell may have inherited some of his father's features, but he didn't lose someone who looked exactly like him. He reached out and saw his mirror image do the same, as if it wanted to stretch its arm up to the surface so Ryan could pull his brother out of the river.

That's who looked back at him. Curtis.

Ryan turned and looked at Lance. "Tell me again."

Lance frowned. "Do we have to go over this?" he said. "You know."

"I want to hear it again. Everything that happened." *Because I wasn't there.* They were always together, but not that day. Curtis left the house without him and took Smokey. He met Lance down by the river that February. *What was so important that he couldn't have waited for him?*

If he had, Ryan thought, *maybe I could have saved him.*

Lance's shoulders slumped as he walked over to the river's edge and plopped himself down on the bank beside Ryan. The others drew in a little closer, but refrained from encroaching on the pair.

"I came over to see Curtis," Lance said, his eyes drifting away from Ryan's. "Just to talk about stuff. He called Smokey and we went down to the river."

"Why there?" Ryan asked, a question he had pondered many times since last February, not once getting an answer.

"No reason," Lance said. "We just wanted to shoot the shit. Talk about stuff."

"Like what?"

Lance sucked in a deep breath. "I liked someone at school, that's all," he said. "Wanted to talk to Curtis about it."

Ryan thought back to sixth grade, how he hadn't thought that much about girls then. But Curtis always acted older. Christ, it was only ten minutes, but his damn brother seemed bigger than him, wiser, more grown up. Ten minutes. But he always held that over him.

"And that was all you wanted to talk about?"

Lance nodded. "Curtis brought his View-Master. Was showing me the *Dark Shadows* reel he had in it."

"And then."

Lance's eyes burned into his. "You know what happened. I told you."

"The rabbit?"

"Yes. It came out of nowhere. A white rabbit. Smokey spotted it. The rabbit took off, sprinted across the frozen river. Smokey went after it."

Ryan gazed out at the flowing river before him, pictured it frozen, motionless, white ice.

"In the middle of the river, the ice gave way. Smokey went in a bit. Before I realized what was happening, Curtis jumped up and raced across the river, yelling to the dog. Still had the View-Master in his hand." Lance looked out at the water. "I yelled for him to stop, but he didn't listen. Too focused on saving Smokey. Before he got to the dog, the ice gave out beneath him."

Ryan pictured it for the umpteenth time as Lance told the story. His brother's arms flailing as the ice ripped apart beneath his boots, his brother dropping into the chilling water, letting go of the View-Master as his hands scrambled to try to grab onto solid ice that kept breaking apart, splashing in a frantic panic.

"He called out to me," Lance said, tears in his eyes. "And then he went under. As I watched, Smokey got up onto the ice from his hole and ran off to the opposite bank. I stared at the empty hole Curtis disappeared into, kept thinking he'd pop back up." He turned to look at Ryan. "Then I ran back to your house to get your parents."

Ryan remembered him coming into the house, shouting in a fear-stricken tone.

Just like that, he thought. *Sitting one moment, gone the next.* He turned to look over his shoulder at Smokey, who was digging at something in the dirt. He hated that dog. Curtis's dog. Not his. But now he was stuck with him.

Russell came over and knelt beside him.

"When my dad died that summer, I never thought I'd get over it," he said. "I miss him, but it seems long ago." He paused. "Though sometimes I can almost feel him in the house."

Ryan remembered the other day in his bedroom when he thought he heard something moving in the bunk bed above his own, Curtis's bed, and a chill rippled through his body.

2

At breakfast at the boardinghouse, Mortimer ignored the idle chatter as he stole glances at Harold Lothrop's eyes. The man did not reciprocate eye contact, in fact quite the opposite; he seemed to go out of his way to avoid the magician's eyes.

The man has demons, Mortimer thought, maybe not unlike his own.

As he tried to read those eyes across the table, his mind drifted back to that night forty years ago at the carnival. Had he seen those eyes out in the audience in his tent? They would have been much younger eyes, but the eyes don't age much, not like the rest of the face and body. Eyes remain constant. Maybe they lose a little of their shine, the colors of the iris fade with time, less sharp.

But they're still the same eyes.

Had these eyes watched him and seen what happened that long-ago night?

Could that be what frightens the man?

Up in his room after breakfast, Mortimer stared out of the arched window facing the quiet street outside. The leaves on the oak tree out front were still mostly green, but a few had turned shades of yellow and orange. He thought about Harold Lothrop.

Mortimer felt sure the man had been in the crowd that night. Every time Harold looked at him, he saw recognition and something else… *fear?* He'd seen what happened, Mortimer figured. It was branded in his mind. How could it not be? He himself saw that night every single day. He could never forget it. The event altered the course of his entire existence.

A decent crowd had filled the tent that night in the Meadows, expecting to be mesmerized by the mystifying feats of the Great Mort Riggor, as he was known on stage. The September night was warm and the air stale inside the canvas tent.

The audience had just witnessed his act of sawing a woman in half and applauded with hoots and gasps, eyes wide in amazement of how he did the trick. The people had no idea that not everything was a trick. Some of it was real magic.

His assistant, a pretty young thing who had her own act with a dozen dancing poodles, helped wheel out the magician's cabinet for his final act of the show. She had to run off to attend to her own performance, but he still had another trusty assistant on standby: his son, Quinn.

The boy was ten and had been with his father at the carnival his entire life. There were several former teachers among the carny folk and they did double duty teaching the young ones during the day. Mortimer's wife, the boy's mother, used to travel with him since before Quinn was born and had been the magician's original assistant.

But after Quinn was born, she tired of the carnival life and took off one night when the boy was only three. She left a note saying she decided to leave at this time, before the boy was old enough to remember her. Mortimer felt a dagger in his heart and didn't know who he felt sorrier for, the boy or himself.

But soon, Quinn's mother was a distant memory and all the boy had as a memento was a locket Mortimer had given him with a photograph of his mother inside. Eventually Quinn stopped asking about his mother, but he always kept that locket around his neck. When it was just the two of them, they became quite a team, the boy able to help with the act more the older he got. And now that night he would help perform in the grand finale.

The magic cabinet stood tall and thin at the front of the stage. Mortimer spun it around so the audience could see all sides of the cabinet, while the boy stood off to the side. The magician opened the door and tapped his wand inside, showing its solid construction.

Mortimer motioned for his son to enter the cabinet and Quinn did so, smiling, without hesitation. Mortimer winked at his son before closing the door, not realizing the fate about to unfold.

The magician gave the cabinet three spins and then brought it to a stop. He tapped three times on the cabinet door and uttered his magic words, ones he'd learned long ago during a visit to a shaman in the Himalayas. When he opened the door, the cabinet was empty and the crowd applauded.

He addressed the crowd.

"Now of course, those of you with mischievous children at home would probably be content with making them vanish."

This brought forth a roar of laughter and a couple of "Hell yeahs!" from several men in the back and even one young woman.

"But I happen to like my son," Mortimer told the crowd, "and need him to help me with my act, so I will bring him back from that dark shadow world beyond."

He spun the cabinet again, this time in a counterclockwise direction, and once more performed the necessary taps with his magic wand and delivered a different phrase of gibberish-sounding words. With a smile, he glanced at the audience as he swung open the cabinet door.

The crowd remained silent except for a couple of shallow gasps from some of the women. Puzzled, Mortimer turned to peer into the cabinet, expecting to see Quinn performing some tomfoolery.

The cabinet was empty.

His breath cut off, as if punched in the gut, and an icy coating slipped around his heart. The boy had not returned.

Mortimer looked to the crowd, which was now grumbling in disappointment, and held up a hand.

"Minor mistake here," he said. "Must have used the wrong magic words." He tried to force a smile as he closed the cabinet door and began spinning it again. He tapped it with his wand and spoke the magic words.

He opened the door and his son was still not there.

The crowd stirred. Some people whispered to each other, clearly wondering if this was part of the act.

"There's something wrong," he said, more to himself than the audience. "I've got the words wrong." *How could that be?* He'd performed this magic trick many times, both with Quinn and his temporary assistant. In the old days, he even performed it with Quinn's mother. The trick always worked.

"What is this?" he cried and frantically shut the door and spun the cabinet again. He tapped his wand. *The words*, he thought. *What were the words?* Did he get them wrong? Now he wasn't even sure what they were. He mumbled what he could remember.

The door opened. The cabinet remained empty.

"My god!" he screamed and turned to see people rising from their seats and heading for the exit. Some of them looked embarrassed for him, others looked scared. "Help me!" he called out to no one in particular. "My son is gone!"

But no one in the crowd offered to help; instead they filed out through the exit in the rear of the tent, the last one being a young man who lingered in the front row, watching him on the stage, a look in his eyes of knowing he had witnessed something unexplained but was not shocked by it.

Eyes that looked just like the ones Mortimer saw earlier across the breakfast table downstairs. Eyes that weren't surprised at the sight of horror.

3

"How did I get here?" the boy asked Mr. Shreckengast.

"Don't you remember?" the master responded.

The boy shook his head.

The two of them stood in the master's room high atop the crumbling mansion, or what was left of its charred structure. Mr. Shreckengast gazed out a broken window bereft of any glass it once held within its frame.

There was nothing out there. Nothing the boy could see. But he often wondered if the master could see something the rest of them could not. He seemed to know what lay beyond the swirling blackness outside the remains of the walls of the house. If he didn't know it, then he sensed it, because he often witnessed Mr. Shreckengast staring out into the darkness, as if waiting for something to appear.

"A door opened in the darkness," the master said. "And a gift from beyond fell into our realm." He turned from the window to look down on him. "Sent to us."

"By who?"

"Don't you remember your father?"

He shook his head as if trying to stir the memory from some dusty bin. It frustrated the boy. As he concentrated, an image appeared.

"A man in a tall black hat," the boy said. He touched the locket around his neck, wondering about the indistinguishable picture inside.

"Yes," Shreckengast responded. "A magician's hat. It must have held such great power to be able to send you from your world of the living to this blackened place."

"He put me in a dark box."

"He sent you on a journey through darkness," Shreckengast said. "And you ended up here with us. That is strong magic. Dark power. What I could do with a contraption capable of such feats."

"Was that really my father?" It didn't awaken any memories. *How could that be?* "Why would he send me away?"

"The power of magic spoiled him," Shreckengast said.

It felt like his life hadn't begun till he woke up here, the boy thought. Though 'woke' wasn't quite the right word. It wasn't like he stirred from a dream or some deep sleep. He didn't just open his eyes upon awakening from a deep slumber and discover himself in this dark place.

He was just here. One moment he wasn't anywhere, and the next he was in this place as if he'd been here all along.

Like the others. The Scamps.

Where had they come from? That he never understood.

"The boys and girls," the boy said, though sometimes the condition of their bodies made it hard to tell the difference. "How did they get here?"

"You don't want to know the answer to that," Mr. Shreckengast said.

"Have they been here a long time?"

"As long as I have." Now, he turned to look back out the window.

"Really?"

"We arrived at this place together. Their souls are fettered to mine." He pulled his gaze from the window and bent down to look into the boy's eyes. He reached a long finger out and stroked the boy's cheek. "But you are here to save us all. To release us from this place."

"I still don't understand how I'm supposed to do that," the boy said.

"Don't you worry," Mr. Shreckengast said. "When the time comes, I will let you know and we will all leave the darkness together."

OCTOBER 5

1

"Today, I have a special guest to introduce," Miss Sheriden said with a smile.

Murmurs erupted from the kids in the class and Ryan sat up with curiosity, shooting a glance at Lance, who shrugged in return.

Miss Sheriden walked over to the storage closet in the back of the classroom. Everyone's attention followed her, and when she emerged, the teacher was wheeling something tall covered in a sheet and attached to a long pole. It looked like a ghost as she maneuvered the contraption all the way to the front of the room. She stood beside the hidden object, taller than her, and looked at the students.

"We are going to learn about one of the most important parts of the human anatomy," she said, flashing an excited grin. She pulled the cloth off, like a magician performing on stage, and revealed a human skeleton.

There were exclamations of "wow" and "cool" and several gasps and a couple giggles.

"The human skeletal system," Miss Sheriden said.

"Is that for real?" Wesley Roark asked from the back of the room.

Miss Sheriden looked into the eyes of the skull and then back at her students.

"This was supplied to us from a medical lab," she said. "So, as far as I know, it's the real deal. This is something we all have inside us, and we're going to learn about all the parts of the skeleton."

Ryan heard a stifled gasp behind his desk, where Russell Mallek sat.

"This poor fellow gave up his body to science," Miss Sheriden said.

Laughter erupted in the room.

"What happened to the rest of him?" Lance asked.

Miss Sheriden's brow furrowed, as she seemed stymied for an answer.

"I guess this is all that was left of him," she said with a smirk.

"*No!*"

The loud voice came from behind Ryan and he turned to look into the gaping maw of Russell, who stood up from his seat.

"That's not real!" Russell said and bolted from the room, leaving a stunned Miss Sheriden and the rest of the class staring at the doorway he exited.

2

Russell leaned up against the brick wall for support, just outside the school's west wing door. His breathing came in rapid pulses; his hands trembled. The air had gone crisp outside this fall morning, and without a jacket, a chill hugged his body.

His reaction to the skeleton surprised him when Miss Sheriden unveiled it. But he knew why. His mind drifted back to two summers ago, when he was ten. His father, a firefighter, worked the late-night shift. Russell used to hear him leave for work in the middle of the night. Most times, he would go to his bedroom window on the second floor of their house on Walnut Street and look out onto the driveway. He watched his father get into his pickup truck and drive down to the fire station.

His father never knew that Russell watched him from the window, and it was a secret thrill to see his old man heading off to work in the middle of the night while most of the town slept. Some nights Russell couldn't stay awake long enough to catch his dad leaving, but usually something woke him, maybe the front door opening and closing no matter how quietly his father tried to shut it.

At the sound, Russell would throw the covers off and race to the window, lifting the shade and peering out. His dad's tall frame strode down the driveway and climbed into the truck. His father would back out of the driveway without putting his headlights on, so as to not let the beams throw any light into the dark house and disturb anyone from their slumber.

As soon as the truck got out onto the road, the headlights would come on, and Russell would watch the vehicle drive away till the red taillights disappeared from view. He'd return to bed and try to imagine what his father's night was like. He'd picture his old man sitting around the firehouse, playing cards with the other firefighters, or lying in the bunks on the second floor, until an alarm sounded and he'd jump to his feet and race to the pole.

Whenever the sirens sounded, Russell always woke up and thought about his father battling a blaze somewhere in town, saving someone's home and possibly their lives.

But one July night two years ago, while Russell looked out the window as his father approached the pickup truck in the driveway, his old man stopped, as if he'd forgotten something. Russell watched, thinking maybe he'd remembered some cookies or something his mother had baked for the boys at the firehouse. His father remained still.

Then he turned and looked up at Russell's bedroom window.

Russell was startled. His father had never noticed him watching before. His old man smiled, and raised his right hand in a wave. Russell waved back. And then his father climbed into the truck and drove off.

He didn't come home that night.

A farmhouse fire in a nearby town. His father trapped. A roof collapsed.

Early in the morning, there was a great commotion downstairs. People had come to the house and he could hear his mother wailing. Russell didn't dare leave his room. The sounds coming from below were too frightening. All he knew was that when he looked out his bedroom window at the driveway, there were several vehicles there, the fire captain's car, a police car. But his father's pickup truck was not there.

Russell lay on his bed and waited. Eventually he heard footsteps and then a door opened. His mother's soft voice called to him.

"Russell?"

He looked up and saw Miss Sheriden standing just outside the school door.

"Are you okay?"

He looked at her, but his lips trembled and he could not speak.

The casket was closed during the funeral service. Russell knew what fire could do. When they got to the cemetery and he watched them place the casket in the ground, he asked his mother what would happen to his father's body.

"He's lying proud in his uniform," his mother told him.

"He's not going to become bones?" he asked.

His mother bent down and looked into his eyes.

"Of course not," she told him. "That's not what happens."

But as he looked at Miss Sheriden and thought about the skeleton in the classroom, his body and mind fought for control over a menagerie of anger, confusion, and fear.

"That's not real," he said to Miss Sheriden. "The skeleton."

She looked confused and took a step closer to him.

"It's nothing to be afraid of," she assured him.

He shook his head. "That's not what happens to us when we die," he said. "We don't become bones."

3

In the same cemetery where Russell Mallek's father was buried, Mortimer Rigby walked the grounds in his black cloak and top hat. If not for it being daytime, his dark figure would seem a foreboding specter wandering among the gravestones.

The cemetery rested on the north side of the river, off Fieldstone Road across from the Meadows, where the carnival that first brought Mortimer to Maplewood had set up. In the four decades since, the old magician could see how much the cemetery had grown, stretching out around young saplings that had now risen into the sky to provide shade for those seeking comfort with their long-lost loved ones.

That's what brought Mortimer to this place. A search. The years had rusted his memory and he couldn't quite be sure what row he sought, so he marched up and down the narrow dirt lanes, eyes scraping across the blocks of granite looking for the right name.

When he finally found it, his heart nearly stopped. His throat went dry and he tried to clear it. The gray granite seemed weathered, lichen crawling across its surface. But the name was still legible: Quinn Rigby.

Of course, the tiny box buried in this plot held something other than his son. The burial was symbolic, something Mortimer felt needed to be done. The only thing in the box under the ground was the one-eyed teddy bear, Orso, that Quinn used to sleep with. Mortimer had buried that in memory of his son, with a vow to keep searching for a way to bring his boy back from that other confined box his real flesh and blood had been interred in.

But that box was gone, no thanks to Rita Stone, and Mortimer hoped to hell that all his effort to seek the solution to his magic trick wasn't lost with it. The new box would arrive tomorrow, and with it Mortimer's last hope to return poor Quinn from whatever damnation he'd inadvertently sent the boy to.

Mortimer took his top hat off and knelt by the grave.

"Soon, my boy," he whispered in a hoarse voice to the empty plot. "It won't be long till I find out if I can get you back." He reached into the top hat and pulled out a bouquet of daisies, tulips, and carnations. He leaned the flowers up against the headstone and stood, his knees cracking as he rose, his bones aching from the long walk from the boardinghouse.

The sooner he accomplished his task in this place, the sooner he could leave.

4

The boy descended a staircase into the basement of the house, a basement that he never realized was there in all the time he had been at the House of Embers. How long that was, he never really knew. Sometimes it felt as if he had only recently arrived; other times it seemed like he'd been here a lifetime. But he didn't even know how long a lifetime was, least of all his own. Time had no meaning here. There was no light, no days, only darkness blurring into more darkness as the house floated on a sea of black.

But he had a reason for going down these stairs. Some of the Scamps had told him about it.

"You're not the only one Mr. Shreckengast thinks is special," one of the older boys had remarked, the one with no eyes. "There is someone else."

"Who?" the boy had asked.

"He keeps him hidden away in the basement."

The boy had set out to find the basement and discovered the staircase. Like everything else, darkness lurked down there, musty, like earth turned from a newly dug grave. When he reached the bottom, he stepped onto a dirt floor. The foundation was made of large granite slabs. Somehow, he could see down here, just like he could see anywhere else in the house above. In such a dark place with no lights that floated in blackness, he never understood how seeing was possible. He searched the basement till he came to a wooden door. He heard a clicking sound on the other side.

"Hello?" he called out, not bothering to try the door to see if it was locked.

The clicking sound stopped.

"Who's there?" a boy's voice called out.

"I heard someone was down here," he said. He grabbed the doorknob, turned it, and pulled the door open. Sitting on the dirt floor was a boy a couple years older than him. Even in the darkness, he could see the boy's pale skin, not blackened and charred like the Scamps. In his hands the kid held some kind of plastic device that looked like binoculars. "What are you doing here?"

The older boy looked up at him.

"I don't know," he said. "I think I'm lost."

"What's your name?"

"Curtis."

"I'm Quinn," he said, wondering how he remembered his name. "How did you get here?"

"I was cold and wet and found myself on the edge of a riverbank. There was an amusement park nearby. I wandered in, but there was no one around. I heard music, but didn't see anyone. Then I found this place."

"There's no amusement park here," Quinn said. "There's nothing here, except this house. If you want to call it that. What are you doing down here?"

"The tall, thin man told me to stay here. The others scared me." He glanced at Quinn. "You don't look like them."

"I'm not," Quinn said. "I came here later than the Scamps, after whatever happened here."

"How did you get here?" Curtis asked.

He tried to explain it to the older boy, but knew he wasn't making much sense. He looked at the device in the boy's hand.

"What is that thing you've got?"

The boy held it up for him to see.

"It's a View-Master."

"What do you do with it?"

"You can watch reels of pictures, like scenic sights, or television shows."

"What are television shows?"

Curtis looked surprised. "Are you kidding me? Don't you have television shows here? Motion pictures?"

"There isn't anything here," Quinn said. "The place is in ruins." He thought for a minute. "Is it like a nickelodeon machine?" He had a glimmer of a memory of putting a coin in a slot and looking through a screen to see silly moving pictures.

"I don't know what that is," Curtis said.

"Can I try it?"

"Well, I don't have any of my reels. I must have lost them. I was looking at *Dark Shadows* but it must have gotten lost in the water."

"So why are you still using it if it doesn't work?"

Curtis stood. "There's still something there when I look in it. But I don't understand it. It's weird." He handed the toy to Quinn and showed him how to use it.

Quinn put the View-Master up to his eyes and looked through the windows. He clicked the button and images appeared. He saw a Ferris wheel and a roller coaster. Then he saw a large gabled house. As he clicked the button, the images of the house got closer. Then he saw flames leaping from the windows. A few more clicks and he saw children on fire, their skin bubbled as they burned. He pulled the toy away from his eyes.

"Do you know what that means?" Curtis asked.

Quinn dropped the View-Master onto the ground and ran from the room and up the stairs.

He went to the master's room.

"The boy in the basement," Quinn said, out of breath. "What is he doing here?"

Shreckengast, seated in a chair, looked at him with fiery eyes.

"He's of no concern to you," he said.

"Where did he come from?"

The master got up from his seat and went to look out the gaping hole in the wall into the darkness beyond.

"He came from somewhere out there."

"Like me?"

"Not quite like you," Shreckengast said. "His heart doesn't beat like yours."

"So, he's not special like me?"

The master came over and stroked Quinn's hair.

"No one here is special like you."

"Then why do you keep him here?"

Shreckengast once again went to the hole in the wall and looked out.

"Because, like you, he came from somewhere out there." He turned to him. "And if he found a way in, then that means there's a way out."

OCTOBER 6

1

When Ryan and Lance strolled down Elm Street toward the boardinghouse with the last two newspapers of the delivery, they noticed the panel truck parked out front of the home. The two boys raced toward it, their curiosity piqued. At the sidewalk in front of the house they spotted the old man in black on the top of the front stoop before the open front doors.

A man lowered a large boxlike object from the truck onto a dolly and wheeled it down the sidewalk to the front steps. The wooden box was tall and narrow and black as coal. It reminded Ryan of a coffin and he thought about his brother Curtis lying in his box the day of the wake. An autumn chill rattled his spine as he remembered staring into the coffin at his twin, seeing his own dead face lying still. *That's what I'd look like if I were dead.*

But it didn't look like me. It didn't even look like Curtis. It looked fake, like an awful papier-mâché cast of him. He shook the chilling image from his mind.

"It's the old man's coffin," Lance whispered into his ear. "For him to sleep in during the day."

"It's daylight," Ryan said. "He can't be a vampire if he's out in the sun." Besides, Ryan thought, it didn't really look like a coffin. It had a door on the front with a black metal handle.

"It's a clothing cabinet," the old man on the front stoop said, as if reading the boys' minds.

Ryan felt another chill cascade down his spine. He didn't believe the old man. This seemed like something else, as he watched the man with the dolly lug the cabinet up the steps to the stoop and set the item down.

"My room is on the third floor," the old man said, motioning inside.

"This is as far as I go," the delivery man said. "I only got orders to deliver it to the address. I'm not lugging it up three flights of stairs."

The old man scowled.

The delivery man took his dolly and went back to the truck. He threw the dolly in the back and rolled down the door before climbing into the cab. As the truck drove off, the boys looked at the perplexed old man. He seemed to study them, Ryan felt, as if sizing them up.

"How'd you boys like to make five dollars?" the old man asked.

Ryan and Lance looked at each other, and then they bounded up the steps, tossing the newspapers aside when they reached the top.

The cabinet was lighter than Ryan expected, which he was grateful for as he and Lance maneuvered the item up the staircase, struggling the most each time they turned one of the corners. The higher up the stairs they went, the heavier the cabinet seemed.

At the second-floor landing, they had to proceed down the length of the hallway to the back of the house where the stairs to the third floor were situated. That staircase was narrower, and steeper than the main one in front. As they made their way up the steps, Lance in the lead and Ryan supporting the back end, Ryan felt his arms strain under the burden.

Now it did seem like a coffin to Ryan and it certainly no longer felt empty. The muscles in his arms flared and his legs felt wobbly as if they might give out.

"Almost there," the old man barked from above as he led the way.

Ryan felt some relief when they reached the third-floor hallway and carried the cabinet past Mr. Lothrop's room to the bedroom at the front of the house. Once inside the old man's room, they set it upright against one wall.

"Here you go, boys," the old man said and handed Lance a five-dollar bill.

"What are you going to do with it?" Lance asked, pocketing the cash in his jeans with a nod and a smile at Ryan.

The old man's weary gaze shifted from Lance to Ryan. He pulled out his wallet and plucked out another five-dollar bill.

"Here's five more for minding your own business," he said in a gruff voice. He handed the bill to Ryan. "Say no more about it. Now, get out."

When they stepped back into the hallway, the old man slammed the door shut behind them.

"That was easy," Lance said as they walked back down the hall.

"Speak for yourself," Ryan said. "My arms are sore."

When they passed Mr. Lothrop's room, his door flung open, giving them both a startle.

"What was that all about?" he asked the boys, though his eyes were drawn to the room down the hall.

Ryan glanced at Lance, remembering the old man's words.

"Nothing," he said.

Lothrop looked down at them. His eyes narrowed.

"Stay away from that one," Lothrop said. "He's not to be trusted."

He retreated into his room and shut the door.

2

Long after sunset, Mortimer Rigby stalked the halls of the boardinghouse checking on the whereabouts of the various tenants. His body felt alive, as if lightning danced along his nerves, igniting synapses like firecrackers. It made him feel youthful, like he had that horrid night so long ago. He hadn't felt as young since. The tragic mishap had sapped the years from his body and mind. Then time did its work.

God, where has the time gone? He thought he had plenty of it to search for the answers and solve the problem to bring Quinn home. But time had run away as well as his son. No. Quinn hadn't run away. Mortimer had banished him to an unknown place by his own incompetence. His fault. All his fault. Not the poor innocent boy's.

Life had punished Mortimer, taunted him as he traveled the world searching out all the mystics and shamans to gain the knowledge to put things right. Magic in the Himalayas had gotten him close to the answer. But it wasn't till he visited the Teatro del Misterio located down a dark, twisted alley in Venice, Italy, when he met a magician who had the answer he sought. The words. The right magic words.

By then, Mortimer looked in a mirror and saw he had grown to an old man.

Where has the time gone?

Would Quinn even recognize him now? Or would he fear this crumbling, wrinkled stranger who drew him out of whatever dark hole his father had sent him to?

And if it had been this long for Mortimer, what did all that time away do to poor Quinn? How was he affected? What was the place like where he had been sent? The magician in Venice had no answer to that, only the right words to bring him back.

If Mortimer wasn't so selfish, he'd leave things be. Don't mess with fate once again. But he was robbed of the only thing in life he loved. And he had come too far, across too much time, through too much magic.

Tonight.

It will be tonight.

In the front parlor room, Wilfred Downey sat asleep in a chair in front of the small black-and-white television. Mortimer had noticed the landlord was an easy dozer. He had at least half a dozen years on him, so maybe that was to be expected, but the man's wife looked only a handful of years younger than her husband, and seemed to have a decade or more of energy than he.

Mortimer had seen Ruth Downey go out earlier this evening with Calvin Armstrong and the Fifers. The four of them piled into Armstrong's station wagon full of gaiety and exuberance, something about a whist tournament at a social club in Manchester. They'd be gone for a while.

Up on the second floor, Mortimer quietly hovered outside the Brown Room. Ravenous snores from Noreen Stich and quiet whistles from the narrow nose of her sister, Pearl, assured him the ladies were not going to be a concern. That left only one person.

Observations from his short stint at the boardinghouse had enlightened him that Harold Lothrop did not sleep with ease. But Mortimer also knew the man's weakness and retreated to his room to retrieve the necessary items that would assist the man this important night. Once collected, he knocked on the door of the Gray Room.

Suspicious eyes of the tenant inside greeted Mortimer with curiosity when the door flung open.

"What do you want?" Lothrop asked.

"I was in the mood for a nightcap," Mortimer said, holding up an unopened bottle of bourbon in one hand, and two glasses clenched in the fingers of his other. "And a spot of company."

"One of those sounds good," Lothrop said, but did not budge from the doorway.

"The rest of the house is out," Mortimer responded, "both literally and figuratively. You're my only option."

Lothrop's lips clenched and the skin on his brow formed waves, but he backed away from the entrance to the room and gestured him inside. Mortimer walked over to a small round table by the window and set down the bottle and glasses. The men each took a seat in the chairs on either side of the table and Mortimer opened the bottle and poured the drinks. He watched the delight in Lothrop's eyes as he poured. *Yes, this is just what the man needs to keep his nightmares away.*

"What's the occasion?" Lothrop asked as Mortimer brought his glass up to clink with his companion's.

"Does one need an occasion?"

Lothrop studied him with hesitant eyes but said nothing.

This man surely had his demons. Mortimer cleared his throat. "Let's just say, time grows short for old-timers like us," the magician said, "and it's nice just to savor the quiet moments like this."

Lothrop grunted, but didn't hesitate to tip the glass back and take a deep swallow. Mortimer refilled his glass, even though it wasn't empty.

"You've been here a long time," Mortimer said.

"The original tenant," Lothrop answered between pulls on the glass. "Back when Wilfred and Ruth first started renting rooms. They bought a big house thinking they were going to have a bunch of kids, but when they couldn't, they decided to rent the rooms instead of letting them sit empty. We were all about the same age." The man frowned. "Now we've all grown old in this house."

"And you never wanted to leave?" Mortimer took tiny sips of his drink, not like the gulps his companion hoisted down.

Lothrop's hand shook as he reached for his glass. "No reason to," he said. "Fine right here."

"No places to go," Mortimer pushed. "No one special to see?"

Lothrop's eyes narrowed. "I see plenty here."

Mortimer refilled the man's glass. "You saw me here," he said as he set the now half-empty bottle down. "Forty years ago." He tipped his glass in the air. "At the carnival."

Lothrop's face went slack, his eyes rounded. "You remembered me?" He seemed credulous, but also suspicious.

"Some eyes are hard to forget," he said as his locked with Lothrop's.

"I was a young man back then."

"We both were," Mortimer said.

"I couldn't figure out how you did it. The trick."

Mortimer froze, his glass seconds from his lips. Something cold wrapped around his heart that dissipated the warmth of the bourbon.

"Which trick?"

"You cut a young woman in half." He took another gulp. "I mean, I know it was a trick, but I still couldn't figure it out. You placed a wooden board under the lady, you drew the buzz saw blade across. The board comes out split, but the lady is fine."

"It's easy," Mortimer said and finished his sip. "I hypnotized the lady, and then used mysticism I learned in Tibet to stop the flow of her blood." He set his now-empty glass down.

Lothrop cracked his first smile of the evening.

"Gah!" he said, waving a hand in the air. "It's all smoke and mirrors, you blokes."

"No," Mortimer said as he refilled the man's glass. "It's magic."

Lothrop gripped his glass tight and his eyes bore into Mortimer's.

"What about the other trick?" he said, and then looked in his glass as if expecting to see some trick in the dark liquid. "The one that didn't work so well."

Mortimer felt the walls of his heart tumble in. He cast his eyes down at his empty glass. No amount of liquor could dull that wound.

"That was the case of a young magician reaching too high," he said in a soft voice barely above a whisper.

"And the boy?"

Mortimer's body hitched as he sucked in air to try and revive his sunken body. "My son."

Lothrop's eyes never left him, but the man said nothing.

Mortimer glanced at the bottle with only a quarter of the liquid left. He stood up.

"I'll leave you the rest," he said to Lothrop. "For now, I'll bid you good night from a tired old magician." With one last trick up his sleeve, he hoped.

Lothrop remained quiet, but as Mortimer left the room and started to close the door behind him, he glanced back in time to see the man reaching for the bottle. As Mortimer continued down the hall toward his room, he felt confident that no one would disturb his task tonight.

3

In the House of Embers, there was a rumbling. Not from some force of nature, or whatever ruled the strange universe where this crumbling structure existed, but from the first sign of excited activity within the dark blackened walls. The boy came running when he heard the master calling, up the flight of crooked stairs to the room where he usually perched staring out into the black. The boy had to dodge other kids, the charred ones who scurried to and fro in a frenzy of madness.

"What's going on?" Quinn asked as he reached the master's chamber. The tall, thin man turned to him and he saw the first smile ever on the man's face.

"It's time," Shreckengast said through shiny teeth. "Our opening is here."

Quinn ran to the gap in the wall and peered out. He saw nothing.

"But where?" He didn't understand.

The master's long strides took him to a broken window.

"There!" he exclaimed, with one long finger pointing toward the distance. "I can see it. The opportunity is now."

"I still don't see anything," Quinn said as his eyes followed the direction of the narrow digit.

"Trust me," Shreckengast said and lowered his arm. "I've sent for everyone. We must make haste."

As he spoke, the others poured into the room from below like scurrying rats. The boy never quite knew how many Scamps there were in this place because they never all gathered at once. Now he could see the dark faces that haunted this place, from the young to ones old enough to be off to college if life hadn't interrupted their journey and deposited them here.

"What do we do?" Quinn asked as he turned to the master for guidance.

"Take hands," Shreckengast commanded. "We must all hold tight if we want to leave this place together."

Quinn watched as the others around him began clasping hands. Soon a long line formed in the room and down along the staircase for those who could not squeeze in up here. One after the other they grasped hands and squeezed.

Quinn looked at them all and then faced Shreckengast. "What about the boy in the basement?" he asked.

The master frowned. "He's not like us," he said.

"I'm not like you either," he said. "Any of you." He gazed at all the scorched faces.

"Time is short," Shreckengast said, a scowl masking his face. "We mustn't dawdle."

Quinn folded his arms across his chest. "If he doesn't come, then I'm not going." He stared at Shreckengast, whose eyes narrowed into sharp points. The boy shivered, not sure provoking the master was the best idea. What if he got left behind here? Should he risk that? *But they can't go without me.* The master said that time and time again. He was the key; he was important.

He saw Shreckengast struggle with the decision, his face a consternation of grimaces.

"Fine!" Shreckengast yelled. "Get the other," he said to a couple of the Scamps down by the bottom of the staircase.

Two boys ran off in the direction of the basement.

"Now, come," the master said and stretched a long arm toward him, palm extended. "Take my hand."

Quinn glanced behind him and saw the two Scamps drag the boy from the basement toward the line. They all held hands. He looked up at Shreckengast and took his offered hand.

A rush of wind brushed his face and before he knew it, the house was gone. Everything disappeared except the blackness and a sensation of floating, or maybe flying, he couldn't tell. He gripped tight to the skinny, bony fingers of the master, afraid of falling.

But falling where? No up or down. He watched the line of children all clinging together like the tail of a kite, and they seemed to be moving without any perception of direction, as if the blackness was trying to swallow them all whole. At the end of the line, he spotted the boy from the basement. His free hand clung to the View-Master, but then it slipped from his grip and tumbled away into the nothingness.

Quinn turned his head and saw a pinprick of light in the distance. How far, he could not tell. No perception here, as if they were in a great vacuum of space, only a space with no light. *Dark matter.*

The point of light grew closer, as if it moved toward them. Or maybe, they were moving toward it. An opening, Shreckengast had called it. But an opening to what? What if they were heading to an even worse place than they had left? Though he could hardly imagine that. As they approached the dot of light, it seemed to crack in two, a long bright line ripping across the darkness, so bright it blinded him and Quinn squeezed his eyes shut. He felt the chain holding the locket around his neck break off and slip away.

Before he reopened his eyes, Quinn felt a change in the air, something fresh that he could suck down into his lungs. His eyelids flung up like a loose shade and he saw it was still dark. But stuff below was beginning to take shape. Wispy whiteness whipped by. He realized they were clouds.

Shreckengast's grip on his hand felt comforting, for now Quinn felt he might fall if he let go. Down below he began to make out great squares of green that seemed to rise at an incredible speed.

We're going to crash, Quinn thought in a panic. Shoot down into the ground and smash into smithereens. He looked at Shreckengast, his face gripped with a delicious smile. Was this all part of the plan? No one had told him anything. Where were they even going?

Their speed slowed and the sensation of flying became more like a feeling of drifting, as if helium balloons were strapped to their waists and hoisting them aloft. The ground below rose and as the boy looked, he saw a great field.

And something more.

Something orange. Lots of somethings.

A pasture of pumpkins. The biggest patch he had ever seen.

Shreckengast turned to him with that secret smile.

"You've brought us far enough," the master said. "Thanks for the ride." He let go of Quinn's hand.

No! Quinn thought, feeling jettisoned. He began to drift away from the rest, as if being pulled backward.

"Don't leave me!" he cried out.

Shreckengast only laughed as he and the others headed down toward the pumpkin patch. Quinn saw the kid from the basement also cast off from the end of the line and spin away in the opposite direction. As he looked below, Quinn saw Shreckengast and the Scamps approach the field of pumpkins, and release hands as they all darted toward the gourds. Shreckengast spiraled toward one great giant gourd, a beast whose shape resembled a human heart.

Quinn was whisked away and once again found himself engulfed in darkness.

4

Mortimer Rigby felt the tremble of the magic words he uttered dancing on the edge of his dry lips, a tingling sensation. The light bulb in the lamp by the small desk against the wall had grown dim, but a tiny bit of incandescence still ringed the room. His heart thudded in his chest like a jackhammer.

Can it be? he thought. *Have I done it?*

He stood before the closed wooden cabinet that looked too shiny in the faded light of the room, not like that weathered pine skin of the original box. But while his ears heard no sound and his eyes sensed no movement, he felt a presence in the room. He took off his black top hat and set it upside down on the desk with fingers that danced with fear.

But what was he afraid of? He'd waited a lifetime for this moment. He should be rushing to the cabinet door and flinging it open. But something stopped him. Guilt, maybe. When Quinn laid eyes on him, would he see the accusation in them for what he had done to his boy? Mortimer was unsure whether he could bear that much of a burden.

But he knew there was no sense delaying the inevitable. He hadn't traveled halfway around the globe and across decades of time that brought him to the precipice of his own end of days to stop now that it was done. He approached the cabinet door, grasped the handle, and yanked it open.

5

Quinn Rigby huddled in the darkness and dared not move. Shreckengast and the Scamps were gone, and he was alone in the black. Even the older kid from the basement had deserted him. Alone. Darkness.

This was not like the House of Embers. Quinn could see nothing here. Whenever he reached out, he touched a hard smooth surface. Trapped.

Am I in a coffin? It seemed plausible due to the confined narrow space he found himself in. But he wasn't lying down. That's what you're supposed to do in a coffin. And he was sitting on the bottom of whatever had imprisoned him. There was little room to move around in here and it was too dark to search for an exit.

What could he do? Wait? Scream for help?

He pounded a fist against the surface in front of him. But there might be no one to help him. Maybe this was what death was like. Maybe it finally came for him when Shreckengast let go of his hand.

Quinn reached up and placed his right hand on his shirt over his heart. He felt nothing. Are you supposed to be able to feel your heart beat? The master could. Quinn remembered Shreckengast placing his bony hand on his chest and telling him he could feel his heart beat. That's how Shreckengast knew Quinn was not like the others. That's why he felt Quinn could be the key to releasing them all.

But Quinn didn't know that meant he'd be abandoned by Shreckengast, cast off once his purpose had been fulfilled. He still didn't understand how he got here, or where 'here' was. He just knew he felt more alone and scared than ever before.

His head lifted.

Footsteps.

He cocked his head toward the direction in the darkness where the sound came from. They were approaching, that he knew. He shifted in his spot.

Something is coming.

Quinn heard the creak of a knob or handle, and then a crack of light appeared as a door in front of him slowly opened.

After so much time of darkness, the little bit of light that entered his confined space bore down on his eyes and he squinted, not wanting to shut them though the brightness tried to force his eyelids closed.

"Oh, my my," came a thick voice. "What have we here?"

Quinn looked up, forced his eyes open, and stared at the largest woman he had ever seen. Something about her seemed familiar.

6

A few blocks away, in the front room on the third floor of the boardinghouse, Mortimer Rigby stared into the empty magician's cabinet and felt his heart drop.

Nothing, he thought. All this time and it didn't work.

His magic was gone.

OCTOBER 7

1

By the sparse morning light that managed to filter through the small iron-grated windows of the basement, Quinn surveyed his surroundings and concluded he had traded one prison for another. Sleep escaped him, even though the woman had set up a cot and left him with a musty blanket before going upstairs and locking the door.

He couldn't see much in the dark, so he curled up on the makeshift bed and tried to cry himself to sleep, but no tears came. In what seemed an eternity at the House of Embers, he had lost all sense of sorrow and sadness. Frustration ruled his emotions after all that time.

Time? He didn't really understand what that meant. Time had no meaning for him there; he doubted it would here. Wherever here was.

Quinn saw a familiarity in the face of the captor. He knew her from somewhere. From sometime before. *Before what?* Not sure. But he felt certain of one thing: *She knew him.*

He saw that in her eyes. A hint of recognition she tried to suppress, but when her eyes grew wide and her lips curled up, he could tell she remembered him. *From before*, he assumed.

Boxes and old furniture cluttered the basement, leaving barely enough room to move around, but Quinn paced regardless as he sought any possible avenue of escape. The iron grates covering the cellar window wells eliminated that possible egress.

From time to time, he stared at the tall cabinet he had found himself in when the woman first opened the door and discovered him. Something about it seemed familiar. He wondered why he ended up in there, and how. He remembered Shreckengast releasing his hand and he drifted away into darkness like a foggy dream.

The door opened at the top of the stairs and he braced himself. Heavy thudded footsteps descended. The woman held a plate in one hand and a glass of milk in another.

"I heard you rummaging around down here," she said when she reached the bottom. "I figured you must be ready for breakfast."

Quinn felt hunger pangs in his belly, something he never experienced in the House of Embers. He stared at the plate in the woman's hand and saw two powdered doughnuts. He did not let himself react to the food, not wanting to give her any satisfaction that he was grateful.

"The bread man just came," she said, "and I decided to purchase some fresh chocolate powdered doughnuts for you because I know that's something little boys like." She pulled her eyes off him to glance around the basement. "Let's find someplace for you to set up."

She waded through the mess and stopped before a small pedestal table covered in old, dusty *Life* magazines. She set the milk down on the edge and used her massive forearm to swipe all the debris off the table, where it clattered onto the floor.

"Here you go," she said as she set the plate down beside the glass of milk. She looked around. "There's a chair here somewhere." She foraged through some stuff and dug up a small wooden chair with a torn seat pad. "Perfect." She set it beside the table.

His stomach gurgled at the sight of the food.

"Come on," she said, impatient. "Don't be shy."

Quinn's desires got the better of him and he moved to the table and sat. He nearly engulfed the first doughnut, an uncontrollable urge overtaking him without warning, leaving his face around his mouth dusted with the white powder. He quickly took a gulp of milk to wash the food down.

The woman hovered over him, watching him with a toothy grin.

"Do you remember me?" she asked, her eyes filled with glee.

Though she looked familiar, Quinn remembered little before his time at the House of Embers. He gazed at her and did not answer; instead he took another bite of the doughnut.

"Does the name Rita Stone ring any bells?"

It meant nothing to him.

"And I know who you are."

He stopped in the middle of a gulp of his milk, a bit running out of the corner of his mouth. His hand shook as he set the glass down.

"I don't know how it's possible," she said. "But I know you are Quinn Rigby." Her body half turned as she glanced back at the tall wooden cabinet in the corner. "And I'm good friends with your father."

2

What went wrong?

Mortimer Rigby eyed his son's grave, his old bones aching from being twisted into a position he hadn't sat in since he was a young man, seated on the grass with his legs crisscrossed. He ran the magic incantation over and over through his mind, remembered everything he learned in his quest to reverse the catastrophic trick he performed forty years ago.

But it didn't work.

The cabinet remained empty when he opened the door and his heart sunk inside his chest like a lead weight. Incompetent fool, he thought of himself. Felt so assured that he had everything right, just like he did those many years ago at the carnival.

Who's the great magician now?

His stomach lurched and he wanted to vomit. His top hat sat on the ground beside him and he reached inside it to pull out a handkerchief, but came up empty. His hand rummaged around the interior of the hat. Nothing. No magic left in there either.

He felt like he had squandered his entire life. Forty years chasing a fool's quest and now he was an old man and had nothing to show for it. No more tricks up his sleeve.

Mortimer stared at the headstone. Here was another lie. No boy lay beneath that marker. Only Orso, an old stuffed teddy bear with a missing eye.

"Where are you, Quinn?" he called to the sky. "What have I done to you?"

He began to cry.

3

Rita cranked up the old Victrola and put on one of her Enrico Caruso records. Among the cracks and static from the worn needle came the booming voice of the Italian opera singer. She turned the volume up as loud as it could go, and the sound bounced around the walls of the house.

She pulled a curtain aside on the front window and watched for the paperboy. She hoped any cries for help from young Quinn in the basement would be drowned out by the music. Right on cue, Rita spied Lance Stanton walking up the front steps. The other boy, Ryan Woodson, stood on the sidewalk across the street. *They're afraid of me.* The boys in the neighborhood. They feared the fat, old carnival lady, maybe thinking she'd eat them for dinner like the old witch in Hansel and Gretel.

When Rita saw the boy mount the steps, she sprung to greet him at the door. His eyes showed surprise by her sudden appearance, and he looked startled by the booming music echoing throughout the house.

"I just love my opera," Rita exclaimed to the mystified young boy as she snatched the newspaper from his paws while her face wore a welcoming grin that bared lots of teeth. *All the better to eat you with*, she thought to herself, and burst out laughing, which only seemed to compound the perplexed look on young Lance's face.

As he walked away and back down the front steps, he glanced back at her only once and she managed to maintain her exuberant smile no matter how uncomfortable until he looked away and ran across the street to join his friend. Beneath the sounds of the orchestra strings and horns, she could hear the faint cry of a young boy's voice from beneath the floorboards only to be drowned out by crashing cymbals.

The paperboy seemed to take no notice and, satisfied he heard nothing, she slammed the door shut and tossed the newspaper aside. She should just cancel the damn thing anyway, she thought, and she wouldn't have to worry about any intrusions that might lead to the discovery of her basement captive.

Rita turned the music down only a slight notch before going into the kitchen to boil some hot dogs. She hated cooking, but knew young Quinn needed to eat. She herself liked eating enough, just not the preparation. She often ordered food to be delivered, but now that she had a guest, she would need to be more careful about that. No unnecessary visitors to the house if she wanted to keep her little secret.

That would mean venturing into town to do her own shopping, and since she didn't drive, it would amount to a lot of exercise, something she did not relish. But being a mother now to a young child came with its consequences, and she'd have to adapt, as reluctant as that made her feel.

Rita turned the music down, unlocked the basement door and brought down to the boy the plate of three hot dogs in buns, lathered in mustard and relish, and a helping of potato chips.

"They won't be able to hear you," she said with a leer as she set the plate on the small table. "Calling for help will do you no good." She smiled. "Come eat." She settled into another wooden chair she had rummaged from the cellar heaps of junk. Rita enjoyed watching him eat, and he attacked the meal with a ravenous fury.

"I was never hungry before," Quinn said between bites. "Eating never even entered my mind where I was. But now my stomach aches all the time for food." He shoved another bite in his mouth.

"Where were you before?" Rita asked as she watched him eat.

"I don't know," he said. He crunched a couple chips in his mouth and took a swig of milk. "Someplace dark." He glanced around the basement. "Darker than this."

"It won't always be dark here," she said. "Once you get used to living with me."

Quinn paused, the back end of a hot dog raised to his open mouth. "Living with you?" His eyes grew wide.

"Yes," Rita said. "I've aways wanted a little boy. I couldn't give my husband kids of our own." She cast her eyes down, hoping he'd spot sadness in them. "That's why he went away." She looked up and brightened her face with a smile. "But now I have you here. And I'll treat you well if you learn to behave." Her smile dropped and eyes narrowed. She leaned her hulking frame forward. "Which means no calling out when the paperboy, or anyone else, comes to the door." She thought about the bread man and his morning deliveries. "Especially if you want me to get you nice treats like those chocolate powdered doughnuts you liked so much this morning."

Rita sat back in the chair. "Your father sent you away. Nobody wants you. Only me."

Quinn finished his last bite. "What do you know about my father?"

"He never searched for you," she lied. "He sent you away and went on with his life." She reached out and patted his arm. "But I won't do that. I won't leave you. I'll always be here for you. You just need to accept that and learn to behave." She removed her hand and watched the fear settle in behind his eyes.

She liked that he was afraid of her.

4

The Woodsons arrived at Hank Swain's farm after Ryan got done helping Lance with his paper route. He convinced his mother to let him go pick out a pumpkin that day. He didn't want to wait till Harvest Fest and take the chance that someone else would get the one he spotted the other day when he and the gang rode their bikes to the farm after school. That's when he caught site of the perfect one. The greatest pumpkin he'd ever seen.

Ryan wasn't even sure why he thought that. But somehow, glimpsing the round orange gourd, it felt like it spoke to him. *Pick me.*

And he needed to get that one. Only that one.

When the car stopped, Ryan bounded out of the door before his father shifted into park. He spotted a few other people milling about in the pumpkin patch. He hoped he could remember exactly where the one he wanted was located. He pictured it the last few nights, trying to conjure the memory of its location in his mind. As he wandered between the irregular rows of pumpkins, he kept his eyes glued to the ground.

He almost tripped over it.

Lying in a nest of green leaves and vines, sat his Holy Grail. He reached down and scooped it up, ripping the vine from its top. He stared at it, admiring its perfect round shape. It felt right in his hand, a warmth transmitting from it to his body as he held it close.

This is the one.

He looked up to seek out his parents and spotted them chatting with Hank Swain by the giant pumpkin the farmer planned to enter in the weight contest. Ryan walked over, keeping his grip tight on his own pumpkin.

"Found one already?" his father asked.

"This is the one I wanted," Ryan answered. He glanced at the giant heart-shaped pumpkin between Mr. Swain and his parents. *It may be big,* he thought, *but it's damn ugly.* Not like his pumpkin.

As he stared at the giant gourd, its shell stretched.

No. Impossible.

It seemed to inflate like a bellows. The palms of his hands grew cold, as if the pumpkin he held was covered in a layer of frost. That chill worked its way from the skin of his palms all the way up his arms, raising goose bumps along his flesh.

"Can we go now, Mom?" he asked, feeling a sudden urge to get away.

"Sure," his mother said and turned to her husband. "Pay the man."

Ryan didn't wait for his father to finish fishing bills out of his wallet before starting to walk toward the car. He glanced to his right to the small shed with its doors wide open and shelves crammed with row upon row of pumpkins. The orange gourds seemed swallowed in the shadows of the shed. Something about the way they sat askew on the shelves made the rest of Ryan's body grow cold.

OCTOBER 8

1

The pumpkin rested on the top step to the Woodson house and the boys gathered to check it out, Ryan beside it, the other three astride their bikes on the front walk.

"How come you haven't carved it yet?" Lance asked.

"Haven't decided what kind of face to give it," Ryan said as he looked at the pumpkin.

"Something scary for sure," Lance said.

"Of course. But it needs to be just right. It's too perfect to take the chance to ruin it."

"Curtis was the best at pumpkin carving," Wesley said, oblivious to the implications of his comment.

Russell shook his head in disbelief.

Lance turned to Wesley. "Moron."

"What?" Wesley asked, his hands raised in a confused gesture.

"It's all right, guys," Ryan said. "He's right. Curtis knew how to carve the perfect pumpkin."

"You'll figure something out," Russell said.

"But more important than that," Lance said, "when are we going to the movies again? *The Dunwich Horror* opened tonight. That's going to be wicked."

"Friday night would be good," Ryan said.

The others agreed.

Russell said nothing. He kept thinking about the skeleton in Miss Sheriden's classroom and now he worried it would pop up in every horror movie he watched. *It's just bones*, he told himself. But deep down he heard another voice tell him: *Just like your father. Nothing but bones.*

He swallowed hard and felt a sudden chill.

Mrs. Woodson came to the front door.

"It's getting dark, boys," she said. "Time to call it a night."

Ryan said his good nights and headed inside. Russell and the others turned around on their bikes and headed off toward their homes.

None of them noticed the pairs of eyes watching.

2

When the boys on the bikes left and Ryan went inside, Eddie Scruggs and Wayne Barnes crawled out from under the drooping curtain of a willow tree's branches where they had been hiding and watching. Eddie's parents expected him home once it got dark and he'd probably get the belt from his old man, hopefully not buckle side. But it didn't matter tonight. He needed the cover of darkness to accomplish his task.

"Come on," Eddie said to the bigger boy and the two crept across Oak Street to the Woodson house. The pumpkin sat on the top front step like a beacon and he aimed his sights straight for it. He quickly looked over the front of the house and saw no signs of the occupants. They stopped in front of the steps.

"That's a nice jack-o'-lantern," Wayne said.

"It ain't a jack-o'-lantern till someone carves it," Eddie replied.

"Oh, yeah."

"But it is a perfect pumpkin." Eddie glanced up and down the quiet street. No cars, no people about. "Let's go." He crept up the steps and grabbed ahold of the pumpkin, wrapping it tight in his arms. "Now!"

The two boys raced down the road past quiet houses of people probably sitting down to dinner, and kept going all the way to Lincoln Street. Once there, they left the neighborhood and crossed over to Stonewall Road and followed it along the river.

"What're your parents going to say when they see you come home with a pumpkin?" Wayne asked. "They'll know you got no money for it."

"Who says I'm taking it home?" Eddie felt a chill as he carried the pumpkin. Maybe it drifted over from the river.

"Let's chuck it in the river," Wayne said with a toothy laugh. "It'll sink right to the bottom."

"No," Eddie said. "I've got a better plan."

"What's that?"

"I'm going to smash it."

They walked in silence except for Wayne's periodic chuckling as they approached the juncture of Stage Coach Road, where the dark outline of the covered bridge stretched across the river. They continued on Stonewall past the Town Green, where Eddie saw a man walking a dog and a young couple canoodling on a park bench.

Nobody paid the two of them any attention and Eddie felt good about that as he lugged the pumpkin wrapped in his arms. Up ahead he spotted his target, the hulking frame of the railroad trestle that crossed the Piscataquog.

"There?" Wayne asked with a grin.

"Yes," Eddie said.

Beside where the road went under the trestle, Eddie and Wayne picked their way up the steep incline of the embankment. Eddie's sneakers, their tread worn to flatness, slipped a couple times on the loose gravel that made up most of the incline, and he almost thought he was going to drop the pumpkin, but managed to maintain his balance.

Wayne reached the top first, and lent a hand down to help Eddie up the last few steps and onto the wooden walkway beside the tracks on the bridge. The two of them walked about a quarter way along the bridge to a spot where Eddie could look down and see they were over the center of the road that ran under the bridge.

A car approached down the road and the two of them instinctively ducked like criminals and waited till it disappeared under the bridge. The soft hum of its engine emerged on the other side and slowly faded as it disappeared around the bend in the road heading north.

Wayne poked his head up first. "Coast is clear," he said.

Eddie stood up and set the pumpkin on the trestle railing. He gazed down at the dark asphalt of Stonewall Road below. He looked at Wayne and smiled.

"Let 'er rip," Wayne said.

Eddie lifted the pumpkin with raised arms. Something felt odd about the weight of the gourd, as if it shifted in his upraised arms. His hands grew cold. With a sudden urge to release his grip from it, he flung the pumpkin downward and then leaned over the railing to watch.

The pumpkin turned in the air during its descent and a streetlight glanced off the gourd, almost casting a glow along its rind. The pumpkin met the pavement with a loud splat and it broke apart, sending pieces in several directions and spraying seeds across the road.

Eddie saw something else.

Maybe it was the stringy innards of the pumpkin. But something dark like oil seemed to leak out of its center when it cracked open, and Eddie could have sworn it swept across the road toward the embankment like a moving shadow. And up it.

"Run!" Eddie screamed.

Wayne assuredly didn't know why, but the bigger boy bolted down the tracks in the direction toward where their rowhouses flanked the railway. For a few seconds Eddie stood frozen, his hands cemented to the railing as he looked down at the gooey mess of the splattered pumpkin, and he sensed that something had crawled from it.

Then his legs moved and he found himself racing along the tracks, wanting more than anything to get home, no matter what punishment awaited him. He caught up to the lumbering Wayne and passed him. He didn't take the time to glance back at his friend, for fear he might see something dark following them.

OCTOBER 9

1

The subtle squeak of a bedspring prodded Ryan from his slumber. His eyes were sleepy in the dawning light of his bedroom as he glanced at the bottom of the bunk above him, where the sound had emanated. He was about to call out, "Are you awake?" but then came to his senses.

But still….

It sounded like something had shifted on the mattress above him, though that couldn't be. A sensation stirred inside him, telling his body to get out of bed and look to see what made the bedspring squeak. He threw the covers off and stepped out. As he straightened upright, he peered into the empty bed of the top bunk.

He felt a tug inside his chest. He reached out and smoothed a wrinkle in the middle of the bed covers. A quick glance at the clock told him he needed to get a move on.

Downstairs he wolfed down his breakfast at record pace.

"What's your rush?" Dane asked.

He made a face at his brother. "Nothing you care about."

"Ryan and his friends are riding their bikes to school today," his mother said, putting some toast on a plate in the center of the table. "Taking advantage of the great weather."

"Indian summer day, the weatherman says," his father piped in before slurping his coffee.

"Good day to get some exercise," Mrs. Woodson said as she turned to Dane. "When was the last time you rode your bike?"

His older brother laughed. "That's for kids. I prefer riding with Wade. I get enough exercise at practice." Dane got up from the table.

"Besides, I need to save my energy for the big game Sunday." He grabbed his school bag, said goodbye to his parents, and headed out the door. The sound of Wade's El Camino rumbled out front.

Mrs. Woodson watched him go with a forlorn look. "I remember when he used to kiss me goodbye before heading to school."

"He's saving his lips for someone else," Mr. Woodson said with a laugh.

His wife gave him a playful slap on the arm with a dish towel. She turned to Ryan.

"You'll still give me a kiss before you leave, won't you?"

"Oh, Mom." Ryan blushed. He gazed at the clock on the wall and jumped up. "Got to go."

When he stepped out the front door, the first thing he noticed was the empty spot on the steps where his pumpkin had been. He looked in disbelief. *What the—?*

"Mom!"

His mother appeared at the screen door.

"My pumpkin's gone!"

His father joined her and shook his head. "Hooligans," he said. "Can't trust anyone these days."

Voices from up the street drew his attention, and Ryan saw Lance, Russell, and Wesley riding down Oak Street on their bikes. They all skidded to a stop in front of his house.

"Someone stole my pumpkin!"

"What?" Lance looked at the steps. "Bastards."

"Language!" Mrs. Woodson said from behind the screen door.

"Sorry."

"What a bummer," Russell said.

"Who'd do that?" Wesley asked.

"Some asshole," Ryan muttered under his breath so his mother wouldn't hear.

Soon the four boys were racing down Lincoln Street past the police station and public library in the Town Square before shooting across Hitching Post Lane to pick up Stonewall Road along the river.

Ryan led the pack, followed close behind by Lance. The baseball card clipped to Russell's front wheel reverberated in the spokes like the rumble of a motorbike as he tried to keep up. Wesley lagged behind.

Up ahead loomed the railroad trestle that crossed over the road. Something in the road caught Ryan's eye. As he got closer, he skidded his bike to a halt. The others stopped beside him as they spotted it too. Pieces of pumpkin shell, seeds and strings of orange lay scattered over the middle of the road.

"Is that your pumpkin?" Wesley asked.

Ryan stared. It could be anyone's pumpkin. There was no way to tell. But somehow, in his gut, he felt sure it was his. His eyes were drawn up to the railroad trestle and the precipice it must have been dropped from.

An unsettled queasiness burrowed into his stomach. His skin felt clammy as if the morning dew stuck to it. He glanced along the road, wondering if whoever did this was nearby. Maybe watching.

He got off his bike, put the kickstand down, and walked over to the broken pumpkin. He picked up a shattered fragment. It felt soft and he noticed a black stain on the orange skin, as if the impact with the asphalt had rubbed some of the tar onto it.

It felt cold and his fingers grew numb, so he dropped it.

It was his all right, he thought.

Before getting back on his bike, he took another look up at the trestle. Something urged him to get on his bike and get away from here.

2

Mortimer stood at the front window in his bedroom, staring down at Elm Street below as a couple of squirrels scampered around an oak tree searching for acorns in the yard on the other side.

Secrets, he thought. Everyone has secrets in this place. He was thinking of the town, but even of the boardinghouse itself. He knew Calvin Armstrong's secrets, and Ruth Downey, as he could hear her footsteps in the wee hours of the night coming a floor below from the back end of the house to the bachelor's room at the front, one floor below his. He could hear the bedsprings and soft moans coming up through the heating vents.

He also sensed the Stich sisters' secrets. Sisters indeed. Mortimer made a living long ago at reading his audience and figuring out who they were and what they wanted. No one could hide things from him.

But this Lothrop fellow was a tricky one. He hid from the world in this house surviving on the royalty checks from reprints of his ghastly stories sold long ago and now collected for a few furtive fans and impressionable young boys who scoured macabre anthologies.

Something made the man stop writing and hide away in this nondescript town that resembled thousands of others throughout New England. Harold never went outside, not in all the years he's spent here, except for that one night when he witnessed Mortimer's show and the catastrophe that followed.

He's seen things, Mortimer contemplated. *He's witnessed events that frighten him and he hides those secrets inside himself and buries them in booze. But what has he seen?* He wondered if it had something to do with this town. Some force here that warped his magic. He never had problems before he came to Maplewood. His tricks were always right at his fingertips.

Mortimer turned and walked over to the desk, where his black top hat lay upside down on it. He pulled the chair out, sat down, and stared into the dark abyss of the hat. *What happened to my magic?*

He waved his hand over the top of the hat and muttered some magic words. He reached inside and felt around. Nothing.

Mortimer leaned back in the chair and released an old sigh.

"Again," he said.

He reached his hand over the hat, waved it around, and plunged his fingers down inside.

He felt something. His hand closed around softness and pulled it out.

His grip held a dead white rabbit. Mortimer's eyes widened; his heart fluttered. A soft moan croaked out of his tightened throat.

Daimon.

It had been at least thirty years since his faithful pet had passed, succumbing to natural causes at the age of twelve and buried long ago in a part of the world he couldn't even remember.

But here its body lay in his tired, old hand, eyes closed. He stroked the soft fur with the fingers of his left hand, the fur a bit mottled, the body not quite entering the stage of decomposition yet. *How can that be? How can it even be here?*

This wasn't magic. This was something else.

He felt a soft thump where the beast's body lay across the palm of his hand.

An eye opened. Red. The iris bleeding into the white.

More thumps from the body vibrated through his palm. Heartbeats.

Mortimer's blood froze in his veins. He jumped up from the chair and dumped the rabbit back into the hat. He stared at that black opening, waiting for a white furry paw to grip its rim and climb up out of it.

Before it had a chance, he struck the hat and sent it sailing off the desk. It hit the wall and bounced along the floorboards. It rolled to a stop on its side.

Mortimer walked over to it with fearful steps. He got down on his hands and knees and peered into the black opening.

Nothing but empty darkness inside.

Something is happening here, he thought, as his heart skipped a few beats. *And it's not magic.*

3

After a breakfast of overcooked scrambled eggs and slightly burnt toast sprinkled with cinnamon sugar, Quinn washed his meal down with the last drops of pulpy orange juice. Rita sat watching him the whole time, making his stomach squirm. Or maybe it was the eggs.

Her face conjured vague memories that frustrated him. At the House of Embers, he couldn't remember much of where he was before he got there, just sporadic glimpses of images. He remembered the sound of calliope music and bright flashing lights. And the smell of straw, that too.

But his father? He couldn't remember anything about him. Or his mother. His brain remained foggy. Shreckengast didn't know where he came from either. It remained a mystery. Quinn assumed he was an orphan the Master took in. But the House of Embers wasn't like a real home.

Quinn glanced around the shadows of the basement. Neither was this place.

"You say you knew my father," he said to the woman leering at him as he wiped sticky orange pulp from the corner of his mouth.

"I knew him well," Rita said.

"Where is he?"

Rita's face was supported by her hands as she leaned on the table with her elbows. Her round eyes seemed to roll in their sockets as she contemplated his question.

"He's been gone a long time," Rita said. "I haven't seen him in years."

Quinn studied her. He didn't trust her, had no reason to.

"Where did he go?"

She shrugged. "Nobody knows."

"Are you lying to me?"

The woman laughed. "Why would I lie to a little boy? I like little boys. I've always wanted a little boy." She leaned closer. "I couldn't give my husband any kids." Her face drooped. "That disappointed him."

Quinn couldn't believe this woman had a husband. "Where's your husband? Is he upstairs?"

"Oh no. He's been gone a long time."

"Did he die?"

"He just disappeared one day," she said with a frown.

Something about that disturbed him, gave him a cold chill as if the basement were suddenly encased in ice. His shoulders shivered.

"Disappeared?" Quinn remembered something. Stepping into a dark box. Eyes upon him. A man in black with a top hat smiling at him as he closed the door and then there was nothing but darkness.

Rita's face shifted as her lips curled up, pushing her pudgy cheeks apart. "You know what it's like to disappear, don't you?"

Quinn felt his throat constrict. The look on her face frightened him. *She knows something.* "What do you mean?"

"Your father didn't want you, Quinn," she said. "That's why he made you disappear."

Goose bumps erupted on his arms. "That's not true," he said. *Is it?* Even if he had a father, would he do something like that? Why?

"I was there, Quinn. I saw what happened."

Quinn jumped up from his chair, the legs scraping against the cement floor with a squeal.

"You're lying to me!" He didn't have a father, and if he did, his father wouldn't have sent him away. Not to a place like the House of Embers with Shreckengast and the Scamps. He wouldn't have done that to him.

"Your father didn't want you, Quinn." She rose from her chair, the expression on her face half grinning, half angry. "Face the facts."

Quinn's lower lip quivered.

"But you don't have to worry anymore," Rita said. "I'll take care of you. You can live here and be my little boy. I've always wanted a little boy of my own."

Quinn nibbled on his lip before speaking. This ugly woman was loony, he thought.

"I don't want to live with you," he said.

She approached him and reached out to grab his upper arm. Her fingers squeezed down like a vise grip till he could feel a jolt of pain in his bone.

"Then you'll stay locked in this basement till you come to your senses!" she yelled, her cheeks becoming flushed. "Be an ungrateful little brat, and you'll be sorry. Learn to accept your predicament, and you can have a nice life here." Her smile returned and the red drained from her face. "I'll treat you special. Like the most precious little boy in the world."

4

Eddie and Wayne walked along the railroad tracks on the way home from school. Eddie knew his parents didn't like him taking this route, but it was the most direct path and since he didn't like taking the bus because of all the jerks on it, this was the easiest way for him to get to or from school. He liked walking with Wayne, the only kid who never made fun of him, and who was big enough that he could protect him from the others at school.

The boys approached the part of the trestle that crossed the river, before it spanned the road on the other side. He stopped. One of the reasons his parents didn't like him taking this route was because his mother said hobos lived beneath the trestle and liked to molest boys. She warned him often, but he never paid her any mind.

As he stared at the bridge, he thought about the other night and what he thought he saw. *That was no hobo*. Something came out of that smashed pumpkin. Something dark had slithered out.

Eddie turned and looked up at the sky. Dark clouds gathered and kicked up the breeze that had blown along the tracks. Storm coming. Wouldn't that be great, right in time for Harvest Fest tomorrow. He hoped it poured on the stupid festival and ruined everyone's fun.

Wayne started across the wooden planks of the walkway across the trestle. He turned when he realized Eddie wasn't following. "Are you coming?"

"Yeah," Eddie said, but did not move.

"Are you still freaked out about last night?"

"No." He eyed the wooden platform that ran along the side of the rails of the bridge. "Not really."

"What did you see last night?" Wayne asked. "Because I didn't see nothing. Just gave me the creeps when you yelled to run. You spooked me more than anything."

"Nothing," Eddie said and began walking. "I didn't see nothing."

But as he started across the bridge, he looked down through gaps in the planks wondering if there were any hobos camping out under the bridge. The planks were weathered and cracked like an old mummy's skin, and you had to be careful when you walked because some of the boards were loose and gaps between them sometimes were big enough to slip the toe of your sneaker into.

He couldn't shake the feeling that something came after him last night. Something dark that moved fast. Something that followed him home. *Does it know where I live now?*

Halfway across the bridge, he turned to look back. The clouds in the sky mushroomed and darkened. He stopped to watch them as they moved above in the same direction as he. *Following us. Following us home.*

Up ahead, Wayne plodded along, his big shit-kicker boots stomping on the planks with a sound that reverberated. Eddie watched him and listened. Another sound came from beneath the walkway. A scuttling noise.

Eddie took a few steps and heard the sound again. It matched his own pace, as if something crawled on the underside of the wooden walkway, replicating his steps. *Following.* Maybe an animal, or a river rat. But what could crawl along the bottom of the boards like that? No animal he knew of. It would take great strength to cling to the underside of the boards.

Eddie stopped and stared at his feet and the noise stopped. He lifted his gaze toward Wayne, who had reached the part of the trestle that now crossed over Stonewall Road. His friend's footsteps faded the farther he got away from him.

When Eddie started walking again, he heard the floorboards creak beneath his feet, but also noticed a scratching sound. He stopped and the noise stopped. He got down on his knees and peered into a one-inch crack between two planks. Below he saw the dark water of the Piscataquog as the river sloshed by.

There couldn't be anything under there, Eddie thought. No way anything could crawl upside down like that.

An eyeball filled the gap between the boards.

Red veins scratched across a cloudy white cornea, an iris black as coal and burning as it looked up at him.

Eddie's heart leapt into his throat so he couldn't scream. He jumped up and raced across the bridge, not caring that the boards rattled beneath his pounding feet and felt like they were going to collapse and pitch him down into the grasp of whatever crawled along the underside.

He didn't know if it was following, but he didn't attempt to look back as he hurried to reach the other side and get home.

OCTOBER 10

1

When Ryan and his friends entered the Town Green on the morning of Harvest Fest, crowds of people mingled among tented booths of farmers, crafters, and other artisans. As Ryan wandered with Lance, Russell, and Wesley by his side, he thought about how much Curtis used to enjoy the festival. He always excelled at the sack races and egg toss. When the twins teamed up for the three-legged race, Curtis was faster and nearly had to drag Ryan along to the finish line.

He'd like it here today, Ryan thought as he scanned the crowd of happy faces.

Curtis would have also liked the movie they saw last night at the Colonial Theater, *The Dunwich Horror*. Ryan liked Lovecraft because it reminded him of a lot of Harold Lothrop's writing. Lovecraft died young but still had more output than Mr. Lothrop. He couldn't understand why Lothrop stopped writing, or why he discouraged Ryan from pursuing the genre. The man turned his back on the success it gave him.

Ryan spotted Becky Williams walking by the crafts tables with Liza and Lindsey in tow. Ryan wanted to go talk to her, but didn't dare. He wouldn't know what to say. Curtis wouldn't have had that problem. Girls didn't make him nervous. How could he be so different from his own twin?

"You should see if she wants to go on a hayride later tonight," Lance said, as if reading Ryan's mind.

Grant Parker, one of the local farmers, gave hayrides at the festival on a wagon pulled by his antique tractor. Most of the younger kids took rides during the day, but the older kids and teens liked the nighttime rides.

"She'd probably say no," Ryan said.

"Can't hurt to try," Lance said.

"Of course it could," Russell said. "She could laugh in his face in front of her friends, and then it'd be all over school."

"But she could say yes," Lance countered.

"Is it worth the risk?" Wesley said. "Think of the worst possible outcome."

Ryan watched Kirby Tressler and some other eighth-graders approach Becky and her friends and chat them up. Ryan hated the way Becky smiled at Kirby. The group of them wandered over to a dunk tank booth where Police Chief Asa Strong sat on a collapsible shelf perched over the water. The overweight chief, who was in his fifties, wore an old-fashioned, one-piece striped bathing suit from a bygone era, the kind that covered the upper and lower torso.

Kirby stepped up to take a chance. As Ryan slinked away with the others, he heard a loud clang and turned in time to see Chief Strong's body plunge into the water tank to cheers from the gathered crowd. Becky jumped up and down and clapped her hands.

Ryan turned away. "Let's find something to do. This festival seems lame this year."

"I know," Lance said. "Let's go over to the newspaper booth and get the scoop on the scavenger hunt contest."

Every October, the county newspaper sponsored a scavenger hunt in Maplewood and announced the list of items at Harvest Fest. They headed over to the booth manned by Monroe Wright, the reporter who, though nearing sixty, still covered the town beat.

"Hey, Mr. Wright," Lance said as they approached the table set up under a tent.

"Hello, Lance, boys," Wright greeted. "Enjoying the festival?"

"It's lame," Lance said. "Nothing here for us."

"Maybe not here," Wright said as he picked up some sheets of paper. "But elsewhere."

"The scavenger hunt?" Ryan asked.

"Yes, indeed." The man passed a sheet of paper into the waiting hands of the four boys. "And what boy wouldn't want to win one hundred dollars?"

"A hundred bucks," Ryan said as he grazed past the rules listed at the top of the page and focused on the list of items below.

"And you get to explore all over town to find the items," Wright said. "But you better get started. Some people might already be collecting."

"Let's book," Lance said and the four of them peeled away from the newspaper man's booth.

"These look hard," Russell said as he read over the list.

"Of course it's hard," Lance said. "It wouldn't be worth a hundred bucks if it wasn't."

"Hey, we should team up," Ryan said. "Then if we win, we can each get twenty-five bucks."

"Sounds great," Lance said.

"But, where do we start?" Russell asked.

Lance looked down the list again. "We need to put our heads together and see who can come up with some of the items easy enough."

"Look at this one," Ryan said, pointing to the page. "A headstone rubbing of the oldest grave."

"That stinks," Wesley said. "Everyone will be down at the town cemetery looking for the oldest grave."

"But the oldest grave might not be at the town cemetery," Ryan said with a smile.

Lance cracked a smile. "That's right," he said. "We know of an even older graveyard, that probably no one else knows about."

"We can hit it first thing in the morning. In the meantime, let's brainstorm about the rest of this list."

"Can we get something to eat first?" Wesley said as he rubbed his belly. "I'm starving."

"Come on," Ryan said. "Let's find some food and then plan how to attack this scavenger hunt."

After grabbing some hot dogs from one of the food booths, Ryan and his friends sat at a picnic table and pored over the scavenger hunt list till a voice interrupted.

"What are you losers up to?"

Ryan looked up to see his brother Dane and Dane's friend, Ben Karney.

"It's the annual newspaper scavenger hunt," Ryan said. "We're going to try and win the hundred bucks."

"Not try," Lance said from across the table. "Win it."

"And split it four ways," Russell said.

"Twenty-five bucks apiece," Wesley added.

"Wow," Dane said. "What math geniuses. Let me see that." He snatched the paper from Ryan.

"Hey! That's mine."

"Just want to take a look," Dane said. He nodded as he perused the items on the list. "Ben and I can find this stuff and that'd be fifty bucks apiece for those of you who don't have your slide rule handy." He turned back to his brother. "Thanks for the sheet." He and Ben walked away.

"No fair," Ryan said.

"See ya, suckers."

"Your brother's a real jerk," Russell said.

"It's all because he's a big jock now," Ryan said, reflecting on the memories of when Dane used to look after him and Curtis. Now with Dane in high school and Curtis gone, it didn't seem his brother paid much attention to him. He wanted to stand up and shout, 'Curtis is gone, but I'm still here.'

"Forget about him," Lance said.

"Right," Ryan said. "We've got to concentrate on this scavenger list. The whole town will be trying to win this, not just my brother Dane."

"Does he know about the graveyard?" Lance asked.

"I doubt it," Ryan said. "We discovered that. I don't think anyone else knows it's there."

"Hope not," Lance said.

"I'm still hungry," Wesley said. "Let's get some popcorn or ice cream."

"Okay," Ryan said. "We can deal with this scavenger list later."

The boys got up from the table and headed toward the food booths on the other end of the Town Green. Before they got there, Lance stopped.

"Look over there," he said, pointing. "It's Rita and the creepy old guy in black."

Russell and the others looked to where he indicated. The pair seemed to be in an intense discussion.

"Do you think they know each other?" Russell asked.

"Maybe she's looking for her next victim," Lance said. "I mean, husband."

They all laughed.

"They don't look like friends," Wesley said.

It didn't appear that way to Ryan. The old man seemed irritated about something, his face bunched up in knots.

"What a strange pair," Lance said. "But that crazy witch doesn't seem afraid of him."

"I'd be afraid of him," Russell said. "He gives me the creeps, all dressed in black like that."

"There's something else odd about him though," Ryan said.

"What's that?" Lance asked.

"Haven't you noticed something different about him?"

Lance shrugged. "Not really."

"I see it," Russell said. "Or rather, I don't."

"What are you talking about?"

"He's not wearing his black top hat."

2

Mortimer Rigby leered into the enormous face of Rita Stone and could feel his blood rise like an overboiling pot, his face flushing.

"You ruined everything," he said, the words squeezing out between clenched teeth as he tried to temper the tone of his voice in the middle of the crowded park.

"I don't have a clue as to what you're talking about, Morty," she responded, which infuriated him further.

"My magic cabinet," he said. "You got rid of my original cabinet and a replacement one didn't work."

Rita snorted. "Maybe you just lost that old magic touch, Morty."

"Do you realize how important this was to me? I've devoted most of my life to this and I've lost my chance to…to…."

"To what, Morty?" Her eyebrows knitted as her face tightened. She took one step closer to him, her large frame causing him to lean back. "To bring your boy back? Did you really think that would work? Do you really think you're that good of a magician? Do you think you're Harry Blackstone?"

He fumbled for a response, but she gave him no respite.

"And what if it did work?" she asked. "Your boy would come back as a middle-aged man and he wouldn't even remember you, and if he did, he wouldn't want anything to do with you after you abandoned him. Is that what you wanted?"

"No," he barked in defense.

"You thought you could have your precious little boy back, but you're wrong." Spittle flew from her mouth as her voice bellowed. "He ain't coming back to you, Morty. Your one last magic trick was the last thing you had up your sleeve. Face it. You're all hocus, with no pocus."

His body drooped as if the weight of her words were dumped on his shoulders.

"Now get out of my way, Morty," Rita said. "I've got some pies to buy."

Mortimer watched her walk away, wishing he could cast some spell to make her inflate till the seams of her skin ripped apart. But maybe she was right. Maybe it wasn't the cabinet. It could be that he had finally lost the magic. Or if it didn't vanish, it quite possibly could have rotted away.

He thought about the rabbit in the hat, poor Daimon. It looked dead, but wasn't quite gone. He hadn't imagined its eyes opening. They looked like vacant eyes, dead lenses into whatever world it had come from. It had gone bad. He had been afraid to put the hat back on, didn't even want to touch the thing. The magic had rotted inside it.

Mortimer glanced around the park as eyes fell on him, wondering what this old man had been blabbering about with the former carnival fat lady. Something rotten indeed. He could taste it. There was bad magic going on in this town. As he turned, his eyes fell on a display of pumpkins at one of the farmer's booths.

He made a beeline for it and noticed the Stich sisters perusing the pumpkins. They didn't notice him at first as he stood before the display of orange gourds on the booth's table and in big wooden crates beside it. Set up on a pallet beside one of the crates, he eyed a giant. King of the pumpkins; the great pumpkin sitting on its throne with a blue ribbon plastered to its top.

"Hello, Mr. Rigby," Pearl Stich said when she noticed him lurking behind her. Her sister, Noreen, hefted a large, round pumpkin that she nestled in the crook of one large arm.

"What are you doing with that?" he asked.

"We're bringing it back to the boardinghouse of course," Noreen said. "To carve later."

"Wilfred and Ruth always let us set up a jack-o'-lantern for Halloween," Pearl said. "We like to sit on the porch and hand out candy to the trick-or-treaters."

"It's our tradition." Noreen held up the pumpkin for him to get a better look at. "Does this look like a good one?"

Mortimer cast his eyes upon the pumpkin. His upper lip curled.

"It's flat on one side," he said.

"We'll make that the back," Pearl said and took some money out of her purse to pay the farmer.

"Now we must find Calvin," Noreen said, "so we can put this in his car. I can't lug this around all day. Have you seen him?"

"No," Mortimer said, and hoped he wouldn't.

"We'll find him," Pearl said to her sister. "Good day, Mr. Rigby."

"Enjoy the rest of the festival," Noreen said.

The two women left with their purchase and he wished he had stopped them. He looked back at the table before him. *Rotten*. Something rotten about these pumpkins. He didn't like their shapes. Not round and smooth. Warped and bumpy. He walked over to the giant pumpkin. It looked like a heart with a deep crease down the middle.

"First prize," the farmer said as he came out from behind the table and extended a hand. "Hank Swain."

Mortimer looked down at the hand as if it were poisonous.

Hank withdrew it.

"Two thousand and thirteen pounds," Hank said. "Almost a state record. My biggest yet. I named her Bessie."

Mortimer eyed the giant pumpkin. It didn't look like a prize to him. The shape was odd, the color pale, as if something had drained the life out of it.

"What's wrong with it?" he asked Hank.

"What do you mean?"

"It's odd. It's not right." Mortimer went back to the table and looked over all the pumpkins. Some had dark spots, as if the pumpkins were bleeding black from the inside. "Something's wrong with them."

Hank's face scrunched up as if insulted.

"These pumpkins are fine," Hank said. "Been kind of a dry autumn so far and the summer was way too hot. Not enough rain got into the soil. But not a bad crop after all."

"Something else got into them," Mortimer said. He could smell something off. "You know what you should do?"

"What's that, mister?"

"Dump them in the river. The whole damn lot of them."

3

Hank Swain thought about the strange old man in black while he towed the trailer of unsold pumpkins back to his farm as dusk fell on the town after the festival ended. At least, his part of the event. Nothing left but nighttime hayrides put on by Grant Parker, who ran a farm down the road from him.

Maybe the old man had wandered away from a nursing home or something. The local one out on the county road brought some of the more able residents to the festival every year. This one probably slipped away from the group. He hoped someone corralled the old man before something happened to him.

Hank couldn't help wonder why the man got so riled up about the pumpkins. He glanced back through his rear windshield at Bessie nestled in the back of the pickup, a blanket thrown over it to keep the night chill off it. He needed to keep it protected till he could harvest the seeds. Those would fetch a pretty penny from some of the other pumpkin growers who would want to top his prize-winning gourd.

He looked farther back at the trailer and the remaining pumpkins he was bringing back to his farm. They looked black in the dwindling light of day as twilight settled over them, like heads bobbing on a dark sea. He sold enough at the festival this year and felt pleased. He had plenty to sell the remainder of the month. After that, the rest would become pumpkin pies.

Once he was back at the farm, Austin Stanton and a couple of his other workers helped him lift Bessie out of the pickup and set it down beside the pumpkin shed. The boys then unloaded the remaining pumpkins and stacked them on the shelves in the shed.

"Thanks for all your help today, boys," Hank said as they piled into Austin's car. "Enjoy the day off tomorrow and the big game." He always closed the day after the festival to recuperate from the big event and let his workers enjoy the annual homecoming game. He'd be open bright and early on Columbus Day. Till then, they all deserved a day off to relax, even though he himself probably wouldn't. Still too much to do to run a farm, especially since he was on his own.

The boys drove off and Hank went to shut the pumpkin shed door, but as he grabbed the edge of it and prepared to swing it closed, he stopped. A pumpkin fell off one of the shelves and landed with a plop on the wooden floor. He stepped inside and stared down at it. A bit of moonlight spilled in through the doorway and provided enough illumination to allow him to see the pumpkin and a long crack that formed when it landed.

One of the boys must have inadvertently placed it teetering on the edge of a shelf and it toppled off. Hank stared at the pumpkins that lined the shelves. These were the worst of the lot. The misfits left behind because they weren't the right shape.

Were those black spots he saw on some of them, or were they just shadows? He stepped further inside to inspect them.

They looked deformed. Flat edges on some. Indentations on others. Not a one was a nice round shape that people liked. They sat awkward on the shelves, tilting to one side or the other. None of them stood up straight. He couldn't imagine anyone having faith in placing these on their front stoop or porch railing.

No. These were bad. Just like the man in black said. They were off. Something wrong with them.

Hank heard a noise behind him and spun around.

A shuffling sound.

He eyed the pumpkins. *Did one of them move?* As he stared in the shadowy darkness of the shed, one pumpkin seemed to lean over to touch the one next to it. *Something wrong. Something not right.*

Hank stepped over to that side. He straightened the leaning pumpkin upright and took a step back.

It keeled over to fall against the one on the other side of it.

Mocking me, he thought. *Playing games.*

The pumpkin beside it seemed to turn, as if it were trying to face him. But it had no face of course, unless you counted those black spots that sort of resembled eyes. *No. Not a face. Not yet.* Not till someone brought it home and took a knife to carve out a crooked grin and hollow eyes.

Then why did it seem to be looking at him?

Hank turned away, but the pumpkins on the opposite shelf seemed to lean forward as if they wanted to leap off the shelves.

No, he thought. *I'm the boss here. Nothing happens without my say-so.*

His eyes scanned the pumpkins. Some had warts and imperfections. Others looked crooked and distorted. They seemed to stretch and twist. Had some of them elongated?

What's wrong with me? He wiped a hand across a sweaty brow.

These pumpkins are worthless, he thought. *Orphans.* No one would buy them. Hell, he couldn't even give these blasted things away. Rubbish.

Hank left the shed, thinking he heard a giggling sound from within as he stepped back outside.

Don't mock me. He looked over his shoulder and glanced back inside the pumpkin shed. *I'll fix you.*

He walked over to his barn and stepped inside. When he came back out, he held a sledgehammer gripped tight in both trembling hands. *I'll show them who's boss.* He returned to the shed and stepped inside. *Damn you all. You'll never get to be a pie.*

Hank swung the sledgehammer. The heavy metal head of the tool slammed into the pumpkins, crashing through their shells and sending orange goo splattering across the walls of the shed. He didn't know how he mustered the strength, but the tool felt as light as bamboo as he swung it back and forth, crashing into rows of pumpkins, shattering their rinds, and sending them tumbling to the floor where pieces lay scattered, orange slime coating his boots.

He only stopped when he heard a loud crack from outside. It sounded like a tree branch breaking. Still clutching the sledgehammer, the mallet head dripping with stringy orange strands, he stepped out of the shed. The sound came from where Bessie lay nearby.

He walked over to his prized pumpkin and stopped. The moonlight cast a glow over the giant gourd. The sound had come from here and as his eyes roamed over the surface of the pumpkin, he noticed a crack had developed along the crease that divided the heart-shaped object.

No.

A rusty liquid oozed out of the crack.

I have to act fast, he thought. *I need to save the seeds.* They were worth a lot.

As he pondered what action to take, the crack widened and lengthened almost to the bottom of the pumpkin. Something began to work its way out of the center of the crack, and at first it appeared to be dark worms wiggling their way out.

Rotten. My prized pumpkin has been infested by worms.

But then he realized they were not worms and the sledgehammer slipped from his hands and dropped to the ground at his feet.

Not worms.

Fingers.

Long black fingers squeezed their way out through the crack. They wiggled, searching for purchase, and then they gripped the edges of the crack and pushed out to widen the opening.

A long narrow head began to emerge from the chasm, lids sprung open to reveal bloodshot eyes above a long, pointed nose. Thin lips parted from narrow teeth in a widening smile.

Hank's bowels unspooled like a coil of rope as the thing spoke.

"Peekaboo."

OCTOBER 11

1

Quinn scavenged through boxes in the basement looking for something to help him out of his predicament, such as a tool to pry off one of the metal grates that covered the cellar windows or break open the door at the top of the stairs. Or better yet, a weapon, preferably sharp or heavy, that he could use to clobber his captor on her head.

What he found was useless. A box filled with Matchbox cars. Another contained parts of a train set. Still another had sets of tiny Airfix military figures. *Didn't anyone in this household own a damn hammer?* he thought, aggravated and wanting to smash something.

He'd tried being nice to the lady, playing along, thinking she'd finally let him upstairs and then he could make a break for it. But she saw right through him.

"Those are mostly Gordon's crap," said a voice behind him.

Quinn nearly jumped out of his skin. He turned to see Rita standing on the basement stairs looking at him. How could he not hear those heavy steps coming down? Or the door being unlocked and opened at the top? He must have been so immersed in his search that he blocked everything else out.

"I boxed everything up after he was gone," she said as she came down the rest of the stairs. Now he could hear the creaking wooden boards strain with each step. She carried a pie in her hands.

"Why did he have all these toys? I thought you didn't have any kids." He sat on his knees before a box.

"Because he was a big kid. He liked collecting things." She approached and stood over him. "Comic books, toy models. To me it was garbage."

"Looks like neat stuff," Quinn said and closed the cover of the box. "Bet he was funner than you."

Rita let out a pent-up sigh. "If you learn to behave yourself, things would be better for you. I would have taken you to Harvest Fest yesterday and you could have had fun. But this behavior..." She pointed at the boxes he had been rummaging through. "...just proves that you're not ready to be trusted. If you can just learn to be my good boy."

"I'm not your boy," Quinn said, nearly spitting the words at her.

"I'm all you got," she said. "I'm the only one who cares about you. Not your father, that's for sure."

"I don't believe you," he said. Some memories of his father had filtered back as he lay in the basement at night before drifting off to sleep. He remembered the magic hat he wore, and pulling things out of it that surprised him. His father had to care for him. But if he did, why hadn't he come to rescue him after all this time?

"He didn't want a brat like you," Rita said. "And I'm not going to tolerate it either." She glanced around the basement. "You've made a mess of these boxes. I should have gotten rid of all Gordon's crap years ago. Now I want you to clean it all up."

"No," Quinn said and sat back on his haunches and folded his arms across his chest. "You can't make me."

Rita's eyes tightened.

"You ungrateful little shit," she said. "And here I brought you a nice blueberry pie from the festival. Is this how you show your appreciation? I saved you. No one else did."

Quinn kept silent. She was right. His father didn't save him. Shreckengast didn't save him. He had nobody.

"You like blueberry pie, don't you?" Rita asked.

He couldn't remember if he did or not, but he nodded.

"That's a good boy," she said. Rita held out the pie with a smile, and then her grin evaporated as she smashed the dessert upside down on the cement floor. Berries and juice and pieces of crust spread out in front of him, some splattering onto his pants. "Now you can lick it up off the floor like the animal you are, if that's how you're going to behave down here!"

Rita turned and trudged up the cellar steps, each big foot stomping on the treads with a thumping sound that echoed in the basement. When she got to the top, she went through the door and slammed it shut. He heard the locks click into place.

2

As Ryan and his friends rode their bikes toward the covered bridge, he could see across the river to the town cemetery. Several cars were parked near the old-town portion where some of the original settlers of Maplewood were buried. He spotted several people kneeling by ancient headstones making their grave rubbings.

There were lots of old grave markers there, many dating back to the early eighteenth century, but he had to smile as they pedaled down the road along the opposite side of the river. They could have those tombstones. He knew of somewhere better.

The four of them turned onto the covered bridge, bicycle tires clattering along the wooden planks sounding as if they'd shake them loose. The bridge spit them out the other end onto Old Coach Road as they headed north. Ryan and the others had left their houses early. He hadn't wanted his nosy brother to wonder what they were up to, because as far as Ryan knew, Dane and his stupid friend Ben didn't know what he knew.

In fact, he often thought no one else knew but the four of them.

As the road inclined, he pedaled harder, switching gears on his three-speed bike to little avail. Lance led them all on his Schwinn ten-speed. Maybe with his cut of the scavenger hunt winnings, Ryan could buy a better bicycle. Of course, he'd need more than his twenty-five-dollar share, but he'd been saving some of the money he earned from helping Lance with the paper route. At least what he didn't spend on comic books.

Ryan spotted the Williams farmhouse up ahead and he followed as Lance turned off the road and into the tall grass of the field before

Becky's family home. Russell pulled in right behind him, his Stingray making its fluttering noise from the baseball card he kept clamped to the spokes with a clothespin. It sounded so loud in the quiet morning that Ryan worried it would draw the attention of Mr. Williams. He didn't like the thought of that. The man seemed angry and mean on a normal day, never mind disturbing his peaceful Sunday morning.

"I thought I told you to take that card out," Lance said as they got off their bikes behind some shrubs.

The long grass was still damp from morning dew and soaked Ryan's sneakers and the cuffs of his jeans. Wesley finally caught up, huffing out of breath, and the four of them hunkered down out of sight of the Williams house.

"I meant to," Russell said, "and then I remembered something." He reached down to his rear tire and removed the baseball card from the clothespin. He handed the bent card to Ryan.

"What's this for?" Ryan asked.

"It's a Carl Yastrzemski card," Russell said. "It's on the list."

"Oh right!" Ryan said, remembering it being one of the items on the scavenger hunt paper. "Thanks." Ryan shoved the card into his back pocket. "One more item off the list."

"We should head to the woods now," Lance said, "before anyone in the house gets up."

"Okay," Ryan said. They left their bikes hidden behind the shrubs and walked through the field toward the wooded area.

As they reached the edge of the back end of the Williams property, they paused at a crumbling stone foundation nearly buried in the ground. They stopped and peered into it. Ryan remembered being told that this was the foundation of an old barn root cellar from when the Williams house had been a farm decades before the family lived here.

Mr. Williams threw all his yard waste, grass clippings, and fallen branches and brush he had cleared from the property into the barn cellar. He had carved a wide flat area behind his house for his kids to practice soccer. Two big nets were set up at each end of the open area.

Ryan peered into the root cellar and saw it was now nearly

overflowing, with a tangled mass of tree branches and brush making a huge deadfall. He saw twisted limbs wrapped in thorny vines.

"I dare you to walk across that," Lance said with a wicked grin.

"No way," Ryan said.

"That'd be crazy," Russell added.

The quiet morning was broken by the sound of a door opening and closing. Ryan looked but could see nothing from the rear of the Williams house. It must have come from the front.

"Let's go," he said.

As they entered the woods behind the barn cellar, Ryan felt a sense of security knowing they couldn't be seen. Ryan and Lance had discovered the old graveyard plot when they were eight. Back then the Williamses hadn't moved to town yet and the old farmhouse was vacant and the barn cellar hadn't been filled up with brush and dead tree limbs. The two of them were exploring the woods looking for a place to build a cool fort when they stumbled upon the graveyard.

Lance said it must have been a private plot for the family who originally lived in the farmhouse. None of the headstones stood upright, all lying on the ground and covered in moss and leaves, and seemed to be sinking into the earth. Most of the headstones were so worn you could not even read the names and dates carved into the stone. The few that still had some letters and numbers visible showed the same family last name, Eaton, and the dates were in the late sixteen hundreds. This was much older than any of the dates in the town cemetery.

Ryan had seen other small family plots on roadsides throughout Maplewood, but they were always in good condition, fenced in and well maintained by the town. This one had three granite posts standing guard at three of the corners of the plot. A fourth stone lay toppled over at the remaining corner like some watch guard who'd collapsed from their exhaustive duty. As far as Ryan figured, no one in town knew about this graveyard. It was as if the plot had been forgotten. At least, until they discovered it. They came out here several times over the years and just hung out, as they were its caretakers and felt it belonged to them and no one else.

"This one," Lance said. He kneeled over a gravestone on the ground. "It's got the most writing you can see."

Ryan removed his backpack and went over to the spot. He got down on the ground and the damp leaves soaked into his knees. He removed the paper scroll and a piece of charcoal and handed it to Lance. Russell and Wesley stood over them and watched.

As Ryan held the paper down over the face of the grave marker, Lance began rubbing the charcoal over the writing carved into the stone. Ryan watched as letters appeared first. One by one they emerged onto the white paper till a name spelled out: *Camilla Abigail Eaton.*

Lance continued to rub with soft, easy strokes, careful not to rip the thin paper. As he rubbed, a date appeared: *Born 1681.*

Below that, Lance scraped the charcoal back and forth and another date appeared: *Died 1692.*

A child, Ryan thought. She was just a young girl when she died. Then it hit him. The same age as Curtis. Eleven. Never to see twelve or anything more. As Ryan thought about being on the cusp of his teenage years and how much he looked forward to how it would feel, he pondered how much Curtis would miss. His insides felt as damp and cold as the soft ground beneath his knees.

Lance finished the rubbing with partial names of the girl's parents coming through the paper.

"Good enough," Lance said and stood.

As Ryan got up, he held out the paper in his arms and admired Lance's work. It looked like a gravestone floating in the air. It felt colder now in the shadow of the woods and Ryan wanted to leave.

3

Eddie walked to the Town Square on his way to the public library. The cobblestone plaza was situated between the streets where many of the oldest homes in the heart of Maplewood stood, behind the downtown business district, and the neighborhood where Ryan and his friends lived, which consisted of a mixture of more nineteenth-century houses and modern homes. A Revolutionary War statue stood guard in the center of the square and four municipal buildings were spread out on the four corners: the library, police station, elementary school, and Town Hall.

Eddie had learned that the latest *Dark Shadows* novel had been released, *Barnabas, Quentin and the Frightened Bride*, and he wanted to see if the library had it. Stupid title, he thought, but he enjoyed the books, even though they strayed from the actual storyline of his favorite TV show. He looked forward to each release, which this year ended up being one every month. His parents wouldn't buy him the books, so he was fortunate the library carried them.

"Waste of money," his father said. "You can get books for free at the library. That's what my taxes pay for."

Eddie looked up at the two-story brick library to gaze at his favorite part of the building. On each of the four corners, though he could only see three from this angle, situated at the edge of the gabled slate roof of the structure, were carved stone library gargoyles.

He always marveled at how weird they looked. One had a face like an owl with a long, curved beak poking down into an open book grasped between its talons. Another was a fat bullfrog, its round eyes bulging and wide mouth gaping over the book in its webbed hands. The third looked like an old man with glasses perched on a humongous nose and a hood from some type of monk's cloak up over the top of his head. The fourth squatted on the opposite corner of the building that Eddie couldn't see from his angle, but he knew it depicted a human figure curled up in the corner, one hand on its chin, the other grasping a book by its spine. Eddie had learned the library had been built in the eighteen hundreds. Whatever architect had decided to include these gruesome gargoyles must have had a sense of humor.

As he headed toward the library entrance, he spied Becky Williams coming down the granite steps alone. Her face contorted as if something had pissed her off. She didn't even seem to notice him as she came barreling by, nearly bumping into him.

"Look where you're going," Eddie said as she passed.

Becky stopped and turned to look back and the expression on her face gave him a jolt.

"Stay out of my way, Eddie Spaghetti," she said.

"What's your problem?" Though he didn't really want to know and could care less what gripe she had.

Becky took two steps toward him, which made him flinch.

"You're my problem," she said. "You and your ugly face."

He glared at her, wanting so much to lash out at this girl who thought the world fell at her feet. He felt like yanking on her hair if he didn't worry his hand might get stuck in it.

"Why don't you go bananas?" was the best he could do.

"Buzz off, Eddie," Becky said, but she didn't budge, as if daring him to leave her space. No, not daring, demanding.

He gave her the best response he could think of when he hooked his two index fingers into the corners of his mouth and pulled back to stretch it wide, sticking his tongue out and crossing his eyes.

"Is that your Halloween mask?" Becky asked with a grin. "If so, you're sure to scare all the trick-or-treaters. I didn't think you could look any uglier."

Eddie held the face and tried to say something but it came out muffled.

"You're such a dork," she said. "Be careful your face doesn't stick that way!" She turned and walked away.

Eddie continued to hold the goofy face for a few seconds longer in case she turned to look back. But as he watched, she left the Town Square heading toward downtown. He released his fingers from the corners of his mouth.

It took a second to realize something was wrong.

The facial muscles around his jaw felt stiff and his mouth remained stretched wide, his tongue still dangling out the open orifice. His eyes stayed crossed and his vision doubled.

What?

He couldn't withdraw his tongue. His hands shot up to feel his face; the skin around his mouth was taut and stiff.

On my god. My face has stuck.

Eddie tried talking, but he couldn't form any words, not with his tongue sticking out. Only a guttural grunt came forth as he tried to squeeze out words without the use of his tongue or lips.

"Smeenh ee fwess." He began to pant as his chest heaved up and down, air sucking in and out of his open mouth. He spun around looking for anyone. The plaza was empty. No one around except for the library gargoyles, but they didn't see him, their lifeless eyes focused on the books held in stone hands.

He heard footsteps. Someone approaching the square from Lincoln Street.

Can't see me like this, Eddie thought, his mind buzzing. *I can't let anyone see me like this*. He darted off in the opposite direction, toward the historic district of town and onto Arbor Lane. *Need to hide*, he thought, till he could figure this out. *Don't want anyone seeing me like this*. It was bad enough that the kids at school made fun of his face; he didn't want to be spotted looking like he did now. A freak.

He cut across the backyards behind Cobblestone Drive, stopping only to duck behind a forsythia bush, its massive tangle of branches and leaves that started to burn red providing ample cover. Eddie tried to catch his breath, but he felt as if he were panting like a dog with heatstroke. He glanced at the houses in front of him and behind him, but could see no one looking out their windows at the strange boy traipsing through their yards.

His mind tried to map out a course home where he'd have the least chance of coming into contact with anyone. Most of the homes in this section of streets belonged to older residents of the town, people who probably kept indoors away from the autumn chill.

Eddie sprinted out between a couple houses and darted over to Carriage Lane to the yard of a house he knew to be vacant. The large home with the mansard roof had been Wickstrom Funeral Home for a long time but closed several years ago and had been empty ever since. He hid behind a large maple tree in the front yard, whose long limbs were still covered in yellow and orange leaves and stretched out almost to the row of windows that looked out from the sloped roofline. He rested for a moment as he tried to catch his breath and plot his next move.

He couldn't believe how hard it was to breathe with his mouth gaped open. His lungs felt like they were trying to work overtime to keep up. He had no idea what happened. It was as if all the nerves in his face went numb. He couldn't feel anything except a cool breeze blowing on a tongue that felt as if it were drying up.

Got to get home, his racing mind yelled. But what then? He couldn't show his face to his parents. His dad might be gone by now to get ready to work at the big game, but his mother would still be home. She rarely left the apartment. It was Sunday, so she'd be glued to the television, so maybe he could get by her in the house and up to his room.

Most of the town residents would be on their way to the game by now, so that was why the streets were quiet. He peered around the trunk of the tree at the house across the street. A carved jack-o'-lantern sat on the stoop. It seemed to be looking right at him. It made Eddie think about the pumpkin he stole from Ryan's front steps and smashed, and what he thought he saw looking down from the railroad trestle.

A maple leaf landed on his shoulder and startled him.

Can't stay here. He looked back at the empty house and the darkened windows and took off from his spot. Down Carriage Lane he ran, coming out onto Washington Street where he turned toward downtown. He came out from behind the drug store on Main Street and tore across the road when he saw no cars coming. His vision made him dizzy as he ran, his crossed eyes creating blurred images of everything.

Eddie squeezed into the alley between the Colonial Theatre and JJ Newbury's, coming out behind them and heading up the hill toward the old train depot. *Almost there*, he thought, as he looked across the tracks at the Box Cars rowhouses.

Please let Mom be knee-deep in some lame movie, Eddie thought, like one of the Ma and Pa Kettle flicks. She liked those. Heck, so did he. It was nice to see other poor people on TV, though they looked like they had a lot more fun as a family than his.

He scrambled across the worn wooden platform of the train station and thought about that morning more than a week ago that he saw the strange man in black get off the train. What he wouldn't give to hop on the train and get the hell out of here.

Eddie ran across the tracks, stumbling on the rails and nearly tumbling face first into the gravel. That would do a number on his tongue, he thought, as he regained his balance and scampered across the street and up to the apartment building.

A woman and young child were leaving the door of the apartment next to his, and while the mother paid no attention, the little girl, who looked about six, caught sight of Eddie's face.

"Eww," she said, pointing at him.

If Eddie could stick his tongue out any further at the girl, he would have, but it was already at its limit, so he turned his head and dashed inside his own doorway before the girl's mother could take notice.

"That you, Eddie?" his mother's voice came from the living room. He could hear Ma Kettle's voice screaming on the television.

Eddie grunted, which was all he could do, and took the stairs two at a time up to his bedroom, slamming the door shut behind him. He flopped down on his bed as he heard a muffled response from his mother that he could not make out.

He lay on the bed, the left side of his head embedded in his pillow, and looked away from the door. With his father at the high school field and his mother immersed in the TV, he had time to ponder what the hell was going on.

A blare of the train horn came roaring from outside and his bed began to shake and the window rattle as the freight train lumbered down the tracks. The train had brought that man in black and things got strange after that.

But it was after he saw, or *thought* he saw, what came out of Ryan's pumpkin when things really seemed to weird out. He felt something was out there, even before the strange thing lurking under the trestle bridge. That was no hobo for sure that he saw peeking up through the crack. Nothing could walk along the underside of the trestle bridge like that. Nothing of this world, that is.

He regretted ever stealing that stupid pumpkin from Ryan's house.

As much as that kid annoyed the hell out of him, Eddie thought he should warn him. He needed to tell someone something was going on. He couldn't hide in his room all day and night and hope his face unfreezes.

But what if it doesn't?

His heart speeded up its beats and the skin on his arms felt prickly.

The sound of the train trailed off outside his window as it continued its journey south out of Maplewood. How much he yearned to be on that train and away from this nightmare.

4

Ryan sat with his parents in the top row of the bleachers at the high school soccer field and craned his neck to see where his friends might be. It was tradition for the family to sit together at the annual Columbus Day weekend homecoming game against St. Bartholomew High School, but for cripes sakes, he was in junior high now. He felt he should be able to hang with his classmates instead. He looked around and saw other students sitting together. Several rows below he spotted Becky Williams with Liza and Lindsey as they cheered Becky's brother, Boyce.

Ryan couldn't care less that Dane was in the game and didn't give a crap about watching. But his parents made a big deal of it now that Dane was starting on the varsity squad. It was barely halfway through the first half and Ryan was bored, his butt numb from the wooden bleachers.

On the other side of the field, he surveyed the high school and thought about how in two years he'd be there. He wondered how different things would be once he and his friends became teenagers. He'd seen the change in Dane from eighth-grader to sophomore and how outward and bold his older brother had become.

Then he thought about Curtis. His twin had died before getting a chance to be a teenager and would forever be a young kid even as

Ryan himself matured. It wasn't fair. He always thought this would be a journey they'd take together and he had been counting on Curtis, the wiser one, to guide him through the process. He was ten minutes older by birth, but always seemed so much more. But now Ryan was passing him by, his brother frozen in time by death.

"Hey you," a salty voice called from behind.

Ryan turned, thinking it came from down below behind the bleachers, calling up to someone in the stands, but the grassy area was vacant.

"You, kid," the voice came again. "In the blue jacket."

Ryan looked beyond the grass to the back of the school grounds, where a chain-link fence separated the schoolyard from the woods that lay between here and the river. A boy stood on the other side of the fence. Ryan looked down at his own jacket as if to make sure it was blue.

"Yeah, kid," the boy said. "You."

The boy looked a couple years older than him, maybe a freshman, because Ryan didn't recognize him from school. Or maybe he came from St. Bartholomew.

"Toss that ball over here," the boy said. "I want to play."

Ryan looked and noticed a soccer ball in the grass about twenty yards behind the bleachers. Must have been a stray ball that got kicked back here during pre-game warmups and nobody noticed. He wasn't sure what the heck this kid wanted with the ball and why he was on the other side of the fence. The boy wasn't wearing a uniform; in fact he was dressed in jeans and a sweatshirt. His blond hair was tousled, as if he'd just fought through a windstorm.

"Get me the ball," the boy said.

Ryan shrugged his shoulders and turned around, ignoring the kid.

"Buddy, toss me the ball," the boy said. "Please, help me out here."

Ryan looked at his parents and then the other spectators around him in the stands. He pretended to watch the game, even seeking out where his brother was situated on the field in relation to the ball the players chased around.

"I want to play," the voice persisted. "Toss that ball over here."

Ryan wanted to get the ball just to shut the kid's annoying voice up. He turned to his father.

"Can I have a dollar for popcorn?" he asked.

"Sure." His father dug a bill out of his wallet. It was a fiver. "Get yourself a soda too."

"Thanks, Dad." Ryan got up and made his way down the bleachers, pausing long enough halfway down to cast a quick glance at Becky before turning away when she noticed him. He heard soft giggling as he continued down.

Instead of heading to the snack bar, he made his way around to the back of the bleachers. He approached the ball, wishing he had the athletic confidence to give it a running kick over the chain-link fence beyond, but not daring since he wasn't sure who might be watching besides the annoying boy on the other side.

"That's it," the boy said when Ryan reached the ball. "Give it here." The boy grabbed the fence with both his hands in anticipation of getting the ball.

Ryan picked up the ball and began walking toward the fence, knowing darn well he needed to be closer if he ever wanted to hurl it over the six-foot-high fence.

"Toss it here," the boy said, his fingers clenching the fence so tight that it made the skin on his knuckles turn white.

Ryan thought from the way the kid gripped the fence that he might begin climbing up and over to this side.

What's he even doing over there?

As Ryan approached the fence, he got a better look at the boy and stopped. He noticed that the white on the boy's knuckles was not from the kid clenching the fence too tight.

It was the boy's bones poking out from the flesh of his fingers.

Ryan dropped the ball and it bounced off his right foot and rolled away. He stared at the boy, whose ashen face gazed back at him with bloodshot eyes. The boy grinned a mouthful of blackened teeth.

Ryan turned and ran, hearing the boy laughing behind him, and forgot all about going to the snack bar, retreating to the bleachers where he didn't mind sitting beside his parents.

"Where's the popcorn?" his father asked.

"All out," Ryan mumbled, not meeting his father's eyes. He huddled closer to his mother.

"Cold?" she asked.

He nodded. Yes, he felt chilled. Not quite as cold as Curtis must have been when he plunged through the ice on the Piscataquog, but he felt a chill in his bones that made him think about the kid behind the fence.

His mother put an arm around him, and instead of feeling embarrassed and worried about being seen by any of his classmates, especially Becky Williams, he felt comforted and brave enough to turn and look back over his shoulder.

On the other side of the fence stood nothing but trees, yellow and orange leaves drifting down from the limbs and floating to the ground.

5

Shreckengast walked down the sidewalk on Carriage Lane, marveling at the historic homes on the street that seemed to mostly have been built in the Colonial period. The street remained quiet, as if everyone in town had somewhere else to be on this warm Sunday afternoon. That was fine as far as Shreckengast was concerned. He needed time to sample his surroundings and get his bearings while he looked for a place to 'set up shop'.

Halfway down the street, he stopped and turned to look at a vacant home. A black iron fence rimmed its perimeter. Two squat granite pillars stood sentry, one on either side of a gate that led to the front brick walkway. The siding of the house, a mottled green, appeared in need of a new coat. Cracked shutters hung askew. A portico supported by four thin columns stood over the front stoop. Two arched windows above the second floor peaked out of the mansard roof like leering eyeballs.

Shreckengast took a deep sniff of air into his flaring nostrils.

This house has a scent, he thought. Not just of dust and mildew, but of something rotten. *Death. This house smells of the end.*

He looked at the inviting front door and noticed to its right a rusted metal post sticking out of the woodwork.

A sign hung there once, he thought. He closed his eyes and looked back in time.

He smiled.

Shreckengast knew what this place had been and it pleased him. With his eyes shut, he could see the sign that once hung on that metal rod: Wickstrom Funeral Home.

Yes, he thought. *This is the place.*

He opened the metal gate and stepped through.

I'm home.

6

The flashlight darted through the streets after sundown, the beam picking up piles of raked leaves and pumpkins perched on porches as Ryan ran down his street. A three-quarter moon lurked overhead as if to assist him if his light weren't strong enough to pry open the darkness.

A game of flashlight tag was what Ryan needed to take his mind off what he saw at the soccer field. *Or thought he saw*. He still couldn't be sure. Maybe those weren't bones poking out through the skin on the boy's knuckles. He could have been wearing some tattered pair of gloves. But those eyes in the pallid face, and the mouth with the charcoal teeth. Something wasn't right about that kid.

"Are you yanking my chain?" Lance asked earlier when Ryan told him about the incident.

"I know it sounds wacked," Ryan said. Of course he wouldn't be pranking them. Especially knowing how sensitive Russell was when it came to bones. How he freaked out at the skeleton in Miss Sheriden's classroom. "Totally unbelievable, but I tell you that kid was messed up."

"Wowsers," Wesley said, his mouth agape.

Later, when Lance suggested they play a game of flashlight tag after dark, Ryan thought it would help him forget that weird scene. But when he got stuck being 'it' and now ran through the neighborhood looking for the others, he realized how much he didn't want to be alone.

Lights were on in most of the houses as people were probably finishing dinner and settling in for a night of *The Ed Sullivan Show*, but it seemed odd that no one else roamed about outside, as if the night kept the residents inside.

Ryan shined his light up and down the street, poking the beam behind bushes and trees, hoping to catch a glimpse of Russell's arm, or Wesley's big butt. Or maybe Lance's dark hair flying out from his head as he raced to get away.

But nobody.

Where did they go? They hid well, concealed by the night and shadows. Shrubs became camouflage, trees barriers. A feeling of someone following him crept into his bones. He was supposed to be stalking the others, so why did he feel like something was tailing him?

Ryan moved between a couple of houses on Oak Street, running through the backyards between them and the rear of the Elm Street homes. Nobody peeked out from lighted windows to see the source of the beam prancing across their lawns. Most people knew kids ran about the neighborhood. As long as no one caused any trouble, there were never complaints.

He cut over onto Elm Street and stopped. There was the Downeys' boardinghouse where Mr. Lothrop and the others lived, including the new resident. The man in black who lived on the third floor in the front of the house. A light shone in the window of that room. As Ryan walked down the street watching it, he saw it darken as a silhouette crossed the frame.

He's there. Maybe he's looking down at me. Ryan turned his flashlight off and ran down to the end of the street. At the corner of Washington, he turned it back on. He looked around but still found no sign of the others. He didn't like this game anymore. He didn't want to be out here alone. He wanted the security of his friends.

A sound made him spin around and look behind him. A rustling in the leaves. Lance, Russell, or Wesley? Across the street was Rita's house.

The lights on the bottom floor were on. So was a light in the basement, though those tiny windows looked weird and not much spilled out. He remembered they had a metal covering over the window wells, a sort of ornamental grate.

He wondered what the lady was doing in the basement. Maybe that's where she kept her husband that no one ever saw. Lance joked that she probably ate him. Ryan doubted she ever had a husband. Or if she did, he probably ran off. Who would want to stick around with that crazy lady?

Then he remembered seeing her at the Harvest Festival talking to the man in black from the boardinghouse. They knew each other and it looked obvious that they weren't on friendly terms. Maybe he could ask Mr. Lothrop about it. The writer must know something about the man in black. He lived right down the hall from him, so he should have uncovered something about the old man's mysterious arrival on a freight train.

A twig snapped.

Ryan turned away from Rita's house. Something stirred in the big forsythia bush down the street. He skimmed his flashlight over red pointed leaves. Was that someone's hiding spot? He took a few steps toward it.

He heard a mumbling sound. Someone trying to suppress a laugh? Got to be Lance. No, he'd be too calm. Wesley. Big ol' Wesley thinking he outsmarted him.

"Come out," Ryan said, trying to make him run so he could tag him with the flashlight beam. "I know you're there."

He took a few steps closer to the bush. A noise came from it and he stopped. It sounded like an animal and he hoped it wasn't a skunk. The sound it made gave him the impression it was in some kind of struggle. It could be hurt. Which would make it dangerous.

I should leave it alone.

He started to walk away when the noise came again, but this time it sounded human. Sort of.

Not exactly words, but the muffled voice seemed to be trying to form words. Someone gagged, he thought. *Had he stumbled into a crime scene?*

"Thrr, sum-hin en le hunkins."

Human, yes, Ryan thought.

"Who's there?" he asked, waving his light around the bush hoping to get whoever was hiding to come out. "What's wrong with you?"

The voice called out, louder but the same gibberish.

"What are you saying?"

"Eerrs shum tin un la hunkins."

Ryan strained his ears and tried to make sense. Almost words, but not quite. He wanted the person to come out, but maybe they couldn't. Or didn't want to. Ryan stayed glued to his spot, not daring to approach, too uncertain about this strange message directed at him.

"Hunkins!" the voice yelled out.

The word echoed in the quiet night. Then it dawned on him.

"Pumpkins?"

The voice in the bush gurgled an affirmation.

"What about pumpkins?" *Is this some kind of joke?* he wondered.

"*Thrr sum-hin ehn ler hunkins!*"

The roar from the bush startled him and drove him back a step. The leaves of the bush rustled and a dark figure tried lurking away. Ryan ran up to the edge of the grass and shone his flashlight at the fleeing figure. It turned to look at him.

Ryan's flashlight beam fell on the face of Eddie Scruggs. But something was wrong with it. Eddie's mouth was stretched open in a twisted contortion and his tongue hung out, wagging in the open cavity. Eddie turned and ran off into the darkness, but not before uttering his senseless phrase once more. It sounded like a warning.

As Ryan stood with the beam of his flashlight growing dim from weakened batteries, he realized what Eddie was trying to say.

There's something in the pumpkins.

OCTOBER 12

1

Eddie Scruggs knew the train schedule by heart. Before sunrise, he got up and pulled the linen pillowcase off his pillow and began stuffing clothes into it. He had no problem getting up that morning, because he never went to sleep. Not because he didn't feel tired; in fact he could barely keep his crossed eyes open. But with his face still frozen in that wide grimace with his tongue lolling out, it made it impossible to nod off.

He hoped his face would correct itself, and even looked into the bathroom mirror down the hall to see if it might be just a nightmare. But the image that looked back at him from the mirror door of the medicine cabinet sent his heart racing. That's when he began to pack a bag and prepared to sneak out of the apartment for the second time in less than eight hours.

Last night, he'd been fortunate to make it out thanks to his parents going to one of the neighbors' apartments to play cards. His mother had checked on him at dinnertime and even brought him a Spam sandwich and a glass of milk in case he felt well enough to eat. Fortunately, she hadn't approached his bed too closely and he kept his face turned to the wall. She set the food and drink down and told him to let her know if he needed anything.

He couldn't answer, only groaned. She assumed he still had a bellyache and left him alone. She wouldn't call the doctor; that might cost too much. He needed something, for sure, but his mother had no clue.

When his parents told him they were going out for the night and wanted to know if he'd be all right alone, he assured them with an affirmative grunt. Eddie waited awhile after they left and then made his way out of the apartment to steal away into the night toward the neighborhood where Ryan and the others lived.

He knew he needed to warn Ryan about what happened with the pumpkin he had smashed. Eddie had no doubt that whatever he saw come out of it caused the distortion of his face. Something had been unleashed that night and he felt responsible. Telling Ryan was the best he could do to make amends.

It took him a while to track Ryan down as he and the others had scattered throughout the neighborhood. Eddie tried to be as stealthy as possible for fear of being spotted by someone. He wanted to alert Ryan, but didn't want anyone to see what had happened to his face. He hoped he got his message through, as difficult as it was to speak with his screwed-up mouth.

Eddie felt he did his best last night, and now, as morning broke, he made his plan to escape. He filled his empty pillowcase with a few clothes and even threw the homemade I Ching wands into it. Who knows, maybe he could really find a way to break through to another dimension, a world that would be better for him than this one. Hell, something had broken through to get here via that pumpkin, so he knew it was possible, not just something on *Dark Shadows*.

He also grabbed his lucky bag of marbles and shoved it into the pillowcase. Before leaving his room, he looked at the Spam sandwich. His stomach groaned and saliva dribbled out across chapped lips, but without being able to close his mouth, he didn't know how he'd be able to eat.

That was going to be a problem. He'd starve to death if he didn't find a way. Just in case, he grabbed the sandwich and put it in the pillowcase. He threw the bag over his shoulder and made his way quietly down the stairs, knowing where each creak was and doing his best to avoid them. It was a holiday, so his parents would sleep in. With that assurance, he reached downstairs and slipped out the apartment door.

As he made his way toward the railroad tracks and the old depot station platform, he thought about how many times he'd dreamed about running away by hopping on a southbound train. He never thought he'd be brave enough to do it. But even now he figured bravery had nothing to do with it. More like fear.

He waited in the dark, wondering what lay ahead for him. Wherever he went, if his face didn't correct itself, there would be no point in his action. But maybe getting away from Maplewood and whatever curse had befallen it, he would return to normal. It was the only chance he thought he had.

In the distance, north of town, came the long bellow of a train horn. He stared in that direction toward the horizon of darkened treetops that looked like rounded mountains. Right on schedule, he thought. If his face could smile, he would have.

As the chugging sounds got louder, he spotted the first sign of the train, emerging from the darkness of the trees on the other side of the river like a slithering dragon, its one cyclopean eye lighting its path. The beast roared again and made a rattling noise as it crossed the iron trestle, the vibrations sure to shake whatever that thing was that walked upside down under the wooden walkway.

The blackened hulk of the engine dragged the freight train slowly through town as it approached the old station. Eddie knew it wouldn't stop; it never did except for that early morning the man in the black cloak and top hat showed up. No, it would not stop, but it moved slowly enough that Eddie was positive he'd be able to hop aboard.

What worried him was that he wouldn't find a boxcar with its doors open. All he needed was a little crack that he could squirm through. But if they were all closed, he'd have to hang on to one of the exterior ladders and ride it as far as he could hold on.

As the train pulled through the station, he got up from where he crouched and approached the tracks. He felt the vibrations in the wooden planks beneath his feet reverberate up through the bones in his legs, and his whole body tingled with trepidation.

He watched each boxcar whisper past him, feeling a pull of air that brushed his stiffened cheeks and tousled his wispy hair. Then he saw it. A boxcar with its doors open about four or five feet, like a mouth waiting to swallow him up. Eddie held his breath, and as the boxcar came by, he ran alongside it, tossing his bag up into the opening and then with his heart pumping, he jumped up and grabbed on to the side of the door.

Eddie pulled himself up into the opening, and then felt himself slip, fearing he would fall back onto the station platform where he would watch the train disappear down the tracks with his bag inside. But he caught a grip and with determination pulled himself up and into the boxcar.

He fell flat on his face, sprawled out on the floor of the boxcar. He glanced up to see large wooden crates stacked on either side of the car. Eddie got up on his knees. His sandwich had spilled out of the bag and lay before him.

I'm finally doing it, he thought, as he made his way to the opening of the door and sat down with his legs dangling out. He wanted to watch the town disappear in the distance. *Good riddance, Maplewood.* So long to his lousy parents and all the rotten kids in school.

He felt his mouth try to smile.

A shuffling sound came from behind, and Eddie's heart paused. A hobo perhaps, hitching a ride like himself. He could hear him stirring, as if shifting position from where he lay.

Maybe Eddie had awakened him from his sleep. He could offer whoever it was his Spam sandwich. A peace offering for letting him share the boxcar.

As a soft sound dragged itself across the floor of the car, Eddie dared not turn around. He didn't want to see what emerged from the darkened interior. He thought about what he'd seen through the crack of the walkway on the railroad trestle a few nights ago, not long after he'd smashed that pumpkin. Whatever that was that day beneath the bridge, it was no hobo. And whatever was approaching him from behind, also didn't sound like it normally walked on two legs.

Eddie's heart stiffened as he sat in the doorway of the boxcar looking out while the sun began to rise beyond the roofs of the neighboring buildings as Maplewood began to awaken. But Eddie felt something else had awakened in this boxcar, and now he regretted thinking he could really escape.

As the sound shuffled closer, Eddie felt hot breath on the back of his neck that raised hackles all along his shoulders and caused the air in his lungs to get caught in his throat. Then something touched his back and traced a cold trail down the length of his spine.

2

Ryan pedaled his bike as fast as his churning legs would pump as the four of them headed up Old Coach Road not long after sunrise. This time, he rode ahead of Lance for a change, with Russell and Wesley bringing up the rear. Russell's wheels didn't make their usual thrumming sound without the baseball card clipped to the spokes.

The others had complained about getting up early on a school holiday, but Ryan had told them last night about Eddie Scruggs and the weird thing that had happened to his face, followed by the warning about the pumpkins. Lance led the dissent about what it meant.

"It's Eddie freaking Scruggs, for cripes sakes," Lance said. "Why would you believe anything he says?"

"You didn't see his face," Ryan countered. "It was horrible."

"It's always horrible," Lance said.

"That's just how he looks," Russell added.

"No," Ryan assured them. "This was different." Add it to the incident with the boy at the soccer game, and it told him something was not right in town.

The only way to find answers was to take a ride to Hank Swain's farm and Ryan ordered them all to meet early in the morning. He felt an urgency, and that's why he rode faster than Lance and the others and didn't even bother to look at the Williams house as they passed, not caring about catching a glimpse of Becky in the early morning light.

No. This was more important than that.

Ryan did cast a glance toward the school grounds as they went by, particularly the area beyond the fence between the soccer field and the woods. No sign of the mysterious boy with the pale face and the bony fingers.

The four of them crossed Deer Pond Road and the street inclined, Ryan's lungs heaving as he pumped his pedals hard, feeling fire burn in his calves and thighs. At the top of the hill, he turned right onto Bittersweet Road. Up ahead he spotted the open fields of the Swain farm. His rear tire skidded as he turned into the long gravel driveway and he felt the bike almost slide out from under him, but the treads caught the dirt and propelled him forward.

Ryan slowed when he saw the Trans Am parked outside the closed gate that barred the rest of the way up the farm's driveway. Lance and the others finally pulled up to a stop beside him.

"Ain't that your brother's car?" Ryan asked Lance.

"Yeah. Austin's working this morning."

Ryan looked over the farmhouse, barn, and fields. There didn't appear to be anyone working.

It seemed quiet until he spotted Austin Stanton coming from the direction of the barn and approaching the fence. He eyed the boys with surprise before hopping over the fence and stopping by his car.

"What the hell are you losers doing here?" Austin asked.

"What do you care?" Lance said.

"I don't," Austin said with a shrug. He looked back at the farmhouse.

"Something wrong?" Ryan asked. Austin seemed tense.

"Just weird," the older teen said. "Mr. Swain ain't around." He looked at his watch. "He's supposed to open soon. I knocked on the door – no answer. Checked the barn – nothing."

Ryan's throat felt dry, and not just from the strain of the ride here.

"Where do you think he is?"

Austin shot the boys an annoyed look. "How the hell should I know? Just weird." He got in his car and started it up. He turned his car around in the driveway and then stopped beside them and rolled down his window. "You idiots better get the hell out of here." He drove off, hitting the gas pedal a bit hard and spitting gravel back at where they stood astride their bikes.

"What do we do now?" Wesley asked.

"We check it out," Ryan said after a glance at Lance, who nodded.

They laid their bikes down in the driveway, approached the gate, and hopped over. Ryan led the way as he headed without hesitation toward the pumpkin patch. There was still a scattering of the gourds in the patch, many of them smaller than the ones Mr. Swain had brought to the festival.

Most of them sold, Ryan thought, thinking about all the people who lugged pumpkins home from the event.

"Check this out," Lance said, excitement in his voice. He stood beside where Mr. Swain's prized giant pumpkin rested. Or what was left of it.

When Ryan approached, he saw the massive gourd was split in two, leaving a crater filled with blackened stringy remnants. An awful stench hissed from its center, and he took a step back and brought his hand to his mouth. He was glad he hadn't taken time to eat breakfast this morning.

"What the hell happened to it?" Russell asked from behind him.

"I don't know," Ryan said.

"He probably gutted it to harvest the seeds," Lance said, though he didn't sound convincing.

"Who would want seeds from that mess?" Ryan said.

"Well, it looks like someone tried to dig something out of it," Russell said.

"No," Ryan said. "Look at the way it's split open. It looks like something *broke* its way out of it."

There's something in the pumpkins.

As he turned to look away, he spotted a sledgehammer lying in the grass.

"Look," he said, and pointed. The steel head of the mallet was orange.

Lance walked over and bent to pick it up.

"Don't touch it," Ryan said. "You'll contaminate the crime scene."

Lance shot him a perplexed look. "What the hell makes you think a crime happened here?" But he didn't bother to reach for the sledgehammer.

"Something happened here," Ryan said. He could feel it – the same eerie feeling he'd had looking at that kid at the soccer field. The same one he'd felt when his flashlight beam caught Eddie's distorted face.

There's something in the pumpkins.

Ryan turned and noticed the doors of the pumpkin shed stood open. Without saying a word, he walked toward it and stopped just outside the entrance. The others followed. They came up behind him and he could feel their panting breaths on the back of his neck.

He looked inside the darkened shed. Smashed pieces of pumpkins lay all over the floorboards. The shelves still held pumpkins, but most of them had been caved in with something. The sledgehammer, Ryan thought.

An oblong pumpkin leaned on the edge of one of the broken shelves that slanted down from where it barely clung to the shed wall. The pumpkin was concave on one side. Ryan thought he saw it teeter on the shelf. He stared at it. It teetered and then pitched forward and fell to the mess on the floor. It landed with a thud, causing Ryan's heart to leap up into his throat. He gasped. The thinnest of cracks appeared in the orange skin. It gave the appearance of a lopsided smile.

Ryan released a breath, pulled his eyes away from the pumpkin and surveyed the mess on the floor of the shed. Something caught his eye, but he didn't dare step into the shed.

"I don't think we're going to find Mr. Swain," Ryan said as he kept his eyes fixed on a mass of orange pumpkin guts and pieces of shell piled on the floor.

"Why not?" Russell asked.

"I think something got him."

"Oh Christ," Lance said with disgust. "You're really starting to freak me out. First the kid in the woods, then Eddie last night with his screwed-up face, and now this. You ain't in a *Dark Shadows* episode. This is reality. Nothing got Mr. Swain."

"Then how do you explain this?" Ryan said, and got the nerve to reach into the shed and pluck something out of the sticky mess on the floor. He held it up for the others to see.

He displayed a small piece of green plaid flannel cloth, its edges torn.

"What is it?" Wesley asked.

"A piece of a shirt," Ryan said. He looked back inside the shed at the broken and battered pumpkins.

"That doesn't mean anything," Lance said.

"Take a closer look," Ryan said.

As all their eyes peered down at the flannel material in Ryan's hand, they noticed a dark red stain on it.

"Is that—" Lance started to ask.

"Blood," Ryan said before he could finish.

3

Quinn stood on a chair, up on his tiptoes, and looked through the cellar window and the honeycombed iron well grate. Through the small openings in the metal, he could see an old man on the sidewalk staring back at the house. The man wore a black cloak over dark clothing. Lines were carved into his face from age, like a timeworn block of granite. He wondered why the man stood there and why he seemed interested in the house.

He wanted to call out to the man before Rita had a chance to put on her bellowing opera records, but he knew it'd be pointless. The man wouldn't hear him unless he broke the glass. If he did that, he feared what his captor might do to him.

The lock on the door at the top of the cellar stairs clicked, and Quinn jumped down from the chair and brought it over to the table before Rita descended the steps. She carried in her arms a large pumpkin nestled up against her bulging bosom. A smile creased her face as she approached the table and set it down.

He stared at it and then back up at her.

"I also got you this at Harvest Fest," she said.

"What for?" he asked. "Am I supposed to eat that?"

"No, silly. It's for Halloween. It is October."

Quinn had vague memories of Halloween from before. *Before what?* Before his father sent him through that door that led to darkness and brought him to Shreckengast and the House of Embers? That seemed a long time ago. How long, he had no idea. Quinn knew he was still the same age, so it couldn't have been that long ago. Why then was it so hard to remember anything before Shreckengast's house? Why could he not remember much about his father?

He did remember pumpkins and Halloween. But he didn't know what he was supposed to do with it.

"You're supposed to carve it," Rita said, as if reading his mind.

He looked up at her, baffled. "With what?"

"This," she said, and laid a knife on the table beside the pumpkin. It had a small handle and a thin blade that curved up toward the end. "It's a filet knife. You must be very careful. It's extremely sharp."

She seemed to delight in saying that, Quinn thought. He hesitated before picking up the blade, heeding her warning. It felt lighter than he expected. He eyed the thinness of the metal blade and then looked at Rita.

His immediate thought was to plunge it into the fat roll that enveloped her neck and make his escape. Now was the best time. The door at the top of the cellar stairs was open. He could cut her and race up them before she had a chance to stop him. While she dealt with the blood shooting out of her neck, he could be out the door and maybe that old man out there, if he was still outside, could help him find the police.

But how hard would it be to cut through that fat? Would one quick stab be enough? The blade was thin, but long. He didn't know if he could get it deep enough in her throat to reach any of the important veins. Or were they arteries? He wasn't quite sure.

Rita's hand clamped down on his shoulder like a pincer, and she squeezed. Quinn screamed as a bolt of pain ran from his shoulder all the way down his arm. His hand flexed and the knife slipped out of his fingers and clattered onto the table.

"Don't get any stupid ideas with that knife," she said through gritted teeth. She released her grip and he slumped down in the chair, feeling dizzy. "I'm doing something nice for you and you need to be appreciative."

"I didn't do anything," he groaned as he rubbed his sore shoulder.

"I could see it in your eyes," she said. "You were thinking something."

Quinn looked at her, wondering if she knew what he was thinking right now.

"Carve your pumpkin," she said. "When it's done, I'll put a candle in it and light it. You were complaining about it being too dark down here at night. That will give you some light."

Quinn picked up the knife and brought the tip of the blade to the side of the pumpkin.

"That's a good boy," she said.

He plunged the blade into the rind.

4

Ryan had never been to Depot Street where the Box Cars apartments stood on the west side of the railroad tracks. His mother always warned him to stay away from the Box Cars. The tenements had a reputation for troubled kids, drugs, and crime. Ryan had no idea if his mother knew the truth about this, but he never had a reason to go there anyway. All his friends came from his neighborhood. The kids from the Box Cars, like Eddie and Wayne, weren't the kind he'd ever hang out with.

As the four boys crossed under the railroad trestle and prepared to turn left on Depot Street, Ryan noticed a police car pulling out of the road and saw Chief Strong behind the wheel. Maybe his mother was right about the Box Cars after all. Ryan rarely saw a police car driving through his neighborhood.

He slowed his pedaling as they rode down the street, feeling a little unsure about being here as the long two-story tenement building loomed ahead, its gray siding dull and fading, windows dusty and dark. Maybe this was a mistake, but he felt the need to find Eddie and see what his warning meant the other night, and what he might know about things happening in Maplewood.

Ryan stopped his bike and the others came alongside and joined his gaze at the building. He had no idea which apartment Eddie's family lived in, and wasn't even sure if there were nameplates on any of the doors. He could just knock on any door and ask, but his nerves kept him glued to his bicycle as his eyes scanned the doors.

"Now what?" Lance asked.

Ryan wasn't sure. Usually, Lance was the one with the ideas. Or Curtis. Yeah, his brother would have walked right up to one of the doors and started banging on it without hesitation. But Curtis wasn't here.

Before Ryan could answer, he spotted Wayne Barnes exit one of the apartments. The bigger boy looked at them with surprise in his eyes and sauntered over.

"What are you guys doing here?" he asked, as if offended that they were treading on his territory.

"We're looking for Eddie," Lance said.

"Why?"

"We just wanted to ask him about something," Ryan said.

Wayne sighed and shrugged his big shoulders. "You're too late."

Ryan had a sudden chill. "What do you mean?"

"Eddie ran away," Wayne said. "Wrote his parents a note and hopped a southbound train."

"What? When?" Ryan's mind raced back to the night before. He remembered seeing the fright in Eddie's eyes when his flashlight beam lit upon him. Despite the distortion of his face, that fear was apparent.

"I dunno," Wayne said. "They found the note first thing this morning, so he must have left last night or early today. Trains are going by at all hours. Police just left. They're going to alert all the towns on the train line going south. At least, that's where Eddie said he was going."

"Why'd he run off?" Lance asked, casting a glance at Ryan.

Wayne shrugged again. "He didn't say anything to me. He was my friend. I don't know why he didn't tell me."

Ryan could see an expression of hurt on Wayne's face, as if he'd been betrayed. "Was anything bothering him lately?"

Wayne stared back at the four of them. Ryan sensed he wanted to say something, but seemed nervous about getting the words out. "He's been spooked the last couple days," Wayne said. "Ever since…."

Ryan waited for him to finish, before realizing he wasn't going to, so he finished for him.

"Ever since he stole my pumpkin and smashed it?"

Again, Wayne seemed surprised. "You knew that was us?"

"Wasn't hard to figure out," Lance said.

"Something scared him that night," Wayne said. "Didn't seem to be the same after that. Had the jitters."

"What did he see?" Ryan asked.

"Don't know," Wayne said with another shrug. "I didn't see anything. But Eddie panicked about something. I just didn't think it was bad enough to make him run away." Wayne reached into his pants pocket and pulled something out. "I found this by the railroad tracks this morning. Eddie's marble bag." He held it up for them all to see. "He must have dropped it getting on the train. He always considered his marbles lucky."

"Guess he's out of luck," Russell said.

"I'm going to hold on to these," Wayne said. "And give them to him when he gets back."

"If he gets back," Ryan said.

"Don't you think they'll find him?" Wayne asked with a frown.

Ryan didn't have an answer for him.

5

As Russell rode with his mother and younger sister out Bittersweet Road toward the apple orchard later in the afternoon, they passed Hank Swain's farm. Russell noticed the gate on the driveway was still closed.

"That's strange," his mother said. "Swain's Farm seems closed. I was thinking we could get a pumpkin on the way back. Strange him not being open today."

"That's okay," Russell said. He sat beside his mother in the front seat, an honor bestowed on him after his father died. He enjoyed not having to sit in the back beside Erin. "I don't need a pumpkin." From the road he could see the pumpkin shed and one door hanging open. Though it was too dark inside to make out its contents, his memory held a vivid recollection of the smashed pumpkins inside he'd seen earlier that morning.

"But we always get a pumpkin for Halloween," Mrs. Mallek said.

"I want a pumpkin!" Erin hollered from the back seat.

"We can skip it this year," Russell said.

"You always like carving them," his mother said to him.

He knew his friends were gathering in Ryan's basement to discuss pumpkins and the things going on in Maplewood, and Russell wished he were there with them, but it had been his insistence that the family go apple picking today, so he couldn't back out.

"I'm getting too old for jack-o'-lanterns," he said, though he knew it wasn't true. The things Ryan said had him spooked and he really didn't know what to believe about what Eddie had said about the pumpkins and some of the other weird stuff in town. But there had to be a reason Mr. Swain smashed up everything in the shed, and who knows what happened to him. If that was really blood on the piece of flannel shirt that Ryan found on the bottom of the shed floor, then where was the rest of the shirt and the guy who was wearing it?

"I want a pumpkin," Erin repeated from the backseat.

Mrs. Mallek looked into the rearview mirror to catch her daughter's attention. "We'll get you one," she said, "even if your brother thinks he's too big to enjoy a jack-o'-lantern."

Russell watched the Swain farm disappear from view and thought maybe they could get a pumpkin from the A&P. Maybe that would be all right.

A bit farther down the road they arrived at the apple orchard. After parking, Mrs. Mallek paid for two half-peck bags at the barn and they strolled off toward the orchard. His mother had wanted to get a full-peck bag, but Russell insisted on having his own bag and she relented. He didn't want to have to stay by his annoying sister.

"I'm going to head down back," Russell said, pointing to the rear of the orchard.

"I thought we'd stay together," his mother said. "You said you wanted to do this as a family event."

"We are," he said. "I just want to find my own trees."

"Okay," his mother said with a shake of her head.

"Good," Erin said and stuck her tongue out at him. His mother and sister headed off to the right and Russell followed a rutted dirt path toward the back of the orchard.

The ground sloped with dips and rises and he followed the winding path through the rolling hills of the orchard, passing trees that were mostly barren of apples. Pretty picked over, he thought as he wandered along the trail, his head up, gazing at the tops of the trees. He passed another family, parents and two kids, clearing out the last of the apples from a nearby tree.

He wished his father were here picking apples with them. Russell missed that, remembering his father hoisting him up on his shoulders so he could reach some of the taller branches. Missed the way his dad laughed. He thought about that night he looked out his bedroom window and saw his father wave.

Did you know, Dad? Did you know you weren't coming home that night? Why did you look up then? Why that night?

Russell brushed away the start of a tear.

His dad wasn't here to pick apples with them. He was in the ground at the cemetery. Russell knew that. But he refused to believe his father was nothing but a pile of bones. *No. That doesn't really happen to people.* The skeleton in Miss Sheriden's classroom wasn't real. It was a prop to teach them science. It had never been a real person, like his dad. He refused to believe that.

Almost at the very end of the orchard, before a stretch of tall field grass, he came upon a tree that still sprouted a fair number of apples on the top branches. A wooden ladder leaned up against the trunk of the tree. It wouldn't be the same as his father lifting him up, but it would have to do. Russell climbed the ladder to a point where he could reach some of the apples. He began plucking the best ones off the branches and deposited them in his paper sack.

The sound of laughter floated through the orchard. He turned from his perch and looked back the way he had come. He no longer saw the family of four. Perhaps they had wandered off to look for another tree. Their voices must have carried in the silent orchard. No one else was around.

Laughter again.

Russell looked and thought he saw someone ducking behind a tree trunk. The kids he saw earlier? But where had their parents gone?

He resumed his picking.

An apple bounced off the tree trunk beside where he stood and dropped to the ground. He looked down at it, seeing it in the grass below. He glanced over his shoulder.

Did someone throw that at me?

He saw no one. What happened to the figure who moved behind the tree? Had they gone off?

Russell shrugged and took another step up the ladder. He reached up and plucked an apple off a branch and dropped it into his bag. The ladder was wobbly and he had a difficult time holding on to the bag with one hand while picking apples with the other. The bag started to get heavy. Just a few more, he thought.

Another apple hit the ladder by his feet.

He turned. Nobody out there.

"Hey!" he yelled. No answer.

Had Ryan and the others dropped by, knowing he'd be here? Were they playing games with him?

Laughter.

Where the heck did it come from? He squinted in the sunlight.

"Ryan? Lance? Wesley?" No response.

"Erin?" No. His sister couldn't throw like that.

Russell looked up at the canopy of the tree. Maybe the apples were falling from above him. But no. That didn't seem likely.

"Whoever it is, stop it," he called out. *No one.* The orchard was still. Now and then a light breeze ruffled some of the tree branches. From another tree an apple dropped and landed with a plop on the ground.

Don't be silly. There's no one there.

Russell looked to his left and spotted a big round apple near the end of a long branch. One last one, he told himself, and then he'd go find his mother and Erin.

The apple was too far out to reach. He looked around, assessing the situation. He hooked the handle of the bag onto the top of the ladder and then climbed off the rungs and onto the thick branch. Using his hands and legs, he shimmied along the branch till he got beneath where the apple hung. He reached up and plucked it from its stem.

Russell looked at the apple. He rubbed it on his sleeve and it shined nice and red. His stomach rumbled and he thought this apple was too perfect to bring home. He took a big bite, hearing the crunch as his teeth cleaved through the skin and into the juicy heart of the apple. Not too tart. The right amount of sweetness. Russell chewed and swallowed. He smiled and then took another big bite.

When he pulled the apple away from his mouth, he saw a dark brown spot from where his mouth had been. Half of a worm squirmed in the opening. Something moved in his mouth.

Russell reared back, released the apple and screamed, spitting out the chunk. He lost his balance and before he could regain his grip on the tree limb, he found himself falling toward the ground. He stuck his left arm out to brace for impact and closed his eyes as the ground rose to greet him. He landed with a thud and heard a loud crack.

When he opened his eyes, he looked at his left arm. Between the wrist and his elbow, a white bone protruded from a bloody patch of torn flesh.

"Bones," he uttered before passing out.

6

Quinn hated when Rita turned out the lights, usually by nine o'clock, because the cellar was so dark. Not much light from the moon could filter in because of the iron grates covering the window wells. He expected he'd be used to the dark after all that time in the House of Embers with Mr. Shreckengast and the Scamps *(how much time?)*, but unlike there, he was all alone here. That's why he was happy when Rita brought a box of wooden matches and let him light the candle she placed in the jack-o'-lantern.

A dim glow seeped out through the triangle eyes and crooked grin of the jack-o'-lantern as it sat in the middle of the table where he ate his meals. He lay on his cot under a blanket that kept out the dank chill in the basement and stared at the beacon of light that illuminated the shadows surrounding him. The aroma of the toasted pumpkin hovered in the stale air of the basement.

As he watched, the jack-o'-lantern watched him back, those triangle eyes aimed at him, that grin seeming to flex with each flicker of the flame inside its wide crooked mouth. Those teeth looked sharp. Quinn hadn't remembered carving a pumpkin before, but it appeared he had fashioned a work of art.

Now if he could only get to sleep.

He worried about whether he should blow the candle out before he got too tired, fearful of it causing a fire. He thought of the House of Embers and the Scamps, victims of a disastrous conflagration. *Don't want to end up like them.* He wondered where they had gone. And where was Mr. Shreckengast? Why hadn't he come looking for him?

Maybe Rita was right. Nobody wanted him.

Except her.

The jack-o'-lantern laughed at this. Quinn knew it was just the flickering flame bouncing shadows around the interior of the pumpkin shell.

Quinn felt sure the flame couldn't spread any farther than that jagged grin. Besides, if he got up to blow the candle out, then he would have to make his way back across the cellar floor to the cot in the dark. He shivered at that thought, or maybe it was only the cold air in the cellar. If only he would agree to behave and be her child, then he could get to sleep upstairs in a normal bedroom.

But that would be giving in, and he wasn't done fighting yet.

Quinn drifted off to sleep.

Sometime later, he awoke in darkness. His eyes searched through the blackness but could only make out shapeless shadows. The outline of the pumpkin rested like a silhouette on the table. The candle inside had gone out.

Somehow, even in the darkness, he could see the pits of the jack-o'-lantern's eyes and the gaping maw beneath it. Had the candle burned down? Or had something blown it out? Maybe Rita had come down. He often heard the creaking of the basement steps as she descended to check on him late at night. He always pretended to be asleep, not wanting any encounter with her.

He'd sense Rita approach his bed and stop beside it. Quinn always remained motionless, keeping his eyelids still, and waited for her to leave. He would hear her labored breath from coming down the steps as she stood beside the cot. Sometimes it seemed to take forever before she'd leave, her breaths deep and sharp. When she finally did go back upstairs, Quinn would release his own sigh of relief.

Maybe Rita had come down here and blown out the candle. It surprised him that he hadn't heard her. She was never quiet when she moved about the house. Otherwise, how else did the candle go out?

As he stared at the pumpkin and his eyes adjusted enough to the darkness that outlines of the items in the basement began to form, he noticed something about the pumpkin. The top piece of the jack-o'-lantern, with the stem, lay on the table on its side, as if someone had knocked it off.

OCTOBER 13

1

Russell sat in Miss Sheriden's classroom Tuesday and stared at the skeleton hanging in the front by her desk. He looked at his left forearm, now wrapped in a plaster cast covered in signatures from school friends and supported by a sling around his shoulder. He thought back to the shock of seeing the bone sticking out of that arm yesterday. He looked up at the skeleton the class had nicknamed Shinbones.

That's inside me. And when I die, I will be reduced to nothing but bones. Just like my father. A skeleton lying in his grave. He wondered how he could ever visit the cemetery and stand over his father's plot, knowing that beneath that six feet of dirt, and within that mahogany casket, lay not his father, but his father's *bones*.

Russell locked eyes with Shinbones and thought, at one time there had been flesh covering those bones, a face over that grinning skill. That had been a human being who walked and talked and maybe even had a family.

Now just bones.

They lied to me, he thought. His mother, the fire chief, and the priest from church, him worst of all. They said his father would be whole and ascend to another world, a better place. But how could he when he would just be bones? Skeletons walking around. What a racket they would make.

He almost laughed at the idea. Almost.

But when he thought about his own bone that he had seen, bloody and protruding from his skin, there was nothing funny. *That's inside me. Bones.*

"Russell," Miss Sheriden said, catching him off guard as he wasn't paying attention to her lecture about the composition of the human skeletal structure. "Would you care to come up here and point out to the class which bone you broke yesterday?"

All eyes in the classroom turned toward him. *How dare she*, he thought. After what he told her last week, how could she even consider that he wanted to have anything to do with that monstrosity? He swallowed hard. If he refused, everyone would make fun of him. Even Booger Barnes would laugh, happy that someone else was a target of ridicule.

Russell rose from his seat and plodded his way toward the front of the classroom. At one point he did a slow shuffle, holding his sling up against his body, pretending he was Lon Chaney from the *Mummy* movies on TV. Everyone laughed, but not at him, at his joke, and that made him smile.

I can do this.

He approached the skeleton, looking up into the dark holes of its eyeless skull. An idea popped into his head, and he grabbed the skeletal hand by its bony fingers and shook it.

"How do you do, sir," he said.

Laughter burst forth in the classroom. Even Miss Sheriden couldn't hold back.

Nothing to it, Russell thought as he gazed over the classroom and basked in the attention.

He felt those bony fingers squeeze back.

Russell's face went slack as something cold crept from the skeletal hand to his, forming an icy grip that traveled along his tingling flesh all the way up his arm and into his chest, where it seemed to form a layer of frost over his heart. He tried to pull his hand away, but the skeleton wouldn't let go. He jerked his hand back and got free, almost toppling the skeleton toward him.

"Careful," Miss Sheriden said as she rushed forward and steadied the skeleton.

More laughter erupted from his classmates. Russell looked out at the faces and the wide grins. Not everyone smiled. Wayne sat in the back row with a shallow expression as he watched the scene play out before him. Ryan's face, too, held a look of grave concern.

"I can't," Russell said to Miss Sheriden. "I don't remember which one." He hustled back to his seat as the laughter subsided.

Miss Sheriden looked confused. "Quiet down now," she said to the rest of the class. She picked the left arm of the skeleton up and pulled it away from the rest of the body. She pointed to Shinbones' forearm. "This is the ulnar bone," she said.

Don't touch it, Russell thought as he watched her.

"It's the one Russell broke when he had his unfortunate accident yesterday."

If it was *an accident,* Russell thought, remembering that someone was throwing apples at him when he was in the tree. As Miss Sheriden droned on about the bone, Russell looked down at the palm of his right hand. The flesh looked red and still felt cold, as if he'd been gripping an ice cube.

2

The boys gathered in Ryan's basement, sitting on the old couch that comprised most of the seating in the section divided off from the rest of the cellar by a partial framed partition covered in drywall. The family's old television had been shoved down here for whenever Ryan wanted to watch something besides what his parents were watching on the main TV upstairs in the living room. The basement TV wasn't hooked up to the aerial antenna on the roof, so it only got two channels, 9, the local ABC affiliate out of Manchester, and 11, the New Hampshire PBS station.

Lance and Wesley were checking out all the people's names who'd signed Russell's cast.

"He even got Becky Williams to sign," Lance said to Ryan.

"You've got to be kidding," Ryan said.

"Maybe *you* should break an arm or leg," Wesley said with a laugh.

"We got more important things to talk about," Ryan said, tired of the distraction. "What the heck happened in the orchard?"

"It's like I told you at school. Someone was chucking apples at me while I was up in the tree."

"Did you see them?"

"Not exactly."

"What the heck does that mean?"

"I saw shadows or something," Russell said. "Like someone was out there, but every time I looked, there was no one there."

"Spooks," Ryan said.

"What the hell are you talking about?" Lance asked, agitated.

"It's like that kid I saw at the soccer game."

"Not that again."

"I'm telling you, he didn't look right. I saw the bones in his fingers."

Russell shivered at the thought.

"And this whole thing with Eddie Scruggs and the pumpkins, and now he's gone."

"He ran away," Lance said.

"Did he? And what about Mr. Swain and the smashed pumpkins and the bloody shirt scrap?"

"What are you saying?" Wesley asked.

"I'm saying Eddie warned me about the pumpkins and now he's gone and Mr. Swain took a sledgehammer to his pumpkin shed. And he's disappeared. There's something not right in town."

"I know what's not right," Lance said as he stood. "We've got a scavenger hunt list and only found two items on it. We'll never get the hundred bucks at this rate."

Ryan felt frustrated. He wished he could make Lance understand. Lance hadn't seen the look of the kid at the soccer field and he didn't see Eddie's screwed-up face. He got up from the couch and walked over to the table, another relic from upstairs that got demoted to the basement.

"The scavenger hunt doesn't seem important anymore," he said. He looked at the two items on the table: the Carl Yastrzemski baseball card and the rolled-up gravestone rubbing.

"How can you say that?" Lance said. "It's a hundred bucks. Do you realize how many comic books you can buy with your share? How many movies we can see down at the Colonial?"

Ryan picked up the gravestone paper. Was he making a big deal out of nothing? Something settled in his stomach with an uneasy feeling these past few days. And it didn't seem a coincidence that Russell fell out of an apple tree after thinking something was lurking in the orchard.

"I can't help feeling that something is wrong here," Ryan said. But maybe Lance was right. Maybe they should just get on with the scavenger hunt and be normal kids again. Eddie ran away. He left a note, for cripes sakes. It was simple as that.

Ryan unrolled the scroll and looked at the gravestone rubbing. His mouth went dry and the basement felt very cold.

"There's nothing wrong in town," Lance said.

Ryan turned to face the three of them. He held out the gravestone paper.

"Then look at this."

The charcoal rubbing they'd done on the paper looked the same. But the writing had changed. It now read:

Curtis Cooper Woodson
Born December 7, 1957
Died February 14, 1970

3

The barn stood silhouetted against the clear night sky as Dane Woodson and his friend Ben crept across the grass at the Parker farm on Hickory Road. The lights in the house were out. Grant Parker and his son, Jacob, lived in the home and Dane assumed the boy would be asleep; he was around ten years old. But he wasn't sure if Mr. Parker would be up. He figured most farmers got up early, so surely that meant they went to bed early. And it appeared he was right.

Wade Droege had dropped the two of them off at the end of the driveway and stayed behind, parked in his El Camino waiting for them in the dark. Dane knew exactly what they were looking for as he and Ben hunched down and scampered along the yard toward the barn.

A constant breeze blew and brushed along the tops of the stalks in the cornfield, creating a whispering sound. Dane glanced that way and saw the cornstalks sway back and forth in the wind. The dark outline of a scarecrow propped up on a pole stood out above the cornfield. The wind blew the flaps of its wide-brimmed hat up and down, but the darkness of the night kept the face hidden.

"I have a bad feeling about this," Ben whispered from behind as they got closer to the barn.

"Keep your voice down," Dane said; even the soft tone of Ben's voice seemed to carry in the quiet of the night. "It'll only take a minute."

They reached the edge of the barn and crept along its side to the front. The wall to the left of the large barn doors held his target. Nailed to the planks of the barn were more than a couple dozen license plates.

"Do you have the flashlight?" Dane asked.

"Here," Ben said and handed it to him.

"Keep an eye out." Dane took the flashlight from him.

"What am I keeping an eye out for?" Ben asked as he stood with his back up to the corner of the barn.

"Any sign of life," Dane said and flicked the flashlight on.

"If I see anything, I'm out of here."

"Just be still. Watch the house in case a light comes on." Dane shined the flashlight beam onto the license plates on the wall. He scanned them, searching for the years of each plate. He had seen these plates many times on the barn when he came with his parents to the Parker farm to get corn on the cob or other vegetables. Every year Grant Parker nailed his old license plate on the wall when he received his new one. He had quite a collection that stretched back many years. They joined some of the plates his father before him had put up on the wall.

"There," Dane said when he spotted one from 1924, the oldest of the bunch. That was just what he needed for the scavenger hunt, the oldest license plate, and he doubted anyone else would find one older than this. Certainly not his brother Ryan and his idiot friends. "I got it."

Ben came up beside him and looked up.

"Can you reach it?" he asked. The plate was higher up on the wall than they expected.

"I might need you to hoist me up," Dane said.

"Can't you just take one lower down? There's still old ones there."

"It needs to be the oldest," Dane said. "We want to win the hundred bucks, so I'm not taking any chances. Give me a boost."

"I still don't like this." Ben interlocked his fingers and held them down for Dane to step into.

"Just keep quiet." Dane felt himself hoisted up until he was at eye level with the 1924 license plate. "Good." He took out a jackknife from his back pocket and leaned against the wall. With one hand still holding the flashlight, he used his other to pry at the nails holding the plate. It took some digging to get the blade under the head of the nail, but fortunately, the aged wood of the barn planks was soft and the nail came out with little effort. He wobbled in Ben's grasp. "Hold me still," he called down.

"You're heavy," Ben said between labored breaths. "Hurry up."

"One more nail," Dane said. He made quick work of it and the plate popped off the wall. "Got it. Let me down."

Ben let go of his foot and he came crashing down to the ground and fell on his butt.

"Thanks," Dane said.

"Sorry," Ben replied as he helped him to his feet. "Let's get the hell out of here."

Dane shut the flashlight off and the two of them made their way back across the grass toward the driveway and the road, where Wade waited for them. A rustling sound to his right caused Dane to stop. He looked toward the cornfield. The wind blew and the stalks swayed back and forth with a soft whooshing sound, as if they were whispering, trying to tell him something.

The scarecrow stood rigid on its pole. As Dane watched, a gloved hand at the end of one arm moved.

No, Dane thought. *The wind*.

He continued after Ben, who was now several yards ahead of him. At one point he looked back over his shoulder. The angle made it seem the scarecrow's head had turned his way, its eyes watching him.

4

In a second-floor bedroom of the farmhouse beside the barn, Jacob Parker lay in bed unable to sleep, trying to remember his dead mother's face. She died three years ago, when he was seven, and sometimes he would dream about her coming to him, and it felt wonderful, but he would awaken with such sadness because he knew it wasn't true, only a dream. Then her face would fade and he would lie in the darkness trying to remember her features.

He'd get frustrated and finally turn on the bedside lamp and look at the picture of her he kept on his nightstand. Then he'd be angry with himself for forgetting what she looked like. How unhappy that must make her. What would she think of him?

On this night, something else had disturbed his sleep. A noise from outside. He got out of bed, went to the window, and pulled the curtain aside. He glanced down onto the barn next to the house and the cornfield beyond it.

Jacob saw figures moving below. Two shadowed shapes by the front wall of the barn. There had been a light, but now it blinked off and he watched the two figures slinking away from the barn toward the driveway.

Should he run and wake Father? Maybe they were robbers.

As he watched, the two figures stopped and peered into the cornfield. Jacob's eyes followed them, wondering what caught their attention. In the middle of the cornfield, on a great wooden post, hung his father's scarecrow. It rose above the cornstalks like a ship's mast bobbing on a darkened sea.

The two figures began moving again and continued down the driveway till they were out of sight. Maybe they got what they came for, or maybe something spooked them and they chickened out. Whatever the reason, Jacob felt he didn't need to disturb his father's sleep.

As he stared out the window, the glow of the nearly full moon shined its spotlight down on the cornfield. Like a performer on a stage, Jacob saw the scarecrow begin to move.

The scarecrow shifted on the post; it twisted one arm free, then the next. It reached behind it and unhooked the spike in the middle of the post. The scarecrow dropped to the ground and submerged into the sea of cornstalks. Jacob watched the swaying of the stalks as the spectral figure moved through the cornfield, away from the house, in the direction the two figures had gone.

Jacob's whole body froze up as if his blood had turned to ice water. He pulled away from the window in horror, his mouth open as he tried to scream out to his father in the bedroom below, but nothing would emit from his clenched throat. He jumped in the bed and pulled the covers up over his head and curled up beneath them, knowing there was no way he'd fall back asleep.

OCTOBER 14

1

Russell ate breakfast Wednesday morning, brushed his teeth, and got ready for school while thinking of the secret he kept from his friends, because he wasn't sure it really happened.

When they'd gathered in the basement room at the Woodson house yesterday, he'd explained everything he knew about his encounter at the apple orchard with the mysterious person laughing and throwing apples at him. It certainly didn't seem to be anything far-fetched. Even though he couldn't see his tormenter, that didn't mean there wasn't anybody there. Anyone real.

He knew Ryan wanted to see ghosts or ghouls in whatever was going on. But it could have been some jerk from school playing tricks on him, hiding behind the trees, and chucking rotten apples at him while he stood on the ladder. Lance understood, even if Ryan didn't want to believe.

But what happened with Ryan's grave rubbing freaked him out. *Try and explain that.* When Russell saw Curtis's name and dates of birth and death, he wanted to tell the others about what he experienced in the classroom with Shinbones.

Russell kept telling himself yesterday that it was his imagination. The skeleton hadn't gripped his hand. Maybe when he grabbed it to shake hands, the fingers got stuck on his. That had to be it. Never mind the cold sensation it sent shivering up his whole arm. That could have been nerves. He felt it best to keep it to himself. No sense letting the others think he was seeing spooks too.

Russell pulled a shirt over his head, stuck his hand through the arm hole and pulled the sleeve over the cast. He could only wear short-sleeve or three-quarter-sleeve shirts now that he had the bulky cast covering his forearm from his wrist to his elbow. As he bunched the sleeve up around the top end of the cast, he looked down.

He had to read it twice to understand what he saw, and wondered why he hadn't noticed it before.

Fifteen minutes later, as he approached his friends at the bus stop, he felt anger build up inside. A joke's a joke, and who doesn't like a good trick, especially during the Halloween season, but this prank was a low blow.

He walked up to Ryan, Lance, and Wesley.

"Who did it?" he yelled, holding his left arm up so all could see his cast.

"What are you talking about?" Lance said.

Russell looked from one confused face to the next.

"Who wrote this on my cast?" Russell's voice squeaked with heightened inflection. It must have happened at school yesterday when everyone was signing his cast. "Who's the wiseass?" He waved his arm around in front of their faces.

"You need to pipe down," Ryan said, "and tell us what the heck you mean."

"Yeah," Lance said. "Take it easy. What gives?"

"This!" Russell thrust his cast before them and pointed.

The cast was covered in signatures:

"Have a nice trip" – Ryan

"See you next fall" – Lance

"Keep on trucking" – Wesley

"Smooth play, Shakespeare" – Becky

"Wowzers" – Wayne

"What a bugga" – Liza & Lindsey

In the middle of all those signatures was one Russell hadn't noticed until he was putting his shirt on this morning. He didn't recall seeing anyone write it and didn't think it was a damn bit funny. But it was written in black ink in the middle of the cast:

"See you soon" – Shinbones

2

After school, Wayne Barnes walked toward the railroad tracks that he followed on the way home. He thought about Eddie. Yesterday he had been the talk of the school when word of his running away had gotten around. Nobody could believe it, least of all Wayne.

Why hadn't Eddie said something to him? He didn't understand why he would take off like that. Eddie was the only friend he had at school. Now he had no one. And today, Eddie was already being forgotten. No one brought up his name. His empty chair stood out like a silent sentinel, but nobody cast a glance at it.

Wayne wondered how far Eddie had gotten on the train and where he'd gotten off. That took balls, that's for sure. But it was also stupid. Did he think the cops wouldn't find him? Chief Strong might not be a great detective, but there must be fuzz all up and down the east coast looking for him. Eventually someone would find him and turn him in. What would happen when Eddie got back to school? If he thought people laughed at him a lot before this, he was in for a rude awakening.

In Wayne's backpack he still had Eddie's bag of marbles. He wanted to hold on to them for his friend so he could give them back when he returned. The least he could do. If only Eddie would come back. He missed him.

Wayne had been walking with his head down, but now he looked up, sensing something. Ahead stood a line of boys and girls between him and the railroad tracks. He stopped.

What the heck?

It looked like more than a dozen, some young, but some older, high school age and even older than that. *What the hell are they doing here? Where did they come from?*

They were standing in his way, about thirty yards in front of him. Wayne stared, puzzled, and then moved off to the left to go around them.

The line moved to block his path.

Wayne stopped.

From this distance, he couldn't recognize any faces, not even the ones who appeared to be his own age. Their clothes looked ragged, their faces dirty, kind of like most of the kids from the Box Cars, but this bunch didn't look familiar.

Who the hell are they and what are they doing here? It pissed him off. Wayne shifted to the right and once again the line moved to impede his way. What kind of game were they playing?

Some of them smiled.

A joke, he thought. *They think this is a joke.* He was in no mood for this kind of crap. Not after the last couple of days.

"Back off!" he yelled at the group.

More smiles among them as they all linked arms.

"Red Rover, Red Rover, send Booger Barnes right over," they chanted in unison in shrill voices that carried across the field toward him.

Wayne felt a chill in the air.

"Get bent!" he yelled back.

"Red Rover, Red Rover, send Booger Barnes right over," they repeated.

Wayne didn't know why they were ragging on him, but their smiles got under his skin. He looked from face to face, trying to recognize someone he knew who might have some issue with him. But their grubby faces looked unfamiliar. A bunch of jerks from another school maybe, kids from Saint Barts still pissed over losing to Maplewood in the soccer game last weekend.

But why pick on Wayne? He didn't even go to the freaking game.

"Red Rover, Red Rover, send Booger Barnes right over."

Wayne felt his blood boil. He flexed his fingers as he eyed the creeps.

"Knock yourself out," he said as he looked for the weak link in the chain in front of him. That was always the key to playing Red Rover. Find the smallest pair and aim for them to break through the linked arms.

Wayne reached a hand back to the side pocket of his backpack and took out the bag of marbles. He gripped it in his right hand. Insurance, he thought. It would make a nice heavy blow if he threw a punch to one of the brats' heads as he was busting through.

I'm bigger than a lot of them, he thought, as he braced his legs for the charge, *especially some of the younger ones. Find the weakest link in the chain.* He eyed the kids in the line as he squeezed the marble bag in his hand.

"Red Rover, Red Rover, send Booger Barnes right over."

Wayne bent forward, almost in a track race starting position, though he had never played sports. With a wild wail ripped from the base of his throat, he sprinted forward, his eyes glued to the linked arms of a young boy and girl in the center of the line. He didn't care if he busted their arms when he broke through. That would teach these jerks.

Their grins seemed to widen the closer Wayne got, the whole lot of them looking like mad fools. He sucked air in through gritted teeth as he chugged across the field, his legs pumping like the wheels of a locomotive, like the one that took Eddie away from town. The wind brushed his hair back from his face.

He squeezed the marble bag tight.

As he got closer, the line of kids seemed to condense. They looked bigger as he got within ten yards of the group.

He noticed something else.

Their faces.

The skin on most of their faces looked blistered and charred. Not dirty.

Seconds before he hit the line, he noticed one older-looking kid had no eyes, only hollowed-out, blackened sockets.

Wayne slammed into a pair of arms.

They did not give. They bent a little, but he could feel the solid bones beneath soft, squishy flesh.

Wayne felt himself falling forward as he lunged, and soon the bodies of the kids were all around him, smothering him, a rotten stench gagging him. Bones poked him as he was swallowed up in a morass of loose flesh that pressed against his body, his face. He tried to scream but when he opened his mouth, he tasted ash.

Before things went black, he felt his fingers open and the marble bag slip from his grip.

3

Jacob Parker went to bed earlier than usual, not long after dinner. His father had asked him if he felt all right as he kept quiet throughout the meal. Jacob told him he was fine and climbed the stairs to his bedroom. He wanted to tell his father about what he'd seen out the window last night, but wondered if it was nothing but a nightmare.

The scarecrow had been back on its perch when he got up in the morning, so what he saw couldn't have been real. He wasn't sure. His father had noticed a missing license plate from the wall of the barn, so that must have been what those two dark figures were up to. Teenagers most likely. *At least that part of last night was real*, he thought.

But what about the rest?

Jacob was homeschooled by his father ever since his mother died. He felt his old man didn't want to be away from him now there was only the two of them. But earlier in the day, he couldn't concentrate on his studies. He was distracted by the scarecrow and whether he had seen it come alive.

As he got into bed, he reflected on the day he and his father made the scarecrow. They had stuffed the red flannel shirt and old jeans of his father's with hay till its body was bloated, then stuffed more hay into an old burlap sack for its head. Jacob himself had sewn two large black buttons from his mother's sewing box for its eyes, and took a thick rawhide lace from an old leather work boot and stitched together a jagged grin for a mouth. He tied an old pair of his father's work gloves onto the end of the scarecrow's arms for hands. They topped it off with a wide-brimmed black hat. His father carried the scarecrow out to the middle of the cornfield where he had made a wooden cross, and the two of them had strapped the scarecrow onto it.

Jacob remembered when his mother came home from the hospital to die. There was nothing more the doctors could do for her; the cancer had ravaged her body, leaving her weak and limp, like a rag doll. Jacob went into her room one time, while she was sleeping, and saw the once robust woman he had known had become thin and frail. He touched her arm, lifted it in an attempt to hold her hand, and it was light. She had felt just like the scarecrow, as if she were stuffed with hay and not made of flesh, bones, and blood.

As Jacob lay in bed, he wondered what could have brought the scarecrow to life. Or had he imagined the whole thing? He stared at the window, but felt too afraid to get out of bed and go to the window to look at the cornfield below. He could picture the scarecrow struggling to remove itself from the post. He didn't want to see that.

Finally, his heart thumping in his chest, he got up and went to the window. The post was empty.

He lay awake for quite a while and watched his closed bedroom door. He stared at the knob, waiting to see if it would move. He thought about going downstairs to his father's bedroom, but wondered if the scarecrow might be somewhere in the house. He lay awake, not daring to move, and listened for the slightest sound, afraid to close his eyes.

Then he did doze, and when he awoke sometime during the night, he gathered his nerves and went to the window. He saw the scarecrow climb back up onto its perch and reattach itself to the wooden post.

Its head turned and looked up at Jacob's window.

It's seen me!

Jacob's mouth gaped open and closed several times, and then finally he found his vocal cords and let rip with a shattering scream.

His father came bounding up the steps and burst into the room.

"What's wrong?"

Jacob, shaken, looked up at the tired old man and began to ramble about the scarecrow. His father sat beside him on the bed and took him in his arms.

"What are you talking about?"

Jacob tried to stop shaking and gulped a few shallow breaths of air. "The scarecrow," he said. "It's alive."

His father looked out the window. "Jacob, it's just a scarecrow. It can't move." He tried to keep his voice calm and soothing.

"But it did, sir – I swear. I saw it tonight and last night."

"Is that why you've been acting kind of strange?"

"I know what I saw."

"The scarecrow is supposed to scare crows, not young boys."

"Well, it scares me."

"Okay," his father said in a calming voice. "How about hopping into my bed tonight? Will that make you feel better?"

Jacob nodded.

And he did feel safer lying on the side of the bed his mother used to sleep on, almost feeling her warm, comforting presence, but also making him miss her terribly and wish she were here to tell him everything would be all right.

His father snored beside him, which also offered its own sort of comfort.

Before drifting off, Jacob glanced at the window that looked out on the same side of the house as his window and wondered if he should dare peek outside. *Where did the scarecrow go? What did it do?*

If he looked out now and it were gone, he could wake his father and show him he wasn't imagining things, that the scarecrow was alive. Somehow.

But he didn't dare look, not wanting to disrupt the comfort he felt lying in his parents' big bed beneath the warm quilt and soft sheets. He drifted off to sleep, trying to push away thoughts of that burlap sack face with its big eyes and crooked leather-lace grin.

5

The gravel crunched beneath the tires of the VW as Elsie Hoover pulled the car off Old Coach Road beside the covered bridge on the north side of the river. Dane Woodson felt something tickling his insides, as if he'd swallowed a wasp. He'd heard this place was a common make-out spot. Now he was here with the most beautiful girl in school.

Elsie looked out the windshield up toward the sky. His eyes followed her trajectory.

"Supposed to be a full moon tonight," she said, "but I don't see it."

"Me neither."

"Maybe we need to step outside."

She opened the door to get out and he did the same. He ached to stay inside the vehicle, thinking that's where anything would happen. Not that he was quite sure what might happen, but he decided to just follow her lead. This was his first real high school date, at least one that involved a car. He didn't count meeting a girl at a school dance and hanging out together till it ended.

"There it is," she said, pointing up.

The moon hung plump in the dark sky, shining a spotlight over them as it lighted up the area around the covered bridge. From where he stood, the inside of the bridge looked like a dark throat.

As he gazed up at the moon, he felt her body lean up beside his. He looked into her eyes. She pursed her lips and bent toward him. The buzzing in his belly sped up. He met her lips and mushed his against hers. *Damn, I hope I'm doing this right*, he thought. Then her lips parted and he felt her tongue slip inside his mouth.

God, he thought, as his tongue found hers. *I'm really kissing her.* After a few warm, precious seconds, their lips parted when the sound of a car approached down Old Coach Road toward town. Its lights spotlighted them brighter than the moon ever could. A car horn tooted before it rumbled through the covered bridge and out the other side.

"Let's go down there," she said, as she pointed beneath the bridge. Her eyes glowed in the moonlight as she smiled.

Her hand slipped into his and she led him down the slope toward the river. He followed her under the bridge, where they sat on the cool ground. Out of the light, her features slipped into a darkened silhouette, and he admired the outline of her face, the blonde hair that fell past her shoulders, and the swell of her breasts beneath her soft sweater.

"No interruptions here," she said with a soft giggle.

"That's right," he said, and felt like slapping himself for not thinking of anything smoother to say. He slipped an arm around her shoulders and leaned in for another kiss. This one lasted longer and when their lips parted, he had to catch his breath. *Breathe through your nose,* he told himself.

Elsie looked into his eyes and brought her lips up again. Once again, the embrace lasted longer than the previous one. His right hand stroked the top of her left thigh and then up across her hip to her waist. Their lips drew apart for a brief second as he felt the saliva building in his mouth. He swallowed and then their lips and tongues came together again.

As his right hand caressed the curve of her hip, he wondered if he should dare more. He braced himself as he brought his hand up to her breasts, feeling the firmness in his palm as he began to squeeze. She did not flinch; in fact, leaned into him more and he let his hand roam over the fullness of what lay beneath her sweater.

A tapping sound came from above.

He felt her body tighten and they pulled apart.

"What was that?" she whispered.

He looked up at the darkened underside of the wooden bridge.

"I don't know," he said in a low voice, annoyed by the interruption. They listened. *Maybe it was nothing*, he thought.

The soft tapping sounded again. *Footsteps.* Someone walking on the bridge above them. The steps stopped for a second and then started up again.

"Someone's up there," Elsie said, pointing up.

"They'll go away," Dane said and paused to listen.

The sound of the steps seemed to fade as they led along the bridge to the other side of the river. *There,* he thought. *Going away.*

But then the steps came back the other way, getting louder as they approached.

"What are they doing?" Elsie whispered. Her eyes rolled up to look above.

Dane followed her gaze up, now irritated that his big moment was being ruined by whoever was walking back and forth on the bridge. Could it be someone from school, one of his classmates? Maybe they recognized Elsie's car and were playing a prank on them.

"I should go check and see what's going on," he said.

Her brows knitted. "Are you sure?"

He sensed she wouldn't feel comfortable otherwise.

"Stay here," he told her. "I'll be right back. Don't go anywhere."

She tried to stifle a giggle. "Where would I go?"

"I won't be long." Dane headed up the incline toward the end of the bridge. Maybe it was just some townie out walking about for some fresh air. But if it was some jerk from school, he was going to be pissed. Dane had a good thing going down there and now someone had ruined it.

He reached the road and stared into the mouth of the bridge. It was dark inside, with fragments of moonlight filtering in through the diagonal slats of the sides of the bridge.

But he saw nothing in there.

Dane entered the bridge with slow, plodding steps, his eyes seeking out the dark sides of the bridge for someone lurking in the shadows. He could hear his own feet tapping on the wooden planks as he walked, and thought Elsie must be listening to them from below. He hoped she wasn't scared.

Scared? What made him think that?

Just because it was night and the moon full and bright and the two of them were under the bridge all alone.... *Or were they?* Someone had been walking on the bridge. Dane could see the opening on the other side and the empty road that spilled out. He continued till he was nearly halfway across the bridge. He heard the water of the river moving below, but other than that, nothing.

Nobody on the bridge but him.

Whoever it had been must have gone.

With a sigh of relief, he turned and headed back across the bridge toward the north side of the river.

He stopped.

His steps had echoed in the interior of the wooden bridge and the rafters above. But other steps joined his from behind. He heard the tap-tap sound as someone approached.

Dane turned to look behind him.

Nobody there. His eyes strained through the darkness. *Nothing*. The bridge was empty.

What the—?

Maybe he had only heard the echoes of his own steps. Of course. He looked carefully at the shadows on the bridge, almost daring one of them to move and reveal a person. But he only saw wooden beams and planks.

He turned back and headed toward the opening.

The steps sounded behind him.

Dane spun around quick, hoping – expecting – to catch someone sneaking up on him.

Still nobody there.

This is nuts. I'm making myself crazy.

He ran to the end of the bridge, this time not bothering to stop and look back, hearing the thumping steps of his feet. He came out of the bridge and scrambled down the embankment to the underside.

He stopped.

Elsie was gone.

A pounding began in his chest. He saw the spot where they had just been sitting, where they were kissing. *What happened?* He scanned along the ground toward the river, the water where his younger brother had been swept away.

Elsie?

What am I going to do? His mind raced inside his skull.

A hand landed on his shoulder and he turned.

"Boo!" Elsie yelled with a laugh.

His heart nearly leapt out of his chest and his hand came up to clutch it and prevent it from flying from his body.

"Jesus!" he yelled.

Elsie continued to laugh.

"Boy, did I scare you," she said when she stopped laughing enough to manage a few words. "You should see the look on your face."

"Christ, you gave me a heart attack!"

She stopped laughing. "You scare easy," she said with a smile.

Dane tried to calm his nerves, which felt on fire. He tried to be cool about the whole thing, didn't want her to think he was a jerk.

"Where were you?"

"I had to pee," she said. "So, I went over to the bushes there." She pointed behind her, over by the riverbank.

"I didn't know what happened to you," he said, feeling a little more in control of his breathing.

"Was there anyone up on the bridge?" she asked.

"No," he said. *Was there?* He couldn't be sure. "No one at all." He hoped.

"I should probably drive you home," she said. "It is a school night."

"Okay," he said, a bit sorry the date was coming to an end when a few minutes ago he felt it was just beginning, but in a way, he wanted to get out of here and back to the comfort of his home. "Let's go."

They got back into the car and as Elsie drove it across the bridge toward town, Dane couldn't help looking at the headlight beams picking their way across the wooden planks, expecting them to light up something that shouldn't be there.

OCTOBER 15

1

In the morning, on Hickory Road, Jacob Parker awoke to an empty bed and began to panic. Footsteps came down the hall toward the open bedroom door and he gasped before seeing his father come to the doorway. He stood there in a blue work shirt and jeans.

"Get dressed," his father said. "I want to show you something."

Once outside, his father led him toward the cornfield.

"But, sir," Jacob protested.

His father stopped and turned. "Come with me. I'm going to show you there's nothing to be afraid of."

Jacob hesitated, but knew he couldn't disobey his father. He looked up at the early morning sun and then out toward the cornfield. The stalks swayed back and forth in the breeze, a congregation bowing in holy worship before the scarecrow on the wooden cross.

Maybe in the daylight it'll be all right, Jacob told himself. *Maybe it only comes alive at night under the bright moon.*

Jacob walked slowly toward the field, his father leading the way. They entered between a row of stalks, dust kicking up from the soft loam beneath their feet. The stalks were brown and brittle, creating a crispy sound as they brushed by their dried leaves. It sounded like whispering.

His breath grew sharper and shallower the deeper they got into the field. Jacob could see the dark figure of the scarecrow looming up as they got closer. He could feel his heart pumping, and his skin grew cold and clammy. He didn't want to do this, didn't want to go near the thing. But his father plowed on and Jacob fixed his gaze on the old man's blue shirt as he pushed through the cornstalks.

There was a small circular clearing in the center of the field where the wooden post rose out of the ground like a tree trunk, as if it had grown there and not been planted by Jacob and his father. Jacob stared at the ground where the base of the post burrowed into the dirt. He didn't dare look up. He wanted to close his eyes.

"Now, Jacob," his father said in a gentle voice. "You remember when we made this scarecrow? You and I together?"

"Yes, sir," Jacob said, still not looking up. He did not want to see those black button eyes or crooked grin.

"We took some of my old clothes and stuffed them with hay from the barn. You were so proud of the face you made. Remember?"

Jacob nodded, but still didn't look.

"Now, you know it's not real. Not alive. You say it moved. Well, it was probably just blowing in the wind. Maybe the strapping holding its arm came loose."

"No," Jacob said, shaking his head. "It came down off the post and took off through the field." He looked up at his father, keeping the scarecrow out of his sight.

The old man's forehead furrowed and he let out a deep sigh. "Just walked off, huh? Just like that?"

Jacob nodded.

"Now how could that be? We didn't even give him any feet."

Jacob turned and looked at the pant legs of the scarecrow, its bottom cuffs tied with twine to keep the hay from spilling out. Jacob shrugged.

"Look at him, son."

Jacob lifted his head, following the pant legs up to where its waist met the red flannel shirt and on up to the burlap sack face with the jagged rawhide grin. The black button eyes stared in silence beneath the black wide-brimmed hat that flopped in the breeze.

"It can't walk, son. Not only because it doesn't have feet, but because it isn't alive. Not like you and me. Don't you see?"

His father stepped onto a small wooden wedge nailed to the front of the post about two feet from the bottom and hoisted himself up in front of the scarecrow, even with it so he could look it in the eye.

Holding on to the left arm of the cross, he took his right hand and began unbuttoning the front of the red flannel shirt. He reached in, pulled out some hay and turned to show it to Jacob.

"See?" he said as he let shreds of the hay slip from his fingers and flutter to the ground.

Jacob stared.

"It's made of nothing but hay," his father said. "How could it possibly be alive if," the old man thrust his hand into the chest of the scarecrow, "if it doesn't even have a heart…."

His father suddenly froze, mouth still open from expelling the last word he had uttered, eyes wide, his right hand still buried deep within the scarecrow's chest.

Jacob knew what his father's right hand was feeling. Something soft and wet and pulsating in his raw, weathered hand.

His father's pale face turned slowly to look down at him, his mouth still drooping, his eyes round and wide.

"Run," his father said. "Run, Jacob! Run as fast as you can!"

Jacob froze, afraid to leave, afraid to stay, but mostly afraid of the look of horror on his father's face.

Jacob pivoted in the soft loam and pushed his way through the cornstalks.

"Run, Jacob!" his father screamed. "And don't look back!"

He didn't look back. His heart pumped as fast as his legs as he tore through the cornfield, leaves of the stalks slapping his cheeks and forehead. He hoped he was going in the direction of the house, but his vision was nothing but a blur of cornstalks as he pushed his way through them, cracking the stalks of some as he knocked them aside.

Jacob could no longer hear his father and tears began streaming down his cheeks, stinging from the whipping of the cornstalk leaves. He heard nothing from behind him, but didn't dare look back, afraid of seeing the dark shape of the scarecrow, its mad grin looming behind him, those worn old work gloves reaching for him.

Jacob's legs grew tired as he ran, and he thought about never finding his way out of the cornfield. *What if I'm running in circles?* He would be chased by the scarecrow throughout the cornfield until his legs could move no more and he collapsed to the ground in a heap at the mercy of that sinister creature.

But he did see the barn and the farmhouse ahead and burst through the edge of the cornfield, screaming because it made him feel better, though there was no one nearby who would hear. Only the scarecrow and his father, and he didn't know if his father was capable of hearing anything anymore.

Jacob raced past the barn, across the lawn toward the house. He leapt up onto the porch and stumbled through the door, nearly collapsing onto the floor. He quickly slammed the door shut, glancing outside and seeing neither his father nor the scarecrow, but only the empty wooden post in the middle of the cornfield.

He threw the bolt on the door and looked around.

What do I do? His mind raced in a wild panic. *God, what do I do?* He wished his mother were here. She'd know what to do.

Hide. That's what she'd tell him. Hide and hope his father makes it out of the cornfield.

Jacob spied the basement door. He ran to it, threw it open and hurried through. He shut the door behind him and nearly fell as he dashed down the wooden steps. Across from the bottom of the stairs sat a long, wooden workbench. He crawled beneath it and leaned his back up against the cold stone slab of the cellar wall. He drew his legs up in front of him and wrapped his arms around them, hugging them to his chest and feeling his beating heart pound against them. Tears ran down his red, raw face, stinging his cheeks. He gasped for breath in the dank, dark cellar as he inhaled mold and mildew, dust, and cobwebs. He felt as if he were choking, but he would not move except for the shaking spasms of his body. He was so exhausted from his sprint, he thought he might pass out.

But his eyes, wide, stared at the cellar stairs leading up to the door to the kitchen. He listened for the slightest sound. There was none. He wasn't sure if fear had made him deaf, or if there really were no sounds within the house. Not even the groan of the furnace, the hiss of the radiators above, or the gurgling of water in the pipes. Nothing but silence, except for his breath, expelled in rapid spasms.

He sat still for what seemed like hours, not daring to move, not willing to make a sound. He was prepared to stay in this position as long as it took. All day and night if he had to, though once it got dark, he thought he might go mad sitting in the blackness of the basement, not knowing if the scarecrow was in the house somewhere, looking for him.

He heard a door shake from above.

The front door.

He gripped his sweaty legs tighter.

A crashing sound came from above, the sound of the bolt ripped from the doorframe, and he heard footsteps creaking on the wooden floorboards of the kitchen. Soft steps. He looked up at the basement ceiling, at the underside of those very floorboards, and he could swear he saw each board dip slightly with each creaking step. His eyes followed those moving floorboards as the steps worked their way around the first floor of the house.

The steps stopped on the other side of the cellar door. Jacob rested his chin on his knees as his eyes glared at the paneled door. He held his breath.

The doorknob turned with a creaking rattle.

The door swung open and light spilled down the cellar steps. A dark figure stood at the top of the stairs.

"Jacob?" his father called out. "It's all right now."

Jacob exhaled with a great sigh of relief and scampered out from under the workbench.

"Father!" he screamed as he bolted up the stairs. "I was so scared."

At the top of the stairs, he threw himself at his father and buried his face into his soft belly beneath the blue work shirt as his father's arms wrapped around him tight.

But the belly was soft and prickly beneath the shirt and Jacob tried to pull himself away when he saw the hay poking out between the buttons, but the arms gripped him ever tighter, and he didn't dare look up into the face, not wanting to see that sewn-up grin.

2

As Becky Williams cut across the cobblestones of the Town Square toward the public library after school, she thought about when she saw Eddie Scruggs on Sunday. He'd taunted her, but she'd given it right back to him. She enjoyed making fun of him because he went out of his way to be annoying. That was the last day she had seen him. She couldn't believe he ran away, and hoped it wasn't because of any of the things she'd said to him. It wasn't like she was the only one who made fun of Eddie. Her friends Liza and Lindsey usually joined in and she often saw Ryan and his friends at odds with Eddie.

He'll turn up, she thought. Kids who ran away usually came back eventually. Didn't they? Of course. Eddie will be back in class in no time and playing marbles on the playground with Wayne Barnes. *Come to think of it*, she thought, *Wayne was absent from school today.*

Becky pushed thoughts of those two geeks out of her head as she prepared to mount the steps to the front entrance of the library. No need for them to waste space in her head; she'd rather reserve those spots for Kirby Tressler.

That put a smile on her face as she glanced up to the stone gargoyles on the corners of the roofline. She never understood why the town built those things into the library building. Sure, the twisted figures held books in their stone hands, but they still creeped her out and seemed an odd choice for the design of the building.

She greeted the librarian at the front desk and strolled past the reading room where the magazines and newspapers were kept. Becky spotted two old men sitting in chairs by a window. They both held newspapers that they lowered as she walked past. Their eyes followed her. She knew her sweater was a bit too tight for her newly developed breasts, but she liked the way Kirby Tressler admired her, so she didn't mind. These two dirty old men, though, were another thing. She felt like walking right up to them and telling them to stick their eyeballs back in their sockets.

The way they held their newspapers up pretending to read while peering over them at her reminded her of the stone gargoyles on the library roof. Their mostly bald heads, with veins and dark spots covering the skin, resembled granite. She turned away from them and marched into the stacks beyond the front desk.

It took Becky no time to find the book she came for: *Are You There, God? It's Me, Margaret*, by Judy Blume. She had heard so much about it from Liza and Lindsey and some of the other girls at school. Everyone was reading it. Becky knew it was about a girl her own age going through puberty with her friends and waiting for her breasts to develop and have her first period. She had to get the book.

Of course, she was already well on her way in the breast department, but felt frustrated that she hadn't had her period yet. Liza and Lindsey had both had theirs already and they assumed Becky had too because of how much more developed she was than the other girls. That's why she'd lied and told them she'd had it. She couldn't admit that she hadn't. Not the way her two friends looked up to her.

Maybe the book would give her some insight on what she was going through. Or maybe it would just be silly fun. She got excited as she pulled the book out, admiring the artwork on the cover of the young Margaret. Becky heard the library originally refused to carry the book sparked by concerns of some parents in town. But they relented and decided to keep it in the adult section of the library instead of the children's room.

Seemed about right to Becky. She felt that's where the book and she belonged.

With a flutter in her tummy, she strolled over to the front desk.

"I'd like to check this out," Becky said as she placed the book on the counter and pulled her library card out of the back pocket of her jeans.

The librarian's smile turned to a frown. "I'm sorry," she said. "With this particular book, you'll need to have permission from one of your parents." The smile came back.

"What?" Becky couldn't believe what she heard. She had a library card. She should be able to take out any book she wanted.

"It's the library's policy," the librarian said in a soft voice. She bent down toward Becky and spoke even softer. "It's because of the sensitive nature of the book." She now wore her serious face.

Becky looked down at the book and the cover with the young girl sitting in her bedroom gazing out the window. Becky didn't know what to say. A glance into the reading room and she spotted the two old men watching her.

"I guess I'll put it back," she said, her lower lip protruding in a pout.

"Just come back with your mommy or daddy and that will be fine."

Becky felt like she shrunk down beneath the counter, almost expecting the librarian to tell her she might find some books to her liking in the children's room downstairs. Becky dragged the book off the counter and walked back into the stacks. She disappeared down one of the rows, not even the one where the book belonged, because she wanted to get out of sight of the librarian's prying eyes as well as those of the two old men.

She gripped the book tight, not wanting to let it go. Becky looked around to make sure she was alone in the aisle, and then shoved the book underneath her jacket. Her body shook as her nerves tingled.

Did she dare?

She wondered what the consequences would be if she got caught. Nothing the library would do would even compare to the punishment her father would mete out. But she felt sure there was no way she'd get caught. *Just walk out of here with your head up, just the way you walked in.* She steeled her nerves, preparing to exit the row she stood in, when movement from behind startled her.

Becky turned to see a man had entered the row from the back. Another old man, this one with white straggly hair and wearing a long trench coat. He smiled at her with missing teeth. Another gargoyle, she thought and looked away. She pretended to browse the books on the shelf in front of her.

"Looking for something to study for school?" the old man said in a raspy voice.

She ignored him. *Not supposed to talk to strangers*, she told herself.

"How about studying this?" the man said.

The oddity of his question lured her to look his way.

He held his trench coat open, and as she looked down, she saw his fly was unzipped and something long, wrinkled, and pinkish stuck out between the zipper teeth.

Becky's eyes widened as she turned away with a gasp. She stumbled out of the row of books into the center aisle. Her legs wobbled. She heard the man snickering behind her and felt she might vomit.

She wanted to run, but with the contraband book beneath her jacket, she didn't want to draw suspicion. Instead, she walked as quick as her weak legs were able, past the front desk toward the main doors.

"Have a nice day," the librarian behind the counter said in a cheerful voice.

Becky didn't answer. She couldn't even find words in her tightened throat. As she headed toward the front doors, she heard the rustling of newspapers from the two old men in the chairs, but didn't turn to look at them. She pushed open the door, out into the draining sunlight and clambered down the stone steps. Her shoes made loud clomping sounds on the cobblestones that echoed in the square as she hurried away from the library.

Did the librarian suspect?

But of more concern, was the old man in the trench coat following her out of the library?

She slowed her steps and gathered enough courage to turn and look behind her. No one had come out of the library. A pigeon flew off the roof, its flapping wings startling her, and she caught her breath before a gasp leapt from her throat.

As she watched the pigeon in flight, she noticed movement out of the corner of her eye.

One of the stone gargoyles lowered the book it held in its hands.

No. Becky thought she imagined it. It was the one that looked like an owl, big, round eyes and long beak pointed down into the stone book it grasped.

It didn't move. You're just unhinged from the pervert in the library. Your brain's a mess.

The frog gargoyle lowered its book. Its head turned to look down at her.

No!

Becky turned her back to the library.

You're not seeing anything.

Across the square she saw the brick elementary school building. Becky thought about when she used to play outside at recess. One of the games she liked to play was Statues. She would have to keep her back to the other kids, who would try to sneak up on her. If she turned around, they would have to freeze, like statues. Anyone caught moving would be eliminated from the game. The game would end if she got to eliminate all the players, or someone got close enough to touch her before she turned around.

Becky stood frozen in her shoes, telling herself the gargoyles were only statues. They couldn't move. She took a few steps and stopped.

She turned.

The frog gargoyle's webbed feet clung to the edge of the roof. Its stone eyes peered out over the book its long, pointed fingers clutched. It looked at her. But it did not move.

She shifted her eyes to the owl. Its eyes looked at the book in its hand. Not at her.

Of course not. It can't see me.

In the back right corner of the building, she could see the hooded gargoyle with the spectacles. Did the pages in its book flutter?

No. Stone can't move. Stone is solid.

Becky turned and continued to walk across the Town Square. The only sound she heard were her own steps.

She stopped and pivoted in a rapid motion.

The gargoyles stood motionless on the roof corners. She watched. Satisfied, she turned and walked away.

But are they moving when I'm not looking? Are they sneaking up on me?

Becky turned.

Did the owl gargoyle wink? Did the frog's mouth sneer? Ever so slightly?

Her eyes shot back and forth. Every time she looked at one, the other seemed to move.

No.

She was being silly. Or was she?

Becky looked at the owl. Her eyes shot back to the hooded man. All stone. All focused on the books in their granite hands though their eyes could not see.

Or can they?

Stop it!

Becky turned and stomped away. But then stopped. What if one of those stone hands reached out and tapped her on the shoulder? Then she would have lost the game.

What would happen to her?

She turned back fast, hoping to catch movement.

Even though she was farther away from the library, the gargoyles looked closer, as if they were leaning out from the edge of the roof, ready to leap off it and come scrambling across the cobblestones after her.

No!

You're made of stone.

She looked at the owl. The frog. The hooded man with glasses. Had he inched along the roofline, closer?

Not real. Not alive.

She waited for movement.

Of course, they would only move when she wasn't looking. That's how you play the game.

One, two, three, freeze.

Becky turned away, took three steps, counted, and turned.

None of the gargoyles had moved.

She turned away again and walked three paces, counting as she went. She turned.

The owl looked at her. The frog looked at her. The hooded man looked at her.

All three had shifted on their perches.

Becky screamed and ran. She scampered across the cobblestones, not caring when the book hidden under her jacket fell out and landed on the stones. Becky kept running and did not dare look back to see if the gargoyles followed.

3

Rita brought Quinn's dinner down to the cellar and set it on the table. He didn't want her to know how hungry he was, so he sauntered over to the table as if he didn't care or appreciate her offerings. He stared at the plate containing a pork chop, mashed potatoes, and peas. He slumped down into the chair.

"Why do you always have to look so damn grumpy?" Rita said. "You should be grateful I feed you."

Quinn eyed her with contempt. "You keep me a prisoner," he said. "How should I act?"

"Like you're glad to be fed," she answered. "Be happy about that."

He picked up his fork, resisting the urge to jam it into her eyeball.

"No knife to cut my pork chop?" he asked.

"When I can trust you with a knife, I'll give you a knife. As for now, just pick it up by the bone and gnaw off it. Like a monkey."

"I don't think monkeys eat pork chops." He grabbed it by the end of the bone, sunk his teeth into the meat and tore off a chunk. It tasted dry in his mouth, overcooked. It took a long time to chew it enough to be able to swallow without it getting stuck in his throat.

"How would you know what monkeys eat? Or do you remember them from the carnival?"

Quinn thought hard. It remained a struggle to remember the past, but he had flashes of a little capuchin monkey with a tin cup. An image of a hurdy-gurdy man with a concertina appeared in his head. It seemed so clear he could almost hear the music and imagine the monkey dancing and holding his cup out for coins.

"No, I don't remember," he lied and took a bite of the mashed potatoes, feeling thick lumps in his mouth.

"Of course not," Rita said. "That's what happens to kids who get abandoned by their parents. They forget. How sad."

Quinn wished she'd go away and not watch him eat. He wanted to have his meal in peace. But she probably wanted to make sure she confiscated his fork as soon as he finished. He tried to eat faster so she could go back upstairs, but the food was difficult to chew and even harder to swallow, except for the mushy peas.

"I'm trying to be the parent you never had," Rita said. "I'm doing my best."

Quinn rolled his eyes at her.

"If you'd learn to accept your plight and be happy here, then I could let you go upstairs and have a normal bedroom and eat in the dining room with me and even watch television. Speaking of monkeys, there's a funny show called *Lancelot Link, Secret Chimp*. There are only chimpanzees in the show and they talk, dress and act like humans. It's hilarious. They're secret agents and fight against a spy ring. You'd love it."

"Sounds stupid," he said before ripping off another piece of pork.

"That's the problem with you," Rita said. "You refuse to behave."

Quinn knew he should pretend to be good and maybe she would give him more freedom in the house and he could plot his escape. But he doubted she would give him much leeway, and it was hard trying to be nice to her. She was a wicked old witch and he wouldn't be at all surprised if she wanted to eat him one of these days.

"What can I do to make you happy here?" Rita asked.

Quinn finished the last of his meal and drained his glass of milk.

"I'm bored," he said when he set the empty glass down and imagined breaking it and shoving the sharp fragments into her face. "And I'm lonely."

"I've offered to play games with you down here," Rita said. "I have Chinese Checkers and Parcheesi."

"I don't want to play games with you." She was already playing games with him. He pushed the empty plate away, leaned back in his chair and burped. As crappy as the meal tasted, it felt good to not have that aching empty feeling in the pit of his stomach. Even if it were temporary. Even if he threw it all up later tonight.

"Things must be better here than wherever it was you came from," Rita said. She leered down at him.

She had asked him many times about the place where he was before he showed up in the magic cabinet in her basement, but he refused to talk, though he often thought about it. He wondered why Mr. Shreckengast had abandoned him. It was because of Quinn that the master and the Scamps got out of the House of Embers, but Shreckengast had cast him aside as if he didn't matter.

Not that he missed the other boys and girls. He never got along with the Scamps, but at least it was some form of companionship, especially the ones closer to his own age. Here all he had was Rita.

"What more can I do to make you happy here?"

"There's nothing you can do," he said. Because he knew she wouldn't do anything for him.

A smile broke over her face and it gave him a queasy feeling. Something was going on inside her head. She leaned forward, bringing her round face closer to his, like a balloon floating toward him. He cringed as he shrunk down in his chair.

"I have an idea," she said as her smile broadened. "How about if I found you a friend?"

4

Ryan lay awake in the bottom bunk in his room, unable to fall asleep. He still felt unnerved about the message Russell showed him on his cast. He thought at first his friend was pulling a prank on them, but the look in Russell's eyes convinced him he wasn't. *So how did that message get there?*

It reminded Ryan about the gravestone rubbing with Curtis's name, date of birth, and death date. No explanation for that either. Or the boy he saw at the soccer game. Or Eddie Scruggs. Too many weird things.

He always relished the macabre storylines on *Dark Shadows*, but he never imagined unexplained things like that in real life. Lance said there had to be a logical explanation. But Ryan wasn't so sure.

The door to his bedroom nudged open and the sound of soft footsteps entered.

They stopped beside the bed and Ryan turned his head. In the darkness, he saw the outline of Smokey. The dog settled down on its haunches on the rug.

"Go away," Ryan said and rolled back onto his pillow. "I don't want you here."

The bedsprings above him creaked.

Ryan lay still. *That wasn't me*, he thought.

He gazed up in the dark at the underside of the mattress. *Is something pushing down on it from above? Is that what made the bedsprings creak?*

In the darkness, the mattress appeared to bulge outward.

Smokey whimpered. Ryan glanced over and saw the dog raise its head and look up toward the top bunk.

Ryan's heart clenched. Something's up there.

Curtis?

No. Curtis is gone. Forever.

Ryan slid out from under his covers. He brought a finger to his lips as he looked at Smokey. The dog eyed him with curiosity, and then lifted its head once more to gaze up at the bed above. A soft whimper squeaked out of the dog's throat.

Ryan stepped up on the end of the railing of his bottom bunk and reached up to grab the edge of the railing above him. He pulled himself up to peer into the top bunk.

What if I see Curtis lying there?

The bed was empty and Ryan breathed a sigh of relief.

Though deep down, he truly wished Curtis was in bed. If ever there was a time he needed his twin's help, it was now.

His right hand reached out to touch the top of the bedcovers to make sure they weren't disturbed and that nothing was there. The covers felt cold.

OCTOBER 16

1

Ryan took his hot lunch tray and sat down at a table next to Lance, with Russell and Wesley seated across from them. He stared at the food in front of him. Fish sticks. Of course, it's Friday – always fish sticks on Friday. Green beans and mashed potatoes. At least the cake looked good. A spice cake with maple frosting.

"Did you hear about Wayne Barnes?" Russell asked.

"No," Ryan said. "What about Booger?"

"Gone missing."

Ryan almost dropped his fork on the floor. "What?"

"I heard about it last class. He didn't show up to school yesterday or today."

Ryan had noticed the empty seat in the back of the room earlier. "What do you think happened?"

"Maybe he ran off to join Eddie," Lance said as he picked up a fish stick with his fingers and shoved it in his mouth.

"Why would he do a thing like that?" Wesley asked.

"Because he's a moron."

"Or maybe something else happened to him," Ryan said. "Like with Mr. Swain and the smashed pumpkins." The thought made him shiver.

"My brother said Swain's farm hasn't been opened since," Lance said. "It is kind of odd."

"Something's happening in town," Ryan said.

"Don't start talking like that again. I'm sure there's an explanation for all of it."

"No one explained this," Russell said and laid his arm with the cast on the table.

No one said a word.

Ryan looked down at the food on his tray with a sudden loss of appetite, except for the cake. As he admired the dessert, Kirby Tressler walked by. The eighth-grader leaned over Ryan's shoulder and stuck his index finger right in the middle of the cake.

"Gonna eat that?" Kirby asked with a laugh.

Ryan rolled his eyes up at the older boy. "Guess not now."

"Great," Kirby said and swiped the cake from the tray. He plopped it onto his own tray and walked to another table, laughing the entire way.

Ryan watched Kirby sit down at a table with Becky Williams and a few others. He cringed at the way Becky draped her eyes all over the boy.

"That's brutal," Lance said.

"The best part of lunch," Wesley added.

"Such a jerk," Ryan said as he looked away and back at what remained on his tray. He began eating. "What does Becky even see in a guy like that?"

"It's simple," Lance said. "He's a jock. That's all that matters."

"It shouldn't," Ryan said. "It's not like we're nerds or anything like that."

"No," Lance said. "We're inbetweeners."

"What does that mean?" Russell asked as he shoved mashed potatoes into his mouth.

"We're not at the top, but we're certainly not at the bottom. We're somewhere in the middle. And nobody pays attention to anyone in the middle."

"Well, it sucks," Ryan said. He stole a glance over at Becky. She looked beautiful as she smiled and laughed, but it sickened him that Kirby Tressler was the target of her attention.

"If you want to make an impression, then you need to make a grand gesture," Lance said.

"A what?" Ryan asked.

Lance set his fork down. "A grand gesture. Something spectacular that would get her to notice you. Something big."

"Like what?"

Lance thought for a minute. "I've got an idea. Tell our parents we're going to go to the Colonial to see that bird movie."

"*The Bird with the Crystal Plumage*," Ryan said. "I don't think it's really about birds."

"Whatever. Doesn't matter. We're not going to the movie."

"What are we going to do?" Russell asked.

"I'll tell you when you get to my house. Bring toilet paper."

2

After dinner at the boardinghouse, Calvin Armstrong loaded Ruth Downey and the Fifers into his station wagon as the four of them were taking a ride to the Rockingham Ballroom in Newmarket to see Ben Baldwin and the Big Notes. The Stich sisters sat on the couch in the front parlor watching *The High Chaparral* on television.

Harold Lothrop sat in the adjoining parlor waiting for Wilfred Downey to kiss his wife goodbye and join him for a game of backgammon. When the theme music from the television show penetrated his ears, Harold got up and walked over to close the pocket doors that divided the two living rooms. Noreen gave him a stink eye before the two doors met to cut them from his view.

When he got back to his seat at the table by the bay window, he gazed out onto the side porch to see Wilfred waving goodbye as the car backed out of the driveway. The old man came back inside and joined Harold, who had the game board all set up.

Wonder if we'll finish before he falls asleep, Harold thought. He looked at the man who was only a year older than him, but seemed more withered. The two of them got halfway through the game before Wilfred dozed off. It always amazed Harold how quickly the man could fall asleep. No wonder Ruth sought entertainment elsewhere. He grabbed his drink and left the table to head up to his room. When he reached the third-floor landing, he paused at his door and cast a glance down the hall to Mortimer Rigby's room.

The old magician had rarely ventured out of his room these past few days. Was there something keeping him inside as well? When Harold did see Mortimer, he noticed the man didn't wear his top hat anymore. *Something odd about that.*

Once inside his room, Harold poured himself a glass of bourbon. He went over to the window and looked out onto the side yard as he took a couple gentle sips.

Something darted behind the maple tree near the sidewalk. Harold set his glass down on the table. Whatever it was peered out from behind the tree. *Looking up at the house, at this very window.* As Harold strained his old eyes, the figure stepped away from the tree where the streetlamp caught it in its glow.

Harold gasped as he recognized it.

Goblin.

Harold gulped down the rest of his drink.

They're out there. And they're coming for me.

As he turned from the window, his body shook like it never had before. At least not since that day he took the train north and first stepped off it in Maplewood.

The night the goblins came after him.

3

The four boys biked north on Old Coach Road in the dark, Lance so far out in front that Ryan could barely see him. It felt weird riding at night. Usually, Ryan always had to be home before dark when he was out on the town, as soon as the streetlamps came on. If his parents knew what he was doing, he'd be grounded for sure. He told them he was going to the movies and then sleeping over at Lance's house.

They ditched their bikes in the same spot behind the bushes near the Williams house. Ryan thought about that trek the other day to the hidden cemetery in the woods when they made the grave rubbing.

What was written on that parchment of paper now lying on the table in his basement made him shiver.

Don't think about it.

Easier said than done.

They huddled behind the bushes and glanced over at the house. The lights were off. That was a good sign, Ryan thought.

"Okay," Lance said as he opened the paper sack he'd been carrying and handed out the rolls of toilet paper to each of them. Three rolls apiece.

"Are you sure this is a good idea?" Ryan asked.

"Of course," Lance said. "When Becky finds out that you toilet-papered her house, she'll know you dig her."

"And if her dad finds out," Russell said, "he'll dig your grave."

Ryan's throat clenched.

"Just keep quiet and be quick and we won't get caught," Lance said. "That means you." He directed his last comment to Wesley.

"Hey, I can be quiet."

"Ssh!" Ryan whispered to him, hearing Wesley's voice carrying in the night.

"Like a bull in a china shop," Lance said.

The four boys ditched their hiding spot behind the bushes and crept across the field toward the Williams' yard. The lights remained off in the house. They gathered at the base of the old oak tree taller than the roofline of the two-story home. Ryan glanced up at the windows on the second floor and wondered which one belonged to Becky. He pictured her lying in her bed, wearing skimpy nightclothes that clung to her curves.

"Snap out of it," Lance whispered in Ryan's ear as he waved a hand in front of his face. "Let's be quick about this and then book it."

Ryan watched as Lance unraveled a few feet of a roll of toilet paper, reached back his arm and launched it toward the top of the tree. About halfway up it looped around a limb and came unspooling toward the ground.

"Bet you can't get higher than that," Lance said as he grabbed the fallen roll off the ground, tore off its tail and prepared to heave it skyward again.

The challenge was on as Ryan and the others began hurling their toilet paper rolls up into the tree as high as possible. Soon the branches of the tree were draped in streamers of the white paper as the old oak tree began resembling a weeping willow.

Lance got another one stuck at an even higher elevation than his first toss and the others tried to top it to no avail. Ryan came close once, but his toilet paper fell a few branches shy of Lance's highest point. Wesley had the worst attempts, his paper reaching only the lowest limbs. A couple of times Ryan couldn't control his laughter at Wesley's frustration. Once, his friend heaved his roll up and the paper didn't unravel, the roll bouncing off the side of the tree trunk and landing back on the ground.

Lance hushed them again, but even he couldn't contain a chuckle.

A light came on in a second-floor window.

"Someone's up," Russell whispered, and the four of them ducked behind the base of the large tree trunk.

"Keep still," Lance said.

Ryan heard a sash raise and he peered around the corner of the tree trunk just enough so one eye could see up to the lit window.

Becky's silhouette was outlined in the glow from the window. Ryan could see the curve of her breasts as she leaned out.

Gosh, he thought, as butterflies fluttered in his belly. Something else stirred inside him, lower.

"Who's there?" she asked in a low voice.

"Crap," Russell whispered.

"Pipe down," Lance said.

"She knows we're here," Ryan said as quiet as possible. Now he felt stupid being caught in a childish prank. What would she think if she found out it was him?

"I can see you behind the tree," Becky said.

She didn't sound mad, Ryan thought, more like excited. Maybe Lance was right. Go ahead, he thought, step out from behind the tree and take credit for this grand gesture and she'll be yours.

"Is that you, Kirby?" Becky asked from the window.

Ryan's heart sank into the churning pit of his stomach. Great, she thinks it's Kirby Tressler. How much worse could this get?

A window lit up on the first floor to give Ryan his answer.

"My dad's up," Becky said. "You better get out of here." She slammed her window shut.

"Busted," Russell said as voices came from the first floor of the house. An outside light by the side door lit up.

"Let's split," Lance yelled.

Before Ryan knew it, everyone cut out from behind the tree and began running. He didn't see the others as he booked it out of there, not paying attention to what direction he headed as long as it was away from the house. He heard the sound of a door opening and a voice yelling behind him that had to be Mr. Williams.

Ryan lost track of his friends and kept running as fast as he could through the dark. His lungs felt ready to burst. He couldn't tell if footsteps followed. He couldn't even see where he was going – everything was dark in front of him – but he felt grass beneath his feet, so that was enough to keep him moving away from the house.

When he suddenly didn't feel anything beneath his feet, he knew he was in trouble.

His body pitched down and when he hit branches that snapped beneath his weight, he realized he had fallen into the old barn cellar at the back of the Williams property. Sticks poked into his body like dull knives as he tumbled down beneath the brush of the deadfall. Twigs scratched at his face, rough bark scraped against the back of his legs, and knobby branches jabbed him in his sides and back. His body sank like a rock in the quagmire of discarded limbs.

His breath sucked out of him when he came to a hard stop on a thick branch that punched into his lower back. It took several seconds before he could get any air back into his lungs. He lay motionless, a thousand aches coursing throughout his entire body, as if someone had worked him over with a jackhammer.

Christ, he thought and squeezed his eyes shut to absorb the pain. He wanted to cry out.

Ryan lay there feeling imprisoned in a cage of tree limbs. He wasn't sure he'd be able to move his body, but he shifted one arm and tried to raise it. He grabbed onto a branch and tried to pull his body up, but it wouldn't move.

Stuck, he thought. *Damn it to hell, I'm stuck.*

He gripped the branch his hand rested on and shook it, but couldn't push it out of the way. He stopped.

A rattling sounded from below.

What was that?

He turned his head to look down, but could see nothing but blackness below.

Ryan could barely see anything above. His eyes strained through the twisted web of branches and limbs to where he could make out a few stars in the distant sky above.

How far down am I? And how deep is this pit?

A scratching came from beneath.

Is that an animal down there? Could a fox or something have made this place its den? His heart raced as he imagined the animal wakened by his sudden intrusion into its lair and coming to inspect him.

Got to get out of here.

He shuffled his body, trying to squirm and get some purchase on the limbs he rested on.

His body sank a few inches further down.

Cripes!

Ryan pulled at his left leg, but it seemed to be entangled in something, as if a rope had been thrown around it. He remembered the other day seeing vines growing out of the pile of deadfall in the barn cellar. Was that what wrapped around his leg?

It tugged his leg down.

Jesus! It's alive!

The vine or whatever it was pulled at his leg and his body sunk more. He flailed his arms.

"Help!" he cried out, hoping Lance or one of the others would hear him. *Which way had they run?* He didn't know. They had scattered in random directions and probably didn't know what had happened to him. "Help me!"

Twigs snapped below him. Something stirred, moving through the branches.

Ryan tried raising his upper body into a sitting position, but heavy limbs blocked his way. The more he squirmed, the more the vines or whatever wrapped around him pulled him down, dragging him deeper into the barn cellar.

An earthy odor worked its way through the wreckage of forest debris. Wet, rotted leaves, moldy bark. *Scratching.* Something climbing up as he sunk down. Pulled down, as if the deadfall was a pit of quicksand, only made of hard limbs and branches instead of wet sand. But it had the same effect.

I'm drowning. Drowning in branches.

The only difference is I can breathe. But what happens when I sink to the bottom and reach whatever it is I'm hearing beneath me?

Something touched the calf of his left leg and worked its way under the cuff of his jeans till it touched his flesh.

He squirmed.

A vine? Or something else.

It moved up his leg.

"Help me, please!" he screamed up at the stars above. The place he wanted to reach.

A bright light shined down upon him and at first he thought one of the stars had fallen from the night sky and landed in the deadfall and would now set fire to the dry kindling and burn him to death in an outdoor oven.

He realized it was a flashlight beam.

"Hello?" The voice of Mr. Williams. "Who's down there?"

"Help me!" Ryan called out. He reached his hands up through the tangle of branches, trying to reach the light and the shadowy figure behind it, his chest squeezed by crushing wood around his rib cage. "I'm here!"

"Grab my hand," Mr. Williams said.

Ryan reached up, but his arm became restricted by a heavy limb, the fingers of his rescuer just out of reach.

Branches shifted beneath him. A shallow breath blew up through the twisted mass.

Ryan stretched his arm up, almost within reach.

The flashlight beam carved a path through the branches and Ryan followed it. The hand above grabbed on to his. It pulled. At first, Ryan's body wouldn't budge, but then the branches resting on him parted and he felt himself pulled upward, twigs snapping, breaking.

As his body rose toward that bright light, he turned his head and looked down.

Toward the bottom of the barn cellar, down among the debris of leaves, chunks of broken bark, and mass of settled sticks, he spotted in the glow of the flashlight beam a large log with a bulging knobby knot pushing out from the trunk. As he heard shuffling from the twigs and branches below, the beam of light poked at the knot and the shadows cast down from the weave of twisted branches, and within it he saw a face.

His heart skipped, his stomach tightened, and the hand above continued to pull him upward. The branches below thrashed and thrust upward.

The face in the knot opened its eyes and looked up at him.

OCTOBER 17

1

Police Chief Asa Strong drove down the gravel driveway of Hank Swain's farm on Bittersweet Road on Saturday morning and stopped at the closed gate. He radioed dispatch to establish his location.

He knew he should contact state police about the missing Barnes boy, but coming on the heels of the Scruggs kid running away and given that the two of them were friends, Asa couldn't quite be sure any kind of crime had been committed.

But now he'd gotten reports that Hank Swain's farm had closed without warning and no one had been able to reach the farmer. Asa spoke to Austin Stanton, one of the teens who worked part-time at the farm, and the boy said there'd been no communication or warning from Hank that the farm was shutting down. Austin said he showed up for work on Monday and Hank didn't have the place open and wasn't around.

Asa remembered talking to Hank at Harvest Fest and nothing seemed amiss. No indication the man was going to take off or any such thing. The chief knew these were tough economic times for farmers, but this was unexpected. Strange.

He put his chief's hat on and exited the car. There was no lock on the gate, so he released the latch and opened it. Asa first went to the front door of the house, where several raps on the brass door knocker produced no results. The barn was his next destination and that proved just as fruitless.

Asa eyed the pumpkin patch when he left the barn. Several round orange gourds lay scattered throughout. He knew this time of year was a big one for Hank for selling his prized pumpkins, some of the best in the region. The farmer had sold quite a few at the festival, but it looked like he had plenty left, with two full weeks remaining in the season. Made no sense he would shut down.

Asa walked over to the edge of the pumpkin patch. *Nope. Made no sense at all*, he thought as he scanned the field. Asa turned and something caught his eye. He got closer and stared at the sledgehammer lying on the ground. Odd for Hank to leave a tool lying about like this.

The chief noticed the open doors on the pumpkin shed. He approached and peered inside. This was even stranger, he thought, as he gazed at the smashed pumpkins inside.

What the heck?

It looked like someone had taken out their frustrations on the contents of the shed. Was that what the sledgehammer had been for? Could be financial issues were piling up and Hank needed to vent.

As Asa went back to his car and left the farm, he figured all he could do was keep phoning the Swain house and checking in on the farm to see if the man returned. But as he drove away, he had an idea to check with some of the other local farmers to see if maybe Hank had given anyone a clue about troubles he was experiencing.

Asa drove up the road to the neighboring apple orchard and spoke with the Crogans, who owned the place. They weren't much help and were just as baffled as he was about the sudden closure of the Swain farm. He got in his car and headed back the way he came, making a turn at the juncture onto Hickory Road and stopping at the Parker farm to see if Grant had heard anything. The Parker farm did close for the season after Columbus Day weekend, he knew. Unlike the Swain farm and the Crogans' orchard, Parker sold mostly corn and other vegetables. His growing season ended this time of year and he shut down right after the holiday weekend.

Asa walked past the barn and went to the side door. He was about to knock when he noticed the door was slightly ajar.

Left open? Strange.

He knocked anyway on the wooden frame and peered through the slight gap into the kitchen. No movement from inside. Asa knocked again, this time on the door itself, which had the effect of pushing the door open a bit more.

"Hello?" he hollered. No response. "Anyone home? Grant?" What was the farmer's boy's name? Johnny? No. Jacob. "Jacob? Anyone home?"

An unexplained open door gave him the authority to enter, he told himself as he stepped into the kitchen.

"Anybody here?" he yelled. Silence. He went farther into the kitchen. He saw another door slightly ajar and crossed over to it. He pulled it open and stared at wooden steps that led down into the cellar. "Anyone down there?" he asked. Once again, no response. "I'll be damned." No evidence of any kind of crime. Not against the law to leave your door open.

Asa decided to leave and had gotten halfway across the kitchen when he spotted something on the wood floor. He bent down and picked it up. A long piece of straw. He tossed it aside and left.

When he got to his car, he looked out toward the cornfield beside the barn. A large scarecrow in a blue shirt and jeans stood propped up on a post above the cornstalks. Beside it stood a smaller scarecrow.

No need to worry about crows anymore, Asa thought as he got into his car and drove away.

2

It had been more than a week since Mortimer had touched his magic hat. It lay on the floor where he'd tossed it last Friday. Now he sat on the edge of his bed after dinner and stared at it, wondering if Daimon would come out again, but there had been no more sign of the white rabbit.

Of course not, he thought. *It's dead. Has been for a very long time.*

Then why did he see it last week? What was the meaning behind its sudden appearance?

This town. Something in Maplewood. A dark force.

The hat stirred. Vibrated.

Mortimer leaned forward. *Something's in there.*

Daimon?

As he watched, he saw dingy white paws reach up from inside the hat and grip the edge of its brim. He leaned back, a hand clutched to his chest. A tremendous pressure gripped his heart and he felt like it might stop.

The rabbit leapt out of the hat onto the floor.

Mortimer's mouth dropped open. The nerves beneath his skin began to tingle.

"What are you?" he whispered.

Daimon stood on its hind legs and looked at him with its red eyes. *Dead eyes.* The rabbit twitched its nose, rocking its whiskers back and forth like paddling oars on a boat adrift at sea. Daimon turned its head toward the door.

Mortimer understood and stood up on shaky legs. It took great effort to walk to the door and open it. The rabbit sprang across the room and out into the hall. Mortimer followed it down the front staircase to the lobby where he opened the front door and Daimon slipped out.

Mortimer followed.

The rabbit ran across the front lawns of the houses on Elm Street and Mortimer kept on its trail on the sidewalk. Every so often Daimon would stop and sit up on its hind legs and look back at him.

It wants me to follow.

The rabbit turned right on Washington Street and kept to the soft grass as it headed west. When it got to the Town Square, its pace slowed as it crossed the cobblestones. The large brick structures of the municipal buildings loomed above as Mortimer kept pace with the rabbit.

The neighborhood of older historic houses between the Town Square and downtown provided brick sidewalks that seemed easier on the rabbit's feet as it quickened into a scamper down to the next corner. Daimon turned right and Mortimer glanced up at the street sign: Carriage Lane.

Halfway down the street, the rabbit stopped. It stood on its hind legs again and sniffed the air. It pivoted and slipped between the bars of a black wrought-iron gate and up a walkway to a large dark house.

Mortimer came down the sidewalk and stopped before the waist-high gate. He looked up at the three-story house.

Daimon was nowhere in sight.

Mortimer wondered where the rabbit had gone.

Had something let it inside? But the house seemed abandoned.

"Why have you led me here?" Mortimer asked as he scanned the dark, empty windows of the house and the crooked shutters that flanked them. "What do you want?"

With no hope of answer, and feeling as if something watched him from those very windows, Mortimer turned and quickly made his way back to the boardinghouse. He didn't bother to look behind him as he walked, though he wondered if anything were following. More than once he thought he heard the soft patter of feet on the sidewalk.

3

In the front parlor of the boardinghouse, a debate raged as usual on Saturday night between the Fifers and the Stich sisters about what to watch on television. Darrin Fifer and his wife wanted to watch *The Andy Williams Show* while Pearl and Noreen preferred *Lawrence Welk*. It didn't matter to Harold, who sat in the back parlor doing the crossword puzzle from the daily paper. But he had to listen to the bickering through the pocket doors, which he had closed earlier to keep the intrusion at bay.

Calvin Armstrong had taken Ruth Downey to the movies at the Colonial to see some lurid thriller Harold had seen advertised. Ruth's husband, Wilfred, was in the kitchen making popcorn on the stove for the others.

The whole house seemed to be in an upheaval when Mortimer Rigby came in by the side door. He looked shaken when Harold glanced up from his paper, face more ashen than usual.

"You all right?" Harold asked.

"Fine," Mortimer said and quickly made his way up the stairs to the third floor.

Harold heard the front bedroom door slam.

The ruckus in the other room had seemed to quiet down once Wilfred entered with a bowl of popcorn, leaving a trail of buttery scent in the air. Harold didn't know which program the group settled on and didn't care.

It must have been during a commercial break when the pocket doors slid open and Darrin came into the room. Harold noticed the man's left eye twitching. He went to the bay window near where Harold sat and looked out.

"Something wrong?" Harold asked.

Darrin continued to stare out the window and appeared to ignore his question before finally turning to look down at him.

"Do you see that policeman out there?"

"A policeman?" He craned his neck to look out the window.

"Yes, near the streetlight. A man with a craggy face in a policeman's uniform just standing there looking at this house."

"Why would there be a policeman out there? You haven't done anything wrong?"

Harold meant it as a joke, but Darrin gave him a nervous look followed by a forced laugh.

"'Course not," he said in an unconvincing tone. "Just strange for a cop to stand outside our house. It's like he's watching us. And he keeps flicking a cigarette lighter. It's weird. Come see."

Harold knew Darrin wouldn't go back to the other room till he indulged his curiosity, so he rose from the chair and stood before the window. He didn't see a policeman out there under the streetlamp watching the house. But he saw something else scurry behind the cover of a maple tree. Green scales and pointed ears.

Goblin.

"I see no one out there," Harold said in a quivering voice. He sat back down.

Darrin Fifer's eyes went wide as he stared back at him.

If the man was seeing things, Harold thought, as he himself saw, then whatever this policeman figure represented, it frightened the poor man.

What are you hiding in your past that's catching up to you? Harold wondered.

Because whatever it was, it was apparently here.

OCTOBER 18

1

Long after midnight, Mortimer Rigby awoke to the sound of scraping wood. His eyelids slid open and he stared at the darkness of the ceiling. A soft patter on the wooden floor of the room caused him to bolt upright. As his eyes adjusted to the dark, he saw movement beyond the foot of his bed, a flash of white fur.

Mortimer crawled to the edge of the bed and peered over in time to see something hop into the black top hat on the floor in the corner.

Daimon's back. The room felt cold. His heart constricted inside his chest. He turned to gaze at the open window where the chill blew in.

Who could have opened that?

2

After church on Sunday, Lance saw Wesley Roark at the bottom of the stone steps. His friend seemed excited. On the sidewalk out front, he pulled Lance away from his family.

"Meet me at the Town Green after lunch," Wesley said, his face plastered with an exuberant grin.

"What's up?" Lance asked.

"The town workers raked all the leaves in the park yesterday, but they haven't picked them up yet."

"So?"

"There's a gigantic pile of leaves beneath the big oak tree," Wesley said, his grin about to cleave his plump face in two. "It's massive. We can launch ourselves from the tree right into it. Know what I mean?"

"That sounds cool," Lance said, though he wondered if Wesley had exaggerated the size of the leaf pile.

"I'll see you down there," Wesley said.

"I'll call Ryan and Russell."

Lance got on the phone as soon as he got home. He called Ryan first.

"I can't," Ryan said, after Lance explained the situation. "Still grounded from my 'grand gesture'."

"Crap," Lance said. "Sorry about that. Thanks for taking the hit for the rest of us."

"Sure thing."

"I bet it'll all blow over."

"I can't help you with the paper route this week too, so that sucks."

"Parents don't get it," Lance said. He promised to tell Ryan all about the leaf pile later. When he hung up, he called Russell.

"I'm not going anywhere near a tree," Russell said. "Even if there is a pile of leaves to land on."

"I get you," Lance said.

"Can't wait to get this stupid cast off so things can be back to normal," Russell said.

"I bet. Well, catch you later."

Down at the Town Green, Lance dumped his bike on the ground near where he spotted Wesley sitting on a limb up in the large oak tree in the center of the park, his red PRO-Keds sneakers as bright as some of the leaves. Beneath the tree was the biggest pile of leaves Lance had ever seen, a mound about six feet tall.

"Can you believe it?" Wesley yelled from the branch.

"It's killer," Lance said as he approached.

"Watch this." Wesley stood up on the branch, wobbled a bit, and then launched himself into a cannonball and slammed smack into the middle of the pile, disappearing.

Lance looked on as the leaves shook with a rustling sound before Wesley popped up out of the side like a surfer emerging from a wipeout. The kid laughed, leaves stuck all over his hair and clothes.

"I'm next," Lance said and raced to the base of the tree. He jumped up to grab the lowest limb and hauled himself up hand over hand like a monkey till he reached the long branch that hung out over the leaf pile. He stared down at what looked like an ocean of leaves.

"Geronimo!" he yelled as he pitched himself off the branch. The leaves cushioned the blow when he landed and consumed him. He swam his way out, trying to keep from laughing so he wouldn't swallow remnants of the crisp leaves. "Wow!"

Wesley was already back up in the tree. This time he did a belly flop into the leaf pile before rolling down its side to the ground like a barrel.

"I don't know how much longer till the city picks up the leaves," Wesley said, "but I could stay here all day."

"I hear you," Lance said and raced back up the tree.

The two boys found creative ways to jump into the pile, giving each other number scores for technique and execution, like some Olympic diving event, each one trying to outdo the other. It was a mild day and soon Lance felt sweat build up beneath his clothes. Leaf crumbs got down his shirt and up his trouser legs, and he scratched the itchy spots. But he didn't care. This was fun and a great way to end the weekend before the school week began.

It also helped him forget about some of the weird things they'd seen in town. The stuff he tried to make logical sense to Ryan that they couldn't quite explain. He only wished Ryan could be here today to enjoy a break from the stress his friend was under. These were the kind of things they always used to enjoy, back when Curtis was still around.

Alive, don't you mean? Of course, he told himself. That's what he meant. He missed Curtis too. Things hadn't seemed the same since he died.

As he stood up on the branch and looked down, he thought about how simple it was to enjoy free-falling from the sky into a soft pile of leaves. This was enough to let him just enjoy being a kid for a while. That's all he cared about now.

He leapt off the branch. When he hit the leaves, he sank down into them, burrowing a hole through the pile that filled back up quickly as if he were never there.

A sharp pain dug into his left ankle.

He winced. *What the heck?* Buried in leaves, he reached down his leg, feeling for the source of the pain. His first thought was it must be a stick at the bottom of the pile. He crawled out from the leaves onto the grass and rolled over into a sitting position. He grabbed his ankle and began rubbing it.

"What's the matter?" Wesley asked from the tree branch above.

"I hit something," Lance said. He rubbed the sore skin beneath his sock. There was no blood on his fingers.

"What was it?"

"I don't know. Maybe a stick." He continued to rub; the pain lessened. He worried it might have been a piece of broken glass from a beer bottle or something. He knew older kids drank in the park.

"Are you all right?" Wesley asked.

"I guess." He stood up and put his weight on the foot. His ankle still felt sore but nothing serious. He looked up at Wesley. "Think I'm going to call it a day."

"You sure?"

"Yeah." He went over to his bike. "You coming?"

"I'm gonna hang here a little more," Wesley said. "Get a few more jumps in. They might take the leaves away tomorrow."

"Okay." Lance waved and got on his bike. He watched Wesley drop down into the leaves before he rode off. He rode down Stonewall Road along the river. Each turn of his pedals brought a stab of pain in his left ankle.

What the heck. What did I hit?

Lance got off his bike and set it down on the ground. He pulled his left pant leg up and his sock down to examine his wound.

On the skin of his ankle, he saw the outline of what appeared to be teeth marks.

A bite?

Not deep enough to draw blood, but the wound showed indentations in the skin in an oval shape.

What did that?

Had a fox or woodchuck burrowed a home into the base of the leaf pile? Or had something else nested under there?

Lance knew he should go back and warn Wesley. If some critter was in the leaf pile, it could prove dangerous. He hopped back on his bicycle and pedaled fast, despite the annoying pain that gripped his left ankle as he pedaled.

He reached the Town Green and rode over to the oak tree. No sign of Wesley. Lance felt relieved, figuring his friend had gotten bored with the activity and went home. As he turned to head back home himself, he spotted Wesley's bicycle leaned up against a nearby pine tree.

The sight of the lonely bike gave Lance an uneasy feeling in his stomach.

He looked at the giant pile of leaves.

"Wesley?" he called out. The only sound was the tweeting of a few birds high up in the trees, and the drop of an acorn.

"Wesley!" he cried out, louder. Movement behind him caused him to turn. A squirrel scurried along the grass. Lance set his bike down and walked over to the leaf pile. He gazed over it, as if looking for some impression in the leaves.

Can you drown in leaves?

He waded into the pile despite his concern that whatever animal had bit him still lurked within the mass of leaves.

If it was an animal.

He stopped. *Don't start thinking like Ryan.*

Lance swished his hands around in the leaves, wondering if his friend could possibly be in there.

And what would you do if your hands touched a body part?

Scream, he told himself. *Scream and run.*

But what scared him more was, *What if something touched him?*

It's just leaves, he thought as he continued to wade deeper into the pile, his hands brushing the leaves out of his way. *There's nothing else in here.*

Then what bit you?

He didn't have a logical answer for that.

"Wesley!" he yelled.

His hands touched dampness. Lance pulled them out of the pile. A mass of wet, sticky leaves clung to his palms. He held his hands up and pulled the leaves off them. *Red.* Something red on the leaves.

Lance backed up. He wiped his hands on his jeans.

Red.

He turned and lunged away to escape the pile. It felt like he was in the ocean and trying to get to shore to escape some ravenous shark. The grass seemed far away, the leaves thicker and hard to push through. He felt like he might get stuck in a quagmire of leaves that would drag him down and under.

He panted as he propelled forward through the mass, wondering if something were nipping at his heels. Something deep within the pile of leaves. Something that had found a home there. Something that wanted company.

Lance reached the grass and sprinted to his bicycle. He hopped on and, despite the pain in his ankle, pedaled furiously all the way home.

3

Ryan saw flashing blue lights in the darkness out his bedroom window right before his mother told him he had a phone call. He went down to the kitchen and took the receiver from his mom.

"Hello?"

"Wesley's gone!" Lance's frantic voice jolted into his ear.

"Gone?" Ryan asked. "What are you talking about?"

"He disappeared," Lance said. "He's missing." Or worse, Lance thought. Something much worse.

"Missing? How?"

Ryan listened as Lance told him about the two of them jumping in the leaves at the Town Green. Lance's voice speeded up as he told Ryan about hurting his ankle and leaving Wesley behind and then going back and finding him gone, but his bike was still there.

Lance talked about something in the leaves and what looked like blood. "I told my parents and they called the cops."

"Get over here," Ryan said. "Come to the basement door. I'll meet you down there."

Within a few minutes, Ryan let a shaken Lance into the basement through the outside door.

"Go over everything again," Ryan asked, his friend's nervous state heightening his own anxiety. Lance told the story from start to finish, including what he thought was blood in the leaves.

Lance began crying.

"I shouldn't have left him," he said.

The upstairs door to the basement opened and Smokey descended the steps. Ryan figured his mom let the dog down here. She was always trying to push Smokey on him though she knew he didn't want the dog around. It looked at him with sad eyes but he ignored it.

"Show me your ankle," Ryan said.

Lance pulled his pant leg up and rolled his sock down. Ryan bent down and examined the oval wound and the soft tears of skin.

"What do you think did that?"

"I don't know."

Smokey uttered a low growl. Ryan noticed the dog staring at Lance's wound.

"What's got into him?" Lance asked as he covered his ankle back up.

"I don't know. He's been acting weird lately."

"There's a lot of that going around."

The two of them sat on the couch. Lance put his head in his hands.

"It's not your fault," Ryan said. He thought of Wesley. Can it really be? Gone? Like Wayne Barnes. And Eddie? No, Eddie ran away. *Or did he?*

Smokey came over and lay on the floor in front of the couch at their feet.

"What do we do?" Lance asked. "Chief Strong has the whole force out looking for him."

"Maybe they'll find him," Ryan said, trying to offer some glimpse of hope.

"Do you really think so?" Lance rubbed tears from his eyes.

Ryan didn't have an answer.

"I think you're right," Lance said.

"About what?"

"I think something strange is going on in Maplewood."

"And do you realize when it all started?" Ryan asked.

"When?"

"When the old man in the black cloak arrived here on the train."

"That's right," Lance said. "A freight train. Eddie saw him."

"And now Eddie's gone."

"Since when does a freight train make stops to let off a passenger?"

"And now he's staying at the boardinghouse," Ryan said. On the same floor as his friend, Mr. Lothrop, Ryan thought. Right down the hall.

"And remember he had us carry that weird box up to his room?"

"Yeah," Ryan said, thinking back. "It didn't seem very heavy. Like there was nothing in it." It had been bulky, but easy to maneuver up the stairs.

"What do you think it was for?" Lance asked.

Ryan shrugged.

"I don't know, but it's about the right size to hold a body."

Smokey lifted his head and his ears perked up. Ryan stared at the dog, wondering what it was thinking.

"Maybe we should go visit Mr. Lothrop tomorrow and pick his brain," Ryan said. The day he had shown the man his short story, Lothrop had warned him against writing horror tales, had talked about the supernatural being something not to be messed with. "Maybe he knows something that can help us."

4

Police Chief Asa Strong sat in his office at night. He finally made the call to the State Police. There was no longer any reason for putting it off. It appeared there might be a child abductor in Maplewood, and that was too big a deal for his small police force to handle.

The sudden disappearance earlier today of Wesley Roark, topped off with Wayne Barnes going missing four days ago, made him realize this just might not be a case of runaway kids. Something far more dangerous could be in their midst. And though he could not make a correlation, the absence of Hank Swain and the abandonment of his farm made him realize he needed experienced outside help, and he hoped the State Police would provide that before things got more out of control.

The Stanton kid said he found what looked like blood in the leaves, but a preliminary inspection of the pile didn't turn up anything. He'd make sure they took a closer look tomorrow in the daylight.

Blood or no blood. One thing was certain.

Something dangerous had come to Maplewood.

OCTOBER 19

1

Though Ryan remained grounded from helping Lance with his paper route, he was able to talk his parents into letting him visit Mr. Lothrop. They thought his friendship with the old man and frequent visits provided a wonderful community service. His mother always lamented that young people don't pay enough attention to senior citizens.

He made the plan to meet Lance there at the end of his paper route. On the walk over, Ryan couldn't get rid of the image of Wesley's empty desk at school. Every classroom they shared confronted him with the same scene: Wayne Barnes' empty seat in the back row, Eddie Scruggs' vacant chair behind him, and now Wesley's abandoned desk. His gut felt hollow.

It also made him think of Curtis. His brother's absence pained him. He heard time heals all wounds, but he couldn't imagine ever not feeling pain from the loss of Curtis. He was a part of him, his mirror image. Ryan felt Curtis should be beside him now; he would know what to do. He would have some answers. Ryan didn't know if he could handle this himself.

He arrived at the same time as Lance on the Downeys' boardinghouse front steps. They were greeted at the door by Mr. Downey, and Lance handed him two copies of the paper.

"Mr. Lothrop upstairs?" Ryan asked.

"In his room," Mr. Downey answered.

There were only two places his old friend would be, Ryan thought. In the back parlor or up in his room. He never went anywhere else.

"Thanks," Ryan said, and he and Lance mounted the stairs.

"Rita is getting weirder every day," Lance said as they reached the second-floor landing.

"How so?"

"Every day I deliver her paper, she's playing really loud music."

They reached the third-floor stairway and began their ascent.

"Music?"

"Yeah, like old people music. Lots of loud horns and strings and some guy singing in a weird voice. And it's not English."

"Strange."

They reached the third floor and knocked on Mr. Lothrop's door.

"Who is it?" the old man called out.

"Ryan Woodson."

Lance tugged on Ryan's arm and pointed down the hall toward the man in black's room.

"Do you think he's in?"

Ryan shrugged.

"If he's not, we could snoop inside his room."

Ryan shook his head. "No way."

The door opened and Mr. Lothrop stood before them.

"Come in," he said, though he sounded irritated. He closed the door behind them. Lothrop waddled over to his chair by the window and sat down. A half-empty bottle of booze stood on the table and he poured some into a glass. "What brings you here?"

Ryan and Lance glanced at each other. *Where to begin?* Ryan proceeded to explain to Mr. Lothrop all the things that had been going on in town, starting with the day his neighbor down the hall arrived. He ended with the disappearance of Wesley Roark.

Lothrop took a swig from his glass and squinted at the boys. "What do you expect from me?"

Ryan's heart sank. He hadn't a clue as to what he expected from Mr. Lothrop, but somehow thought his experience as a writer of the macabre could shed some light on the events in town. Maybe this was a mistake.

"I don't know," Ryan said. "On my last visit, you said you've seen real magic and horror. That's why you don't go outside."

"Silly ramblings from an old man," Lothrop said and took another sip. "Plus, I drink too much."

"Unexplained things are going on in Maplewood," Ryan said.

"And something happened to our friend," Lance added.

Lothrop's wrinkled stone face stared back at them. It reminded Ryan of one of the library gargoyles.

"If there is something happening in town," Lothrop said, "what makes you think I can do anything about it?"

"You've seen it before," Ryan said. "That's why you don't leave this house."

The man leaned forward and pointed a finger at them.

"And you should stay home too," he said and leaned back. "Especially after dark."

"What do you know about your neighbor down the hall?" Lance asked.

"He used to be a magician in a traveling carnival," Lothrop said. "The same carnival where Rita Stone-Thurlow worked as a sideshow fat lady. Mort Riggor, Prestidigitator, he called himself. Or maybe still does. I don't know. Dark magic. Stay away from him."

"Why?" Ryan asked.

"Because I'm an old man and you should listen to your elders." He looked out the window and squinted as if trying to make out something down below.

"Is he in his room now?" Lance asked.

"Think I heard him rumbling about in there earlier," Lothrop said. "I don't care about him."

You're lying, Ryan thought. The magician bothered Lothrop. Ryan could tell by the way he twitched when the man was mentioned. *Dark magic.*

"We should get going," Lance said.

They both got up. Mr. Lothrop looked at them with genuine concern etched on his face.

"Be careful, boys," he said.

Out in the hallway, Ryan began to head to the stairway, but

Lance grabbed his arm and pointed to the closed door at the end of the hall.

"Listen," Lance said.

Ryan heard faint sounds of someone rummaging about behind the door.

"Let's go," Ryan said, anxious to get back home. Not because he wanted to heed Mr. Lothrop's warning, but because being home made him feel safe.

"I have an idea," Lance said. "I'll tell you outside."

Ryan didn't like the sound of that, but before he could protest, Lance ran down the stairs. Ryan followed, wondering what brilliant idea had gotten into his friend's head.

Outside, he caught up with Lance, who crossed the street and stopped beneath a large maple tree.

"What's going on?" Ryan asked.

Lance looked up into the branches of the tree and then back across the street at the boardinghouse.

"This should be perfect," Lance said and jumped up to grab the lowest branch and hauled himself up.

"What are you doing?"

"Come on," Lance said, looking down at him. "We can spy on his room from up here."

The idea seemed crazy, but there was no stopping Lance now, so Ryan climbed up into the tree and followed the path of branches till he reached near the top.

"The view is perfect," Lance said.

Ryan settled into the fork of a limb and looked across the street. They were at almost the same height as the windows of the third-story room of the boardinghouse where the magician lived. One large rectangular window with an arched top situated just beneath the peak of the roof, with two smaller windows on either side. The yellow and orange leaves that remained in the tree provided camouflage to keep them hidden, but allowed enough clearance to see across to the house.

"This is perfect," Lance said.

Lance rested on a branch a couple feet higher than Ryan's. The shades were up in the window and Ryan spotted movement in the room. He saw the old man move back and forth before the window, as if pacing.

"Can you see that box we helped carry up?" Ryan asked.

Lance craned his neck. "Kind of, off in the corner."

"What else can you see?"

"A bed, not much else," he said. "At least, there aren't any bodies in the room."

Ryan swallowed hard and it hurt his throat. He thought about Wesley. He ached to think of something bad happening to his friend. He didn't want to believe it. Not yet. Not while there might be a chance he was okay.

"This is pointless," Ryan said. "We're not getting anywhere with this."

The old man came to the window and stared out.

Ryan leaned back against the trunk of the tree, as if trying to blend in with it to hide. As the magician stared out the window, Ryan got the sensation that he sensed he was being watched. It almost seemed like the magician looked right at the tree they were hiding in, searching for them.

"Don't move," Ryan said in a whisper, though no one was down on the street to hear him. But maybe the old man could. Maybe he had strange powers.

"Why?" Lance asked.

"I think he sees us."

The magician stood at the window for several minutes before Ryan saw him grab something out of the closet, his black cloak, put it on and exit the room. A minute or two later, Ryan looked down and saw the man emerge from the front door of the house and stroll down the sidewalk toward Washington Street.

"Let's go," Ryan said and started to move from his perch.

"Wait," Lance said. "I have another idea."

Ryan sighed. He felt drained from this ordeal already. "What now?"

"You stay here," Lance said. "I'm going to check out his room." He began to climb down.

"What?" This was crazy. "No way!"

"Keep an eye out on the road to see if he returns." Lance was already halfway down the tree.

"What good will that do?" Ryan said. "It's not like I can warn you or anything."

"I'll keep checking out the window," Lance yelled back up when he reached the lowest branch and dropped to the ground. "If you see him come back onto the street, just shake the branches and I'll know."

Before Ryan could protest, Lance ran across the street and disappeared through the front door of the house.

2

Lance greeted Mr. Downey when he got inside and made up some excuse of forgetting something in Mr. Lothrop's room, then hustled up the stairs to the third floor. He slipped quietly past the writer's room and down the hall to the bedroom at the front of the house. He turned the doorknob and pushed the door open.

He stuck his head inside and glanced around, as if worried someone else might be in the room. But that was silly, of course. The man rented the room by himself. Lance stepped inside and closed the door gently. He went to the front window and looked out across the street at the maple tree. He could see Ryan partially concealed by the sparse orange and yellow leaves that clung to the branches. Maybe it hadn't been such a good hiding spot. He waved and Ryan shook the branch above him. Half a dozen leaves fell from it and twisted in the air on their way down to the ground.

Lance turned and his eyes took in the room. It wasn't much different from Mr. Lothrop's. A queen-size bed on one side wall, a small desk and chair opposite it, a tall bureau on the interior wall next to a closet door.

And the wooden cabinet that stood in one corner.

Lance remembered how light it felt carrying it up the stairs to this room. It seemed empty then. *What about now?*

He approached it. He turned to look out the window at the branches of the tree. They weren't moving. He turned back to the cabinet and took a deep breath.

Lance hesitated, thinking about what could be in there. What if he opened it and found the bodies of Wesley and Wayne Barnes stuffed in there?

I have to know.

Did this newcomer to town who arrived at the start of the month have something to do with the missing kids and the strange events in town? He wasn't a vampire, like Lance joked on that first day, because the man walked in the daylight. But what if he were something worse?

What had Mr. Lothrop said? *Dark magic.*

Lance grabbed the knob on the cabinet.

He told himself there would just be clothes in there and nothing more. Nothing sinister or diabolical. Just shirts and pants.

He pulled the door open.

Empty.

He breathed a sigh of relief and closed the door.

Another thought struck.

Why does the magician have an empty cabinet? What did he plan to put in there?

A headscratcher, but nothing to dwell upon. Lance turned and something caught his eye out the window.

The branches of the maple tree were shaking.

Shit.

He moved to the door and spotted the black top hat.

It lay on the floor. Something moved inside it.

Time. Not much time.

Lance hurried over and picked up the hat. He peered inside but only saw the black lining of the interior.

He'd expected to find something in there. He reached his hand in.

A thud from downstairs sounded. The front door.

He's back.

Before he withdrew his hand, something wet touched his fingertips.

He pulled the hand out quickly, staring at his fingers as if to make sure they were all still there, and then he tossed the hat onto the bureau.

Lance rushed to the stairs and headed down, taking two steps at a time. When he reached the second floor, he hurried down the hallway to the front staircase. Halfway down, he encountered the magician and stopped.

"What are you doing here?" the man asked.

A lump stuck in Lance's throat. What if the magician wouldn't let him leave? What if he dragged him back upstairs and stuffed him in his cabinet? Or worse yet, what if he made him reach his hand back into that hat?

"No-nothing," Lance stammered. "Just visiting Mr. Lothrop."

The man grunted and moved up the stairs past him. Lance raced down the rest of the stairs and out the front door. He sprinted across the street to where Ryan stood on the ground beside the trunk of the maple tree.

As the two of them took off down the street, Lance wiped the wetness on his fingertips on his jeans. He didn't turn to look back; the magician might be watching him from his window.

3

The Maplewood Public Works dump truck with the leaf-collecting machine in its bed was parked beside the tall oak tree in the middle of the Town Green. The engine of the big machine rumbled as a town worker stood beside the truck and held the large flexible intake hose. He began sucking up the leaves from the huge pile beneath the tree.

Police Chief Asa Strong stood near the truck and watched. Earlier, a State Police captain and a couple of the department's officers had gone through the park with a thorough search looking for any evidence but had come up empty. Not even a sign of any blood the Lance kid said he found in the leaves. This was the last known place the Roark boy had been seen, as reported to him by Lance Stanton.

Word was out in town about the missing boy, but no one else had contacted the police about witnessing anything. Strong figured there had to have been other people in the park on Sunday afternoon, though he knew a lot of folks were probably home watching the Boston Patriots being shut out by the New York Giants. Though the team stunk and had only won one game so far, it was their first year in the NFL, so many like him still enjoyed spending their Sunday afternoons at home watching.

Despite that, someone must have seen Wesley Roark. The Stanton kid said he came right back to the Town Green after leaving and his friend was already gone. But Roark's bike was still in the park, now confiscated as evidence by the State Police. The Stanton boy couldn't explain why he suddenly returned to the park, and in fact seemed a bit evasive when Strong talked to him. Something seemed to spook the boy.

But just like the Barnes boy, Roark had vanished without a trace or witness. Into thin air. It didn't make sense. Maybe the Staties would figure it out. They had a lot more resources and experience for something like this than his own small department.

Strong continued to watch as the vacuum hose sucked up the brightly colored leaves and the large pile began shrinking. It was more than half gone when the worker stopped and laid the hose down. He went over to the machine and turned it off.

The sound of the engine still rumbled in Strong's ears before the park became quiet. He and the worker approached what remained of the pile. A flash of red caught his eye that was brighter than the red of the fallen leaves. He bent down for a closer look.

On the grass in a spot where the leaves had just been cleared lay a red canvas PRO-Keds sneaker, its laces still tied.

OCTOBER 20

1

Lance tossed newspapers onto front stoops as he walked down Washington Street, wishing Ryan was with him. It wasn't fair for Ryan's parents to ground him. Lance was the one who suggested toilet-papering Becky Williams' house. Ryan shouldn't have been the one punished. He also wished Ryan were here because he dreaded delivering the newspapers to the boardinghouse because of the old magician.

Something was in that black hat. His hand touched something wet.

He knew it wasn't blood, but it made his stomach queasy and his encounter with the man on the stairs made him leery of running into him again. He planned to toss both newspapers on the front steps and run back home as fast as he could.

Speaking of strange people, he thought as he approached Rita Stone-Thurlow's house, music blaring from it, the same as yesterday and all last week. Music unlike anything Lance ever heard before. *Why all of a sudden?*

He approached the front steps, hoping she wouldn't come to the door. At the end of her walk, he tossed the paper and watched it land on the third step and then bounce back off and onto the walkway. He turned to go, then decided to get the newspaper and put it properly on the top step near her door. Lance didn't want any complaints filed down at the newspaper office and spoil his perfect record.

He grabbed the bundled paper and gave it a quick loft onto the landing, where it came to a stop near her doormat. Good, he thought, and turned to go. He stopped when he heard something strange about the man singing in the awful music blaring through the closed windows.

Something seemed different about the voice, a screech interspersed throughout the vocals. He thought the record might be skipping, but the robust music flowed without a hitch. He turned his head toward the house, trying to hear better.

As he focused on the house, movement caught his eye and he looked down toward the foundation. Through the black metal grate of the cellar window well, he spotted the face of a young blond-haired boy.

The kid's mouth was open as he screamed.

That's what's wrong, Lance thought as he approached the house to the right of the front steps. This kid yelling through the glass basement window undercut the voice of the singer on the record just enough to be barely audible.

As Lance got closer to the window, the boy disappeared, but not before he noticed a mask of fear on the young kid's face. Lance knelt by the window well and peered through the grate. The glass window beyond was coated in dirt and dust, which made it difficult to see.

What happened to the boy? Is he in trouble?

Lance stood and looked at one of the first-floor windows. No sign of movement inside the house. Rita must be around, otherwise the music wouldn't be playing. Could she not hear the kid screaming in the cellar?

What's the boy doing down there?

Rita had no children that he was aware of. And no husband anymore either. So where had this kid come from? And why was he trying to get Lance's attention?

Lance worked his way around the side of the house, trying to see inside the basement, but each window was encased in grime and behind the metal grates. He moved around to the back of the house. A rusted bulkhead was flanked by two more grated window wells. As he contemplated what to do next, an unsettling thought crept into his head.

What if Rita was the one snatching kids, not the old magician? She was large enough and strong enough to out-muscle a boy, even one as big as Wayne Barnes. If Lance could provide the clue to solve this mystery, he'd be in all the papers. How cool would that be?

If only he could just get a glimpse inside that cellar and be sure.

Lance crept up to the window on the left side of the bulkhead and bent down. He pushed his face right up against the metal grate to try and get a better look through the dusty window.

A loud clang rattled as the bulkhead doors flung open.

Lance turned and, as he started to rise, looked right into the face of Rita Stone-Thurlow, her eyes wide, face flush and mouth opening as she roared like a wild animal. Lance stood frozen in fear, and then turned to flee. Before he could take a step, her large arms reached out and grabbed him.

Lance struggled as the beefy arms wrapped around him and held him tight, squeezing the breath out of him. His vision went blurry and he thought he might pass out.

Before everything went black, he felt himself being dragged down the bulkhead stairs into the dark cellar.

2

After supper, while working on homework at the desk in his room, Ryan noticed the flickering of blue lights outside his bedroom window. The first time, he ignored it, but when it happened again several minutes later, he got out of his chair and went to the window. A police car drove slowly down Oak Street past his house and out of sight.

He left his room and went downstairs, where his mother hung up the phone in the kitchen and locked eyes with him. Hers appeared red and wet. Ryan remembered that look before, when she told him what happened to Curtis. He stopped two steps from the bottom of the stairs, his feet not wanting to move any farther.

"What is it?" he asked, the words stuck in his throat.

His mother rushed to meet him. She grabbed him by both shoulders and those red eyes burned into his.

"Lance has gone missing," she said in a strained voice. She pulled him into her arms and wrapped them around him.

Several minutes later, Ryan found himself sitting on his front steps and staring down the road at the Stanton house on the corner of Oak and Walnut. Local and State Police vehicles were in the driveway and out front of the house.

It can't be. Not Lance. Wesley first, now Lance. It's not real. Lance can't be gone. Not him.

Ryan's mother came to the door a couple times to check on him and ask if he needed anything.

No, he told her. Lance was all he needed. He wanted his best friend.

Dane even came out and sat by him for a few minutes on the steps. His older brother didn't say a word. Didn't have to. Ryan knew what they were both thinking. The feelings from that day last winter when they both lost a major part of their lives. After a while, Dane patted him on the shoulder and went inside.

Ryan wanted to walk down the street to Lance's house. He could tell the police about the magician and the mysterious box they helped carry up the stairs to his room. Had the man seen them spying on him from the tree across the street from the boardinghouse? *Is that why he went after Lance? Will he come for me next?*

Ryan knew the police wouldn't listen to him. Not when he would tell them what happened to Eddie Scruggs. Not about the warning concerning the pumpkins and what they found at Hank Swain's farm. Not about the boy at the soccer game with bones poking out of his fingers or how the words on the gravestone rubbing changed.

The characters on *Dark Shadows* believed in supernatural occurrences without hesitation, but that wasn't real life. If he walked down to the house on the corner and started babbling to the authorities about what he and his friends had been witnessing the past several days, they would think he was making it all up.

He couldn't believe it himself.

His father came to the door and asked him if he wanted a coat.

Ryan hadn't noticed how cool it had gotten now that the sun was down.

"No, thanks," he said. "I'm fine."

"I don't want you staying out here too long."

Ryan had no idea what time it was.

"I won't," he said. He figured his parents were worried about him being outside after dark. But what did it matter? Both his friends went missing in broad daylight, Lance while delivering newspapers right here in the neighborhood. If Ryan wasn't grounded, he would have been with Lance and maybe this wouldn't have happened. He felt like telling his parents that.

He could feel his father's presence at the front door, watching him, worrying over him.

I should have been with him. We should have been together going from door to door. He wondered how far Lance had made it on his route. All the way to the last stop at the boardinghouse, where he might have encountered the magician? Or somewhere in-between?

"You don't have to go to school tomorrow," his father said.

"Okay," Ryan responded. He heard his father's footsteps retreat.

No more homework tonight, he thought as he stared down the street.

What's out there in the night? He looked at the trees that lined both sides of the road as a light breeze blew through their limbs, making the branches sway. Leaves fell and drifted to the ground to join the ones already scattered across the lawns.

Ryan thought maybe he should have accepted the offer of a jacket. He wasn't sure if it was because of the coolness of the night, but his whole body began to shake.

3

Lance awoke in a dark space. His head ached. His body throbbed like he'd been through the wringer. He tried to reach up to rub his head, but he couldn't move his arms. That's when he realized they were restrained behind his back by a rope. He felt the bristles of the fibers rubbing against his wrists as he struggled with the bindings.

As the darkness in the space around him cleared, he could tell he was in a basement. His memory flooded back. *Her basement.* He felt something hard and cold pressed up behind him and it dawned on him that he was tied to a lally column in the cellar. He tried to scream for help, but couldn't because of a gag in his mouth tied around the back of his head.

Out of the darkness, a figure moved toward him.

It was the young blond boy.

Lance stared at him in wide-eyed amazement. *This kid can help me.*

The boy reached toward him and pulled the gag out of his mouth.

"Thanks," Lance said, relieved to be able to breathe normally. "Who are you?"

"I'm your new friend," the boy said with a smile.

"What?" Lance's head felt woozy and he wondered if he had passed out or been knocked out by Rita. "Can you untie me?"

The boy shook his head. "I can't do that."

"What do you mean?" Lance didn't understand. "I can help you get out of here if you untie me."

"There's no way out," the boy said. "She won't let us."

The kid's gone crazy, Lance thought.

"Who are you?"

"My name's Quinn."

The boy didn't look frightened. Not like Lance, whose stomach felt twisted in a knot. He wondered where Rita was and how much time he had before she returned.

"What are you doing here?" Lance continued to struggle with the knot, but it only irritated his wrists more.

The boy shrugged. "I just found my way here," he said. "By accident, I guess."

The kid made no sense.

"Don't you want to get out of here?"

"I'd like to. But where would I go?"

Lance stopped struggling and sat still. "Where are your parents?"

"My mom ran off a long time ago," Quinn said. "For a long while it was just me and my dad. But then he sent me away and I ended up in a different place."

"What kind of place?"

"The House of Embers," Quinn said. "Where Mr. Shreckengast took care of me and the others."

"The others?"

"The Scamps. We all lived in the House of Embers."

"Where the heck is that?" Lance's head spun from the boy's nonsensical explanation.

"Out in the darkness," Quinn said. "Somewhere."

"And how did you get here?"

"I'm not really sure," he said. "There was an opening in the dark and we kind of floated out. I woke up in that." Quinn pointed.

Lance turned his head to look. A tall wooden cabinet stood up against the foundation, surrounded by a lot of boxes. His eyes went wide. It looked just like the cabinet in the old magician's room at the boardinghouse, except it appeared older and more worn.

"And you're here all by yourself?" He thought of Wesley and Wayne.

"Yes," Quinn said. "Rita takes care of me and feeds me."

"Isn't there anyone looking for you?"

"I keep hoping Mr. Shreckengast comes to find me," he said, his eyes downturned. "But I'm afraid he's forgotten about me."

"They'll come looking for me," Lance said, trying to reassure himself.

"The police already stopped here," Quinn said.

"They did?"

"While you were knocked out. That's why Rita gagged you and tied you up. They went door to door asking about you. She told them you delivered her newspaper, but she never saw you. Then they left. They'll probably forget you. Like everyone forgot me."

"What does she want with us?" Lance asked. He thought about how large Rita was and worried she'd cook and eat him. Maybe that was how she stayed so big.

"She wants children," Quinn said. "She told me she couldn't have any of her own."

"That's crazy."

"She grabbed you so you can be my friend."

"Stupid," Lance said. He'd find a way out, he told himself. He just needed to think a bit.

"Don't you want to be my friend?"

"Don't be such a dork," Lance said. His eyes roamed around the basement, taking in his surroundings.

"What's a dork?"

"Take a look in a mirror someday." When he was outside, he had noticed the metal grates covered all the window wells. They must be bolted to the foundation, so even if he broke the glass, he wouldn't be able to remove the grates. The door at the top of the stairs was probably locked. Besides, she was up there. But what about the bulkhead? He craned his neck and found the cement steps to the bulkhead were behind him.

"It's padlocked," Quinn said when he noticed where Lance's attention was drawn. "I told you, there's no way out."

Lance looked at the kid's lonely eyes.

"You don't want to stay here, do you, Quinn?" he asked.

"No," the boy said. "Not really."

"Then we'll work together and find a way out."

"Maybe Mr. Shreckengast will come after all," Quinn said and the thought seemed to lift his spirits.

Lance looked into the boy's face. Whoever this Shreckengast was, he didn't sound like someone who'd be very helpful. In fact, the whole thing about the man and the so-called House of Embers seemed made up. Maybe this kid was crazy after all.

OCTOBER 21

1

Ryan was glad his parents let him stay home from school Wednesday as there was no way he could even think about concentrating on class assignments with everything going on. Still no word on Lance. His friend remained missing. The police activity at the Stanton house had dwindled to a slight trickle, and then to nothing at all.

His mother suggested they walk down to visit the Stantons. She baked an apple pie in the morning and thought it would be a nice gesture.

Yeah, Ryan thought. *A 'grand gesture'*.

He accompanied his mother as they walked down Oak Street, feet swishing through the red, yellow, and orange leaves that carpeted the sidewalk like an autumn cornucopia. Ryan thought about how much he loved the fall season, with its crisp, breezy weather, colorful foliage, Halloween decorations and the scent of burnt pumpkin from candles planted in jack-o'-lanterns on neighbors' front steps.

Now the sight of one of those grinning pumpkins sent his heart into palpitations.

There's something in the pumpkins.

Eddie warned him before he vanished. Did he really run away or had something bad happened to him? Would they ever know? Ryan should have foreseen it. All the horror shows and movies he watched, comic books he collected, and stories he read – and wrote – should have made him an expert. He imagined something like this happening in Maplewood every time he put pen to paper to write one of his lurid tales. He should have seen it coming from that first day of October when the man in the black cloak and top hat arrived in town. He wrote about these things and the people in the stories never believed it until it was too late.

Ryan just hoped it wasn't too late for Maplewood.

He thought of someone else who wrote about supernatural happenings: Harold Bertram Lothrop. Ryan had paperback collections of his best tales. Lothrop knew about these things. Ryan had seen that in the old man's eyes. That's why he hid out in Maplewood and let his typewriter become caked with dust.

The man is afraid of something.

Two days ago, Ryan and Lance visited him and Lothrop offered no help. Now, Lance was gone and Ryan still believed the writer could be useful. He needed to see him, but his mother would never let him leave the house alone.

Ryan felt numb at the Stanton house as he and his mother sat in the living room with Lance's parents. They graciously accepted the apple pie with half-hearted smiles and then the four of them sat and chatted. The adults did all the talking. His mother offered Lance's parents hope and prayers.

Hope was all Ryan had. He wanted to say something, but he felt awkward in the presence of the adults. He wanted to do more. He needed to see Lothrop. He would be able to help.

Their visit was brief and once back home, Ryan pleaded with his mother to let him go to the boardinghouse.

"Absolutely not," his mother said. "Before your father left for work, he gave explicit instructions that you are to remain home."

"But I just want to go see Mr. Lothrop," he said. "It's important."

He followed his mother from room to room as she dusted the woodwork with a not-so-white rag and a can of furniture polish.

"It's admirable that you spend time with senior citizens," she said. "Not enough people pay attention to them. But I don't understand why it's so urgent to go over there."

"He knows things," Ryan said, realizing he was failing at making his mother understand. "He's seen a lot."

"If Mr. Lothrop knows something, he can tell the police."

"That's not what I mean," he said, trying to keep calm.

"Then I don't know what you're talking about." She paused in her housework to put her hands on her hips. "Can he help find Lance?"

Ryan lowered his eyes. "Not exactly."

"Then what can he do?"

He shrugged. "Nothing, I guess."

"That's what I thought." She continued with her housework and Ryan went up to his room.

He kept his bedroom door closed so Smokey couldn't come sticking his sad muzzle in. Ryan didn't feel like company, especially of the four-legged kind. He poked through his comic books but felt no ambition to read. He didn't even think he could get interested in watching *Dark Shadows* later that afternoon and he never missed an episode. He had his own dark shadows going on in real life and nothing else seemed important.

Ryan ate lunch at the kitchen table with his mother and Dane. Tuna fish sandwiches. His parents let his older brother play hooky from school as well, though he wasn't sure why that was necessary. Ryan imagined a lot of parents let their children stay home after the latest developments.

After lunch, Ryan waited for Dane to get off the phone with his girlfriend, and then he called Russell, another homebody today. Russell sounded scared and Ryan didn't blame him. He was frightened too, afraid of never seeing Lance again. This was like Curtis all over again, and the pain from that had never left no matter how much he tried to return to a normal life.

"Did you hear the newspaper called off the scavenger hunt?" Russell asked.

Ryan hadn't, but it didn't surprise him. No sense having kids running all around town looking for items on the list.

"And the town canceled trick-or-treat," Russell said.

Another thing Ryan couldn't begin to care about at this point. Nothing seemed to matter now, just his friends.

His mother came into the kitchen after he hung up the phone. She had her coat on.

"Where are you going?" he asked.

"I've got an appointment at the beauty parlor," she said. The place she went to get her hair done was in a salon in a private home on Arbor Lane in the neighborhood between the Town Square and downtown. It was walking distance. "You can come with me and sit in the waiting room and look at magazines, or you can stay here and your brother will watch you."

The thought of the beauty parlor waiting room sounded painful.

"I'll stay," he said.

His mother called to Dane and he came down the stairs. He wasn't happy when she told him the plan.

"Elsie is coming over and we're going for a ride," he said.

"This isn't a holiday," she said. "You're both only staying home because there's some maniac snatching kids."

"I can take care of myself," Dane said. "And I won't be alone."

"Where are you going?"

Dane shrugged. "Just cruising around," he said. "Nowhere particular."

"Probably some place to go necking," Ryan said.

His brother turned to him. "Like you'd know." He looked back at his mother. "I don't want to watch the twerp."

"No name calling." His mother tried sounding stern. She put her hands on her hips and looked at Ryan. "I have an idea. I'll walk you to the Downeys' place on my way to the salon. You stay there until I come back to get you when I'm done."

"Great," Ryan said.

"Perfect," Dane said and headed back upstairs. "Elsie should be here soon."

"I'll get my jacket," Ryan said.

"And one more thing," his mother said, stopping him in his tracks. "Get the leash. You're taking Smokey with you."

Ryan's shoulders slumped. "Aw, Mom."

"That dog needs to be walked more," she said. "Plus, he's a good protector."

Didn't protect Curtis very well, Ryan thought, as he went to grab the leash. Smokey must have heard his name because he bounded into the kitchen with tail wagging. By the time Ryan and his mother had gotten outside, the dog was nearly pulling him down the street. He had to keep a firm grip on the leash. They walked in silence down Oak and turned up Walnut. At the next intersection they turned left onto Elm Street.

As they walked by his bus stop, Ryan thought back to the first day of the month when he and the others saw the man in black for the first time. Lance joked about the old man, but no one was laughing now. If he did see him at the house, it might not be a bad idea to have Smokey along.

When they reached the boardinghouse, his mother turned to him. "Now, you stay inside until I come get you," she said, a stern look on her face.

"Yes, ma'am," he said.

"Your father's probably not going to like me doing this, so you better stay put."

With that, she was off. Once out of sight, Ryan turned to head up the front steps. Smokey pulled back on the leash. Ryan turned to look down at him. The dog dug its heels in and wouldn't budge no matter how hard he tugged on the leash.

"What's the matter, boy?"

Smokey looked up at the house. Ryan followed the dog's gaze all the way up to the third-floor window of the front bedroom. The magician's room.

The dog knows something's wrong here. It senses it.

"I guess you can stay out here," he said. He pulled Smokey over to an old metal hitching post by the edge of the road and tied the leash to it. "Lie down and be quiet." Ryan watched the dog circle around and lie in the grass. Satisfied, Ryan headed up the front steps.

Mrs. Downey opened the front door when he knocked, a genuinely surprised expression on her face.

"Shouldn't you be in school?" she asked.

"Stayed home," he answered. "Someone's snatching kids."

"Oh, that's right." Her face reverted to disgust. "That's horrid. Then why are you out?"

"It's okay. My mom walked me here. I need to see Mr. Lothrop."

"Come on in," she said as she swung the door open. Before closing it, she stuck her head out and looked up and down the street as if making sure no child-snatchers were about.

Up on the third floor, Ryan knocked on Mr. Lothrop's door. He kept a cautious eye on the door at the end of the hall while he waited.

"You again," Lothrop said when he opened the door. "Don't you have anything better to do than visit old relics?"

Ryan entered the room without a response or invitation.

"Come on in," Mr. Lothrop mumbled and closed the door.

Ryan was already seated on the edge of the man's bed by that time and waited for him to take his seat by the window.

"What is it this time?" Mr. Lothrop asked.

"My friend Lance has gone missing."

"Is that why we didn't get the paper yesterday?"

Ryan felt he might fall apart and start blubbering. His lower lip trembled, but he gritted his teeth to steady his nerves.

"I'm scared," he said once he unclenched his jaw. "You said before that there's real horror out there. I think it's here in Maplewood."

Mr. Lothrop's eyes drifted out toward the window as if he wanted to change the subject. When he spoke, he did not look at Ryan.

"I know it is," he said, and his voice came from deep within his throat, as if he had to force the words out of his mouth. "I'm sorry about your friend. He seemed like a nice kid."

"What have you seen?"

"I've seen things that can't be explained in my lifetime."

"Is that why you don't go outside?"

The old man nodded. "When I came here as a young man, I was pursued by goblins."

"Goblins?" The only goblin Ryan knew about was the Green Goblin villain in the Spider-Man comic books he collected.

"Little creatures," Lothrop said, "with vicious teeth and razor claws. I believed they killed several of my writer colleagues, though everyone else thinks it was just a series of accidents." He finally relented and turned to face Ryan. "But I know better. I got off here on the train thinking I could hide from them. But I fear they've discovered me here."

The mention of the train made Ryan think of the man in black who arrived on the first of October.

"What about your neighbor down the hall?" he asked.

Lothrop flinched. "What about him?"

"He came here mysteriously," Ryan said. "He has that weird wooden cabinet Lance and I carried upstairs to his room." Lance told him the cabinet was empty when he searched the man's room. But something else happened there that Lance wasn't telling him. Something that spooked him. He had seen it in his friend's eyes, just as he could see it in Mr. Lothrop's eyes now.

"He's a dark force of his own. I haven't quite figured him out yet." Lothrop leaned forward in his chair and his voice lowered. "He delves in dark magic, so you best stay away from him."

A sudden knock on the door startled them both. Ryan almost jumped out of his skin. Had the magician sensed them talking about him and come to investigate?

"Who is it?" Lothrop called hesitantly.

"Darrin," came the answer from the other side.

"What do you want?" Lothrop made a face that almost made Ryan laugh.

"I need to show you something."

Lothrop shot Ryan a curious look and shrugged.

"Come on in."

The door opened and Mr. Fifer entered. Ryan noticed he looked jittery, his face damp with sweat.

"Well?" Lothrop said.

Fifer crossed the room and stood next to Lothrop's chair by the window.

"I need you to tell me what you see out there," Fifer said.

"This again?"

Ryan watched the pair with curiosity.

"Look," Fifer said, "and tell me if you see a policeman out there with a cigarette lighter."

"I don't want to look," Lothrop said.

Ryan noticed the writer's face twitch. Something seemed odd. Earlier the old man kept glancing out the window and now he acted afraid to look.

"Just look for me," Fifer said. "And see if the policeman is there."

Lothrop hesitated before rising from his chair and turning to look out the window onto the side yard. Ryan watched his eyes widen and his mouth grimace.

"There's nothing out there," Lothrop said when he turned to face Fifer.

"Are you sure?" Fifer's face drained of color. "You don't see anyone?"

He's lying, Ryan thought. He could tell Lothrop saw something out there and it frightened him. He had no idea why Fifer thought a cop was watching the house, but whatever Lothrop saw, it probably wasn't a policeman.

"There's no cop out there," Lothrop said.

Fifer's face went red, and he turned and stormed out of the room, slamming the door behind him. The old writer now turned to Ryan, who didn't like the look of distress on his face.

"Come here," Lothrop said. "Look out the window and tell me what you see."

Ryan didn't want to budge from his seat on the end of the bed.

"Please," the old man pleaded.

Ryan got up and dragged himself over to the window. He focused on Lothrop's wary eyes before bringing his gaze to the window and down to the sidewalk below, where a figure stood looking up at them.

"Do you see a little critter with green scaly skin and pointed ears?" Lothrop asked.

Ryan's eyes widened when he saw the figure below.

It can't be!

His insides felt as if a pair of icy hands rested on his heart, nearly causing it to stop. Outside on the street, he heard Smokey bark. At first, he couldn't move. His whole body felt numb. When he turned to go, Lothrop grabbed his arm.

"Do you see it?" the old man yelled.

"No," Ryan said and tried to pull his arm from the man's grip.

"Then what *do* you see?" The bony fingers dug into the flesh of Ryan's upper arm.

Ryan thought about the mirror image looking back up at him.

"It's my brother Curtis," he said and pulled free from Lothrop's hand and raced out of the room and down the stairs.

When Ryan burst out of the front door, he saw Smokey straining on his leash, trying to pull it from its mooring on the hitching post. The dog whimpered and whined as it stared down the sidewalk just beyond the boardinghouse's driveway.

But when Ryan looked, he saw no policeman, nor a little green creature, and certainly not his dead twin brother. *No one* was there.

That didn't stop Smokey from trying to break free as the dog looked toward that empty spot.

2

Rita brought dinner down to the basement and set it on the table. Quinn looked down at the two plates of spaghetti. He watched as Rita went over to where Lance remained tied to the post, the gag back in his mouth. Quinn had put the rag back between Lance's teeth the second he heard the door unlock at the top of the stairs. He didn't want to get Rita mad.

"Do you think you can behave yourself enough to eat?" she asked. "You must be starving."

Lance looked up at her but gave no signal. Rita reached down and undid the gag.

"Wait till my dad gets ahold of you," Lance said.

Quinn cringed. He wanted his new companion to be able to eat dinner with him.

"Your dad has no idea where you are," Rita said.

"The cops will find out."

"They've already come and gone," she said.

"What have you done with Wesley?" he asked. "Where is he?"

Rita scrunched her nose up. "I have no idea who you're talking about. I don't know anyone named Wesley. Do you want to eat or not?"

Quinn caught Lance's eye and nodded his head. He mouthed the word 'please'.

Lance looked up at Rita. Quinn figured the boy must be hungry.

"Okay," Lance said to her.

Rita went around behind him and untied the rope that bound him to the pole. She stepped back and Quinn could tell she was prepared to muscle Lance to the floor if the boy tried anything funny. He didn't. Instead, he sauntered over to the table, sat down and immediately began shoveling forkfuls of pasta into his mouth. It looked to Quinn as if he hadn't eaten in a month. Quinn sat down and joined him, feeling famished himself.

"There's my two boys," Rita said with an enormous smile. "Happy tummy, happy heart." She left and went upstairs.

Lance finished before Quinn and wiped his mouth with a napkin. As Quinn hurried to catch up, Lance walked around the cellar surveying his surroundings. He turned to look back as Quinn scarfed down his last bite.

"She's wacked, you know," Lance said.

"She said she was going to get me a playmate."

"Total bananas." Lance went over to the front basement wall and looked up at the window. "I'm not here to be your friend."

"Those windows are nailed shut," Quinn said. He'd seen Rita pound the nails in the first day he got here. "Besides, even if you got the window open, the metal grate is blocking the opening."

Lance came back to the table, grabbed a chair, and dragged it over to the wall. He stood on the chair and examined the window, feeling along the edges of the glass with his fingers.

"But if I can get it open, maybe we can call for help when someone passes by." He looked back at Quinn. "Anyone come visit here regular?"

"The bread man early in the morning," Quinn said, thinking of the yummy doughnuts Rita got from the man. Only if Quinn behaved of course. "But she plays her opera music real loud so no one can hear anything else. And the paperboy. But that's you."

"My friend Ryan is my backup when I'm not available to deliver the paper. Mr. Wright would have contacted him. Ryan should have come by earlier this afternoon." Lance looked out the window. "I wonder why he didn't come." He looked at Quinn. "Anyone else come by?"

"Some strange old guy stopped by," Quinn said, "but he just stares at the house from the walk."

"What's strange about him?"

Quinn shrugged. "Just that he stands there staring at the house. Plus, he's all dressed in black, with some kind of cape on."

Lance's eyes widened. "The magician," he said. "They're probably in cahoots."

"My father's a magician," Quinn said.

"And where's your father?"

"I don't know." Quinn thought back, trying to remember the last time he saw his father. He could only picture his face as a door closed between them. "He sent me away."

"That sucks."

"But Mr. Shreckengast saved me."

"And where's he?"

"I wish I knew."

Lance got down from the chair and began looking through some of the boxes. Quinn jumped up from his seat, worried they'd get in trouble.

"Those belong to Rita's husband," Quinn said. "She won't like you messing with his things."

"And do you know where he is?"

"No," Quinn said. "She said he's gone away."

"Some people think she ate him," Lance said as he continued to poke around the stacks of boxes, lifting lids and peeking inside. "She's a monster, or a witch. Or both."

"She hasn't tried to eat me yet," Quinn said.

Lance gestured at the empty plates on the table.

"Maybe she's trying to fatten us up first."

Quinn felt an uneasy rumble in his belly. He looked down and poked at his stomach with an index finger as he wondered if he'd gained weight since he'd been here. When he looked up, Lance was back on the chair with what looked like a trophy in his hand. A figure of a man in a bowling pose topped the trophy. The next thing he knew, Lance smashed the window with the base of it and cleared the glass away.

"Oh, no," Quinn said. "Now you've done it. She's going to be real mad now."

3

When Lance heard the door unlock at the top of the cellar stairs, he got down off the chair and brought it back just before Rita came down the steps.

"I see my hungry boys enjoyed their dinner," she said with a grin.

"Thank you," Quinn said.

Rita looked at Lance but he chose not to say anything. She hadn't glanced toward the broken basement window yet, and he prayed she wouldn't notice it.

"You'll learn to be grateful," she said. "Now I'm going to need to tie you back up."

"No," Lance said and glanced toward the stairs on the other side of where Rita stood, wondering if he could make it past her and up the steps. He knew he could outrun her, but it was a matter of getting past her first.

"You have to earn my trust, young boy," she said and lumbered toward him.

She moved faster than he expected and grabbed him as he tried to get by. He struggled in her grip but her arms were like powerful pincers and she held him tight and dragged him back to the pole. He tried lashing out with his feet but she smacked him across the head with the open palm of her hand and he went woozy. In a few seconds, his hands were bound behind him and she tied the gag back in his mouth.

"I would have skipped the gag if you weren't being such a twat," she said, spittle flying into his face. "Chew on that while you sleep. Maybe you'll think better in the morning."

Once she went upstairs and turned the light off, the basement went dark. Lance heard a match strike and saw Quinn had lit the candle in the jack-o'-lantern on the table.

"It's the only light she lets me have at night," he said. Surprisingly, it lit up a good portion of the cellar, though draping the edges in eerie shadows. Quinn came over and took the gag out of Lance's mouth.

"I'm sorry," Quinn said.

"Bring the chair back over to the window and see if anyone comes by."

"No one ever passes by this house at night."

Lance felt his heart sink.

"I wish it were Halloween night, then there'd be lots of kids going by for trick-or-treat," Lance said. Though he knew Rita never turned her light on for trick-or-treaters because none of the kids ever stopped at this house. Most were afraid of her. She probably wouldn't hand out candy anyway, wanting to keep it all to herself so she could stuff her fat face.

"What's trick-or-treat?" Quinn asked.

"What?" Lance was bewildered by the question. "You've never heard of trick-or-treat?"

"No."

"Haven't you ever celebrated Halloween? It's the best thing about October."

"The carnival season was usually wrapped up in October," Quinn said, "and we'd all head to Florida for the winter. I don't ever remember celebrating Halloween, or whatever this trick-or-treat thing is."

"It's the best," Lance said. "All the kids dress up in costumes and go door to door and people hand out candy."

"I like candy," Quinn said. "That sounds like fun."

"And who doesn't like fun?" came a deep voice from outside the basement window.

Lance looked over, startled, and saw a pale face in the dark with a long, sloping nose peering through the metal grate on the window well.

"Mr. Shreckengast!" Quinn called out with excitement.

4

Quinn dragged the chair over to the basement wall and climbed up on it. Shreckengast's face looked like jigsaw pieces from the pattern of the grate.

"You found me!" Quinn said, excited, not even thinking about his voice carrying upstairs.

"I've been looking everywhere for you," Shreckengast said in a soft voice. "I've had my Scamps scouring all over town."

"Have you come to rescue me?" Quinn's heart fluttered. He felt he was dreaming and worried he'd wake up and be alone. "There's a mean old lady keeping me prisoner."

"I can get you out," he said. "But I'm going to need you to do something for me."

"Anything," Quinn said with glee. "I'll do anything to be free from this horrible basement. What do I need to do?"

"I want you to get me your father's magic hat."

Quinn's head spun. "My father? But where would I find my father?"

"He's here, my boy. In this town. Not far from this very house."

Quinn couldn't believe what he heard. His father. Here. All this time. And he hadn't come looking for him? Rita must have been right. His father sent him away on purpose and no longer wanted him around.

"What do you want with his hat?"

Shreckengast smiled. "I want its magic. If it was powerful enough to help transport you through the barrier into my world, then that's magic worth having." His grin looked like it would crack his face in half. "The things I could do with that."

Quinn thought for a moment about something Lance said. He turned to look back at the boy who watched him from where he remained bound to the column.

"Is he able to help us?" Lance asked. "Can he get us out?"

Quinn looked back through the window. "I'll get the hat for you. But there's something I'd like."

"Anything, my child," Shreckengast said.

"I want to go trick-or-treating," Quinn said. "Like other kids do."

Shreckengast nodded and pressed his lips up close to the metal grate. "That's a splendid idea. Halloween is the most fun time of year. I've found a new home for us and the Scamps and we're going to have the best Halloween ever. You all can go trick-or-treating and I'm going to make the most amazing fun house and entertain the entire town. It'll be a Halloween they'll never forget."

"Okay," Quinn said. His whole body tingled with anticipation. "But how are you going to get me out?"

"Easy. I have a little bit of my own magic." Shreckengast placed his long, skinny fingers through holes in the grate. Quinn saw blue sparks flow out from his fingertips and run along the borders of the grate. Then he lifted the grate away and tossed it aside as if it were made of cardboard. "Voila!"

Quinn felt a sudden rush of air as the freedom of the world outside the window flowed into his body and nearly lifted him off his feet.

Shreckengast extended his right hand through the window. "Let's go play."

"Hey!" Lance shouted from the middle of the cellar. "What about me?"

Quinn looked back, and even in the dim light of the basement, could see the fear and panic in Lance's eyes. He looked back at Shreckengast.

"Can you let my new friend out too?" he asked.

Shreckengast pursed his lips. "Is he a good boy?"

"I think so," Quinn said with a glance back at Lance.

"You can untie him," Shreckengast said. "But he can't come with us."

"Why not?"

Shreckengast's eyes narrowed as he looked through the open window at Lance.

"Because he's not like you and I," he said.

Quinn jumped down from the chair and ran across the basement to where Lance sat. He began untying his bindings.

"Who is this guy?" Lance whispered.

"He took care of me," Quinn said as he struggled with the knots binding Lance's wrists. "In that other place."

"But he said your father is here, in Maplewood."

Quinn finished with the knot and the older boy stood up.

"Wouldn't you rather be with your father, instead of this guy?" Lance asked.

"He sent me away and didn't come for me," Quinn said. "He didn't want me. But Mr. Shreckengast does."

Both boys ran over to the window. Lance hoisted Quinn up and out through the opening. Quinn turned back and grabbed Lance's hand and helped the boy through. In the front yard, the air smelled fresher. Quinn marveled at all the stars in the sky.

"Come, Quinn," Shreckengast said. "Let's be quick. The others are waiting for us."

"Are you sure you want to go with him?" Lance asked.

Quinn looked at him. "He's all I got," he said.

"I'll look after him," Shreckengast said to Lance. "As I always have." He looked at Quinn. "We must go now. I have a special place for us. And we're going to have so much fun."

Quinn looked at Lance and nodded. The older boy seemed confused. His face looked strained. Then Lance turned and ran off down the street. Shreckengast took Quinn's hand and led him away in the opposite direction.

OCTOBER 22

1

A convoy of blue lights rolled down Oak Street, turned onto Washington and continued before stopping in front of Rita Stone-Thurlow's house near the intersection with Maple. Chief Strong got out of his cruiser and hooked up with the lieutenant and sergeant from the State Police. It was their investigation, but he had jurisdiction in Maplewood as chief of police, so he led the way up the walk to the front door. A swarm of officers, both state and local, followed.

Strong noticed the discarded metal grate from the basement window well lying in the grass to the right of the front stoop. It matched what the Stanton boy had told them. Before he reached the steps, the sound of opera music bellowed from deep within the house.

He knocked on the door. No answer, so he knocked again. Strong had the warrant to search the property in his front pocket. No need to wait for an invitation. He tried the front door and found it unlocked. Strong entered the house and the others filed in behind him.

The deafening music reverberated among the walls. Rita sat in a chair in the living room eating chocolate-covered cherries from a box. She looked at them and flashed them a smile whose perimeter was smeared with melted chocolate and deep red cherry juice. Strong looked around the room at the plethora of Hummel figures lining shelves on all four walls. Rita made no attempt to rise from her chair. Strong walked over to her and pulled the paper from his pocket.

"I have an arrest warrant for you, Rita Strong-Thurlow," he said.

She gazed up at him and the smile disappeared.

"Did you find my boys?" she said. "They're missing. I need you to find them. Two wonderful boys."

"Can someone find that music and shut it off?" the State Police lieutenant barked from behind him.

In a few seconds, the house went silent, though Strong thought he could still hear the music in his head. He looked down at Rita, finding it hard to believe this pathetic-looking woman kidnapped Lance. And if she took him, she must have snatched the other missing boys.

"Lance Stanton is safe," Strong said. "Where are the others?"

"It's like they disappeared," Rita said, her glassy eyes looking up at him. "They came out of nowhere, and vanished into thin air." Her eyes went round. "Like magic."

"We're going to need you to come down to the station," Strong said. "We have a warrant to search your house. And we'll need to ask you some questions about the other boys." No response from her as she set the empty box of chocolates down on the table beside the chair and wiped her mouth with the back of a hand, the chocolate smearing around her lips like a clown's greasepaint.

Behind him, Strong heard the lieutenant instruct some of his men to commence searching the house. Officers went both upstairs and down into the basement.

"I just wanted a boy of my own," she said, her voice distant as if talking to someone else. "I couldn't give my husband Gordon any kids because of my condition. That's why he's not around anymore, because I couldn't give him children. One day he was here." She looked up at Strong. "And the next day he was gone. Vanished. Like magic."

Strong took handcuffs of his belt, but then looked down at her arms. With the size of her wrists, he didn't think it possible for the handcuffs to fit her.

"Please stand up," he said. "We need to take you to the station."

Strong had his own problems with his girth, but the build of Rita as she stood up from the chair made him take a step back. He didn't know what he'd do if she lunged at him. He signaled for a couple of his men to take her arms and walk her out to one of the patrol cars. He followed her out onto the front steps and watched her being led down the walkway.

Rita turned to look back at him.

"Whatever you do," she said and started to cry, "please don't disturb my flower garden in the backyard."

Strong felt his heart sink. He'd better tell the lieutenant that they should bring in a cadaver dog.

2

Ryan raced down Oak Street unable to believe the news. When he caught sight of the Stanton house, his feet picked up speed. Lance must have been looking out the window, because he came out of the house as Ryan got there and met him on his front porch.

"I can't believe it!" Ryan resisted the urge to throw his arms around his friend. "My mother told me this morning, but I thought I was dreaming."

"It was crazy," Lance said, beaming. "I almost can't believe the whole thing myself."

Ryan felt lost for words. He thought his friend was dead and gone forever, and here he stood before him, plain as day.

"Damn Rita," Ryan said. "Who would have thought?"

"Unbelievable," Lance said. "I know."

"I need details." Ryan had a million questions.

"I've got tons to tell you."

"I've got to get to school though," Ryan said. "My parents won't let me stay home another day."

"I'll meet you at your house after school," Lance said. "We've got lots to talk about."

"I'm supposed to do your paper route. My parents wouldn't let me do it yesterday. Too afraid."

"Yeah, I heard Mr. Wright had to do it," Lance said with a grin. "Can you imagine? He's the Maplewood bureau chief for the paper and lead reporter, and he had to do my paper route."

"Yeah, nuts."

"And get this, he wants to interview me for the paper about my experience." Lance brimmed with excitement. "I'll make the front page!"

"Damn," Ryan said. "That's cool."

In the excitement of Lance's rescue, Ryan forgot about one of the most important things.

"Any word on Wesley?" Ryan asked.

Lance shrugged. "Nothing. He wasn't there and Rita didn't say anything about him."

"I heard the cops are all over her house."

"I'm just glad to be out of that nightmare."

"I should get going so I don't miss the bus," Ryan said.

"Tell Russell and everyone at school I'm okay," Lance said. "I'll see you guys afterward."

"Meet me at my house," Ryan said. "After I finish your stupid paper route."

Ryan raced up the street toward the bus stop, excited to tell Russell the good news. Crazy Rita. Who would have believed it? But it still didn't answer a lot of questions. What about Eddie and the pumpkins? What about the kid at the soccer game? What about what he thought he saw at the bottom of the old barn cellar on the Williams property?

And what about seeing his dead brother Curtis yesterday afternoon?

No. This didn't answer a lot of things.

3

Rita sat in a small room at the police station wondering what was taking so long. She must have been in here for hours already. She squirmed in the seat, which was too small for her fanny and not at all comfortable. While she waited, she tried to go over in her mind what to tell them.

She felt sure that Stanton boy had blabbered to the cops about everything she did. But what about Quinn? She tried to think how she could even begin to tell them about the mysterious boy who showed up in the magic cabinet after forty years. And he was still the same age as when he disappeared at the carnival that day. She couldn't tell them that. Why, they'd think her mad.

And you know where they'd send you, don't you, Rita? To the funny farm. That's where they send the crazies. No need to let them think you're crazy. Because you're not.

Chief Strong and those State Police men wouldn't have the slightest idea of how to understand magic. But she knew it was real. She'd seen the boy materialize in the cabinet in her basement. Magic was the only way to explain that.

No way she could tell the police about Quinn. As far as she was concerned, she would tell them only about snatching Lance from her backyard. Why, the boy was trespassing. Of course. He was wandering around in her backyard and peeking in her windows. Probably hoping to catch her naked. She knew what little boys liked. Many years at the traveling carnival taught her that. Little boys and little men, always the same. They all like the same thing, wanted to see the same thing. Coming around for a peep show. She remembered the gawkers lining up for the hoochie-coochie tent salivating to catching a glimpse of some young girls' boobies.

Didn't matter now that Rita's breasts hung down to her belly button. That Stanton boy was peeking in her windows in her backyard, so she had every right to protect herself and grab a hold of him before he did something they'd all regret. She could tell Chief Strong she was waiting till the morning to report him to the police, but he must have gotten free in the middle of the night.

Not her fault. It was the boy's fault.

As for Quinn? She knew nobody named Quinn. Must have been the Stanton kid's imagination. Boys make up a lot of things. They have very vivid imaginations. And they lie.

Yup. That's right. That's what she'll tell them.

It's all a big mistake. She's not crazy.

Rita thought for a moment. Then remembered she probably shouldn't have mentioned anything about her flower garden.

4

Lance's parents sat outside the office of Monroe Wright at the newspaper's Maplewood bureau downtown while Monroe interviewed the boy. Lance's father initially had insisted on being there for the interview, but Lance managed to get his parents to wait in the lobby. He wanted to do this himself. Lance felt nervous, but Mr. Wright softened his tough exterior and made the boy feel at ease.

"Anytime you feel uncomfortable about what we talk about," Wright said, "we can take a break."

He provided a glass of water and Lance had already taken a couple big gulps to slake his dry throat. Once he felt settled in his seat, he shared his experience of being kidnapped by Rita Stone-Thurlow as Mr. Wright took notes.

Everything that happened at the house on Washington Street came flowing out of him and he tried to remember all the details. He worried he talked too fast for Wright to keep up, but the older man's pencil scratched across the paper, only pausing long enough to flip the page over.

Wright interrupted a few times to clarify some points and ask a few questions. But mostly he listened and took notes. When Lance finished, Wright slapped his notebook shut and set it on the desk along with the well-worn nub of the pencil.

"This stranger appeared at the basement window out of nowhere?" Wright asked.

"Yes, sir," Lance said.

"And it wasn't this Quinn boy's father?"

"Nope. The boy said his father abandoned him."

Wright lit up a cigarette and leaned back in his chair, billowing a cloud of smoke up into the ceiling. Lance couldn't help but suck in some of the tobacco scent.

"And the boy left with this man?"

"Yes."

"Of his own free will?" Wright scratched the top of his gray-stubbled head. "He didn't seem afraid?"

"No," Lance said. "He wanted to go with him."

"And you've never seen this Quinn before?"

"Nope."

"You told the police all this, correct?" Wright asked, his face puzzled.

"I sure did," Lance said. "They were very interested in that part. Especially the State Police guys."

"I'm sure," Wright said. "I'll be talking with Chief Strong later. I know the State Police fellows will never give me any information, but Strong and I go way back. He'll tell me things."

Lance said nothing. He felt he'd told Mr. Wright everything he could about his time in captivity.

"Were you scared?" Wright asked.

Lance squirmed in his seat. He glanced out the office window into the lobby where his parents waited. His mother smiled and his father nodded. Lance looked back at Mr. Wright.

"A bit," he said. "I guess." Though he thought he tried to stand up to Rita, the woman had unnerved him. She was off her rocker.

"And this mysterious man who rescued you?" Wright asked. "Were you scared of him at all?"

Lance thought for a moment. Last night already seemed off in the distance. He thought about the tall, thin man with the long nose and narrow eyes.

"Not really," Lance said. "But I knew not to go off with him."

"Why is that?"

"There was something creepy about him," Lance said.

"And you said this boy Quinn referred to him by name?" Wright asked. "Because he knew him."

"Yes, sir," Lance said. "He called him Mr.…" He tried to remember the name. It was a long, weird name, unusual. "Shrecken-something. I think." He thought hard. "Shreckengast! That's it. That's what he called the man."

Lance noticed Wright's mouth tightened and his eyes widened.

It was as if the newspaperman recognized the name.

5

In the basement at Ryan's house, he, Lance, and Russell went over all the events of the past few days. Lance told them both the story of his kidnapping and escape. Ryan noticed Lance fidgeting on the old worn couch and his eyes kept drifting over to the steps that led up to the door to the backyard.

"Are you okay?" Ryan asked.

"Yeah," Lance said, suppressing a nervous smile. "Just feel a bit weird."

"How so?" Russell asked.

"Being in a basement is kind of giving me the shivers a bit," Lance said. "After all that time tied up in Rita's cellar."

"Oh, shit," Ryan said. "I didn't even think about that. Let's go hang in the backyard."

Lance nodded. "Yeah, I think that'd be better."

As they got up to go, Ryan glanced at the table with the two items they had collected for the now-canceled scavenger hunt. They hadn't gotten very far, just Russell's Yaz card and the rolled-up gravestone rubbing from the old cemetery. He wondered if it still had Curtis's name and death date on it, or if it had reverted to the original name. He didn't dare look.

Too many things left unexplained.

That's the point he tried to drive home when they got outside and sat on the top of the picnic table, feet resting on the bench seat.

"It still doesn't all add up," Ryan said. "Rita doesn't explain everything. Not the kid I saw at the soccer game."

Russell held up his left arm. "Yeah, she didn't write the note from Shinbones on my cast."

"You're bringing up stuff that probably has a logical explanation," Lance said. "Because you want to believe there's something more sinister than Rita. She was a crazy lady who kidnapped some kids and the cops caught her. You want this to be like some episode of *Dark Shadows* or something."

"But what about Mr. Swain and the pumpkin shed?" Ryan asked.

"The old bugger probably popped a cork," Lance said. "Had some kind of breakdown, smashed his pumpkins and took off."

"This," Russell said, once again holding up his cast.

"Some kid in class must have written that as a joke when we were all signing it, and you just didn't notice."

"The thing in the old barn cellar at the Williams house?" Ryan asked. "It looked like a face."

"An animal," Lance said. "A fox or a coon, maybe a fisher cat. It was dark, you were scared. Your imagination got the better of you."

"Eddie's face and his warning about the pumpkins?"

"Eddie's a freak who always makes stupid faces. And he was just trying to scare you." Lance jumped off the table onto the grass and turned to face them. "It's almost friggin' Halloween. All kinds of kids are trying to scare each other."

"What about the gravestone rubbing?"

Lance paused. Ryan stumped him. No logical answer or way to explain it away. Damn if Lance didn't try.

"Our imagination," he said. "I bet if we unrolled that parchment now, it would have the name we rubbed from the tombstone. Let's check right now."

Ryan didn't want to. He couldn't bring himself to look at that paper because he was too afraid of what he'd see. Plus, he hadn't told them the biggest unexplained mystery.

"I saw Curtis yesterday," he said.

Lance's mouth dropped open.

"What?" Russell asked.

"Outside the Downeys' boardinghouse," Ryan said. "I saw him from Mr. Lothrop's window looking up at me."

"You didn't tell us that," Lance said. "What happened?"

"I ran downstairs, but when I got outside, he was gone. But Smokey was barking at the spot where I'd seen him."

"A ghost," Russell whispered.

"What did he come back for?" Ryan said.

"It can't be," Lance said. "It's probably normal to see someone you've lost."

"It's more than that," Ryan said. "Something is wrong here. I know it."

"It would be easier if we could blame it all on Rita," Lance said and sat back down on the picnic table with his head in his hands.

"What about that Quinn kid in the basement?" Russell asked. "Where did he come from? No one knows him."

"He said his father abandoned him," Lance said. "He told me his dad was a magician."

"That man at the boardinghouse is a magician, Lothrop told us." Ryan felt everything started when that mysterious man arrived.

"Maybe he's the kid's father," Russell said.

"No." Lance shook his head. "Too old."

Something occurred to Ryan and he turned to Lance. "You said there was a tall box in Rita's basement that looked like the same one in the magician's room at the boardinghouse?"

"Yes, but older-looking."

Ryan thought about a book he had read last fall, Ray Bradbury's *Something Wicked This Way Comes*. He told the others about the book and the carousel that could make you younger or older when you rode it forward or backward.

"Maybe the magician uses the cabinets to change his age," Ryan said. "From young to old or back again, like in the book."

"How does Rita fit in?" Russell asked.

"Mr. Lothrop said they both came from the same traveling carnival, and they both stayed in Maplewood when it left. We saw them arguing at the Harvest Festival. They knew each other."

"Maybe there's a connection," Lance said.

"And what about that mysterious man who let you and Quinn out?" Ryan asked. "Could that have been the younger version of the magician at the boardinghouse? And he came and got his son?"

"No," Lance said with an emphatic shake of his head. "This guy was too tall. Couldn't be him."

"Then we're back to square one," Russell said.

The back door opened and Ryan looked up to see his mother letting the dog out into the yard. She looked over at the boys and waved.

"I don't know why you can't take Smokey out when you go outside," his mother said. "The dog needs to get outdoors more."

"We're kind of busy, Mom," Ryan said and wished his mother would understand he didn't want the dog around.

"Just throw him a stick or something," she said. She waved at Lance. "So happy you're back, Lance."

"Thanks," Lance said.

Ryan's mother went back inside. Smokey wandered out into the yard, but instead of going over to the picnic table where the boys sat, the dog plodded over toward the maple tree with a tire swing hanging from a limb. The dog began whimpering and staring at the tire.

Ryan watched Smokey lie down on the grass, but he kept his head up and stared at the swing. The tire twisted slowly on the rope. Smokey whimpered louder.

"What's wrong with your dog?" Russell asked.

"The tire swing," Ryan said.

"What about it?" Lance asked.

"It's moving."

"It's just from the breeze."

Ryan looked from one boy's face to the other. "But there's no wind blowing."

The boys went silent and stared at the tire swing, the one Curtis and Ryan had hung two summers ago. It stopped moving and Smokey got up and walked over to it, his snout sniffing the air around the tire.

"What did you say that guy's name was?" Ryan asked. "The one who let you out of that basement."

"Shreckengast," Lance said, hanging his head back down.

"I wonder where he came from. And where did he take the boy? I wish we knew something about him."

Lance's head popped up. "I think someone might know."

"Who?"

"Mr. Wright at the newspaper," Lance said. "When I mentioned Shreckengast, there was something about the look on his face that made me think he was familiar with that name."

OCTOBER 23

1

Chief Strong's feet hurt from standing most of the day in the backyard of Rita's house. Law enforcement members circulated among the leaf-strewn lawn watching the activity. Strong would have rather been anywhere but here. A thorough search of the interior of the house had turned up nothing. No sign that the missing Wayne Barnes and Wesley Roark had been here.

And no clue to the identity of the boy known only as Quinn who went off with the mysterious rescuer identified by the Stanton kid as someone named Shreckengast, an identity no law official had been able to locate. The boy and man had vanished into the night.

Strong felt glad the State Police remained in charge of the case, and all he and his officers needed to do was provide security at the crime scene and crowd control. Passersby had come along Washington Street to gawk at the house, either by automobile or foot, and his patrolmen kept them moving along. He hoped they'd get things wrapped up here before the kids got out of school and they'd have to deal with those curiosity seekers.

The beeping from the metal detector jolted Strong out of a daydream. The detectorist the State Police had brought in stood in the middle of Rita's flower garden.

"Strong signal here," the man said to the State Police lieutenant.

In an instant, officers with shovels came forth and digging began. Strong grabbed onto his belt, hiked his pants up, and walked over to the garden. He stood in the background but made sure he had a good sight line into the hole that was being dug, though he really didn't want to see the decomposed bodies of one of those kids. Because regardless of the State Police being in charge, Strong knew he'd be the one tasked with bringing that awful news to the parents. This was still his town and citizens that he was responsible for.

"Got something," one of the diggers said.

Strong crept closer.

The shovels were dropped as men got down on their knees and began carefully brushing aside dirt with their hands. Strong stretched his neck to get a better view and saw gray, maybe a hip bone.

"Look at that," someone said.

Strong took another step forward, though the comment wasn't directed at him. Everyone closed in around the object in the dirt. Strong could see partial skeletal remains, but also noticed what caused the metal detector to beep and knew immediately who lay in the ground beneath Rita's garden.

Wrapped around the hip bones in the dirt was the rotted remains of a leather belt, clasped together by a rusted metal belt buckle in the shape of a dollar sign.

2

When he got back to the police station to prepare Rita's transport to District Court for arraignment, Strong tried to wrap his head around the skeleton found in the woman's garden. The State Police remained at the scene awaiting the coroner and forensics personnel.

What a mess, Strong thought as he felt acid churning in his stomach. They'd probably have to dig up the rest of the woman's flower garden and who knows how much more of her backyard to look for the bodies of the missing boys. But the skeleton they found with that signature belt buckle told Strong one thing for sure: Rita's husband never left town like the woman had claimed many years ago.

That was him buried in her garden, and that opened a whole other can of worms in the case.

"Good afternoon, Chief," Sergeant Rolek said from behind the front desk.

Nothing good about it, Strong thought as he headed to his office with the sole purpose of accessing the bottle of antacid tablets he kept in the top drawer of his desk. The discovery of the body was going to bring more attention from the news outlets. Wouldn't surprise him if even the Boston television stations sent a camera crew up. He didn't need that. He wanted to hurry up and get Rita to her arraignment and then they could cart her off to the county jail and she'd be out of whatever hair he had left under his police cap.

"Feed our lady guest?" Strong asked Rolek.

"Sure did," the sergeant said. "And boy can that girl eat."

"What's she doing now?"

"Think she might be napping," Rolek said. "Hear all kinds of heavy breathing coming from downstairs."

Strong stepped into his office and popped a couple tablets into his mouth, chewing them with vigor as he walked to the dispatch room and grabbed a cup of black coffee to wash them down. He waved to Miss Dove, who handled the calls coming into the station.

"Guess I'll have to wake her up," Strong said as he grabbed the keys to the cells in the basement and headed toward the stairs. With most of his department out at Rita's house, Rolek and Miss Dove were the only ones left at the station. Strong planned to drive Rita to the courthouse himself. He hoped it would be his last interaction with her. Till the trial at least.

He bounded down the stairs and as he reached the bottom, he heard labored breathing coming from the hall along the row of three cells. Rita had been stashed in the last one. Strong didn't think it was snoring he heard. It sounded more like an animal coughing up a hairball. As he reached the end of the hall, he saw why.

Rita hung by the neck from a strip of cloth torn from her dress and tied to a crossbar at the top of the cell door. Her throat made a gurgling sound.

"Jesus!" Strong called out and rushed toward the cell door. "Rolek!"

He unlocked the cell and swung the door open with Rita still attached to it. Her eyes bulged out in a face turning a shade of slate.

Strong reached up toward her neck to try and get to the binding, but the cloth was sunk into the flabby fat of her neck. He was about to call out again for Rolek, figuring maybe the sergeant hadn't heard him, when Rita's arms shot out, grabbed a hold of him and pulled him into the mass of her enormous bosom.

Her arms felt like thick steel and wrapped around his back, pulling him into her fat. His face was mushed into her chest and he couldn't breathe. He struggled to break free, but it only caused her to squeeze him tighter. It felt like the bones in his spine would crack.

I'm suffocating. His hands tried to find purchase on her body to push away. But it was no use. She had him pinned against her and the flesh of her breasts beneath her dress pressed into his face, smothering him. His nasal passages were blocked. He couldn't open his mouth to shout for help. *I'm going to die like this.*

Strong kicked his feet, trying to break free of her grip. He couldn't see anything, his eyes buried in her chest. Dizziness swept over him as he frantically tried to draw in air. His body felt like it was being sucked into her blubbery mass and the flesh folded around him as if her large body was absorbing his.

He heard a snapping sound and thought his spine had finally buckled. But then he felt himself falling and Rita's body was going down with him. The chief realized the cloth around her neck must have snapped.

As he hit the cement floor, Rita's entire weight came down on top of him and he felt himself slipping into unconsciousness.

3

Ryan and Russell helped Lance with the paper route after school, and then the trio headed downtown to pay Mr. Wright a visit at the newspaper office. Lance still felt the rush from the school day when everyone in his classes treated him like a returning war hero. They all wanted to know about the terror of the kidnapping and the miracle of his escape. Even Kirby Tressler came up to him in the cafeteria at lunch to slap him on the shoulder and give him an affirmative head shake, the first time an eighth-grader paid any attention to him.

What most of them wanted to know was how he had gotten out of the house. Lance told them all they'd have to read the exclusive story Mr. Wright wrote about him that would be in today's paper. He didn't want to try explaining the mysterious Mr. Shreckengast.

But Mr. Wright might have answers.

The secretary greeted them at reception, and a minute later Wright came out to escort them into his office.

"Are you here for some extra copies of your page-one debut?" Wright asked as he lit a cigarette and billowed smoke across his desk. "Or were you curious about the big news?"

Lance hadn't thought of getting more papers with his interview.

"What news?" Ryan asked.

"Why, hadn't you heard? Rita Strong-Thurlow hung herself in the police station jail. I just got back from the station and interviewing the chief."

"Is she dead?" Lance asked, barely comprehending the stunning development. One day she's feeding him spaghetti and tying him up, the next day playing her own game of hangman.

"Nearly," Wright said. The cigarette dangled from the corner of his mouth as he leaned forward onto his paper-strewn desk. "Chief said he saved her when he found her hanging in her cell and cut her down. She was unconscious though when the ambulance took her to the hospital. Chief Strong seemed pretty shaken up."

"Wow," Ryan said. "That's a bummer."

"Serves her right," Lance said.

"I'll be checking on her condition later on with the hospital," Wright said. "I'll need to get an update for tomorrow morning's edition."

Lance dreamed of someday getting to write cool stories like these. That was if he wasn't in a combat zone somewhere reporting on the action.

"Chief said she looked comatose when they hauled her out. Blood to the brain must have been cut off for a while. She won't be making it to her arraignment." Ashes from the newsman's cigarette dribbled onto the desktop. "But tell me why you're really here."

Lance stiffened in his seat. "I wanted to ask you about Shreckengast."

Wright folded his arms across his chest and eyed the boys.

"Something very strange about that man," Lance continued. "And you had a reaction to his name."

Wright stubbed out his cigarette and stood from his seat. "Come with me."

The three boys trailed him out of his office and to a door that led to the basement. Lance hesitated a bit at the top of the stairs, reflecting on his recent experience in the cellar, but felt comfortable enough with this adult leading him down that he quickly followed.

"The police have had no luck finding anyone named Shreckengast," Wright said as they descended. "Nor that boy Quinn you described. As if they vanished into thin air. The State Police wonder whether he was in cahoots with Rita. It seems odd how he'd take off with this boy. No record of any missing boy. No one by the name Shreckengast anywhere in the vicinity."

"But you know someone by that name, don't you?" Lance asked.

They reached the bottom of the stairs. Wright flicked a light switch and Lance glanced around the room filled with shelves holding giant books.

"Welcome to the morgue," Wright said.

Ryan backpedaled as a bolt of fear pierced his body. *Morgue?* That's where dead bodies are kept. Had Mr. Wright lured them down into the basement on purpose? Was he part of the child abductors along with Rita and the mysterious Shreckengast? Ryan was about to turn and flee back up the stairs when Lance grabbed him by the arm. He must have read his mind.

"Relax," Lance said. "The morgue is where they keep all the old newspapers."

Ryan breathed a sigh of relief, though his nerves felt jittery.

"Could have come up with a better name," he said.

"Not all the old issues," Wright said as he ventured into the room and the boys followed. "This paper started in the late eighteen hundreds. The real old ones are kept in the main office in Manchester. Our little news bureau here has them collected as far back as 1920." He brought them over to one of the large bookcases.

Ryan read dates on the spines as his eyes scanned the shelves. "Wow, so long ago."

"When the paper was a weekly, they would bind a whole year's worth in one volume," Wright said. "When it became a daily, they would bind about a month's worth at a time.

"These books have all those years of newspapers?" Russell asked.

"Neat, isn't it?" Lance said.

"But why?"

"To have a record library," Wright answered. He led them through the stacks. "Plus, they're used for research. Of course, we have the microfiche machines now and the papers all on film. But some of us old-school journalists like to look at the real thing." He stopped and pulled one of the large volumes off a shelf. "Here's what I'm looking for."

It looked heavy, Ryan thought as Wright carried it over to a nearby counter and set it down. He saw the date said 1927. The boys gathered around.

"One has to be very careful with these books," Wright said, as he opened the cover and began turning the news pages one by one. "They're very old and delicate. These are historic artifacts. That's why I don't smoke down here." He winked at them.

"What are we going to find in here?" Lance asked.

"Maybe an answer to your question," Wright said. "You asked me if I knew the name Shreckengast. That's a very uncommon name and one that would be memorable if it ever got stuck in your head. Have you ever heard of the Pine Island Pond Amusement Park?"

"No," Ryan and the others said in unison.

"Not surprised," Wright said. "It's been gone for more than forty years."

"Since 1927," Ryan said and pointed at the dates on the newspaper pages.

"Yes," Wright said. "Like most amusement parks, it started out as a trolley park."

"What's that?" Russell asked.

"Back in the days of the trolleys, the companies that ran them had parks at the end of many of the streetcar lines on the outskirts of the bigger towns where people could get away on the weekend for recreation and picnics. The Pine Island Pond Park was south of Manchester on the Litchfield-to-Goffstown Trolley line. It had promenades and picnic groves and eventually a roller-skating rink and pavilion for dances and music performances."

"I heard trolleys used to run right through Main Street in Maplewood," Lance said. "I heard the tracks are still there beneath the asphalt."

"True," Wright said. "But with the advent of the automobile, trolleys eventually went the way of the dinosaurs. The trolley parks began to lose their allure as people could now drive anywhere they wanted to go. Many closed, others ended up becoming amusement parks to attract more business."

"Like Canobie Lake Park in Salem," Ryan said. His parents took them there at least once a year in the summer.

"Exactly," Wright said. "That started out as a trolley park too. Amusement parks, though, required a lot more land, so the people who bought the Pine Island Pond Park and wanted to turn it into an amusement park needed more space. Especially for parking, since patrons would be coming in automobiles now instead of the trolley. A great tract of land beside the park was owned by a local family and they sold it to the developers and the Pine Island Pond Amusement Park was born. They had bumper cars, a Ferris wheel, flying scooters, a carousel, a dark ride from the Pretzel manufacturer, those were popular, and an old wooden roller coaster called the Mammoth."

"Sounds cool," Lance said. "Wish it were still there. That would be a shorter ride than Canobie Lake."

"What happened to it?" Ryan asked. This story must be leading somewhere. Wright kept flipping the newspaper pages, but Ryan saw nothing that meant anything to them.

"One of the rides was a walk-through funhouse called the House of Phantasmagoria," Wright said.

"Like the House of Seven Gables at Canobie Lake," Ryan said. "That's my favorite."

"Exactly," Wright said. "The landowner who sold his property to the amusement park company did so on the condition he could have a funhouse constructed that he would operate."

"Let me guess," Ryan interrupted. "This man's name was Shreckengast."

"That's correct," Wright said. "Ezra Shreckengast, who had inherited all his land from his parents when they passed."

"That's bonkers," Lance said.

"Why is the amusement park no longer there?" Russell asked.

"It's sort of still there," Wright said. "A few remains of it anyway. You see, in 1927, there was a fire in the House of Phantasmagoria that killed seventeen people." He finally turned to the front page of the newspaper that had a blaring headline titled: *Funhouse Horror.* A smaller subhead beneath it: *More than a dozen killed in amusement park conflagration.* A photograph beneath the headlines depicted the charred frame of a burnt-out building. "Killed mostly kids, teenagers, a few college students. Some escaped, but most were burned to death."

"Holy smoke!" Russell said, not seeing the irony in his comment.

"How'd it happen?" Lance asked.

"One of the survivors said they saw someone using a cigarette lighter inside the funhouse," Wright said with a shrug, "maybe to light their way in the dark. Who knows. After that, lawsuits followed and the place was abandoned. A fence was put up around the park during the litigation and the owners went bankrupt. A few other amusement parks around New England bought some of the rides and carted them off, but the rest were left to rot. And are still there."

"That's horrible," Ryan said, thinking burning to death must be worse than what his brother Curtis suffered in the frigid waters of the Piscataquog River.

"There actually are a couple residents in town who escaped from the fire," Wright said. "I've tried to interview them for stories about it every time an anniversary comes up, but they refuse to talk about it. Can't say I blame them."

"Who are they?" Lance asked.

"Darrin and Lydia Fifer," Wright said. "They live over at the Downey boardinghouse on Elm Steet."

"I know them!" Ryan exclaimed. How many times had he gone into that house and seen them, but never knew they experienced this horrific event?

"But what about this Shreckengast guy I saw the other night?" Lance asked. "Was that his family that ran the funhouse?"

Wright turned a couple pages to where the story of the funhouse fire continued. With the jump page was a photograph of a tall, thin man with a narrow face, long nose, and pointed chin.

"That's him!" Lance yelled and pointed his finger at the picture. "That's the guy who let us out of Rita's cellar."

"But that fire was over forty years ago," Ryan said.

"He'd be an old man now," Russell added.

"Doesn't matter," Wright said as he shook his head. "Ezra Shreckengast died in the funhouse fire."

4

After dinner at the boardinghouse, most of the guests retired to the front parlor to watch the local news, probably to see if the only New Hampshire television station out of Manchester had any developments on the arrest of Rita Stone-Thurlow. Mortimer grabbed the Downeys' newspaper and settled in the back parlor, unable to believe what became of his former carnival companion.

He closed the pocket doors dividing the room to shut out the clatter of the idiot box and settled into one of the chairs by the side bay window, ignoring Harold Lothrop, who remained seated in the chair opposite and constantly looked out the window to the side yard and street.

Mortimer gazed at the picture of Rita being led by police into the station house in the Town Square. Her face looked a fright, as if aghast that her photo would be taken under such unflattering circumstances. He gave kudos to the journalist who dared to get close enough to photograph her. She looked like she could bite someone's face off.

What did it all mean? He might have thought she was capable of unspeakable cruelty, but never imagined she'd kidnap kids. His eyes pored through the story till he got to the part about the Stanton boy and his miraculous escape from what the paper termed a 'house of horror' along with an unknown and unaccounted second boy known only by the first name Quinn.

Mortimer's fingers trembled; the newspaper shook in his hands.

Quinn?

Is it possible?

He read on. The Stanton kid described the boy as younger, with light blond hair and said that the kid told him he was ten.

It can't be.

Mortimer's heart sped up. It felt like it was bouncing off his rib cage. *How could this be? My Quinn? Oh my god, could it really be Quinn?*

His mind raced around inside his head like a squirrel gathering nuts as Mortimer picked up pieces of a puzzle that had been strewn across the floor. *The magic cabinet.* Rita said she got rid of it long ago. What if she lied? When he performed the trick earlier this month, it hadn't worked.

Or had it?

If Rita lied to him and still had the cabinet, then maybe the trick worked.

Maybe Quinn did return.

Only not in the new cabinet Mortimer had purchased and brought to his room. It only made sense that Quinn would return to the original cabinet.

It worked. It had to. The magic worked and Quinn was here. But where?

He read the rest of the story, flipping to the jump page with fury and learning the mysterious boy left with a man only known by the name Shreckengast.

Who the hell is that?

He must get to Rita somehow and find out. He lowered the newspaper to his lap only to be met by the staring eyes of Harold Lothrop across from him.

"You all right?" Lothrop asked. "You look pale."

Mortimer didn't answer. His mind struggled with how he could get to Rita.

The pocket door slid open and Calvin Armstrong poked his head out.

"Latest development in the news," he said, as if the two men were waiting to be informed. "Rita Stone-Thurlow hung herself in jail."

Mortimer looked up at him, aghast, as he let the paper slip through his fingers and fall to the carpet.

"Taken to the hospital in a comatose state," Armstrong continued. "This story just gets better and better. About time something interesting happened in this town." He turtled his head back inside and slid the door closed.

Can't be, Mortimer thought. He needed her. Needed answers. Then it hit him. The Stanton boy. He looked at Lothrop.

"Where's that boy live?" he asked. "The newspaper boy?"

"Over on Oak Street," Lothrop said. "Why?"

"We need to chat." Mortimer jumped up from his chair and left the room. He was out the door and down the street in a flash.

5

Ryan and Russell sat with Lance on the front steps of the Stanton house on the corner of Walnut and Oak, discussing the revelations revealed at the newspaper office.

"Now do you believe?" Ryan asked Lance. "Something strange is happening in Maplewood. Something unexplainable."

His friend shook his head as if trying to disperse disbelief from his thoughts.

"That guy, Shreckengast," Lance said. "That picture in the paper looked exactly like the man I saw."

"Are you sure?" Russell asked. "I mean, that was an old newspaper. The picture was grainy."

"It was him." He looked at Ryan. "It said he died in the fire. But maybe he escaped."

Ryan sensed his friend clutching at straws. "And didn't age?"

Lance put his head in his hands. "It couldn't be."

"The question is," Ryan said, "what do we do now?"

"I don't know," Lance said.

"I have an idea," Ryan said. "The three of us help you with your paper route in the morning, and then we take a bike ride."

"Where to?" Russell asked.

"That amusement park," Ryan answered. "Pine Island Pond. The remains are still there."

Lance looked up. "But that's got to be twenty miles away at least. That'll take—"

"A couple hours to get there," Ryan finished. "That's why we get an early start. And pack a lunch. Probably won't get back till late afternoon. Give us plenty of time to explore the place. Tell our parents we're going riding for the day. I heard it's gonna be nearly seventy degrees tomorrow. Tell them we want one last bike ride before the nice weather ends."

"And where do we tell them we're going?" Russell asked.

"We don't."

"What do you think we'll find there?"

Ryan shrugged. "Who knows? But if the remains of that funhouse are still there, maybe we can find a clue about something."

"I don't know," Russell said. "You sure we should?"

"It's what the Hardy Boys would do."

"Worth a try," Lance said. "At the very least, it'll be good to get away from here for the day."

"My mom will kill me if she finds out," Russell said.

"Then don't let her," Ryan told him.

After they came to an agreement on the plan, Ryan looked down Walnut Street and saw the old magician coming their way.

"Look," Ryan said with a nod in that direction. The others turned to see.

"Here comes your Barnabas Collins," Lance said.

"You guys thought he was behind the kidnappings," Russell said.

"I still have my doubts about him," Ryan said. "He gives me an eerie feeling." He wondered where the old man was heading, but then the guy spotted them and Ryan had his answer. The man's face seemed bunched in a snarl as he approached the walkway. The three of them stood as he arrived. The old man's face looked pale. Maybe he hadn't gotten his supply of blood for the day.

The magician stopped and looked at Lance.

"You," he said as he pointed a shaky finger. "You're the paperboy?"

"That's me," Lance said. "I delivered to the Downey house today, so don't say you didn't get a copy."

"I saw the paper," the man said. "Read the story about you. That boy you mentioned. You said his name was Quinn?"

Lance nodded.

"Did he say where he came from?"

"No," Lance said. "He wasn't sure. At least, he didn't make much sense. Said something about his parents abandoning him, or sending him away. Something like that."

The old man scowled. "And when you got out, he went off with that man you mentioned?"

"Shreckengast," Lance said. "Quinn said something about the man had taken care of him before he ended up there."

"What business is this of yours?" Ryan asked, noticing the man didn't seem so scary any more. In fact, he appeared almost helpless. Or lost.

The old man ignored him. He reached inside his cloak, pulled something out and held it up to Lance's face. A photograph.

"Did he look like this?"

Ryan and Russell both peered over Lance's shoulders to get a glance at the picture. It was an old photo, sepia-toned with yellowed edges.

"That's him!" Lance said.

Ryan nearly stepped back from the look on the old man's face, halfway between enlightenment and bewilderment.

"I must find him," the man said and stormed off down the street.

"What the heck was that about?" Russell asked. "Why does he have a picture of that kid?"

Lance turned to face them. "He knows him. That Quinn boy."

"Maybe it's his grandfather," Ryan said. "Maybe that's why he came to Maplewood, to find this kid."

"It's kind of weird that nobody's found the boy," Lance said. "I wonder what that Shreckengast guy did with him?"

6

Mortimer roamed around town, his brain straining with the myriad of thoughts bouncing in his skull. *Quinn, here? Could it be? Still a boy after all these years. Is it even possible? Rita lied to me. Keeping the boy stashed in her basement. Kidnapping other boys in town. What does it all mean?*

And who's this Shreckengast the Stanton boy said Quinn went away with?

And where did they go?

Mortimer felt the weird presence in town. He sensed at Harvest Fest that something was wrong with the pumpkins the farmer was selling. Something rotten in them. Now he heard that man had mysteriously run off. *Or had he?*

Mortimer didn't want to go back to the boardinghouse right away. He couldn't face sitting at the dinner table with the others. Not with the jumble of thoughts in his head. That Lothrop guy would know something was up. The writer had been acting weird lately, always staring out the window with a frightened look on his face.

Why did the man never leave the house? What was he afraid of that he tried to escape in the bottom of a bottle?

And Fifer? He too had the habit of looking out the window with a nervous jitter. What was eating him?

No, dinner at the boardinghouse was not going to do tonight, so Mortimer went downtown and consumed a miserable meal at a local dinette. He sat at the end of the counter and ate a dinner of warm meatloaf with a mushroom gravy, mashed potatoes – instant, judging by the taste – and cold peas. A meal unfit for a king of magic.

Mortimer would have chuckled at the thought if his insides weren't eating at him from something besides the greasy meatloaf. He had performed a great feat of magic and hadn't even realized it. Maybe the last illusion he had up his sleeve. No, wait, there had been more than that. He succeeded in resurrecting Daimon when he pulled his long-dead rabbit from his magic hat. *But not really dead, was it?* More like some abomination spawned from the dark corners of prestidigitation.

Thoughts of Daimon brought back the memory from last weekend when he followed the rabbit to that vacant house. Of all places.

Mortimer paid his bill, leaving a less-than-modest tip, and rushed out of the dinette. He hurried down Poplar Street. Night had fallen and the streets were quiet, except for the swishing of crusty leaves as his feet swept him along the sidewalk. He turned left on Carriage Lane and walked until he came upon the vacant house halfway down.

The house was dark. Not a light or sign of life behind its blackened windows. He unlatched the metal gate and it screeched when he swung it open. The house seemed to grow as he walked down the stone pathway toward it, as if the old boards and timbers stretched to tower over him, preparing to swallow him whole.

Mortimer hesitantly ascended the front steps and knocked on the front door. He took a cautious step back before returning down the steps and looking at the darkened windows on both sides of the front door. He examined the other windows on the first and second floors, too.

In each window sat an uncarved pumpkin. In the darkness of the house's interior, the pumpkins looked blacker than orange. Though no faces had yet been carved into them, he couldn't help feeling they were looking out the windows at him. Watching him. He backed away from the house a few more steps.

"Quinn!" he shouted as he gazed up at those two arched windows at the top that poked out of the mansard roof and seemed like eyes looking down at him. "Quinn!"

His voice echoed in the silent night. He gazed around the street at the other homes on Carriage Lane. Windows were lit in each of them and he imagined families behind those doors going about their normal business on a Friday night, unaware of what might have taken hold in this vacant house among their homes.

He called out Quinn's name one more time and wondered if the neighbors would hear his cries and look out their windows and wonder what this lonely old man was doing screaming a name in the middle of the night.

"I'll be back," he whispered, and fled the neighborhood, anxious to get back to the boardinghouse and the safety of his room on the third floor. As he passed through the plaza of the Town Square, his eyes were drawn to the library. Gargoyles perched on the corners of the roof seemed to spy on him and follow his wobbly steps along the cobblestones.

Mortimer was relieved when he reached the boardinghouse and entered through the driveway side door. He heard a clattering of dishes as Wilfred Downey cleaned up in the kitchen. Mortimer started to go up the back staircase but Darrin Fifer grabbed him by the arm.

"Hey," Fifer said. "Did you see anybody out front?"

"What are you talking about?" He shot the annoying man a look of contempt.

"A policeman?" Fifer said. "Did you see a policeman out front watching the house. Maybe flicking a cigarette lighter?"

"Let go of me," Mortimer said and ripped his arm from the man's grasp. "I saw nobody out there. Not a living soul." He hurried up the staircase.

As he reached the end of the third-floor hall, he noticed his door was ajar.

I didn't leave it like that. He remembered how much of a rush he had been in when he'd left the house, but he felt certain he hadn't left the door cracked open. Had someone gone in his room? Lothrop, he thought, snooping around. The writer was suspicious about something for sure. Or maybe Armstrong. That guy was always poking his nose in where it didn't belong.

Mortimer pushed the door open slowly, so as not to rattle its creaky hinges. He scanned the darkness, shifting left and right, looking for something out of place. He stepped inside. Everything seemed normal. He removed his cloak and hung it on the coatrack to his right. Nothing out of place.

He closed the door and saw the figure hiding in the dark behind it.

A young boy whose blond hair still shone in the shadows of the room's corner.

The boy held Mortimer's magic top hat in his hands.

"Quinn?" Mortimer whispered over the sound of his thumping heart. *It can't be. But it is.* He recognized that same lost look in the boy's eyes the day he sent him into that magic cabinet. "You're alive."

"I don't know you," the boy said.

Hearing his voice caused a great swell in Mortimer's chest. It had been so long since he had listened to the sound of his son talking. He heard Quinn speak many times in his dreams all those years he searched for his son, but that never seemed real. Not like this. Not like now.

"It's me," Mortimer said, his voice cracking as he struggled to talk. "It's your father."

The boy's eyes widened, first in surprise, then shock, but they soon narrowed with suspicion.

"You're not my father," Quinn said. "You're an old man. My father is young. You're a liar." The boy moved toward the door.

Mortimer reached out and grabbed the boy's arm. No, he thought. He couldn't lose him again.

"Wait," Mortimer said.

The boy looked at him with eyes that burned.

Something moved within the magic hat.

Mortimer's eyes dropped down to that dark empty opening. Something shot out. White mangy fur and red, blood-glazed eyes.

Daimon, he thought. Or what it had once been.

The rabbit sank its teeth into Mortimer's forearm.

He screamed. He released his grip on Quinn's arm and the rabbit let go and disappeared back into the hat. Quinn bolted out the door and down the hall. Mortimer grabbed his right arm; a throbbing pain coursed through it and blood leaked from the bite. He heard the pounding footsteps as the boy ran down the back staircase.

Mortimer stumbled back toward his bed, dizziness sweeping over him. He looked at the wound and the blood oozing out of it. A fogginess flooded his head and he felt he might pass out, so he sat on the bed. The pain in his arm burned right down to the bone. Mortimer didn't notice at first that someone else had entered the room until he looked up and saw a figure standing in his doorway.

Lothrop.

The writer stepped into the room and stood over him, looking down at the wounded arm.

"I'll go get a bandage," Lothrop said. "And then we'll talk."

OCTOBER 24

1

Three boys on bicycles pedaled at a steady pace down the country road, aware of the nearly three-hour journey ahead. Backpacks were loaded with sandwiches and each carried a canteen of water either slung over a shoulder or strapped to their fender. Lance had plotted the route beforehand and kept the map folded up in his pack.

Route 114 would be quicker, Lance told them before they departed, but it was a state road busy with traffic. His less-traveled route stuck to secondary roads. Although they were more winding, which would add to their mileage, they were safer.

"Less likely to attract attention," Lance had said.

Who he felt would have been paying attention to them, Ryan wasn't sure, but he trusted his friend. When they first reached the edge of the town line of Maplewood, Ryan pulled over.

"What's up?" Lance asked as he and Russell came to a stop alongside him.

Ryan gazed back the way they had come.

"Just thinking," he said. "I've never ridden my bike this far from home before." He gazed at the long road ahead lined with trees whose remaining leaves burned with red, yellow, and orange flames like torches lighting the way.

They pushed on, past houses and rolling fields of farmland, and sometimes through long stretches of woods. They were grateful when the road declined and they could coast down the hills, giving their legs a chance to rest, but agonized when they came to a hill.

No matter how low a gear they shifted into, they struggled to get up it without relenting, getting off their bikes, and walking.

During necessary breaks, they chugged water from their canteens and enjoyed a snack of corn chips or pretzels. Then back on the bikes and on track, hoping to reach the remains of the Pine Island Pond Amusement Park by lunchtime.

The morning had been cool but the day warmed up; the weather forecasters had predicted it would hit the seventies by midafternoon. A brisk wind blew against them as they rode, but once the sun cleared the trees overhead, the rays took away some of the chill. They stopped from time to time for a water break and to double-check the map.

"How much farther?" Russell asked. "My arm's itching." He poked a finger under the cast to get at a hard-to-reach spot.

Lance studied the map. "Shouldn't be long now," he said before folding it back up and shoving it into his backpack. "Let's go."

Ryan wasn't sure what they expected to find when they got there, but he hoped it was worth it. The exhausting ride only made him think about how much he dreaded the return trip. It would seem twice as long he figured, and he knew from how many hills they rode down that going back was going to consist of a lot more uphill climbs.

As they got closer, Lance took the lead and he seemed to have generated some newfound energy that made it difficult to keep up. Must be close, Ryan thought, and then Lance went off-road and came to a stop near some railroad tracks. Lance glanced back and waited for them to catch up.

"There's a trestle here," Lance said. "We can cross the Merrimack. The park should be on the other side."

As they followed him along the rutted trail that led to the railroad bridge, Ryan couldn't help but think it looked like the trestle in Maplewood. He thought how strange it would be if they had gone on one big loop and ended up back where they started.

But he trusted Lance's map-reading skills and sense of direction, and as they crossed the wooden walkway alongside the rails of the bridge, Ryan noticed how much bigger this river was than the one in

Maplewood. The river looked far below, but the sound of its rushing water washing around the bridge's pylons made it sound like the river would rip the trestle from its moorings, and Ryan couldn't wait to get across to the other side and safely back on land.

A side road on the other end of the railroad bridge led them down a narrow, wooded lane that came abruptly to an end. Through the trees, which were mostly bare, Ryan saw a rusted metal chain-link fence about eight feet high. Beyond that, he saw the curved track of a roller coaster winding through a thicket of trees and shrubs.

Ryan felt a rush whip through him, as if he were on that ride, his stomach lurching as it raced around a hairpin curve. They looked at each other and smiled.

"It's really here," Russell said.

"Let's eat first," Lance said.

They agreed and broke out their sandwiches, but Ryan had little interest in his Fluffernutter as all sense of hunger had left him with the anticipation of exploring the park. He made quick work of the sandwich, as did the others, and took a few more gulps of water.

They stashed their bikes in nearby bushes and climbed the metal fence, attacking it like an obstacle course on an Army training base. Russell had some difficulty with his bad arm hampering him, but they all made it over and dropped to the ground.

The other side of the fence ushered in a feeling of foreboding in Ryan's gut that replaced the exhilaration he felt before they entered the park. He thought of the funhouse fire article in the newspaper Mr. Wright showed them. The image of those lost souls burning to death in the blaze made him realize that, no matter what strange happenings were occurring in Maplewood, if there were ghosts, they'd surely be here.

"Where do we look?" Ryan asked Lance.

"Maybe there's a sign with a directory or something," Lance said, "showing the layout of the park." He pointed. "Head this way for now."

As they passed the remains of the wooden roller coaster, Ryan followed the vines that weaved their way up through the wooden support posts to the top of the curved track, as if they were trying to pull the tracks down to the ground. The ride beyond the track showed him nature must have succeeded there. A jumbled pile of wood and metal stacked upon itself was all that remained. It lay like kindling waiting for a match.

"Amazing," Lance said as they passed it.

Ahead stood a Ferris wheel, devoid of its passenger cars, only an old spoked wheel frozen in rust. Next down the weed-choked path came the dodgem-car ride, a skeletal frame all that was left of the roof over the attraction. Beneath sat the ride's cars, their colors faded, discarded among a floor of dried dead leaves. The poles that had reached up to the ceiling of the attraction where it got its electricity now lay bent over on the ground, absent of any spark that had once brought the vehicles to life.

The boys stood against the rail where eager riders would have waited for their turn and stared at the abandoned cars.

"What a waste," Russell said with a shake of his head.

"I can't believe they just left everything here like this," Ryan said. "All these years, this stuff just sitting here."

"Hey, look," Lance said. He pointed toward a sign. They ran over to it. The sign depicted the layout of the park with animated drawings of each attraction. The pictures were faded and the paint chipped and missing in spots.

"There," Ryan said, pointing to the upper left-hand corner. He had to fill in some of the letters from what he remembered from the newspaper article Mr. Wright had showed them. 'Mr. Shreckengast's House of Phantasmagoria'. The drawing was a typical spooky multi-gabled house with ghostly things hovering about it.

"Let's go," Lance said, and they ran off.

When they got to the location, they stopped and stared in silence.

Ryan had no idea what to expect, nor understood what they hoped to accomplish with their mission. It seemed like they had to take some kind of action to make them feel like they were doing something. Anything.

All that remained of the funhouse was a cement foundation filled in with dirt.

"That's it?" Russell asked in disbelief. "All that way for this?"

"What a bummer," Ryan said.

"They must have hauled away the ruins from the fire," Lance said.

"After they dug out the bones of the victims," Ryan said. He immediately realized his mistake and turned to Russell, who looked upon him with his eyes wide and mouth open. "I'm sorry, Russ, I didn't mean—"

Russell turned away and walked off.

"It just slipped out," Ryan said as he went after his friend. Russell looked about to cry and maybe didn't want the others to see. Ryan caught up to him. His eyes looked wet.

"Ever since Miss Sheriden brought that skeleton into class," Russell said, "I can't stop thinking about what happened to my dad."

"I know."

Russell pointed over to where the funhouse once stood.

"My dad died like those people," he said, his voice elevated. "And everyone lied to me about the fact that he wasn't going to turn into a set of bones like that. But it's all lies. We're all going to be just bones someday. All of us." He snuffled up some snot and wiped his eyes.

The foundation of the funhouse stuck up about a foot out of the ground. Ryan looked and saw Lance step over the cement line in front of them and enter the interior.

"What are you doing?" Ryan asked.

"Looking for clues," Lance said. "You know, like the Hardy Boys would do."

"What do you think there is to find?"

Lance shrugged. "I don't know. Anything."

Ryan and Russell joined him and soon the three of them had found sticks and were poking in the dirt, kicking up rocks, sifting through the sand. They spent nearly half an hour at it before Ryan got bored and figured the whole thing was pointless.

Till Russell found something.

"Hey!" he called out and dropped to his knees. He began digging with his good arm and pulled something from the dirt.

"What is it?" Lance asked as he and Ryan rushed over to his side.

"It's a cigarette lighter," Russell said. It was caked in dirt. He rubbed it against the leg of his jeans to try and clean it off.

"Does it still work?" Ryan asked.

"I doubt it," Lance said.

Russell opened the top and flicked the wheel with his thumb. Nothing. Not even a spark. He closed it and turned it over in his hand a couple times, admiring it.

"It's got writing on it," Russell said and stood up.

"What's it say?" Ryan asked.

Russell held it up to his eyes and rubbed more dirt off.

"Just initials. D.F."

"Let's save it," Lance said. "Good work, Russ."

They continued poking through the dirt and Lance was the next to find something. It appeared to be an oval locket, no longer attached to a chain. The others gathered around him as he pried it open. A picture inside was too faded to discern anything, but it might have been a woman. He tucked it in his pocket.

They continued searching for a little while longer until Ryan decided he'd had enough.

"I think we should head back," he said, not looking forward to the grueling ride home. He already felt exhausted.

"I guess," Lance said.

"This whole thing was a bust," Ryan said. "I just want to go home."

As they were leaving the foundation, Ryan stubbed his sneaker on something buried in the dirt and nearly tripped.

"Wait," he said and bent down to examine what it was. The others watched as he dug in the dirt. "What the hell?" He pulled out an old View-Master toy.

"Oh, shit," Lance said.

Ryan brushed the dirt off and held it up in the light to examine it.

"I'm not even going to say it," Lance said.

Ryan knew what he meant. This was the same kind of toy Curtis had in his hand when he ran across the frozen river after Smokey. But it couldn't be the same one, of course. That one was at the bottom of the river somewhere. What Ryan couldn't understand was what this toy was doing here. At the time of the funhouse fire, this toy hadn't even existed.

So how did it end up here?

Though there was no disk in it, Ryan felt the urge to hold it up to his eyes and look through it. He started to raise it up to his face when Lance's voice stopped him.

"Maybe we found these things for a reason," his friend said. "Like we were meant to find them."

"Like someone helped us find them?" Ryan said and looked up at the others.

Is that you, Curtis? Are you trying to tell me something? Do you know something about this place?

They stashed their loot in their backpacks and went back out to the fence and climbed over. On their bikes they began the long ride home. Ryan felt a renewed sense of energy, maybe from the item in the pack on his back, and he couldn't wait to get back to Maplewood.

2

Mortimer barged into Harold's room, startling him and causing him to spill the bourbon he had been pouring into his coffee mug. Harold sat at the small table by the window in his bedroom and wiped the drops off it with the back of his hand.

"Jesus H. Christ!" Harold said. "You nearly scared me to death."

"Did you see it?" Mortimer yelled as he waved the newspaper around. "Did you see the morning paper?"

"Of course I did." He gestured to the edition lying on the table.

"She hung herself." Mortimer sat down on the end of the bed, the newspaper crumpled in his lap. "She's dead, or nearly dead, comatose, brain-dead." He waved his arms in the air. "It makes no difference. Bottom line is, there's no way to talk to her anymore."

Harold's tired eyes examined the man. They were tired for a reason. Harold hadn't slept well last night, not after the talk they'd had when he'd finished bandaging Mortimer's arm. The magician had broken down and told him what had transpired since the night he'd arrived in Maplewood, which culminated in his attempt to bring his son back from wherever his bungled magic trick had sent him forty years ago.

The discovery lurking in Mortimer's room last night confirmed his magic trick had worked all too well. It had brought back Quinn. *And something more.*

"What do we do now?" Mortimer said and put his head in his hands. The newspaper slipped from his lap to the floor.

"Remember what I told you last night?" Harold thought about the things that had been happening. He thought about the goblin who appeared almost every night outside his window and all the other strange things Ryan and his friends had experienced. "You created an opening when you brought your son back. And something horrible slipped through with him."

3

Shortly before midnight, Ryan lay awake in his bottom bunk. A car sounded outside, which he recognized from its putt-putting engine as Elsie's Bug as she dropped Dane off after their Saturday night of carousing. He envied his brother enjoying normal fun while he and his friends were caught in some supernatural quagmire.

For what else could it be?

He gazed over at his desk where the View-Master rested. They didn't just find these objects by accident, he thought. They were drawn to them. If he could only understand why.

Ryan heard the front door open, close, and then his brother's footsteps coming up the stairs. After a brief stop in the bathroom, the next sound was his brother's bedroom door closing. He thought about approaching Dane in the morning and letting him in on the things he and the others had discovered, and the things they couldn't quite explain. Maybe they needed an older person's perspective. Mr. Lothrop hadn't been as much help as he'd hoped. The old man was hiding things. Something scared him. He thought about Miss Sheriden, but she was a science teacher. She'd find logical explanations for the things he couldn't explain. And there was no way he would try and talk to his parents. They would not be of any use. So, maybe Dane could help. He'd ask the others tomorrow what they thought.

With his brother in bed for the night, the house grew quiet again. Ryan threw his covers off and walked over to his desk and stared down at the View-Master. He picked up the toy and turned it over in his hands. He had cleaned it up when he got home earlier today but it still looked old and worn. He brought it up to his eyes.

Without a viewing reel inserted, he didn't expect to see anything. He didn't.

He pulled it away from his face.

"Why did I find you?" he whispered.

A scratching came at his door that startled him and he nearly dropped the toy. He recognized the sound and walked over and opened the door enough to let Smokey in. He didn't want the dog in here but knew he would annoy him all night if he didn't let him in.

The dog went to the center of the room and sat. His head lifted and looked toward the top bunk bed.

Ryan still held the View-Master in his hands. Goose bumps rose along his bare arms. He contemplated for a second before raising the toy to his eyes and aiming it in the direction of the top bunk. He pressed down on the lever on the side of the toy, as if advancing the next frame.

There was nothing there.

OCTOBER 25

1

Lance and Ryan arrived at the boardinghouse after some of the residents had returned from church services. Mr. Downey answered the front door.

"What are you doing here?" Wilfred asked. "They didn't decide to start having a Sunday paper, did they?"

"No," Lance said. "Thank goodness. It's the only morning I get to sleep in."

"We're here to see the Fifers," Ryan said.

"Darrin and Lydia?" Wilfred's face showed surprise, as they'd never interacted much with the only married tenants of the home. "What on earth for?"

"School project," Lance said.

The old landlord looked baffled, but ushered them in.

"They're in the front parlor," he said and then vanished down the hall toward the back of the house.

Lance and Ryan entered the parlor smiling at the Fifers, who were seated on the couch watching television. Lance recognized an old Abbott and Costello film on TV, *Hold That Ghost.*

"Hello, boys," Lydia said as they both greeted them with curious glances.

Lance noticed Darrin was tapping his left foot nervously.

"We were wondering if we could talk to you about something?" Lance said.

"Us?" Darrin looked confused. "What about?"

Lance and Ryan sat on nearby chairs.

"The funhouse fire at Pine Island Pond Park," Ryan said.

The faces of both Fifers turned ashen. Lydia gave her husband a desperate look.

"What are you talking about?" Darrin said in a halting voice.

"Mr. Wright at the newspaper office told us you both survived the fire," Lance said. "I'm writing a historical piece on it for a class assignment and thought it would be great to have an eyewitness account." It was all a lie, but he figured it sounded plausible.

Darrin got up from the couch and went to the hall entrance, looking down it to see if anyone was nearby. Then he went to the pocket doors that separated the two parlor rooms and closed them, even though there was no one on the other side. Before returning to the couch, he turned the volume down on the television.

"I wish Monroe Wright had kept our business private," Darrin said. "He had no right to let you boys know about that."

"Can you tell us about it?" Lance asked. He had brought one of the reporter's notepads that Mr. Wright had lent him a while back and took out a pencil.

"We don't like to talk about it," Lydia said. Her face reddened and she appeared on the verge of crying.

"It must have been horrible," Lance said, trying to prod the Fifers, a tactic he learned from Mr. Wright.

"More than anyone your age needs to hear about," Darrin said, more agitated. "What kind of class assignment is this? Don't you kids have more important things to learn? I should go down to the school and talk with the principal."

"You didn't see how the fire started, did you?" Ryan asked.

Darrin shot up from the couch.

"You want to know what I saw?" he said, his voice heightened. "I saw kids on fire, screaming in pain."

"Dear," Lydia said, looking up at her husband and patting his arm.

"No," he said to her. "They want to know." He looked back at the boys. "I was just a graduate student. Lydia and I were dating, preparing to get married as soon as I finished classes. We were out having a fun day, and then it all turned horrible and the next thing we knew, we were fighting for our lives to get out of that death trap. We crawled over the bodies of the dead and the ones who were going to be dead as soon as they stopped screaming. We were lucky to get out of that hell alive." Sweat dripped from his face as if he could feel the heat from the inferno as he told the story.

Lance had stopped writing, afraid to capture any more details from his horrid story. He didn't know what to say and was glad Ryan spoke next.

"Did you see anyone with a cigarette lighter?"

Darrin's face froze. For a moment, Lance didn't think it would unlock. But it did.

"Who sent you here?" Darrin asked, his eyes darting between Lance and Ryan. "Did you see a policeman out front?"

"What?" Lance asked, befuddled. "No."

Lydia stood and grabbed on to her husband's arm. She looked at the boys with a gentle pleading.

"I think we've said enough," she said and led her husband out of the room and upstairs.

Lance stared at Ryan in disbelief and then glanced at the television, which was still on, though the sound was turned down too low to hear anything. On the screen he saw a hidden door open in a wall and a figure with a sheet over it step out.

"Let's go," Ryan said, and Lance didn't have to think twice.

Out on the sidewalk, Lance felt he could breathe again. "That was something," he said.

"Yeah, strange," Ryan said. "And are you thinking what I'm thinking?"

"What's that?"

"The cigarette lighter Russell found at the funhouse site yesterday," Ryan said.

"What about it?"

"The initials on it were: D.F."

2

Dark fell early since Daylight Saving Time ended after midnight the night before. The sun had set before it was even five o'clock. After a dinner of shepherd's pie that Mortimer shoveled down his throat as quick as possible, he found himself making his way down Elm Street toward Washington.

Where *her* house stood.

He doubted the police were keeping the place under watch now that the 'Witch of Maplewood', as some called her, lay dormant in the hospital in Manchester. How much longer her wicked body would cling to life, he no longer cared.

What he wanted was to get a peek inside her basement.

Mortimer needed to see for himself if indeed Rita had his original magic cabinet hidden down there. He must know. Maybe there was some way for him to redeem himself for all he had wrought upon this town. Harold Lothrop had been right. This was all his doing and he must try and rectify it. He had suffered enough losing Quinn. There was no need for the residents of Maplewood to undergo the torment inflicted upon them by his carelessness.

He passed houses where the smell of burning leaves was lifted into the sky from the smoke pouring out of metal barrels. The scent of toasted pumpkins filtered out through the eye-slits in carved jack-o'-lanterns perched on the railings of neighbors' front porches. If only the people in the houses knew the danger behind those glowing eyes.

The house lay ahead.

He stood on the sidewalk in front of it like he had many times before. Flimsy yellow caution tape lay crisscrossed over the front door, looking no less like the Halloween decorations on some of the other houses in the neighborhoods.

Do Not Enter.

Mortimer ignored the sign and the entire front entrance and made his way across the grass to the back of the house. He needed to be as inconspicuous as possible; he didn't know what nosy neighbors might be poking their beady little eyes out their windows at the crazy lady's house. In the backyard he became enveloped in the shadows. He hoped maybe the bulkhead doors to the basement might be unlocked, or easy enough to break into.

He approached the bulkhead and prepared to reach for the handle when the doors opened.

Mortimer stepped back, his heart given a sudden jolt. *The police?* He looked for somewhere to hide. But it was too late. As he looked at the man who came up the bulkhead stairs, there was no doubt the man was aware of his presence.

Mortimer's heart got its second jounce in a matter of seconds. The tall man dressed in black, thin as a stovepipe, who emerged from the basement wore Mortimer's magic top hat on his head. The man smiled at him when he stepped out of the bulkhead.

"You," Mortimer said as he pointed a shaky finger.

"Ezra Shreckengast," the man introduced himself. "I've been expecting you."

The man stepped aside and Mortimer heard more commotion coming from Rita's basement. Another figure appeared, a young man whose face looked like he was rising out of the burning sulfurs of hell. He held on to one end of a long wooden box that he lugged up out of the cellar. The other end was upheld by another young man, or teenager, with similar disfigured features.

The item they carried like a coffin was his magic cabinet.

"What are you doing?" Mortimer rasped with shock.

"Acquiring some things I need," Shreckengast said.

"Those are mine." Mortimer eyed him with contempt. He wanted to lunge at the man, but knew nothing of his powers. He sensed lethalness in the man's sly eyes.

"They are yours no longer," Shreckengast said. "I have need of this hat and that box. There are many things I want to accomplish with them."

"My son," Mortimer said. "Where is Quinn?"

"Oh, you mean the boy you abandoned?" His smile grew wicked. "The boy you sent away to a dark place for a lifetime?"

"That wasn't my fault," Mortimer said, though he knew different. "It was an accident."

"That's why this hat and box needs to stay in the hands of someone who can appreciate their powers."

Mortimer felt tears build up in the corners of his eyes. "I just want my son."

Shreckengast motioned to the pair, who set the cabinet upright on the ground. He walked over to it and opened the cabinet door.

"Enter the cabinet," Shreckengast said and gestured at the darkness inside. "It'll take you right to your son." He smiled.

Mortimer wished he could wipe that grin off the man's face. But he knew he wasn't capable of it. Just an old man without any magic powers left up his sleeve. He gazed inside the cabinet. Something swirled in the shadows.

It's a trick. He backed up a step. *This man can't fool even an old magician like me.*

"What are you waiting for?" Shreckengast asked. "Quinn is expecting you."

"No!" Mortimer backed away some more. "This isn't over." He turned and fled the yard. Behind him, he could hear Shreckengast's voice trailing after him.

"Of course not. I've only just begun."

OCTOBER 26

1

Miss Sheriden walked up the aisles of the classroom as she handed out the pop quiz. Russell took a sheet, set it on his desk and stared at it. One simple page. On it a diagram of a skeleton.

"I want you to label all the major bones of the skeletal system that you can identify," Miss Sheriden said. "Write the name beside the figure and draw an arrow indicating the bone."

Bones, Russell thought as he examined the diagram. The song went through his head.

Shinbone connected to the thighbone; thighbone connected to the hipbone.

He looked up at the front of the classroom where Mr. Shinbones hung from his rack. He imagined the empty eye sockets following Miss Sheriden with lust as she walked up and down each aisle of seats until she finished distributing the worksheets.

Russell glanced around to where Wesley Roark's empty chair remained. No test for him. Not now. *Not ever?* Lance had been rescued, but what about Wesley? Yesterday had been a week since his disappearance from the park. Russell refused to believe something had swallowed him up in that pile of leaves.

He gazed down at the cast on his left arm. Ulna. That's the one he broke. He wrote it down on the paper and drew an arrow to the bone. Radius, the other lower arm bone. Beneath the cast, his skin began to itch, as if an army of ants had marched under the cast. He stuck the eraser end of the pencil between the flesh and the cast and scratched.

Russell began labeling the leg bones on the diagram. *Do the easier ones first*, he thought, *get them out of the way*. Miss Sheriden walked back to the front of the classroom. As she passed his desk, he lifted his eyes to follow her movements, the way her hips shifted from side to side.

He wondered what her bones looked like beneath the curves of her skirt and blouse. His eyes moved over to Mr. Shinbones propped up next to her desk.

Its eye sockets looked back at him.

No. You weren't looking my way before.

Cold air seeped down from the overhead vents and settled onto him, slipping down through his shirt and into his flesh, chilling him right to the bone.

Bones.

His bones.

He poked his left arm with the end of his pencil, above where the cast ended. He had seen his bone when it poked through the flesh, bloody and white. He looked back up at Shinbones. No, he wasn't looking at him. The skeleton gazed off a couple rows to the left, probably at Becky Williams. Her bones had their own set of curvature, different than most of the other girls in class. Most of them were skinny, beanpole bodies.

How can everyone's bodies look so different, when we're all just flesh thrown over these same kinds of bones? It didn't make sense. *Scrape away the flesh, and we're all bones.* All the same. An army of skeletons marching around the planet.

The people from the funhouse fire were piles of bones. How did they identify them? How could the authorities tell one set of bones from another? They were so many charred sticks in a fireplace.

Like his father?

When the burning house collapsed on his dad, no one could save him. How long did it take before they pulled his remains out of the ash? *Bones.* That's his dad now. *Just bones.*

Russell labeled some more answers and then gazed down at the cast. *Coming off soon.* His eyes roamed over the scribbles from classmates till he saw the message from Shinbones.

See you soon.

He glanced back up at the front of the classroom and once again the skeleton was looking at him.

2

At the junior high school after dark, one man still toiled at his job. Mr. Scruggs, the custodian, always mopped the hall floors on the last Monday of the month. He didn't mind staying late into the night on that day, because he preferred working when there weren't any bratty kids around, or the snooty teachers and administrators. He had the building to himself and liked it. He took his time with the floors, sometimes not getting home till nearly midnight.

Scruggs felt guilty about staying so late with the Missus home alone now that Eddie was gone. No one seemed to talk about Eddie anymore, since he was only a runaway. No one cared. He doubted the police were working very hard at finding him. Everyone had moved on to the missing kids, Wayne Barnes and Wesley Roark. His Eddie had been forgotten, and that got under his skin. He pulled a small flask of whiskey from his work pants and took a deep swallow. It wasn't fair, he thought. No one looking for Eddie.

He killed the lights in the west hallway and pushed his bucket and mop down to the next juncture. He needed to dump the dirty water and refill the bucket. He whistled as he walked past the rows of lockers that lined the halls.

A sound, like a crack, came from somewhere behind him. He stopped whistling and turned back the way he came.

The darkened hallway looked empty.

Scruggs liked the peace and quiet in the night at the school. It seemed strange to hear a noise. He pulled the flask back out and took another sip. He kept his eyes focused down the hall as he screwed the cap back on.

A clicking sound.

He turned around and looked down the hallway.

Did it come from that way?

When the school was quiet and empty like this, it was hard to tell where sounds came from. Even his own steps and the squeaky wheel of the mop bucket sometimes echoed like they were coming from the opposite side of the school.

A sound came from around the next corner. Clicking like heels on the tile.

A teacher coming back for something they forgot? No. The doors were locked from the outside and he had the keys.

Scruggs left the bucket and mop and walked to the next juncture. He leaned up against the wall and peered around the corner.

In the shadows at the end of the hallway stood a figure.

Scruggs strained his eyes. He blinked several times, not believing what he saw.

The dimness of the hallway provided just enough light to see the white outline of the figure. All he saw were bones.

He remembered the skeleton in that foxy Miss Sheriden's room. Had some kid dragged it out in the hallway as a Halloween prank? But he would have noticed it earlier, and now there was no one here but him. Or so he assumed.

He figured he'd have to drag the skeleton back into her classroom.

The clicking sounded again and Scruggs watched in awe as the skeleton began walking toward the other end of the hallway. It reached the doorway, pushed on the bar, and headed out into the night.

OCTOBER 27

1

When Ryan filed into Miss Sheriden's classroom along with the other students, he knew something was wrong right away.

Missing.

As he took his seat, he looked up to the front of the class to the metal stand that stood beside the teacher's desk. The skeleton wasn't hanging from it. Kids chattered as they made their way to their seats. Miss Sheriden stood behind her desk.

"As you may notice," she began, "Mr. Shinbones has gone missing." The look she gave was not one of amusement.

Ryan turned to look at Russell and noticed he had grown pale.

"I'm assuming someone swiped my skeleton for a Halloween prank," Miss Sheriden continued. "I'm very displeased about this theft of school property. I paid for that item out of my own pocket. I'd appreciate it if anyone in school knows the whereabouts of Mr. Shinbones, they return it immediately, or face dire consequences."

Ryan kept trying to get Russell's attention, but his friend looked as if he were in a trance. Miss Sheriden segued into dispensing the papers from their quiz yesterday on the human skeleton. He noticed Russell barely glanced at his paper when she set it on his desk. He wished there was a way to snap him out of it.

After the final bell rang, Ryan and Lance caught up with Russell outside in line for the bus.

"Are you okay?" Ryan asked.

Russell still clutched the exam paper in his hand.

"What do you think happened to Shinbones?" Russell asked.

Ryan shrugged. "It's like Miss Sheriden said. Pranksters. Probably someone from the high school."

"You don't really believe that, do you?"

"It's possible." But he doubted it himself. "I can ask Dane at home if he heard anything."

"More important," Lance said, "are we going to the *Dark Shadows* movie tomorrow after school?"

In all that had been going on, Ryan kept finding it hard to think about the movie. He had been waiting a year for it, ever since first hearing they were making a film out of the show. Now tomorrow was opening day and he wanted to see the first showing, which would be the four p.m. matinee.

"I don't want to miss it," Ryan said, though he felt a twinge of guilt that Wesley wasn't around. He wondered if it would still be right to go.

"What about Wesley?" Russell asked as if reading his mind.

There was an awkward silence.

"We'll go again once he turns up," Lance said in his most optimistic tone.

Russell cocked his head. "Do you really think he'll be found?"

The bus pulled up.

"Anything is possible," Lance said. "We've been waiting for this movie. Maybe it'll be good to get our minds off things for a couple hours."

"And spend it watching a vampire trying to take a bride?" Ryan said with a laugh as he thought about the movie poster down at the Colonial.

"An act of unnatural lust," Lance said, quoting the tagline on the poster as they began boarding the bus. "What could take our mind off things better than that?"

2

Chief Strong sat in his office when Pauline, one of the administrators, told him he had a visitor. He didn't often get visitors unless it was that pesky Wright fellow from the newspaper. He'd already given him all the information he could on the case of the missing kids and told him to ask the State Police if he needed anything more.

"Who is it?" Strong asked. He didn't feel like being bothered.

"A Mr. Ezra Shreckengast," Pauline said.

The name jolted Strong to attention. That was the fellow who let the Stanton kid out of Rita's basement and then wandered off with the unknown boy. He was beginning to believe the kid had fabricated the whole far-fetched story.

"Show him in," Strong said.

The chief didn't know what to expect, and when the tall, thin man walked in, his eyes went to the black top hat perched on the man's head. The man's thin mouth cracked open as he sat in the chair on the other side of Strong's desk.

"Shreckengast?" Strong queried, just to be sure he had heard his administrator correctly.

"Ezra Shreckengast," the man said and extended a hand.

Strong shook it and was surprised by how cold it felt.

"A lot of people have been looking for you," Strong said. "I'm surprised you showed up here like this."

"I go where I'm needed," Shreckengast said.

Strong glanced again at the man's hat and wondered if he was going to take it off. Apparently, he wasn't.

"I have lots of questions for you," Strong said.

"I hope we both can accommodate each other's needs."

Strong didn't know what to make of the guy. He pondered calling the State Police captain in charge of the investigation, but decided the captain had shut him out of enough of the case, so maybe he should see what he could decipher on his own.

"You're not from around here, are you?"

"Not lately," Shreckengast said. "I've been away."

"What brings you to Maplewood?"

The man smiled. "I'm in the amusement business. I like to entertain, children especially."

"Oh," Strong said, wondering what that meant. "Are you planning to set up some kind of shop in town?"

"I am currently establishing a place in your lovely town," Shreckengast said. "And that's why I came to see you. I need some cooperation from who I see as the man in charge around here."

"Well, we got this business of what happened out at the Stone-Thurlow house that you became involved in," Strong said. "We'll need to take care of that."

Shreckengast leaned forward on the desk. "That is no longer of any concern," he said. "You'll be best to forget all about it."

"What?"

"What I want to talk to you about is Halloween."

"I beg your pardon?" Now, Strong felt maybe he should have called the State Police.

"It is my understanding that you canceled trick-or-treat in town this year."

"Of course," Strong said. "We had a few child disappearances and I needed to think about the safety of the community."

"Don't you remember how important trick-or-treat is to children?" Shreckengast said.

"Of course. Sure, but—"

"Think back to when you were a child," Shreckengast said with a wave of the fingers of his right hand. "What did you like to dress up as for Halloween?"

Strong remembered. His mind backtracked to a young boy of twelve. When the worries he had today didn't exist.

"I liked the Lone Ranger," he said. "I used to go see the serials when they played before the main feature at the Colonial. I used to dress up as the Lone Ranger every Halloween."

"I bet you enjoyed that," Shreckengast said.

"I always wanted to be a Texas Ranger."

Shreckengast removed his top hat and set it upside down on the desk between the two men. He gestured at it with his long, thin fingers.

"Go ahead," he said. "Reach in there and see what you find."

Strong stared at the hat and then looked up into the mesmerizing eyes of the man across from him. He reached his hand toward the opening in the hat, but then hesitated, his fingers trembling.

"Don't be afraid," Shreckengast said. "It's not going to bite."

Strong reached into the hat, down into its depth, and felt something hard and smooth with unusual contours. His fingers grasped the item and he withdrew his hand from the hat. He looked down at what lay in the palm of his hand and his eyes widened.

It was a star-shaped badge with the words Texas Ranger imprinted on it.

Strong's mouth dropped open. He looked up at Shreckengast.

"Is this some kind of trick?" Strong asked.

"No trick," Shreckengast said. "Magic."

"I don't understand." He fingered the points of the star.

"You don't have to understand," Shreckengast said. "Just believe. Believe in the magic of Halloween."

Strong stared at the badge and smiled.

"Don't you want all the children in town to enjoy Halloween?" Shreckengast asked.

The chief nodded, still so enamored with the object in his hands that he couldn't tear his eyes away from it, fearful that, if he did, it would be gone.

"Of course," he said.

"Then you'll reinstate trick-or-treating in town?"

"Yes, I will."

"That's all I ask," Shreckengast said as he stood from the chair. He grabbed the hat and put it back on his head. "For the children, of course."

"Of course," Strong said. "The children."

"I want this to be a Halloween they'll never forget."

"Never forget."

"Unlike my visit here, which you'll forget ever took place."

"What visit?"

"Thank you for your time." Shreckengast smiled and turned to leave the chief's office. "I'll see you on Halloween."

OCTOBER 28

1

The news filtered throughout the entire school day but didn't reach Ryan's ears until study hall period with Mr. Lange. Studying rarely occurred in those periods but it gave the students time to chat. Lance came into the classroom with the news.

"Did you hear?" he said as he sat by Ryan and Russell. They had moved the front of their three desks together as Mr. Lange didn't care what you did in study hall as long as students kept the chatter to a minimum.

"What's the lowdown?" Ryan asked, curious.

"Trick-or-treat's back on," Lance said. "Someone heard on the radio that Chief Strong rescinded his cancellation."

"That's big news," Russell said.

"They must think the danger is gone," Lance said.

"But we know better," Ryan said. "Don't we?"

"Do we?" Lance said. "I mean, nothing has happened the past few days. No one's gone missing."

"It's not over. Something is still out there."

"So, are we going trick-or-treating or not?" Russell asked. "Because I only have a few days to figure out a costume."

"I think we should," Lance said. "I mean, next year we'll be eighth-graders. We'll be too old. This year could be our last time to go trick-or-treating. Forever."

"I never thought of it like that," Ryan said.

"Are you boys talking about trick-or-treating?"

Ryan looked over at Becky Williams, who had been eavesdropping on their conversation as she sat nearby with Liza and Lindsey.

"What about it?" Russell said in a defiant tone.

Ryan wanted to crawl under his desk.

"You kids do that," Becky said with a laugh. "Us girls are going to Kirby Tressler's Halloween party. That's where all the cool kids will be." Liza and Lindsey giggled behind her.

"Just be careful," Ryan said.

"Oh really?" Becky laughed again and turned away.

"Forget them," Lance said.

Easier said than done, Ryan thought. He'd never felt farther away from Becky than he did right now. He couldn't compete with an eighth-grader. Besides, he had more important things to worry about.

"Maybe trick-or-treat will give us a chance to see what's happening around town. Poke around that night. See if Mort Riggor, Prestidigitator, is up to anything. See if we can't find this Shreckengast fellow. If he really exists."

"Oh, he does," Lance said. "And I'd like to find out what happened to Quinn. Whoever he is, wherever he is."

"But we are going house to house for candy, right?" Russell asked.

"Might as well," Lance said. "We can discuss it some more after the movie today."

That's right, Ryan thought. Today was the day *House of Dark Shadows* opened. With everything going on, he was still excited to see it.

2

At the Colonial Theater, the three boys pitched in to get a large bucket of buttered popcorn and three Cokes, and then entered the theater. A sparse crowd for a Wednesday afternoon was spread throughout the cinema.

"Front row?" Lance asked.

Ryan nodded and led the way down the aisle to the first row, where they settled into three seats smack in the center. The screen loomed large above them. Ryan turned to look at the rows behind. No one even close to them, which was good if they decided to comment throughout the movie, which Lance usually did. He enjoyed interacting with the screen.

As he scanned the theater seats, he noticed groups of people clustered here and there. One young man with a crew cut sat by himself in a middle seat about halfway up the rows, a big tub of popcorn perched on his lap. Ryan couldn't imagine going to the movies by himself, no matter how bad he wanted to see a film. He felt lucky he had his friends who liked the same stuff. Ryan only wished Wesley was here.

The coming attractions started and the three of them dug into the popcorn. By the time the *Love Story* preview finished, so was the popcorn and Ryan set it down on the floor by his seat and settled back to enjoy the show.

Seeing the show's television characters come to life on the big screen amazed Ryan. He felt a giddiness inside and a sense of awe. Willie Loomis opening the coffin in the secret room of the mausoleum and releasing the vampire Barnabas Collins after two hundred years. Everything went along just like the story in the show. Barnabas becoming enraptured with Maggie Evans; Dr. Julia Hoffman discovering his secret and trying to help cure him.

But the blood soon began to flow. This was a more vicious, cruel Barnabas. When he attacked Carolyn Collins in a rage of fury, Ryan heard a loud laughing from behind. He turned to look over his shoulder and could see the silhouette of the crew-cut man in the dark shaking with laughter.

"Get her good!" the man yelled up at the screen. "Suck that bitch." More cackles.

Later in the movie, Professor Stokes, Roger Collins, and the police cornered the vampire Carolyn and Stokes hammered a stake through her heart while the others held her down. Blood spurted forth from her chest.

"Right between the tits!" a voice boomed from behind, followed by laughter.

Ryan turned to look back. The man had moved several rows up toward the front and he could see him better in the light from the movie projector's beam but couldn't make out his face. The man kept shoveling handfuls of popcorn into his mouth between outbursts of laughter.

Ryan hoped the man wasn't going to be an annoyance throughout the whole movie.

Later, during a scene where Barnabas aged into an old man from one of Dr. Hoffman's injections, the vampire throttled Julia and attacked Maggie, ripping into her neck with his fangs. Ryan couldn't believe how much bloodier this was than the show.

Laughter once again erupted from the man in the theater.

"Kill them bitches!" the man yelled.

His voice sounded closer and Ryan peeked behind him. The man had moved his seat again and only sat about a dozen rows behind them. *What the heck is up with this guy?* It irritated him that the man was closer to their seats.

As the movie built to its climax, characters began dropping like flies.

"They're killing everyone," Lance said beside him. "There won't be any Collinses left."

Not only were the family members being killed off, but they were becoming vampires. It wasn't just Barnabas who Jeff Clark had to worry about as he tried to protect Maggie Evans. Roger was a vampire, Professor Stokes was a vampire. No one was safe.

Ryan heard crunching behind him. He turned to look over his shoulder. The man was now five rows behind him, chewing popcorn with his mouth open. In the light from the movie screen, Ryan could see the young man grin. Before the screen went dark during a night scene, Ryan thought the man made eye contact with him.

But Ryan couldn't see the man's eyes. Most of his face had been lit up, but the eyes were in shadow.

Ryan felt on the edge of his seat as the movie culminated with Barnabas holding a wedding ceremony for him and Maggie. The movie got its bloodiest when Jeff Clark crashed the event with a crossbow. Willie Loomis got his with a wooden stake fired from the crossbow intended for Barnabas. Blood filled the screen.

"Let the red flow!" the man cried out from behind.

He sounded even closer, Ryan thought. *Had he moved his seat again?* He sounded right behind him. Ryan tried to focus on the action on the screen. Willie was still alive and picked up a bloody stake and attacked Barnabas, plunging it through the vampire's back. Jeff Clark jumped in and shoved it till it burst out through Barnabas's chest.

Ryan, Lance, and Russell all screamed in joy at the excitement on the screen. Ryan couldn't believe Barnabas was being killed.

"Booo!" the man from behind cried out. "Don't kill him! He's the star!"

Ryan felt the man's breath on the back of his neck as he spoke.

As Barnabas lay in a pool of blood on the screen, Ryan turned to look back.

The crew-cut man sat in the row directly behind him.

The light from the movie screen lit up the seats.

Ryan saw the man's laughing face, his teeth spattered with popcorn bits.

But it was his eyes that shook Ryan with terror.

In place of his eyes, the man had yellow and black cat's eye marbles in each socket.

The man continued laughing, a rotten stench exuding from his breath, and those cat's eyes bore down on Ryan.

Ryan screamed and leapt from his seat. He ran toward the exit door to the left of the movie screen. He heard Lance and Russell calling out behind him. He didn't want to turn to look back, but hoped they took his cue and followed before the marble-eyed man grabbed them.

He burst through the exit door and out into the alley behind the theater. The sun had gone down. He ran a little bit before stopping and leaning up against a brick wall to catch his breath. Ryan glanced back at the theater door that closed behind him. He waited to see if Lance and Russell would come through it.

Or would the marble-eyed man come out that door into the darkened alley?

The door opened.

Lance and Russell came out.

"What was that all about?" Lance asked when they got to where Ryan leaned hunched over by the alley wall.

"There was something in there," Ryan said. "We've got to go before it comes after us."

He saw the confused look on his friends' faces, but didn't want to waste time to explain. Right now, he needed to get them away from the movie theater.

OCTOBER 29

1

After the day's episode of *Dark Shadows* ended, Ryan shut the television off in the basement. Lance and Russell sat on the couch with dejected looks on their faces.

"Now that we've seen the movie," Lance said, "the show seems tame."

"I can't think about it much," Ryan said. "All I think about is that creepy guy in the theater."

"I didn't even hear him," Russell said.

"I don't know how you couldn't. He was so freaking loud."

"And you said he had marbles for eyes?" Lance asked.

"Yup. Cat's eyes. Like the ones Eddie won from me on the school playground."

"Do you think Eddie didn't run away?" Russell asked. "Maybe something else happened to him."

"Like Wayne and Wesley," Lance added.

"Do you think they're dead?"

"I don't know," Ryan said. "But we have to do something. We need help. Someone older."

"Like who would believe us?" Lance said.

"Mr. Lothrop would. We could go see him. And what about Mr. Wright? Or Miss Sheriden and Mr. Lange?"

"No adult is going to believe us," Lance said.

"Mr. Lothrop would," Ryan said. "He's seen stuff. I know it."

The cellar door opened and Dane descended the stairs with the dog following behind.

"Mom says to take Smokey for a walk before dinner," Dane said.

"Can't you?" Ryan didn't want to walk the stupid dog.

"Elsie's picking me up. We're going out to the A&W."

"Must be nice."

Lance motioned to Ryan with a head jerk toward his brother. Ryan understood what he was indicating.

"Hey," Ryan said as Dane started back up the stairs. He stopped and turned back.

"What?"

"Have you been noticing anything strange in town this past month?"

"Besides you idiots?" Dane cracked a smile.

"I'm serious," Ryan said. "Besides Wesley's disappearance and the others, haven't you seen that there's been some weird shit happening?"

Dane stepped down to the bottom of the stairs and stared hard at his brother.

"Listen, I know you guys have been through a lot. But what are you trying to say?"

Ryan didn't know how to explain it to him. "Like there's some unnatural force in town causing weird things to happen."

"I heard you freaked out at the movie theater yesterday. What happened?"

"There was someone in the theater," Ryan said. "Or something. Didn't belong there."

"Maybe you should cut back on some of this horror shit," Dane said. "It's messing with your brain."

"Show him the parchment rubbing," Lance said. He pointed at the table where the gravestone paper lay rolled up along with the baseball card from the failed scavenger hunt.

Of course, Ryan thought. The tombstone that had changed from the original name to Curtis's name. He went over to the table and grabbed the roll.

"We went out to the old cemetery in the woods behind the Williams house on Old Coach Road," Ryan said. "We wanted to find the oldest gravestone for a rubbing for the scavenger hunt. We did one on a headstone from the sixteen hundreds. But a few nights later, we looked at it and it had changed." He unfurled the paper and held it up for all to see.

Dane's eyes narrowed as he looked at what Ryan showed him.

"What the hell is wrong with you?" He turned to go. "Just walk the damn dog." He marched up the stairs.

"That went well," Ryan said. He looked at Lance and Russell on the couch. They had dumbstruck expressions. "What's up with you guys?"

Lance pointed at the parchment in Ryan's hand. "You need to look at that."

Ryan turned the paper around to see the rubbing. The charcoal outline of the tombstone was the same, but the name had changed once again.

RYAN WOODSON
BORN 12/7/1957
DIED 10/31/1970

2

After dinner at the boardinghouse, while the others gathered to watch the news, Lothrop sat at the table by the bay window indulging in a glass of bourbon when Mortimer took a seat beside him.

"What are we going to do?" Harold asked the magician.

"I think I know where they're hiding," Mortimer said. "There's a vacant house near downtown. I sense things there. Dark things."

"You think that's where your son is?"

"I believe so. I followed an old friend there one night. There's something very ominous about that place."

Harold raised a shaky glass to his lips. The more he heard, the less he wanted to know.

"And you want to go there?"

"I do, but I don't want to go alone," Mortimer said. "The place scares me."

"If you find your son," Harold said, "what are you going to do with him?"

Mortimer shot him a befuddled gaze. "What do you mean? I'm going to save him."

Harold took another swallow from his drink to give him courage for what he wanted to say.

"You know you can't save him," Harold said. "You have to do what's right."

"What are you talking about? I've waited forty years to get my son back."

"There's only one thing you have to do," Harold said. "As hard as it'll be. Your son is the key to getting rid of what he brought back with him. And there's only one way you can do that."

"I don't like what you're insinuating." Mortimer stood from the chair.

"You must send your son back."

3

Ryan lay in bed that night unable to sleep. He stared in the darkness at the bottom of the bunk above him.

A bedspring creaked from the top bunk.

It sounded like someone shifting on the mattress.

He looked over at his desk and the View-Master atop it. There had to be a reason he found it, a reason it ended up at the abandoned amusement park. He got out of bed, cast a glance at the top of the bunk bed and saw the drawn-up covers. *Nothing there, of course.* He went over to the desk and picked up the View-Master. He held it up to his eyes and peered through the viewfinder.

An image formed. He saw ice. The river. He saw Smokey.

Ryan clicked the lever down.

He could see the middle of the frozen river and the dog struggling in a hole in the ice.

He pressed the lever.

Now he could see the dog running off, safe to the other side. But the view was from the hole in the ice, the lip of the frozen edge at eye level.

He pressed again.

All he could see was murky water. Dark.

He pressed once more.

The scene showed him a riverbank. In the distance, beyond the trees, he could see the top of a Ferris wheel, rusted, devoid of its carriages.

Ryan pulled the View-Master away from his eyes, wondering what it all meant. Had he just watched his brother's death? Did Curtis send him those images?

The bedsprings creaked behind him.

Ryan turned and stared at the empty top bunk. The covers were smooth and neatly drawn up. He raised the View-Master to his eyes once again and clicked the lever.

A lump appeared beneath the covers on the top bunk.

His heart caught in his throat and he tore the View-Master away from his eyes.

The bedcovers on the top bunk remained smooth.

The bedsprings squeaked.

OCTOBER 30

1

Wilfred Downey stared out at the oak and maple trees in the side yard of the boardinghouse. Most of the limbs were bare and on the ground beneath the branches lay a carpet of orange and brown leaves becoming crisper as the days of October waned. A few of the limbs still had the last leaf holdouts, waiting for a stiff breeze to dislodge them.

Previous years, the newspaper boy and his friend came around to rake and Wilfred paid them well. It didn't appear they were going to offer to help this year. He had seen little of them the past few days and no hint that they were interested in continuing their chore. Maybe as they got older, they found better things to occupy their days.

Wilfred grabbed a rake from the garage and strolled out into the lawn. It was quiet at the boardinghouse and he figured it'd give him something to pass the time while the others were away. Calvin had taken Ruth, the Fifers, and the Stich sisters for one last foliage ride of the season down to the Monadnock Region and would be gone most of the day. Not much left for the leaf peepers this time of the year, Wilfred had told Calvin, but it was an excuse to get out of town and he chose not to go. He didn't care for long car rides anymore and he'd probably just fall asleep.

He wished he had the energy his wife possessed. Wilfred was only three years older than Ruth, but most days he felt a decade older. He wished he didn't tire so easy. He'd love to go out on the weekend with his wife and the others, but he always felt too worn out. But he never wanted to deny Ruth her fun, so he appreciated that Calvin offered to take her out now and then. The two of them were going out tomorrow night to the Rockingham Ballroom for a Halloween dance and Wilfred was happy for her. Ruth loved to dance and God knows he had no strength in his legs for that. He'd be asleep long before they got home, but he'd be happy she would have fun.

Wilfred saw Mr. Rigby head out toward town earlier, so that only left Lothrop in the house, as usual. Wilfred did not understand Lothrop. He'd heard about agoraphobics, but it seemed incredible to spend nearly your entire adult life cooped up in one place.

As he waded into the leaves in the yard, Wilfred turned back and looked up at the third floor of the house and saw Harold sitting at the window in his room watching him. He wondered if the man envied the rest of them, who had no issues venturing outside. Wilfred raised his hand and the man waved back. To each his own, he thought. None of them had much longer to live anyway.

Wilfred began raking, amazed at how many leaves came from a single tree. These trees were probably more than a hundred years old and towered over the roof of his house. The branches formed a huge canopy that gave the side yard lots of shade in the summer. Now the skeletal limbs looked naked, shed of their garments as the autumn chill settled in.

He raked one section into a nice big pile and then moved on to another area. Wilfred worked slow, not wanting blisters to form on his hands. He had all day anyway. No need to rush. Nice easy strokes with the rake, dragging the leaves into another pile, the grass beneath still green.

Wilfred left that mound and moved on to another section. He figured once he got all the leaves into piles, he could drag the old metal barrel out and start burning them. He loved the smell. As he continued raking, a breeze kicked up without warning. He looked back and saw the leaves from his previous piles scattering.

Damn.

The tops of both piles had been decimated and the leaves dispersed along the cleared grass. He went back and re-raked the areas that he had just swept clean. Wilfred then moved on to the next area. He got a third pile done and moved across to where the tall oak tree stood and began raking beneath it.

A big gust of wind blew through and began scattering leaves from the piles beneath the maple trees.

What the hell?

The wind died out as suddenly as it started, but now leaves lay spread over the areas he had just cleared. He walked back, dragging his rake and shaking his head. The local weatherman had said nothing on the morning news about today being breezy. As Wilfred stood among the leaves, the air now was still.

His arms ached, but he raked the mess back into his original piles. His breathing became a bit more labored. Maybe this wasn't such a good idea, he thought. He wanted to get this taken care of before dark, but the wind caused it to take longer than he expected.

Wilfred raked some more, but it felt pointless as the wind came along without notice and blew his piles apart, scattering leaves across the yard. If the wind was going to blow this hard, he wished it would be enough to blow all his leaves into the next-door neighbor's yard. That would make things easier.

Pain burned its way across the back of his shoulders. His knees ached. Blisters built up on the palms of his hands. The wind gushed through the yard and now he barely had any piles to show for all the work he had done.

The sun would be going down soon and he felt he should start thinking about preparing dinner, but he didn't know if he even had the energy for that. Rest, he thought. A little rest to give him a second wind. He laughed at the thought. Wind was the whole problem today.

He didn't have the energy to even head back into the house and thought he needed to sit for just a minute to catch his breath. He dropped the rake and settled down into a soft cushion of leaves and leaned his back up against the coarse bark of one of the maples.

Just need to close my eyes for a second. Then I'll head back inside.

The wind blew leaves across his legs, covering them like a blanket.

2

Harold watched his landlord from his perch, looking out his bedroom window as the old man raked leaves. At first, he chuckled when the wind began blowing the piles apart and sending the leaves in every direction. But then Harold noticed something.

When the wind gusts came and dispersed the leaves, the branches on the trees themselves did not move. Watching the limbs on the trees in the yard and all along the street, Harold would have sworn it wasn't windy out.

Yet the leaves on the ground were blowing everywhere.

What kind of wind just runs along the ground?

No wind he had ever seen.

He kept a close eye on Wilfred, wishing the old man would surrender to the inevitable and come inside. His hopes faded when the old man sat down and appeared to be taking a nap leaning up against the trunk of a tree. The wind continued to blow and the leaves began covering the man.

Something else stirred the leaves.

Harold watched one of the piles and it appeared something was inside it, moving around. He noticed the same thing in the other piles.

Something was in the leaves.

Harold stood from his chair and unlocked his window. He thrust up the sash and yelled out. "Wilfred!" he cried. "Wake up!"

The old man did not stir.

Damn.

Things were burrowing their way through the leaves toward where Wilfred lay.

I need to do something. There was no one else there to help.

He rushed out of his room and headed down the stairs as fast as he could without falling. On the second floor he took the back stairs that dumped him out by the side porch door. He opened it and looked outside.

Wilfred lay asleep beneath the tree. Leaves swirled all around him.

God, Harold thought, as he stood in the open door. A rush of nausea swept over him and his stomach cramped up.

I haven't stepped foot outside since 1930, he thought. *Can I even do this?*

He looked at the helpless Wilfred and knew he had no choice.

Harold didn't know what else to do. He took one step out onto the porch. Just crossing that leg over the threshold sent a rush of dizziness to his head. He felt unbalanced, as if he might tip over. He closed his eyes, sucked in a deep breath, and braced himself for the next step. His left foot joined his right on the porch.

He opened his eyes. He was outside.

I'm out. I'm really out.

Harold swayed on his feet. He eyed the handrail on the steps a few feet away that led down to the driveway.

I can make that.

He willed his feet forward and just before he felt himself begin to tumble, he grabbed on to the handrail to steady himself. He sucked in more breaths to rejuvenate his lungs, which felt like shrunken balloons.

Harold pictured himself falling down the steps and landing face-first into the asphalt driveway.

No. One step at a time. He counted them as he went down and soon found both feet on the driveway. His whole body felt covered in goose bumps. He looked over to the yard where Wilfred lay. He wanted to call out to him again, hoping the man would hear him now that he was closer, but he didn't have enough air in his lungs to speak.

Quick. Must act quick.

He spotted movement beneath the leaves. He glanced to the right, past the garage to where the sun dipped down into the horizon.

Not much time left. Darkness approaching.

Harold gathered all the strength his aged body could muster and rushed across the driveway and into the lawn. He pushed through the leaves that swirled around him from a sudden gust of wind. He spied the rake Wilfred had dropped and bent down to grab it.

"Wilfred!" he cried out, now that he was only a few feet from the man. Wilfred's eyelids fluttered.

Harold turned and saw movement beneath the leaves and swatted at it with the rake. He heard a squeal followed by a scurrying rustle. He rushed over to Wilfred and kicked the man in the shin. "Get up!"

Wilfred opened one eye and looked up at him. "You're outside?" he said in a sleepy voice.

"It's not safe out here," Harold said and nudged the man's leg again. "We have to get inside. Hurry!"

He helped Wilfred to his feet and took his arm. Wind swept through the yard, throwing leaves in their faces. The two men supported each other as they made their way across the yard.

Harold heard a chattering from behind and looked over his shoulder. He saw beady eyes and glistening teeth in one of the piles of leaves.

Goblins. He hurled the rake at them and tugged Wilfred along. Once at the driveway, Harold dared to look back again. The sun had gone down and bathed the yard in shadows. One of the creatures peered out from behind a tree.

Harold stopped, still ahold of Wilfred, and stared back at the critter.

"You can have me!" he shouted. "But you can't have him!"

Wilfred looked befuddled. "What is it?'

"An old acquaintance," Harold said and hurried his landlord up the steps and through the side door. Once inside, he shut the door and locked it.

Harold looked out the door's window at the side yard but saw nothing but leaves swirling in the wind.

3

At night in the Wickstrom House, Shreckengast sat in what had once been the funeral home's main viewing room in a high-backed velvet-covered wooden chair like a king on his throne. He wore the magic hat. In a smaller chair on his right sat Quinn. On another chair on his left sat the rabbit, Daimon, its red eyes motionless in its sockets. Several of the Scamps sat in chairs facing them as if awaiting a wake. At the head of the room sat an empty coffin, its lid open. On the other side of that stood the wooden magic cabinet.

"Tomorrow is our opening night," Shreckengast said with a smile. "Everything is prepared."

"Halloween?" asked Quinn.

"That's right."

"And you said I can go trick-or-treating?"

"Of course," Shreckengast said. "I promised you, and I always keep my promises."

"I can't wait."

"You have a special task to perform," Shreckengast said. "It's very important."

"But I still get to trick-or-treat?"

"Yes, my boy."

"Won't I need a costume?" Quinn asked. "I don't have anything."

Shreckengast turned to the boy. "What would you like to dress up as?"

Quinn shrugged. "I don't know. I haven't seen many costumes. Except the one my father used to wear on stage."

"A magician's costume." Shreckengast smiled. "That would be perfect." He removed the hat from his head and reached inside. He pulled out a black cape and handed it to Quinn. "Just your size." He reached in again and pulled out a flat, round object. With a flick of a wrist, he popped it open and it was a smaller version of his own magic hat. "I think this should fit you just right." He placed it on Quinn's head. "There, you now have your costume."

Quinn stood and put the cape on. "I feel like a real magician."

"You are one," Shreckengast said. "And tomorrow you will be performing all kinds of tricks."

"What's my special task?"

"Check inside your hat."

Quinn removed the hat and reached inside. He pulled out a handful of rectangular pieces of paper.

"What are these?"

"Tickets to the funhouse, of course," Shreckengast said. His grin grew wide.

Quinn looked at the writing on the tickets:

Wickstrom House of Phantasmagoria
13 Carriage Lane
Free Admission

"What do I do with these?"

Shreckengast ran a finger gently down the side of Quinn's cheek.

"You will hand them out to the trick-or-treaters," he said. "So that everyone can join in on the fun night we have planned. It'll be a Halloween to remember."

OCTOBER 31

1

Ryan inserted the plastic fangs into his mouth and looked at himself in his bedroom mirror. He drew the black cape around him, turned to Lance and bared the fangs.

"You look just like last year," said Lance, dressed in a red devil costume. "And the year before."

"If this is going to be my last Halloween, I'm not going out without a fight."

"Don't believe that stupid gravestone rubbing."

"So, what's the plan?" Russell asked.

Ryan looked at him, surprised he decided to dress up in a skeleton costume. The left sleeve of his dark shirt with painted bones was rolled up above his cast. He noticed earlier that Russell had used a pen to scratch out the message from Shinbones.

"We go out like a typical trick-or-treat night," Ryan said, "but we're really looking for that Quinn kid. Lance said Shreckengast promised him he could go trick-or-treating. We find Quinn and he'll lead us to Shreckengast."

"And then what?" Lance said.

Ryan shrugged. "I don't know. I'm making this up as we go along. We can stop at the boardinghouse and see if Lothrop can help."

"What about the magician?" Russell asked.

"I don't trust him," Ryan said. "He could be a part of all that's happened." He looked at Lance. "You have that locket from the amusement park?"

Lance nodded.

"And I have the lighter," Russell said. "But it doesn't work."

"Don't matter," Ryan said. "There's a reason we found these things, so I think we should bring them." He picked the View-Master up from his desktop, remembering what he thought he'd seen the other night. He stuffed it inside the empty pillowcase he was using for a trick-or-treat bag.

Ryan's mother appeared at the open doorway.

"You boys look great," she said.

"Thanks, Mrs. Woodson," Lance said with a wave of his red rubber pitchfork.

"Dracula again," Ryan's mother said as she eyed her son.

"It's not Dracula," Ryan said in exasperation. "It's Barnabas Collins." He held up the plastic wolf's head cane for her to see.

"Whatever," his mother said. "It's the same thing every year. Couldn't you go as something different for a change? How about a clown or something?"

"Mom," Ryan said. "Clowns aren't scary."

"But they're fun," she said. "I have a favor to ask. I want you to take Smokey with you."

"What? No way!"

"I would worry less," she said. "I know things have calmed in town since Rita's arrest, but I just feel you'd be safer."

Lance looked at Ryan. "Might be a good idea."

"Fine," Ryan said, though he wasn't happy.

"You boys better get going," Mrs. Woodson said, "before all the good candy is gone."

"Yeah," Russell said, "and we get stuck with a box of raisins."

They went out into the hallway as Dane came out of his bedroom dressed in a Boston Red Sox uniform and cap. His left eye was blackened.

"Who are you supposed to be?" Lance asked.

"I'm Tony Conigliaro," Dane said. "He's my favorite player." He pointed at the makeup on his face. "See, I've got the black eye from when he was hit in the face by a pitch in '67."

"Lame costume," Ryan said.

His brother tapped him lightly on the chest with a wooden baseball bat he held. "As long as I look good, that's all that matters, Count Chocula."

"It's Barnabas Collins!" Ryan yelled.

"Oooh, scary," Dane said with a laugh as he waved his arms before he headed down the stairs.

"All of you, out," Mrs. Woodson said and ushered them along. "Go have fun."

Down in the kitchen, Mr. Woodson emptied bags of candy into a big metal bowl. Ryan and the others each grabbed some candy and shoved it into their bags. Ryan got Smokey's leash and hooked it to the dog's collar. Smokey's tail wagged.

"Be safe too," Mr. Woodson said to them. He looked directly at Dane. "You especially."

"I'll be at Kyler Lavory's Halloween party all night," Dane said, "so no worries."

"I'll always worry," his father said. "Home by midnight."

When they got outside, Elsie Hoover had already pulled into the driveway in her Bug. She stepped out of the car and Lance gripped Ryan's arm and squeezed.

"Hubba hubba," Lance whispered.

Elsie was dressed as a Playboy Bunny. Dane paused in the driveway and turned to them with a smile and a wink. He kissed Elsie and they both got into the car.

"She looks like she stepped out of one of my dad's magazines," Lance said.

"One foxy mama," Russell said. "Your brother is damn lucky."

"Think he's jumping her bones?" At that, he turned to Russell. "Oops, sorry."

They all started laughing.

"Let's shove off," Ryan said.

Trick-or-treaters marched up and down Oak Street going house to house. As they headed down the street, Ryan stopped and looked the other way.

Down the sidewalk, a lone figure stood dressed as a ghost with a white sheet over it and two black round eyes. Ryan paused. Smokey took a few steps in that direction but Ryan pulled back on the leash to stop the dog. The ghost figure made no attempt to go to the nearest house. It seemed to be watching them.

"What's the matter?" Lance asked when he noticed Ryan had stopped.

"I don't know," Ryan said. "Nothing, I guess." He pulled on the leash to redirect Smokey and they continued toward Walnut Street.

Ryan couldn't help but look back over his shoulder and saw the ghost figure now moving in the same direction.

2

Mortimer stepped into Harold's room without the courtesy of knocking. The writer had been seated by his window looking down at the street at the trick-or-treaters parading up and down the sidewalks. Little did they know what lurked out there, he thought, knowing what he saw in the leaves yesterday. *Goblins.*

"We need to go to that house," Mortimer said from the doorway. "I need to find Quinn and get him away from there, but I don't want to go alone."

"I'm not going anywhere," Harold said with a leering eye cast at his fellow tenant. "It's not safe out there. Not tonight of all nights."

"That's why it must be done tonight," Mortimer said. "For all our sakes. If we don't end this, I don't know how we'll get through the night or what will be left come morning."

A bottle stood by an empty glass on the table beside where Harold sat. He poured some of the brown liquid into the glass.

"This is how I plan to get through the night." He raised the glass to his lips.

"Coward," Mortimer said and slammed the door as he left the room.

True, Harold thought as he gazed back out the window. *But I have good reason to be one. I've seen too much.*

He listened to Mortimer's footsteps as he headed down the hall back to his own room. The magician started all this, he thought, it was up to him to finish it. He took another swallow of his drink, hoping to be numb and asleep before long.

The rest of the house was quiet except for the muffled sound from the television downstairs in the front parlor that filtered up through the metal heating grate in the floor of his room. Calvin Armstrong had taken Wilfred's wife, Ruth, out to a Halloween ball, and the Stich sisters were sitting on the front porch dressed as witches and handing out candy to the trick-or-treaters, so that left the Fifers watching TV. He didn't know Wilfred's whereabouts.

Harold felt content to stay in his room and watch out the window. No sign of anything yet, but he planned to man his post as long as possible. He refilled his glass and wondered if he'd pass out before anything happened.

The window was open a crack to let in cool air that felt a refreshing balance to his warm insides from the bourbon. As he brought the glass to his lips, he heard a rustling sound outside. He paused, the glass an inch from his mouth.

A rattling of leaves.

Harold set the glass down and rose from his chair. He raised the window up and the screen as well. He leaned out the window and looked down.

The ivy woven through the trellis anchored to the side of the house shook.

Something there.

His eyes adjusted to the darkness outside and what bare light was cast into the driveway from the closest streetlamp. Wood squeaked. Leaves rustled.

Something climbing up the trellis.

He spotted dark shapes down below. Tiny clawed fingers gripping crisp vines; scaled skin; pointed ears; slitted eyes that glowed red in the night.

Goblins.

Harold slammed the window shut and locked it. He pulled the shades down.

They've finally come for me, he thought, thinking back to the night on the train platform in Portsmouth those many years ago. He had tossed his manuscript out the train window, but it didn't matter. They still wanted him; wanted to finish the job they started.

No, he started it, with that damned manuscript. All his friends met tragic ends and now it was his turn.

He had hidden away long enough. Yesterday, he dared to venture outside, and now it had spelled doom for him. They had found him. The fears of his past had caught up with him.

Harold picked up the bourbon bottle and drained the last of the booze. *One last dose of courage.* He held the empty bottle by the neck, figuring it could be a weapon. What use it would be against sharp claws and teeth, he did not know. His options were limited. He backed away from the window and stood in the middle of the room, gripping the bottleneck tight.

He could run, but what would be the point? Where could he go where they wouldn't find him? Even Maplewood had proved not far enough away. Time to stand and fight.

Harold glanced around the room and his eyes fell on his dusty typewriter on the desk. He thought about Ryan and his friends and how they had sought him out for help, but he had failed them. They knew something was happening. They saw things they couldn't explain, came to him, and he had shunned them. He wished there was something he could do.

He walked over to the desk and sat down. He set the empty bottle beside the typewriter and blew dust off the keys. Harold opened a desk drawer, withdrew a blank piece of faded white paper and inserted it into the typewriter.

Harold began to type.

A sound of rasping metal came from behind. He stopped typing and turned to look. His eyes fell on the heating grate in the floor by the wall. He got up from the desk, grabbed the bottle, and walked over. He kneeled on the floor by the vent.

Banging sounds came from deep within.

They found another way in. His grip tightened on the bottle.

The screws on the metal grate began turning, unscrewing.

Clever little bastards, Harold thought.

His heart pounded as he watched the screws untwist one by one and the metal grate cover popped open.

3

As the boys worked their way down Walnut Street, crisscrossing the road to stop at each house and collect candy, Ryan scarcely paid attention to the sweets deposited in his bag. His eyes focused on the trick-or-treaters they passed, hoping Lance would be able to spot Quinn. Lance had spent less than two days in a darkened cellar with the mysterious boy. Would he even be able to recognize him, especially if he were dressed in costume? It was worse than looking for a needle in a haystack.

Most of the younger elementary school kids Ryan observed wore store-bought costumes with plastic masks: Frankenstein, Werewolf, Witch. A lot of the older kids dressed in homemade costumes: Pirate, Hobo, and, yes, even a few clowns. Rarely did he see any other seventh-graders. Maybe they were too old for trick-or-treat. The rest of his classmates were probably at Kirby Tressler's party, especially Becky. Ryan tried to picture what kind of costume she was dressed in, and imagined her in Elsie's Playboy Bunny outfit.

They stopped at the juncture with Maple Street. Russell had already dug a Sky Bar out of his bag and lifted his skull mask to chomp on it, chocolate and caramel smeared on the corners of his mouth.

"This is hopeless," he said between bites.

"We've got to keep looking," Lance said. "He's out here somewhere."

"My bag's half full already," Russell said. "At least something good will come of this."

"Remember what's important," Ryan said as he looked down the street they had come. "Collecting candy is not the objective." As he surveyed the trick-or-treaters, he spotted the kid in the ghost sheet again.

Following us?

The kid seemed to float down the sidewalk and now he stopped as if waiting for them to move. Ryan hadn't noticed the kid going up to any houses and he didn't appear to even have a trick-or-treat bag. He couldn't quite tell as the sheet covered the kid's arms and hands.

What's he doing here?

Could it be Quinn? Lance had said the boy in Rita's basement was ten, but the kid in the ghost sheet looked almost as tall as Ryan. Smokey took a few steps in that direction and a whimpering sound came from the dog's throat. Ryan pulled back on the leash.

"Guys," Ryan said. "Check this kid out. The one in the ghost costume."

"What about him?" Russell asked.

"I think he's been following us. Maybe it's Quinn."

"No," Lance said, and Ryan noticed he wasn't even looking at the ghost.

"Why not?"

"Because I think I see him." Lance pointed across the street. "There, in the magician costume."

Ryan looked in that direction and saw a young boy in a cape and black top hat handing out pieces of paper to trick-or-treaters.

"Come on," Lance said and led the way across the street.

Ryan had to tug on the leash to draw Smokey's attention away from the ghost kid.

"Quinn!" Lance yelled from the middle of the road.

The kid in the magician costume looked up. He must have recognized Lance, because as soon as he saw the three of them approaching, he bolted down Walnut toward the Town Square.

"Get him!" Lance yelled and the three of them raced after the boy.

Smokey sensed the urgency and took off. Ryan was barely able to hold on to the leash as he ran behind the dog. Soon the two of them passed Lance and were gaining on the boy.

Quinn ran out onto the cobblestone plaza of the Town Square with Smokey and Ryan on his tail and Lance and Russell not far behind.

Ryan struggled to keep up with the dog and the handle of the leash ripped out of his grip. The dog took off after the boy.

Halfway across the plaza, past the Revolutionary War statue, Quinn's top hat fell off his head and bounced along the cobblestones before landing on its side. The boy stopped and turned to retrieve it when he noticed Smokey nearly upon him.

The dog must have sensed something, Ryan thought, because it dug in its heels and came to a stop just before the hat. Smokey bent his head down to sniff the opening of the hat. Ryan approached in time to see white-furred claws stretch out of the hat and grab on to the dog's snout.

Smokey let out a howl, and then whatever was inside the magician's hat began pulling the dog inside.

Ryan stopped short at first, stunned by the sight. The dog's front legs pushed back as its head was pulled inside. Its paws lost their purchase and slipped inside the hat along with its upper torso.

Ryan couldn't move, numb from the unreal scene playing out before him. It was impossible for Smokey to fit inside the small top hat, but right before his eyes he saw the dog's body being dragged into it, as if it were made of Silly Putty. He dropped his bag of candy, dove for the leash that lay on the cobblestones behind the dog, and grabbed on.

Smokey was dragged further into the hat, pulling Ryan along the cobblestones as he held on to the leash. Lance and Russell had caught up and each grabbed on to one of Ryan's legs.

The force from the other end felt too strong. The leash ripped through the palms of his hands. Ryan looked up in time to see Smokey's tail wagging furiously before the back end of the dog disappeared into the darkness of the hat, followed by the trailing leash.

Quinn bent down and picked up the top hat and placed it on his head. He looked at Ryan with a smile, turned, and ran off.

Ryan lay on the cobblestones staring as the boy disappeared into the neighborhood beyond the square. His lungs felt like balloons that had been squashed flat and he realized two large cobblestones were pressing into his chest. He could barely breathe. He turned to gaze back at Lance and Russell, who had both let go of his legs and had looks of awe on their faces.

"Smokey's gone," Ryan said when he got enough breath to speak. "Did you see that? He's gone."

"Oh shit," Lance said. "I can't believe what I just saw."

"What do we do now?" Russell asked.

Ryan didn't have an answer. This was too much for him to take. He had just lost his dog. No, not his. Curtis's dog. Smokey gone in an instant. He sat up on the ground but couldn't move any further. He felt helpless.

"I can't do this," he said and felt his eyes moisten. "It's too much."

"We should go after him," Lance said, looking across the way to Poplar Street, where Quinn had run.

"We need help," Ryan said. "We can't do this ourselves."

"There's no one to help us."

Ryan glanced behind to the other side of the square and the figure standing on its edge.

"Yes, there is." He stood up. "Look."

The others turned to see...the kid in the ghost sheet.

"Who is that?" Russell asked.

"I have an idea," Ryan said. He stepped over to where his trick-or-treat bag lay, reached inside, and withdrew the View-Master. He held it up to his eyes, faced the kid in the ghost sheet and clicked the lever. A bright light flashed through the viewfinder and Ryan could see the face of the figure beneath the sheet. *His own face.*

"What is it?" Lance asked, but his voice felt another time zone away.

"Wait here," Ryan said and walked across the square to where the kid in the ghost costume stood. He stopped in front of him and stared into those black eyes. He could see nothing behind them. Ryan reached up and pulled off the sheet.

He stared into the mirror image before him.

No, not exactly his face. A younger version.

Curtis.

"I've missed you," Ryan said.

"You've gotten older," Curtis said, a tinge of envy in the tone. "I'm the older one, by ten minutes, remember."

"I do."

"It's not fair," Curtis said. "You're taller too. Older than me and bigger than me. That's not supposed to happen."

"How are you here?" Ryan asked, one of many questions he had, but worried that he wouldn't have enough time to ask them all. He wasn't even sure how this was possible. Or why.

"I've been adrift," Curtis said. "Got lost along the way."

"Why are you here?" That was the important question.

"You needed help," Curtis said. "There's danger here."

"I'm in way over my head. I don't know what to do, who to turn to."

"There's always our older brother," Curtis said.

Ryan shook his head. "He's in another world."

Curtis laughed and it felt good to hear him laugh, Ryan thought. There was comfort in that.

"I know the feeling," Curtis said. "But big brothers are supposed to be there for you. I know that because I'm your bigger brother too."

"Not anymore," Ryan said.

"Don't remind me," Curtis said. "It's not how it's supposed to be. I'm supposed to be older. But now, you'll grow older and soon you'll be a teenager and you're going to experience lots of things I never will."

"Not if I don't survive tonight." Ryan thought about the gravestone rubbing.

"There's help waiting for you," Curtis said. "At the Downeys' boardinghouse. Don't be afraid to take help when it's available. You can't do this alone."

"I wish you were here to help." Ryan couldn't find the words to tell his twin how vexed he felt about the situation.

"I can't help you now," Curtis said. "I have my own path to find."

"I'd help you if I could," Ryan said and resisted the urge to reach out and touch his brother, but feared he wouldn't feel anything.

"I've got all the help I need now," Curtis said and held up his right hand, which gripped a dog leash.

Ryan looked down and saw Smokey at the end of the leash standing next to Curtis.

"But, how?"

"My dog," Curtis said with a smile. "Always was, remember? I got to pick him out and I got to name him. Because I was the older one. By ten whole minutes."

"That's right," Ryan said.

"Smokey will help me find the way," Curtis said. "Good luck tonight. You'll know what to do."

"Do you want this?" Ryan asked and held up the View-Master.

Curtis took it from him. "This might help. Thanks." He turned to go, with Smokey leading the way. "I'll be seeing you."

Ryan's words caught in his throat and before he knew it, Curtis and Smokey became swallowed up by the night. Tears leaked from Ryan's eyes and he wiped them away just as Lance and Russell came alongside him.

"What happened to the kid in the ghost costume?" Russell said as he picked up the empty white sheet with the cut-out eyes laying on the cobblestones.

"Who was it?" Lance asked.

"Someone from the past," Ryan said with a sniffle.

"What do we do now?" Lance asked.

Ryan turned to the two of them.

"Trick-or-treat is over," Ryan said. "Time to get down to business. First stop, the boardinghouse to see Mr. Lothrop."

4

Becky Williams walked into the basement of Kirby Tressler's house dressed in a black Danskin bodysuit that hugged her budding curves. Whiskers were painted on her face and she wore a black headband with pointy cat ears. A long tail was attached to her backside. In tow behind her were Liza and Lindsey dressed as Thing 1 and Thing 2 from the Dr. Seuss books.

"Wow!" Kirby said as she descended the stairs into the finished basement, with an orange shag rug and dark pine paneling. "You look awesome, like a wild animal."

"I'm a black cat," she said with a giggle.

"Perfect for Halloween." He led her and her friends through the large room to the refreshment table stocked with bowls of chips, popcorn, and liter bottles of soda. He poured her and her friends drinks.

Music blared from a turntable at the other end of the room that held a stack of 45s. Becky recognized 'Monster Mash', and hoped there would be better music than that in the pile.

"I'm glad you came," Kirby said.

"Me too." She motioned to Liza and Lindsey to make scarce and they drifted off to mingle with the crowd. She didn't see many other seventh-graders there and felt emboldened to be here.

They chatted for a while and then Kirby went off for a minute to talk to some of his buddies. Becky floated around the room, complimenting some of the girls and boys on their costumes. She got a lot of admiring looks from the boys and liked it.

Kirby turned the music down and announced they were going to play a game.

"Seven Minutes in Heaven," he said to cheers and a few jeers, followed by laughter. He told everyone interested in playing to write their names on slips of paper he had at the food table and then put them into one of the bowls based on gender. "You're playing, right?" he asked Becky.

"I've never played before," she said. She'd heard of the game and it made her a little wary, but also excited.

"It'll be fun," Kirby said and wrote her name on a slip of paper and dropped it into the bowl.

Becky goaded Liza and Lindsey into signing up as well.

"Everyone knows the rules, right?" Kirby asked the crowd. "Draw names and a couple goes in the closet for seven minutes in the dark." Most of the kids nodded in acknowledgement. "And whatever happens in the dark stays between the two of you." He laughed and everyone joined in. "Let's see who goes first."

Becky didn't know the boy and girl whose names Kirby drew, but the crowd cheered and the two of them marched off to a closet at the end of the room. The girl, dressed as a Native American, waved goodbye and the boy wearing a cowboy outfit made a gesture like he was slapping her bottom. The crowd roared with laughter and the door closed. Someone set a small kitchen timer to seven minutes and placed it on an end table near the closet door.

The party continued while several people watched the closet door. One boy put his ear up against it, which brought loads of laughter. When the timer dinged, the door open and everyone cheered.

Becky had no idea what they were being applauded for and assumed maybe the couple had just been kissing or something. She wondered how well they even knew each other.

"Next couple," Kirby said as he drew names. "Look, I got my name." He waved it in the air. "Let's see who the lucky gal is." He drew a name and read it aloud. "Becky Williams!"

Becky blushed but stepped forward, glad Kirby hadn't drawn some other girl's name, especially Liza or Lindsey. That would have made her jealous. Kirby took her hand and led her to the closet door. He turned to the crowd.

"If we're not out in seven minutes," he said, "don't come knocking!"

The crowd cheered and Kirby led Becky into the closet. When the door closed behind them, she couldn't believe how dark it was inside.

"I can't see a thing," she whispered, not wanting those on the other side of the door to hear.

"Let's sit," Kirby said.

Becky let go of his hand to maintain her balance while she dropped to the floor and sat cross-legged. She could feel his presence across from her. The little light that framed the seams of the door allowed her to see the outline of Kirby.

"You look stellar tonight," he said in a low voice.

"Thanks," she said and felt warm at the sentiment. "What do we do in here?" Seven minutes, she thought. That shouldn't take long.

"Can I kiss you?" Kirby asked.

She was hoping he would. "Okay."

Becky leaned forward and the shadowy figure did the same. She wasn't sure how their lips would find each other in the dark, but they met and she felt his pressed against hers. It felt nice but only lasted a few seconds before she pulled back. She wasn't sure if she should part her lips and let him put his tongue inside. She wanted to know what that felt like.

"That was nice," Kirby said.

"Yes. You can do it again." She wondered how many minutes had gone by.

Kirby leaned forward and as their lips met, she felt a hand on her belly. She opened her mouth and felt his tongue slip inside and meet hers. The hand on her belly rose toward her chest.

Becky pulled back.

"What are you doing?" she asked.

"I thought we were making out," Kirby said.

"Okay," she said. "Yeah, sure. But your hands."

"I wasn't doing anything with my hands."

Becky didn't want him to get carried away, but still wanted to make out more. There must be only a few minutes left. She wished they had more time in here.

"Take my hands," she said. That way she'd be sure they wouldn't wander. He grasped both her hands in his. They leaned their heads forward and their lips met and parted. His tongue was all over hers and she flicked hers around it, enjoying how warm and wet it felt.

Hands moved up her bodysuit and touched her breasts.

Becky backed away.

"Kirby!" The hands lingered. "I didn't say you could touch me there." It did feel nice though and she let them caress her.

"Becky," Kirby said. "You're holding both my hands."

He squeezed her hands to prove it and she felt them in her grasp.

But there were still hands on her body.

Becky screamed.

She pulled her hands out of Kirby's grip and got up from the floor. Something still touched her and she stumbled to the closet door, frantically searching for the handle. When she found it, she burst through the door into the basement still screaming.

Kids were laughing. Liza and Lindsey came rushing to her aid.

"What's wrong?" Liza asked.

Becky pointed toward the closet. "There was someone in there with us!" she cried. It couldn't be though. She saw the empty closet when she first stepped inside. "Someone touched me!"

A girl went up to the open closet doorway and peered inside. She turned to Becky.

"Where's Kirby?"

Becky looked at the stunned girl's face. What was she talking about? Becky approached the closet and peered inside.

Empty.

Becky screamed and ran for the basement stairs. She didn't stop screaming even when she got outside and ran down the street.

5

Hackles rose on the back of Ryan's neck as he walked down Elm Street alongside Lance and Russell. His whole body felt like it had been sunk in a tub of ice, so cold he could feel the blood in his veins pulsing slowly like slush. His breath felt strained and he realized the plastic fangs in his mouth interrupted the flow of air, so he spit them out onto a nearby lawn.

"Was it really him?" Lance asked after a while.

"Yes," Ryan said, unable to believe it himself. It seemed a dream. He couldn't shake the chill.

Ahead stood the boardinghouse where the Stich sisters sat on the front stoop, pointed black witch hats perched on their heads as they handed out candy to the trick-or-treaters parading up the walk.

"Let's go in the other door," Ryan said, and his friends followed him up the driveway to the side porch. The light in Mr. Lothrop's third-floor room was on, but the shades were drawn. Ryan noticed Mr. Armstrong's car was gone, so knew some of the tenants were out. He didn't bother knocking or ringing the doorbell, instead opening the door, and stepping inside. The kitchen to the left was dark. The parlor room to the right had one lamp on. Mr. Downey sat in a chair snoring.

The pocket doors between the two rooms were closed, but Ryan heard the muffled sound of the television set on the other side and wondered who might be in there. He tamped down his curiosity and marched up the back stairs with Lance and Russell right behind. On the third floor, he stopped at Mr. Lothrop's door and knocked.

No answer.

"Maybe he's asleep," Russell said.

"I saw his light on." Ryan put his ear against the door and listened. No sound. "Mr. Lothrop," he called out softly. No response. Ryan turned the handle and opened the door.

The room appeared empty, the bed still made. Maybe he was downstairs watching TV, Ryan thought.

"Look," Lance said and brushed past him into the room. He leaned down and pointed to shards of glass from a broken bottle on the floor.

An uneasy feeling crept inside Ryan's gut. He scanned the room looking for anything else out of the ordinary. He spotted the typewriter and a piece of paper rolled up in the carriage. He knew Mr. Lothrop hadn't touched that typewriter in decades. Ryan walked over and noticed dust had been brushed off. Ryan saw letters were typed on the paper and bent down to get a better look.

"Did he leave a message?" Russell asked.

It gave Ryan's heart a jolt, because he hadn't realized that his friend had crept right up behind him.

"Yes," Ryan said.

"What does it say?" Lance asked from the middle of the room.

Ryan read out loud the message typed on the paper.

It preys on your imagination

"What does that mean?" Russell asked.

"It knows how to scare us," Ryan said.

"You guys want to check this out," Lance said.

Ryan turned and walked over toward the far wall where Lance knelt next to a vent hole in the floor. A metal cover lay discarded nearby.

"This is the heating vent," Lance said.

Ryan leaned over and peered into the hole.

"There's blood down there," Lance said.

Ryan could see streaks of red running down the inside of the vent. It looked wet and fresh.

"I think I know where Mr. Lothrop went," Lance said.

No, Ryan thought. *It can't be.* It felt like something gripped his heart and squeezed. As he turned to look away, not wanting to think about what happened here, he saw a tall, dark figure standing in the doorway and nearly jumped out of his skin.

"Is he gone?" Mortimer Rigby asked and then stepped into the room.

"What do you know about it?" Lance asked.

"Harold was afraid of something," Mortimer said. "I tried to enlist his help, but he was too scared."

"Help with what?" Ryan asked.

"Save my son and stop the madness in town."

"Who is your son?" Lance asked.

"His name is Quinn," Mortimer said, his face sagging with grief.

"You're Quinn's father?"

Mortimer looked at Lance and a spark brightened his eyes. "You! You're the one who was with him at Rita's house."

"Yes."

Mortimer rushed over and grabbed Lance by the arms. "Did he seem okay?"

"I guess," Lance said, pushing the man's hands off him. He eyed the magician up and down. "You're a bit old to be his dad."

The man smirked. "It's kind of a long story. Let's just chalk it up to bad magic."

"What do you know of that man Shreckengast?" Ryan asked.

Mortimer shook his head. "Nothing. Only that he has my son and is doing wicked things in town. He's got a hold of some dark magic and I fear what he plans to do with it."

"Do you know where he is?" Lance asked.

"I think so," Mortimer said. "A vacant house not far from here. On Carriage Lane."

Lance turned to Ryan. "That's got to be the old Wickstrom Funeral Home. That place has been empty for years."

"I need to find my son. Will you boys help me?"

Ryan remembered what Curtis had told him about someone at the boardinghouse able to help him. He assumed he meant Mr. Lothrop, but maybe not.

"Yes," Ryan said. "We'll help."

Lance reached into his pants pocket beneath his costume and pulled out the locket he found at the amusement park. He held it up to the magician.

"Do you recognize this?"

The old man's eyes went wide. He reached out and grabbed it from Lance's grasp.

"That belonged to Quinn," Mortimer said. His shaky hands pried the locket open. He frowned. "This is a picture of my wife, Quinn's mother. It's faded. Can't hardly see her." He closed the locket. "But she's never faded from my memory." He looked at Lance. "Where on earth did you find it?"

"That's a long story too."

"Which we don't have time for," Ryan said. "We need to go to the Wickstrom House."

"Yes," Mortimer said. "I've waited long enough."

Ryan suggested to his friends that they leave their trick-or-treat bags in Mr. Lothrop's room, one less burden to carry.

"But what about all my candy?" Russell asked.

"We'll come back for it," Ryan said, hoping that indeed would be the case. He and Lance left their cane and rubber pitchfork as well. As they headed downstairs, Ryan said he wanted to call his brother.

"Dane might come and help us."

"Are you kidding?" Lance said as they reached the front hallway. "He's at a party with that hot chick. He ain't going anywhere else."

"We'll see about that."

Mortimer showed him the phone closet and Ryan stepped inside. He thumbed through the phone book until he found the number for the Lavory house out on Old Coach Road. The phone rang several times and Ryan thought no one would answer. But then someone picked up, a male voice.

"I'm looking for my brother, Dane Woodson," Ryan said. "It's urgent."

"Hey, Ryan," the voice said. "It's me, Ben Karney. Dane's out in the barn with everyone else. Big party here. You're lucky I heard the phone. I came into the house to use the bathroom. Do you know how hard it is to pee when you're wrapped up as a mummy?"

"Can you get him?" Ryan asked, exasperated. "It's a matter of life or death." He hoped that sounded important.

"Sure," Ben said. "Hold on."

Ryan gave the thumbs up to the others and waited. It took forever before he finally heard his brother's voice on the phone.

"This better be good," Dane said in a perturbed tone.

"It is," Ryan said. "There's some bad shit going down in town. Evil stuff."

"Are you yanking my chain?" Dane said. Ryan could hear the frustration building up in his brother's voice.

"This ain't no joke," Ryan said. "I saw Curtis tonight."

"What the hell are you talking about?"

"I mean it. Curtis appeared. There's a really bad dude at the Wickstrom House and we're going there to stop him. He's behind the disappearances in town and all the other weird shit that's been happening. Curtis knows. He said you'd want to help."

"Listen," Dane said, and Ryan could hear the anger in his voice. Or maybe it was only frustration. "This is really messed up. Are you all right in the head? Should I call Mom or Dad?"

"No!" That was the last thing Ryan needed. "It's all true. I swear. We're going to the Wickstrom House on Carriage Lane. Me, Lance, and Russell. And Mr. Rigby. He's like a really old magician."

"Who?"

"No time to explain everything," Ryan said. "We're going there and I need you to come help us." He felt time was wasting. "That's where we'll be. So come if you can." He hung up the phone before Dane got another word in. "Let's go," he said to the others when he stepped out of the phone closet.

As they headed to the front door, Lance stopped.

"Do you guys smell something burning?" he asked.

Ryan took a deep breath. It smelled like some of the times the town dump caught fire.

"Yeah," he said. He looked at the opening to the front parlor. "I think it's coming from in there." He could hear the noise from the television but nothing else.

As he stepped into the room, followed by the others, he could see the silhouettes of two people sitting on the couch in the glow of the television screen. It looked like Mr. and Mrs. Fifer. They did not move or acknowledge their presence in the room. They sat on the couch facing the television.

"Hello?" Ryan said. "Is everything okay?" No response. He moved around to the front of the couch.

Oh shit.

Darrin and Lydia Fifer didn't move because they couldn't. Their two bodies were burnt to a crisp, like charred logs.

"What the hell!" Lance exclaimed.

"That's what you smelled," Ryan said. "Them."

Mortimer approached and looked at the two bodies.

"What did this?" he asked. "There's nothing else burned, not the couch or the rug. Only their bodies."

"How could that be?" Lance said.

"I think I'm going to be sick," Russell said.

Ryan thought about Russell's dad and how he died. This wasn't something he needed to see.

"Go out to the hall," Ryan said, and Russell left the room.

"Why did this happen to them?" Lance asked.

"More of Shreckengast's work," Mortimer said. "He's raining hell down on this town."

"I think there's a reason for this," Ryan said. "The lighter Russell found at the amusement park. It had the initials D.F."

"Darrin Fifer," Lance said.

"I think the reason they didn't want to talk about the funhouse fire was because he was the one who accidentally started it."

"So that means," Lance said, "that he killed Shreckengast and all the others."

"And they're back," Ryan said.

"And it's all my fault," Mortimer said. "My magic trick brought them all here."

Ryan had no idea what the man was talking about, but didn't want to waste any more time. "Let's get out of here."

Screams came from outside. It sounded like young kids. But it didn't sound like the joyful cry of Halloween cheer. It sounded like fear.

When they stepped out the front door, Ryan turned to the Stich sisters, sitting on the stoop. They looked like statues.

"Oh, no," Ryan said. He waved a hand in front of their faces but they didn't blink. "Something's wrong with them." He leaned closer and reached out to touch Pearl. He shook her arm and it felt like paper. He stepped back and looked at the others.

"What is it?" Lance asked.

"They're like husks," Ryan said. "As if they were made of papier-mâché or something."

"Or like a hollowed-out pumpkin," Mortimer said. "No one is safe. Not even the innocents."

"Then we better get going," Ryan said. If they saw any more things like this, he might lose his nerve. As it was, his heart pounded in his chest and his nerves felt jittery. "Let's get to the Wickstrom House."

He imagined worse things waited for them there.

6

Dane walked into the barn behind Kyler's house where Santana's 'Evil Ways' blared from the stereo against the back wall. He looked for Ben and Wade, who were with Elsie over by a large tin tub of water filled with apples. Elsie got down on her knees as she awaited her turn to bob for the fruit. The party had been rocking and everything was copasetic till the phone call from Ryan screwed it up.

"What's wrong?" Ben said when he approached. He must have read Dane's face.

"It's Ryan," Dane said. "He's flipping out about something."

"Is it serious?" Wade asked.

Dane shrugged. "You never know with these twerps. He said he's seen Curtis tonight, so that can't be good."

"Don't you think he's just yanking your chain?" Ben suggested.

"I don't think so. He sounded messed up. Said some crazy shit is going down at the Wickstrom House."

"That place is empty," Wade said. "Don't suppose they broke in there or something? Some kind of Halloween prank?"

"This didn't sound like a prank. I'm worried about the little shit."

Dane wasn't planning to leave, despite his concerns. He'd brought a condom in his wallet and Elsie hinted it would happen tonight, but he didn't like the sound of his brother's voice. The kid sounded on the edge, or maybe even over it. What he said on the phone made no sense. Dane felt he should have paid more attention to how Ryan was feeling about Curtis's death. Heck, it pissed him off sometimes that he barely thought about the loss himself these days.

Elsie turned to look up at Dane. "Hold my ears," she said. She removed her bunny ears and handed them to him. She brushed her hair over her ears and turned back to the tub.

Dane watched as Elsie put her hands behind her back, and bent over to stick her face into the water near the bobbing apples. Her body began to shudder and tremble, as if in a spasmodic fit.

"Elsie?" Dane called out and moved toward her.

Kyler Lavory must have noticed something because he rushed over and put his hand in the water near her face, as if he thought she were drowning. He yelled and pulled his hand out. Flaps of loose skin dangled off the end of his fingertips.

Dane grabbed Elsie's shoulders and pulled her face out of the tub of water.

An ear-shattering scream ripped from her throat as Dane turned her shoulders to look at her, an image he would never forget.

The flesh from her beautiful face had been stripped off, down to the bone of her skull in spots, exposing pulsing red muscles and tendons that tried to work her jaw so her mouth could scream. Her eyes searched for his, but they were only sizzling orbs that leaked milky pus.

"It's like acid!" Kyler cried, holding his wounded hand out as some kids rushed to his side.

Teens wailed and ran from the barn in a frenzied panic, not sure what was happening.

Elsie's scream died out as sudden as the pulling of a plug, and her body slipped from Dane's hands and collapsed to the floor in a heap. He stared at her motionless body. Blood seeped from loose strips of skin on her face and pooled around her blonde locks.

Dane felt the urge to vomit. He ran from the barn, over toward Wade's Gran Torino and bent over. His stomach lurched and he heaved a gusher of everything he'd consumed till now.

Ben and Wade came over to him.

"What the fuck was that?" Ben cried, looking back at the barn.

"Elsie, for Christ's sake!" Wade said. "She's...." He couldn't finish.

Dane straightened up, but held one hand onto the back of the Torino to steady himself. His knees felt like they were about to buckle. He spotted his baseball bat in the vehicle bed where he had left it earlier and grabbed it.

"We've got to go," he said to the others, trying to compose himself. He gripped tight to the end of the bat for security.

"What? Where?" Ben asked.

"The Wickstrom House," Dane said. He spit and wiped his mouth, still tasting the vomit. "Ryan said weird shit was happening there." He pointed back at the barn. All the other party-goers stood outside by cars not knowing what to do, some crying. Dane didn't know what had happed to Kyler, but now he didn't care. "That shit that just went down in there. That must be why."

"But what about Elsie?" Ben said.

Dane tried to suppress tears. "I can't help her anymore." He spit again, the taste in his mouth bad. "But I can try and help Ryan."

7

Ryan stood on the sidewalk in front of the house at 13 Carriage Lane and stared in awe when he saw the long-vacant former funeral home was now occupied. In the windows of all three stories of the building, staring back at him with fiery eyes, were jack-o'-lanterns glowing from burning flames within them. An uneasy feeling crept inside him and settled in the pit of his stomach like a nesting snake.

Lance and Russell kept silent beside him, equally stunned at the sight. Mortimer stood behind them and though he towered over the trio, Ryan sensed that even the old magician felt insignificant in the presence of the Wickstrom House.

At the front right corner of the house stood a tall maple tree that nearly eclipsed the roof. It still held half of its autumn leaves, bright yellow and almost glowing from the luminescence of the bright jack-o'-lanterns in the windows.

Before Ryan had a chance to say anything, a pair of young trick-or-treaters brushed past him and raced up the walkway to the house, tickets grasped in their tiny hands.

"Stop!" Ryan yelled, but in an instant the kids were swallowed up through the open front door. He turned to look up at Mortimer. "We need to get in there." He regretted the words almost as soon as he said them.

"Agreed," Mortimer said, not taking his eyes off the house. "But not through the front door. I'd rather find a less obvious entrance."

"Okay," Ryan said. "We'll follow you." The old man didn't make him feel safe, but he was all the help they had. Mortimer led the way across the yard, but Ryan stopped when he realized Russell wasn't following. He turned to look back, as did Lance and Mortimer.

"Are you coming?" Ryan asked. Russell's eyes looked dazed.

"I can't do it," he said with a vigorous shake of his head. "I'm sorry."

"We stick together," Lance said.

"I'm not going in there," Russell said.

Ryan walked up to him and put a hand on his shoulder. "That's all right. You don't have to." He could see the despair in his friend's eyes. Who could blame him? Hell, Ryan was scared to death, but felt he had to do something. "You stay out here, by the gate. Keep any other kids from coming to this house. That can be your job. Warn them there's danger inside."

"Okay," Russell said with a nod.

Ryan thought of something. "Give me the lighter, just in case."

Russell dug it out of his pocket and handed it over. "It doesn't work."

Ryan could see the relief in Russell's eyes already. "If my brother Dane shows up, tell him we need his help inside."

"I can do that," Russell said and took up position beside the granite post the front gate was attached to. Next to it was a large shrub that left him concealed in shadows.

A good hiding spot, Ryan thought. He'd rather have Russell's help, but as scared as the boy was, he'd be no use. Ryan joined the others and Mortimer led them toward the corner of the house.

"Look," Lance said as they passed under the maple tree. He pointed up.

Ryan craned his neck and saw something hanging in the tree. It looked like a stuffed dummy, a cheap Halloween decoration. But as the figure twisted on the rope attached to its neck, he saw the face and recognized it.

"That's Chief Strong," Ryan said.

"Shit," Lance said. "Is he dead?"

The arms lay limp at the body's side, the head leaning on one shoulder as if the neck could no longer hold it up.

"Looks like it," Mortimer said, no surprise in his voice.

As light from one of the flaming jack-o'-lanterns cast its rays toward the tree, Ryan could see a star-shaped badge pinned to the chief's chest.

"If the police aren't any help," Lance said, "how can *we* do anything?"

"Because we have some idea of what we're up against," Mortimer said. He pointed up at the chief's body. "Don't let that discourage you." He gestured for them to follow and led them around the house.

In the backyard, lit jack-o'-lanterns looked out the rear windows of the house as well. Ryan felt the glowing eyes watching them. Mortimer approached the bulkhead basement doors at the back of the house.

"We can go in through this way," he said.

"What if it's locked?" Ryan asked, hoping it would be.

Mortimer reached down to the handle and pulled the door open. "Shreckengast isn't going to lock anyone out of this place. He wants people to enter."

"That's what I was afraid of," Ryan said as he thought maybe Russell had the better idea.

"Come on," Mortimer said and descended the steps into the basement.

Ryan shot Lance a cautious look and then followed the magician, becoming engulfed by the darkness below.

"Last time I entered a basement through a bulkhead was not a fun time," Lance said before following the others.

Ryan had never experienced such complete darkness and wished some of those lit pumpkins had been set up down here to at least shed some light. He reached out and grabbed on to Lance's arm to make sure he wasn't all alone.

"Is that you?" Lance whispered.

"Yes," Ryan said in a voice just as soft. "Sorry."

"That's okay."

A light came on, a dim bulb in the basement ceiling. Mortimer stood beneath it with his hand on the chain that turned it on.

"That's better," he said as he looked around the basement.

A long counter stood on one wall with a massive porcelain sink embedded in the middle, looking big enough to take a bath in.

"Look at that," Lance said as he pointed at the sink. "It's huge."

"That's where they would wash the dead bodies," Mortimer said.

"Gross," Ryan said and turned away. They went through a door into another section of the basement.

A large, cylindrical black metal furnace squatted in the middle of the basement, large pipes like octopus arms rising from the top and stretching out across the ceiling. On one wall nearby was set a large bin, its door open, revealing a small pile of black coal. A chute led to the rear wall to the outside. A short, square shovel with a wooden handle stood beside the bin. Mortimer walked over to it and picked up the shovel.

"I'll feel much better with a weapon," he said to them as he tested the heft of the coal shovel. "Shall we head upstairs and see what we find?"

They ascended the staircase with Mortimer in the lead. Each step produced an agonizing screech that sounded like the wooden steps were being rent in two. *So much for sneaking into the place*, Ryan thought. Whoever inhabited the house could hear they were coming.

The door at the top of the stairs opened into a small foyer with three other doors.

"One for each of us," Mortimer said with a smirk.

"No," Ryan said. "We don't separate." He'd seen enough scary movies to know better.

Mortimer gripped the shovel tight and chose the middle door. When they stepped into the room, Ryan nearly lost his footing. The floor in the room was slanted and pitched downward to the right at an angle.

"What the hell," Lance said.

"I don't like the looks of this," Ryan said. "Maybe we should go back and try another door."

Mortimer turned but the door behind them was locked. "Guess there's no going back."

At the far end of the tilted room was the only other door, pitched at an angle even with the floorboards. Ryan stepped carefully, following the outer wall and keeping his hand on it to maintain his balance as the three of them walked along the perimeter of the high end of the room toward the door on the opposite wall. Several times Ryan felt his sneakers slip on the varnished floorboards but was able to keep himself from falling.

"This sucks," Lance said from behind.

"Take your time," Mortimer said. "Plant each foot carefully."

"Yikes!" Lance yelled.

Ryan turned to see his friend's feet go out from under him and Lance went crashing to the floor and began sliding down the slant.

"Watch out!" Ryan yelled, afraid Lance would crash into the wall at the bottom of the tilted floor and break something.

But before he reached the bottom, a section of the floorboards sprung up, like a trapdoor, and Lance fell screaming into the abyss. The boards fell back in place.

"Lance!" Ryan screamed. He got down on all fours and began scampering down the slope toward where his friend had vanished.

"Stop!" Mortimer yelled at him.

Ryan looked back up at the magician. "We've got to find him. He has to be back down in the basement."

"The door's locked," Mortimer said. "We must push forward."

"We can't just leave him!"

"He's on his own now. He can only help himself."

Ryan looked down at the floorboards where Lance had disappeared, seeing no way to pry them up. He pounded on them, hoping Lance would hear him. No response came.

"We need to go," Mortimer said.

Ryan looked up at him as the magician gestured for him with his free hand, the other still clasping the shovel. Ryan crept along the lower edge of the slant, looking back several times to where the opening in the floor had closed, wondering what had happened to Lance. He reached the bottom of the far wall at the same time Mortimer reached the top. They both made their way to meet at the crooked door.

Mortimer turned the knob and pushed it open, and they both tumbled out into a darkened hall. A fluorescent purple glow filtered down from the top edges of the walls, reminding Ryan of the glow from the black lights his brother had in his bedroom.

The hall stretched as far as the eye could see.

"This is impossible," Ryan said. The hall looked longer than the actual house.

"I don't think the inside of this house is the same as the outside," Mortimer said as he walked down the hall.

"How could that be?" Ryan said as he followed.

"Shreckengast possesses some dark magic. One can only imagine what he's capable of doing."

Ryan remembered Lothrop's warning.

It preys on your imagination.

As they proceeded down the hall, Ryan saw framed portraits hanging on both sides. They were young people, kids, teens and young adults, their faces burned and blistered, flesh peeling, distorted. Grotesque.

"These must be the victims of the funhouse fire," Ryan said as he paused in front of one particular picture that looked familiar. He examined the scarred face, the black holes of the sockets that no longer held eyes. He recognized the crew-cut hair.

The young man from the movie theater.

"Restless souls," Mortimer said, surveying each portrait as he passed. "Shreckengast's legion."

Ryan thought about Mr. Fifer, sure he had been the one to cause this. He felt the lighter in his pants pocket. Still there. He met the empty eye sockets of the portrait in front of him.

The eyes blinked.

The young man's portrait now had the marble cat's eyes.

"What the—" Ryan started to say before the man in the picture smiled and began to laugh.

Ryan stepped back but a hand from the portrait reached out and grabbed his arm. The crew-cut man leaned forward and snickered as he climbed out of the painting. His grip on Ryan's arm tightened and Ryan felt his blood vessels would burst.

"Help!" Ryan screamed. He tried pulling away from the man, who now stood in the hall, but he would not let go. Ryan fell to the ground and the man leaned over him, staring down with those cat's eyes, his teeth chattering with laughter. Ryan could see pieces of popcorn stuck in the man's teeth.

Thunk!

The sound echoed in the hall as Ryan saw Mortimer swing the shovel into the back of the crew-cut man's head. The two marbles popped out of the man's eye sockets and shot across the hall. The marbles hit the wooden floor and rolled toward the other end.

The impact of the shovel also caused the man to lose his grip on Ryan's arm. He staggered above him but didn't fall over. The man reached out, waving his hands around as if trying to find Ryan.

He can't see us.

"Come on," Mortimer said. He grabbed Ryan's hand and lifted him to his feet. They raced down the long hall past the last of the portraits.

Ryan looked back to see the man's head spin in their direction. He began chasing them down the hall. The farther they ran, the more the hall appeared to shrink in size, the walls closing in, the ceiling lowering. At the far end, Ryan spotted a door.

"Hurry," Mortimer said.

Ryan didn't dare look back, but could hear the footsteps of the man. They reached the door, which appeared to be half the size of a normal door. Mortimer had to hunch over as the ceiling nearly reached the top of his head. Mortimer opened the door and shoved Ryan through, then followed.

The room they ended up in had no doors. Even the doorway they had come through no longer existed. Ryan spun around and looked at all four walls. Fluorescent paint covered the walls in swirls and twisted shapes. The glow from the paint provided the only illumination in the room.

"There's no way out," Ryan said, fear bubbling up inside him. Lance was gone, Russell left outside, and now he and Mortimer were trapped like rats. At least maybe the crew-cut man couldn't get in here.

"There's got to be an exit," Mortimer said and began pounding on the walls.

Ryan went over to the opposite wall and felt along it with his hands, noticing the textured surface of the paint. Maybe there would be some way to trip a secret door. There were lots of those in the Collinwood mansion on *Dark Shadows*. Secret passages, the stairway into time. There had to be something.

The wall moved where Ryan had his hands. He pushed and a section of the wall opened.

"Here!" he exclaimed and stepped through, glad to be out of the trap.

"Wait!" Mortimer called out from behind.

Before Ryan realized it, the wall slammed shut behind him, separating the two of them. He pounded on the wall.

"Mr. Rigby! Can you hear me?"

No response came.

Ryan couldn't find a release or mechanism from this side to open the wall.

On my own now.

8

Russell kept concealed, squatting down between the front gate's granite post and the evergreen shrub. He had his skull mask back on and had already scared a few young trick-or-treaters away from the Wickstrom House. The cast on his left arm itched and he wished he could scratch the raw skin beneath. He looked down at it and by the light from the nearest streetlamp he could still see the message from Shinbones he had crossed out. He couldn't wait to get the cast off.

He heard a couple of older voices approach the gate. Girls. He heard the rusty squeak of the gate and saw three figures enter. Two wore Thing 1 and Thing 2 costumes from Dr. Seuss, complete with big blue wigs. The third was dressed as a cat and Russell recognized her.

"Becky!" he shouted as he jumped up from his hiding spot.

The girls turned and squealed.

"Who the hell are you?" Becky asked, furious.

He pulled off his mask. "It's me, Russell."

"Why are you hiding in the bushes?"

"Trying to scare little kids?" Liza asked.

Russell ignored her. "What are you doing here?"

"We got tickets to a haunted house," Lindsey said.

"I'm still not sure I want to go," Becky said. "I've had enough frights for one night."

Russell could see concern in her eyes. "I thought you were at Kirby's party."

"Something really creepy happened there."

"I'm sure it was just a prank," Liza said.

"Yeah," Lindsey chimed in. "He must have had one of his goons hiding in the closet."

"It seemed real," Becky said. "Maybe we should just go trick-or-treating instead."

Liza turned to look up at the Wickstrom House. "This will be fun. It's Halloween. Look at all those jack-o'-lanterns in the windows. We're supposed to be scared."

"And we have free passes," Lindsey said, waving a ticket in her hand.

"You don't want to go in there," Russell said.

"Why?" Becky asked. "You think it's too scary for me?"

"It's not that. There's some bad stuff in there. Trust me."

"Why should I believe you?" Becky looked around. "And where are your stupid friends? Where's Ryan and Lance?"

He pointed up at the house. "In there."

"Waiting to scare us?"

"There are scarier things than that in there," Russell said. "You all need to leave now."

"You're not ruining our fun," Liza said. She took Lindsey's hand and Thing 1 and Thing 2 skipped up the walkway to the front door and went inside.

"Wait for me!" Becky hollered and ran after them.

"Crap," Russell said as he watched the black cat disappear into the house. Ryan wasn't going to be happy with him.

He returned to his hiding spot and wondered what was going on inside the house. He felt guilty for chickening out and knew he'd never live it down. Ryan and Lance would be sure to remind him about it, if they even wanted to still be friends with him. He just didn't want to end up like Wesley, disappearing into a pile of leaves never to be seen again. He wished this night would be over.

The leaves of the shrub beside him shook.

Something rested on his right shoulder.

He turned to look and saw a skeletal hand on it.

"Shinbones," he gasped.

9

Mortimer pounded on the wall where Ryan had disappeared and even swung the blade of the shovel against it a couple times but it didn't budge. No sound came from the other side.

Gone, he thought. He had brought two young boys here and he'd lost them both. Who knows what had befallen them. *Irresponsible.* His negligence had cost him his own son, and now the loss of two more boys was on his hands. He couldn't even remember their names.

This has to end. He knew what must be done.

Mortimer continued feeling the surface of the walls surrounding him, looking for a seam or some mechanism to get him out of the sealed room. On the back wall, he felt something give and he pushed hard. The wall opened. It wasn't the same way the boy had gone, but it was an exit nonetheless. Mortimer went through and walked down a dark corridor that ended up in a large parlor.

At the far end of the room, Shreckengast sat in a large chair, the magic hat on his head, surrounded by candelabras topped with flaming candles that lit up the room. Behind him lay an open casket on display. In the coffin, he recognized the body of Harold Lothrop. What Mortimer saw to the right of Schreckengast caused his heart to flame.

Quinn.

All these years, all this time.

Mortimer staggered forward on legs that felt rubbery and weak. He dragged the shovel, which made a deep scraping sound along the wooden floorboards. He stopped before the chairs and noticed an old friend, Daimon the white rabbit, fur now mottled, seated in a chair on Shreckengast's left. The rabbit sat up on its hind legs and bared its teeth. Beside the rabbit's chair stood Mortimer's magic cabinet.

"Quinn," Mortimer uttered with a wispy breath.

"I knew we'd be meeting again," Shreckengast said. His mouth spread in a sly smile.

"Who is this?" Quinn asked, turning to Shreckengast.

"I want my son," Mortimer said. It came out as a plea, though he intended it to be a demand.

Shreckengast rose from his chair and pointed at Mortimer. "This fragile old washed-up magician is your father."

Quinn looked at him, his mouth round in bewilderment, and Mortimer's heart ached at the painful look in the boy's eyes.

"It's true, my son," Mortimer said.

"That can't be my father," Quinn said.

"This is the man who sent you on that long journey into darkness," Shreckengast said. "To where only I could save you."

"My father is a young man," Quinn said in disbelief.

"Time has robbed me of my life with you," Mortimer said, pleading. "I made a foolish mistake and sent you somewhere unknown. I've tried all these years to get you back. You don't know how much I've missed you."

Shreckengast looked at Quinn. "Couldn't have tried very hard. Waited forty years and then, poof, just like that, he was able to bring you back." He looked at Mortimer. "Maybe you never really wanted him back."

"Oh, I did." Mortimer groaned. "And now I want to make amends for all that I've wrought." He spotted confusion on the boy's face. Mortimer took out the locket from his pocket and stepped over to Quinn's chair. He opened the locket and handed it to his son. "That's your mother. She gave that locket to you when you were eight."

Quinn looked at the faded picture inside. "I can't see her. I can't even picture her." A teardrop rolled down his face. He looked up at his father. "I can't picture *you.*"

"Did you send his mother away too?" Shreckengast asked. "Put her in a magic box?"

"No." Mortimer's shoulders slumped at the thought of his wife and how she'd left them in the middle of the night. "No."

"He's an imposter," Quinn said and stood up from the chair. "You should give him to the Scamps."

"No," Shreckengast said. "He is your father. But what's worse, he is a lousy magician."

"Give me my son," Mortimer said, "and I'll leave this place."

Shreckengast laughed. "You can have your son."

"What?" Quinn looked at the tall, thin man. "What are you saying?"

Shreckengast looked down at the boy. "I don't need you anymore. I've got everything I needed from you. You're not like me and the Scamps." He reached out and placed his hand on Quinn's chest. "Your heart is still beating. You don't belong with us." Shreckengast turned to Mortimer. "Take him."

"You can't do this!" Quinn's voice cracked with terror. "Don't let him!"

Shreckengast walked over to the magic cabinet and opened the door. He gestured inside.

"Take him and go into the cabinet. You can go anywhere you want through there." He smiled again. "That's the only way I'll let the two of you leave."

Mortimer stared at the cabinet and its dark interior. *A trap. But what choice did he have?*

None.

He approached Quinn and took the boy by the arm. His son tried to pull away.

"Leave me alone! I'm not going with you."

"This is the only way," Mortimer said. "We can be a family again."

"You're not my family!"

Mortimer's eyes felt ready to burst like a stopped-up pipe.

"I must right the wrongs I've made," he said. He dragged Quinn toward the cabinet. As he passed Daimon, he paused and looked down at the rabbit.

"He stays with me," Shreckengast said. "I've grown fond of the furry little critter."

Mortimer knew this wasn't his Daimon anymore. As he dragged Quinn past Shreckengast, the tall man took the hat from Quinn's head.

"You won't need that anymore," Shreckengast said. "No more magic for you."

"You said I could go trick-or-treating!"

"Halloween has something else in store for you." His eyes bored into Mortimer's as he held the door open.

Mortimer still held the shovel and wanted to smack it upside the man's face, but he didn't think it would do any good. The man wasn't human. Besides, he knew he would need the tool where he was going.

He pushed Quinn inside the cabinet and stepped in behind him. The last thing he saw before the door closed was the wicked grin on Shreckengast's face before darkness engulfed the inside of the cabinet.

10

Wade Droege's El Camino pulled up in front of the Wickstrom House and Dane and Ben hopped out. Dane looked up at the house and the jack-o'-lanterns in all the windows.

"This better not be a prank," Dane said. "Or I'll murder the little bastard." He thought about what happened to Elsie back at the party and his muscles tensed.

"I don't feel so good," Ben said.

Dane looked at him. "Are you scared?"

"No," Ben said. "Something doesn't feel right inside me."

"Did you get car sick?" Wade asked. "What junk did you eat at the party?"

"I think my wrappings are too tight," Ben said. He tugged at a couple of the rags that made up his mummy costume.

"Let's just get in there and find my brother and see what's going on."

The three of them entered the gate and walked toward the house. Ben fell a few steps behind.

"Guys," he said and bent over, holding his belly. "Something's wrong with me."

Dane stopped and turned around, annoyed. "What the hell is the matter with you?"

"I don't know. I feel like I'm burning up and suffocating at the same time."

"Just pull yourself together," Dane said. He could see Ben's eyes through the slit in the wrappings on his face. They burned like embers.

"I feel funny," Ben said. "Something hurts bad."

"Jesus Christ," Wade said.

"I need to get these wrappings off!" Ben cried. "They're smothering me!"

"What?"

"Help me!" Ben said, his voice strangled.

Dane dropped the baseball bat. It clattered on the stone walkway.

"Let's get him out of those," he said to Wade.

"Hurry!" Ben cried. "Please hurry!"

Dane and Wade grabbed edges of the torn white rags that wrapped Ben's body. They began unraveling and unspooling them as fast as they could. Ben had grown silent and Dane worried he'd passed out. They worked in a flurry, pulling and unwinding the strips of rags.

When they finished, they had a pile of rags on the walkway. *But no Ben.*

"What the fuck!" Dane cried, looking all around. He still had some of the rags in his hands.

"What just happened?" Wade asked, his eyes like saucers.

Dane looked down at the pile of rags, unable to comprehend why Ben wasn't in them.

He began to believe what his brother had told him. First Elsie and now Ben.

Dane grabbed his baseball bat from the ground and ran into the Wickstrom House.

11

Ryan heard organ music in the darkness and followed the sound. He wondered why he couldn't see any windows in the house, the ones with the lit jack-o'-lanterns. The place seemed like one dark corridor after another. Mr. Rigby's words came back to him: *The house isn't the same on the inside as it is on the outside.*

A trick? Magic? Perhaps some evil spell caused by this Shreckengast guy?

Ryan made his way through the shadowed hall and at last saw a glimmer of light coming from an alcove ahead where a soft glow spilled out along with the notes of an organ. The music sounded somewhat familiar.

Where do I know that from?

He approached the opening with caution and gazed in. A teen boy sat at an organ, his hands on the keys. Ryan looked at the kid's hands and noticed the bones on his fingers poked out through tears in the skin. He glanced up at the face and recognized the boy as the one he saw that day at the soccer game.

The kid turned and grinned at him.

The music seemed familiar because Ryan recognized it as the theme music to the opening credits of *Dark Shadows*.

"Want to play?" the boy asked. He pulled back on his arms and his wrists detached from his hands, which continued to play the organ. The boy swiveled on his seat, held up the bony stubs of his arms, and began to laugh.

Ryan recoiled and ran away from the room, down the corridor. A strobe light began flashing and made him feel like he was running in slow motion. His head felt dizzy from the bursts of light and dark.

Something moved up ahead.

He stopped.

A ragged white rabbit in an open doorway sat up on its hind legs, staring at him. Its eyes simmered like burning coal.

Ryan wondered what it was doing here.

The rabbit turned and ran through the doorway into the next room.

Ryan ran after it. When he entered the room, his feet went out from under him and he fell on his ass. A jolt of pain burned up his spine. The floor felt cold. He heard a cracking sound, and hoped it didn't come from his own bones. As he tried to stand, the floor felt slippery. He managed to get to his feet and looked down.

In the bursts of light from the strobe, he saw the floor was made of ice.

Beneath the surface, water rushed by.

Ryan looked across to the other side of the room, where the rabbit stared back at him from another doorway.

You tricked me, you sneaky bastard.

The rabbit ran off.

The ice groaned and creaked beneath him. Ryan stood still, afraid to move.

Beneath the ice, he spotted a figure, deep down, floating by in the flowing water. When the body turned in the current, he saw its face.

No. Not possible.

He remembered the typewritten note Mr. Lothrop left in his typewriter.

It preys on your imagination.

Not real, Ryan thought. *This is not real.* He closed his eyes. *None of this is real.*

The chill seemed to be sucked out of the room. Ryan opened his eyes and looked down at darkened wood floorboards. He swallowed, though his throat felt dry, and then raced out of the room into another corridor.

A light beam bounced around at the other end and Ryan steeled himself for what might be coming next. He wondered what had happened to all the trick-or-treaters who might have been lured into this place and what fate they had met.

A tall, dark figure approached, shining a flashlight beam. The light fell on Ryan's eyes and he shielded them from the glare.

"Who is that?" a man's voice called out. The figure approached.

Ryan squinted through the glare and recognized Mr. Williams, Becky's dad.

"Ryan Woodson?" Mr. Williams said.

"Yes," he answered. "What are you doing here?"

"I'm looking for Becky," Mr. Williams said. "She's lost in here somewhere."

No, Ryan thought, a wave of panic engulfing him. She was supposed to be at Kirby Tressler's party. *How did she end up in this place?*

"Have you seen her?" Mr. Williams asked.

"No," Ryan said, grateful to have another adult around since he'd been separated from Mr. Rigby. "I haven't seen her at all."

"Are you sure?"

Why did the man doubt him? It sounded like an accusation.

"I've seen the way you look at her," Mr. Williams said, his voice deepening. "I know you watch her."

"No, sir," Ryan said, wondering what the man was talking about.

"Sure, you do." He stepped closer. "You're like a little letch who can't keep his eyes off her."

Ryan took a step back. "I don't know what you're talking about," he said, unsure what had come over Becky's dad.

"You're keeping her here, aren't you, you little snot!"

"I haven't done anything!" Ryan yelled.

"You probably want to put her in one of your sick little twisted stories that you write."

"That's not true!" Ryan took another step back. He looked around for somewhere to run. Something was wrong with Mr. Williams.

"I know what you wrote about me," the man said, growing angrier. "Your stupid little 'Jack-o'-lantern Man' tale. You think I don't know about that? You made me a monster."

"I didn't." Ryan's body shook. "It's just a story."

"You want to see a monster?" Mr. Williams stepped closer. He held the flashlight up under his chin with his left hand so his whole face lit up. With his right hand he grabbed the top of his head and pulled up.

The skin slid off his head like a mask, revealing a jack-o'-lantern head beneath, flames blazing inside behind the triangle eyes and the crooked carved grin.

"Time to eat!" the creature said. The pumpkin mouth widened.

Ryan screamed. His back bumped up against a wall behind him and he realized he had no place to go.

Something blurred out of the darkness from behind the jack-o'-lantern man. The pumpkin head flew apart, bursting into pieces. Sticky wetness splattered across Ryan's face. Bits of flame floated in the air before flaming out in smoky tendrils that drifted to the floor.

The now-headless body in front of Ryan collapsed to the floor. Behind it stood someone in a baseball uniform.

"Dane!" Ryan yelled. He'd never been more excited to see his older brother. His friend Wade stood beside him dressed as a Revolutionary War soldier.

"What the hell was that?" Dane said, wiping sticky orange wetness from the barrel of his baseball bat. "That wasn't even human."

"I'm so glad to see you," Ryan said, his heart racing.

"Something weird's going on in here," Wade said.

"You don't know the half of it," Ryan said. "I've lost Lance and Mr. Rigby. Don't know what happened to them. And I think Becky Williams might be in here somewhere." He looked down at the headless heap, not sure what to believe.

"Let's get out of here," Dane said.

"No," Ryan said. "We can't go now. We need to finish what we came here for."

"Finish what?" Wade asked.

Ryan raised his hands up. "This place. We need to stop whatever's happening here. We need to stop Mr. Shreckengast."

"I don't know what you're talking about," Dane said. "I just know we lost Ben outside and whatever happened here is freaking me out. We've got to go."

"They won't let us leave," Ryan said.

"Who?" Wade asked.

"Shreckengast and the other sick things in here. We need to stop them. To save everyone."

"And how do we go about that?" Dane asked.

Ryan looked down at the smashed bits of the jack-o'-lantern on the floor, lit up by the flashlight that lay nearby. He remembered the warning from Eddie Scruggs.

There's something in the pumpkins.

He thought about the lit pumpkins in all the windows.

"Smash the pumpkins," Ryan said. "The ones in the windows. Smash them all." He didn't know for sure if that was the answer. But he had no other solutions.

"Do you see any windows?" Dane asked as he gestured around him.

"We need to find our way out of this maze," Ryan said. "It's like a walk-through funhouse, like Shreckengast's House of Phantasmagoria at the Pine Island Pond Amusement Park. It burnt down, but he recreated it here at the Wickstrom House."

"How do we find our way out?" Wade asked.

"I know the way out," a voice called from down the darkened hall.

Dane spun around, and held his baseball bat up as if he was going to swing for a home run. A red figure came walking down the hall, an outline of horns on its head.

Ryan picked up the flashlight and aimed it down the corridor toward the familiar voice.

The flashlight beam fell on the face.

"Lance!" Ryan cried.

12

Becky followed Lindsey in the dark, thinking the funhouse lame. The last display they saw depicted a bloody, naked woman strapped down on a log being driven into a buzzsaw. But it all looked too fake. A plastic mannequin that didn't look the least bit real.

Now they approached a wooden door with a crescent moon cut out in the middle. Becky had seen doors like that on outhouses up north when her parents took the family camping. Gurgling sounded from the other side of the door. The three of them took turns peeking through the crescent window.

When Becky got her chance, she looked in and saw a toilet bowl. Two hands stretched out from inside it as if someone were drowning in the toilet. She could hear rushing water and the muffled cries of help. She pulled away from the door.

"That's just gross," she said, her lips frowning. "Not scary at all."

"Let's try in here," Liza said and walked into a room off the corridor.

Becky and Lindsey followed. Becky saw bookcases lining all four walls of the room. As she twirled around to take it all in, the room seemed to stretch, the bookcases reaching up to the ceiling, giving the effect that the floor was sinking like an elevator. She felt dizzy and went over to lean up against one of the bookcases.

Her eyes surveyed the titles on the bindings. *Something Wicked This Way Comes*, *The Haunting of Hill House*, *I Am Legend*, *Rosemary's Baby*, and *Goblins*. The last one was by someone named H.B. Lothrop. *Scary books*, she thought, and wondered if the whole library was filled with those.

Becky gazed up toward the ceiling and noticed the gargoyles perched on top of each of the bookcases. The same ones from the Maplewood Library in the Town Square. She retreated toward the middle of the room.

"I don't like this," she said, a sensation of something crawling in her gut from the thoughts of the last time she saw these stone figures.

"What's the matter?" Lindsey asked.

"We need to leave," Becky said.

"Shouldn't something scary happen in here?" Liza asked, ignoring her pleas.

Becky shifted her eyes from one gargoyle to the next, watching to see if any of them moved.

Statues, she thought. *They're playing the Statues game like before.*

Becky couldn't keep all four in view at the same time. As soon as she took her eyes off one to look at another, she caught movement out of the corner of her eye from the one before. The room became dizzying as she turned from one to the next. Her stomach churned. She knew it was risky, but she took her eyes off the gargoyles to seek out her friends.

"We need to go," she said.

Thud!

Becky spun around at the sound. The frog-like gargoyle had jumped down from the bookcase and landed on the floor behind Liza.

"About time something happened," Liza said cheerfully.

"You don't understand," Becky warned. "Get away from it."

"It's just a creepy frog," Liza said as she took a step toward it.

"Not really that scary," Lindsey said.

"I wonder what it's supposed to do." Liza stepped closer.

"Don't!" Becky yelled.

The frog's mouth opened and a long red tongue shot out and wrapped itself around Liza's leg. She screamed as it pulled her to the floor, her blue Thing 1 wig flying off her head.

"Help!" Liza yelled as the tongue pulled her toward the frog's mouth.

Becky froze, unable to move.

Lindsey rushed forward and tried to grab Liza's outstretched arm, but it was too late. The frog's tongue pulled the girl into its open mouth and then clamped shut. Liza's screams were cut short, followed by the sound of crunching bones.

"Oh god!" Lindsey cried, looking like she was about to vomit. She fled the room.

Becky stared at the frog. Their eyes locked. She didn't dare move.

I'm a statue, she thought. *I'm still as a statue. It can't get me as long as I don't move. That's the rules of the game.*

Another thud sounded to her right. She didn't react, as hard as the temptation was. The only thing she allowed herself to move was her eyeballs, and she rolled them to her right and could barely glimpse the hooded gargoyle now down on the floor as well.

If I watch it, that means it can't move.

A sound behind her signaled the owl gargoyle had now joined the fray.

I'm surrounded. I can't keep my eyes on all of them.

Becky managed to look toward the open doorway where Lindsey ran. *Too far?* Could she get there in time if she sprinted? The sick thing in her stomach coiled up. She heard scraping on the floor behind her.

I can't keep this up. I can't keep my eyes on all of them.

Becky sprung from her frozen state and lunged toward the door. She heard the gargoyles follow.

13

Mortimer and Quinn stepped out of the darkness into a familiar spot.

"Where are we?" Quinn asked.

"The town cemetery," Mortimer said as the two of them walked down a path between the headstones.

"Why did you bring us here?"

"I need to show you something." Mortimer still carried the coal shovel.

They arrived in front of a grave. Quinn stared at the headstone.

"Is that my name?" he asked.

"Yes," Mortimer said. "But of course you're not buried there."

"Who is?"

"You'll see." Mortimer began digging.

"I didn't want to come with you," Quinn said. "I wanted to stay with Mr. Shreckengast."

Mortimer paused and looked up at his son. He knew he'd made a disaster of things.

"I'm sorry I sent you away like I did," Mortimer said. "But I'm even more sorry about bringing you back like this. It wasn't supposed to be this way." He leaned on the shovel, already tired from digging. "None of this is your fault. But things must be rectified." He continued digging as Quinn looked on. Mortimer hadn't realized how deep he had buried the thing.

When the blade of the shovel hit something, Mortimer stopped, got down on his knees and brushed the dirt away to reveal a small wooden container about the size of a breadbox. He lifted it out of the hole and placed it on the ground. He crawled up out of the grave.

"What's in it?" Quinn asked, excited with curiosity.

Mortimer opened the box and pulled out the teddy bear with the missing eye and ripped seams spilling stuffing.

"Orso!" Quinn cried.

"You remember," Mortimer said, surprised. He wasn't sure how much Quinn knew of his past life. His real life.

Quinn took the teddy bear from his father and hugged it.

"Of course I do. I missed him so much." He held the bear out at arm's length. "He needs a bit of fixing."

"The years haven't been kind to him," Mortimer said.

"Thank you," Quinn said, as his eyes met his father's.

Mortimer's heart sank. His hands trembled. His mouth went dry as he tried to form his next words.

"I need you to do something for me," Mortimer said. He thought about what Harold Lothrop had said to him.

"What?" Quinn asked.

"You need to send him and the others back."

"Mr. Shreckengast? And the Scamps?"

Mortimer nodded. "They don't belong here and they've done terrible things."

"But how do I do that?" Quinn asked.

"I love you, my son. Please remember that."

Mortimer took the teddy bear from Quinn and grabbed his son around the waist. He held tight as he pressed the stuffed bear against Quinn's face. The boy struggled and Mortimer squeezed his arms, keeping Orso pressed over Quinn's mouth and nose. He hoped his arms had enough strength left in them.

"I'm sorry," Mortimer said. Tears streamed down his face. "This is the only way you can take them back. Lead them away from this place to where they belong."

Quinn's struggles lessened and soon his body went limp. Mortimer laid the boy down.

"Oh god!" Mortimer cried, his chest heaving. He couldn't stop the tears. He placed his face down on the chest of the boy's unmoving body, and sensed no heartbeat. "God, help me!"

It took him several minutes to regain his composure, but the whole time the tears did not stop. He placed Quinn's body in the empty grave and laid the teddy bear in his arms. Mortimer then stepped into the grave and began shoveling the dirt back in.

When it was nearly filled, Mortimer lay down inside next to Quinn and began pulling the rest of the dirt over him till he too was buried. He felt in the dirt for his son's limp hand and grasped it.

I'll be there to help you, my son, he thought, as his breath weakened and he waited to suffocate.

14

"I thought you were a goner," Ryan said to Lance. "Where have you been?"

"Finding a way back up here from wherever that trapdoor sent me," he said. "This place is crazy."

"You said you know the way out?" Dane asked.

"Not *the* way out," Lance said. "*A* way out." He looked at Ryan. "Lothrop's note."

'It preys on your imagination.' The line was emblazoned in Ryan's mind.

"This isn't real," Lance said, raising his arms and gesturing around the room. "We're imagining it. None of this is real."

Ryan remembered what happened in the room with the frozen floor. "He's right. We just need to focus on the fact that our imagination is being fooled with."

"That's it?" Wade scoffed.

"We can do it," Ryan said.

The four of them huddled together. Ryan shut his eyes. "We do not believe," he said.

"We do not believe," the others repeated.

"None of this exists." Ryan tried to concentrate, block out all the bizarre corridors and nightmarish scenes since he entered the house. "We're not in the House of Phantasmagoria." He opened his eyes.

The walls around them began to fade. They shimmered and then vanished. The four of them stood in a large empty room, the only light coming from the lit jack-o'-lanterns sitting on the sills of the windows that looked out onto the front yard of the house.

"Wow," Dane said as he scanned the room. "Unbelievable."

"We should go now," Wade said.

"No!" Ryan knew there was lots to do. "We still have to find Shreckengast and stop him."

"I thought you said none of this is real," Dane said.

"The funhouse wasn't real, but Shreckengast is. Or rather, he's unreal."

"I'm confused," Wade said.

"He lived long ago, but he died." Ryan didn't know how to explain it to them.

"He came back," Lance added. "He used magic or something unnatural to do all these things. And he's killed people, kids. He'll do more if we don't stop him and his helpers."

"How do we do that?" Dane asked.

"For starters," Ryan said, "we smash all the pumpkins. They got here through them; maybe it'll drive them away."

"Let's go," Wade said.

The four boys scattered and ran to different windows. Dane used his baseball bat to smash a jack-o'-lantern to smithereens. The chunks splattered across the empty floor, flame spitting out. Wade grabbed one and hurled it into the nearest wall. Lance did the same. Bits of fire from the insides of the pumpkins burned like torches where they landed.

The four of them ran across the foyer to the next room, a large parlor, where more pumpkins filled the windows. While the others got busy, Ryan walked to the back of the room where a pair of giant candelabras flanked an open coffin on a cloth-covered pedestal. Near the coffin stood a tall wooden cabinet like the one the magician owned.

Ryan approached the coffin and noticed a body lay inside. As he got closer, he recognized the lifeless, pale face of Mr. Lothrop. The face appeared distorted, as if it had been squeezed in a vise. Something moved on the old man's body, and at first Ryan thought he might be still alive.

But the light of the candles revealed three small, green-scaled creatures with pointy ears sitting on the body, their heads buried in Lothrop's belly. They must have heard Ryan's footsteps, because all three of them lifted their heads and looked at him. Their sharp, jagged teeth in their crescent grins were streaked with blood.

God! Without hesitation, Ryan ran up and slammed the coffin lid down, trapping the critters inside. He heard their claws scratching. Ryan backed up. He looked at the candelabra nearest him and kicked it over. The flames ignited the cloth on the pedestal and soon the whole coffin was engulfed.

Ryan turned to see Lance, Dane, and Wade had smashed the rest of the pumpkins in the room. But flames now raced up the curtains along the windows.

"We can't stay here," Dane said when he saw the conflagration. "We need to get out."

"But there's more jack-o'-lanterns upstairs," Ryan said.

"It's too dangerous," Dane said, both brave and frightened. "This old place is going to go up like a matchbox."

A young girl screamed from above and the four of them raced to the bottom of the grand staircase. Ryan recognized the girl running down the steps in a costume out of a Dr. Seuss book.

"Lindsey!" Ryan cried as she reached the bottom. She seemed surprised and thrilled to find them. "What are you doing?"

"Something horrible got Liza, and it's after Becky!"

"Becky's here?" Ryan hadn't believed the thing that looked like Becky's father.

"She's upstairs!" Liza said. "Someone has to help her! I couldn't."

Ryan started for the stairs but Dane grabbed his arm.

"You can't go up there," Dane said. His face showed he meant business.

"I have to help her," Ryan said.

"This place is going to be an inferno any minute." Dane looked around at the flames coming from the other room.

An inferno, Ryan thought. *Like hell*. "Someone has to save her."

Dane looked at the others, and Ryan could see confusion in his eyes as he tried to decide what to do.

"Wade, you and Lance get this girl outside." He looked back at Ryan. "I'll go upstairs with you. But be quick."

"Thanks," Ryan said.

"Hurry," Lindsey said. She grabbed a hold of Lance's hand and Wade led them out the front door.

"Let's go," Dane said, and Ryan followed him up the staircase.

At the top of the stairs, Ryan didn't know which way to turn. The landing split off toward two separate halls.

"Maybe you should go that way." Ryan pointed left.

"No," Dane said. "We stick together."

"We can cover more ground."

No flames had reached this point, so Dane relented and turned left.

"Smash any pumpkins you see," Ryan shouted before departing in the opposite direction.

"A lot of good that's done," Dane yelled back.

Ryan worked his way down the hall, poking his head in every room he came to. At the end of the hall, he opened a door on the left and looked inside. A figure sat huddled on the floor, arms wrapped around her legs, head on her knees.

"Becky!" Ryan called out.

She looked up with tears in her eyes, but a smile broke across her face when she recognized him.

"Ryan!" She jumped up and looked about to leap into his arms, but she stopped and looked around the empty room. "There were books in here. And those creepy things from the library. What happened?"

"No time to explain," he said. "This place is on fire." He extended his hand and she took it. Nothing ever felt so good. He led her out of the room and began shouting Dane's name as they made their way back down the hallway toward the stairs. He spotted his brother from the other end, coming toward them.

As they were about to meet on the second-floor landing, something emerged from the shadows behind Dane.

"Look out!" Ryan cried and let go of Becky's hand.

His warning came too late. A figure in a blue shirt and jeans, and wearing a wide-brimmed black hat, lunged at Dane, grabbing him by the arms from behind. Ryan saw the thing's face, only a burlap sack with black button eyes and stitching that formed a crooked mouth. He'd seen this thing before, lashed to a pole in a cornfield at the Parker farm.

Ryan stood frozen.

Without hesitation, though, Becky ran forward and grabbed on to one of the scarecrow's arms and tried pulling it away from Dane. Ryan came to his senses and jumped in, latching on to the other arm. He felt the straw beneath the clothes, but couldn't believe the strength the creature had.

Together, the two of them pulled the scarecrow off Dane. Ryan fell backward and the thing landed on top of him. Its head turned and its face drew within inches of his own. The crooked stitching of its mouth began to stretch, the threads popping as something started to emerge from the burlap. Sharp, pointed teeth burst out of the burlap mouth toward Ryan's face.

He sensed Becky and Dane trying to pull the thing off him. The scarecrow swung one arm back and knocked the two of them to the floor. The scarecrow's black eyes bore down on his and Ryan felt he was looking into a darkness like no other. The jaws got close.

This is how I die.

Ryan struggled, trying to get his right hand between him and the creature to keep the jaws at bay. He felt something in his pants pocket and remembered what he carried. He reached in and pulled out the cigarette lighter from the amusement park ruins. He flipped the top open and pressed his thumb to the wheel.

This thing has been buried in the ground for forty years, Ryan thought. *What are the chances it'll ever work?*

Imagination.

That was the key.

He imagined it would light, concentrating as hard as possible as the scarecrow's sharp teeth inched closer to his face.

He pressed down on the wheel and a flame sputtered, sparked, and then flourished. He held it up to the scarecrow's arm that pinned him to the floor. The flame leapt onto the clothing and ignited the straw.

The scarecrow jumped up, its jaws opening in a roar as its body became engulfed in flames.

A wave of heat erupted toward Ryan, who scurried backward till he was stopped by the bottom of the steps leading to the third floor. The scarecrow waved its arms in a flurry and flames soon overwhelmed the landing. Ryan looked up and saw the walls around the staircase ablaze. A wall of fire separated him from his brother and Becky.

"Ryan!" they both screamed over the roar of the flames.

"Get out!" Ryan yelled. They still had a chance to escape. He craned his neck to look up the stairs behind him, the only way out.

"Make your way to the roof!" Dane yelled.

"Okay!" Ryan could barely see the two of them through the flames and the billowing smoke crawling across the ceiling.

"Take this just in case!" Dane tossed his baseball bat through the flames and Ryan surprised himself by catching it.

He watched as his brother and Becky disappeared down the stairs. He prayed the fire wasn't too bad below and they could get out without any trouble. He also wasn't sure what might still be waiting for them down there.

Ryan backed away from the fire and ran up the stairs to the third floor. Halfway up, he turned to look down. The scarecrow lay in a burning heap at the bottom of the stairs. A wall of flames grew up to the ceiling.

Something moved on the other side.

At first Ryan thought Dane had stayed behind and was trying to find a way to save him. But he saw the silhouette of a tall figure through the flames and could see the outline of a top hat.

Shreckengast.

The man stepped through the flames as if it were a downpour of rain. Not a lick of flame clung to him. He stopped and stared up the stairs at Ryan.

"You!" he bellowed. "You meddling little prick. You ruined everything."

No, Ryan thought. He stood frozen on the staircase as Shreckengast ascended, his dark eyes burning like embers.

"You won't escape!"

Ryan turned and ran up the rest of the stairs. He banked right at the top and fled down the corridor. His feet felt like he was running in mud – slow, unable to get traction. He burst through a door into the nearest room.

Hide.

That was all he could think to do.

The room faced the front yard. A lit jack-o'-lantern rested on the sill of an arched window. Outside he could see the branches of the maple tree. He looked around the room and spotted a closet door. He rushed over to it and hid inside. The small interior was empty and he sank down on the floor and gripped the bat, his only weapon, and waited in the dark.

Footsteps sounded from somewhere on the third floor. The hallway.

"Come out, come out, wherever you are," called Shreckengast in a singsong voice.

The footsteps sounded closer and Ryan heard them enter the room.

"Hide-and-seek is one of my favorite games," Shreckengast said. "Because I always win."

The footsteps approached the closet.

Ryan stood and clung to the baseball bat, ready to strike when the door opened.

Something wet dripped from above and landed on his cheek. He reached up and wiped it away.

Deep breaths sounded behind him and Ryan realized he wasn't alone in the closet.

His heart pounded as he turned to look.

Something large and dark filled the closet. It towered over him, a big, round head nearly touching the closet ceiling. Its mouth opened and something dripped down on Ryan's face and he realized it was saliva.

"Aha!" Shreckengast yelled as he yanked open the door.

The little light that spilled in from the flaming jack-o'-lantern in the window was enough for Ryan to see what stood over him. The thing was encased in brown fur, but there were ragged seams where its shoulder was attached, as if it were sewn on, and part of its side split open, revealing white stuffing.

But what Ryan couldn't take his eyes off was the bear's one button eye and the dangling thread where a missing eye had been.

Not a real bear, Ryan thought, but when it opened its jaw, he saw a mouthful of sharp teeth.

He bolted from the closet and bumped into Shreckengast, who grabbed him and tossed him to the floor. The bat flew from Ryan's grasp and rolled across the floor.

"Your time is up," Shreckengast said as he approached.

Ryan looked up and understood that the man had not noticed the thing that had stepped out of the closet.

The bear looked even more enormous in the room. It stood on two legs and plodded toward Shreckengast. Something about the way it looked at Shreckengast made Ryan realize it wasn't one of his creatures.

"You're the one who's out of time," Ryan said with a smile. "Take a look behind you."

At that moment, perhaps Shreckengast heard the soft steps of the bear, because the grin on his face shriveled and he turned to look. His head leaned so far back to take in the full height of the bear that his top hat fell off his head and landed on the floor.

The bear's jaws opened, wider than any real animal could possibly manage.

"Noooo!" screamed Shreckengast.

The bear wrapped the man in its arms and the huge mouth fully engulfed Shreckengast's head, muffling the man's scream.

Ryan watched as the bear began sucking in the man's entire body and looked away when he could stand to see no more.

Somehow, someway, Ryan felt Mr. Rigby was responsible for this. *Magic,* he thought. Because when he looked back, Shreckengast and the bear were no longer there.

What was there were flames, rushing in from the hallway like a runaway tide.

Ryan got up and went to the window. He picked up the jack-o'-lantern and could feel an intense heat from within. Not a candle flame, but a burning ball of fire.

He hurled the pumpkin through the window.

It left a small hole of jagged glass and broken grille. Ryan grabbed the baseball bat and smashed out the rest of the window. He threw the bat down and stepped out onto the mansard roof.

Smoke billowed up from the burning floors below. He heard sirens in the distance, so he knew rescue was on the way, but the flames told him he couldn't wait for help. He looked at the branches of the maple tree, nearly touching the house.

Ryan leapt, grabbed on to a branch, and held tight as it swayed from his sudden weight. He crawled along the limb till he reached the trunk. Fire began spitting out the window behind him. Flames ignited some of the leaves closest to the house.

Ryan began climbing down the tree as the treetop burned above him. He hurried, though he made sure of each grip. No way did he want to fall now. Not when he was so close to escape. He kept gazing up and seeing leaves on branch after branch exploding into flames.

The muscles in his arms ached, but he felt strength in them he never thought he had as he climbed hand over hand down the tree. As he looked below, he saw Lance at the base of the tree looking up.

"Hurry, Ryan!" he hollered.

Ryan looked up and the flames were rushing down the tree toward him. He dropped down another couple branches. He reached the branch where the corpse of Chief Strong hung from the noose. He glanced at the man's dead eyes for only a second before continuing his descent.

Something gripped his arm.

Chief Strong had grabbed him. The man's eyes were all white, but somehow, they saw into his own. Ryan tried to pull away, but the grip held tight. Up above, the flames spread down the tree, branch after branch. He could feel the heat. Down below, the ground was close.

"Come on!" Lance yelled as he jumped up, trying to grab Ryan's legs to help.

Ryan jerked his arm back, but couldn't pull free of the dead man's grasp.

"Stay with us," Strong said. "You'll like it here."

The flames swept down to the branch above them.

Ryan spotted the Texas Ranger star badge pinned to the chief's shirt. He reached out and pulled it free, then stuck the pin end into the dead man's left eye.

The hand let go of Ryan's arm, and at the same time he felt Lance grab on to his right foot and pull. Ryan released his hold on the branch and felt himself tumble down, landing with a thud on the ground next to Lance.

Up above, the flames swallowed the corpse of Chief Strong. Lance pulled Ryan to his feet and hurried him away as the entire tree became engulfed.

Firetrucks arrived on the street and firefighters began spilling out of the vehicles and racing to hook hoses up to a nearby hydrant. Police cars arrived, their blue lights flashing.

Ryan looked up at the burning Wickstrom House and knew the firefighters would not be saving it. He saw kids running out of the front door and rescuers rushing to help them out. At least some were making it out, Ryan thought, but who knew how many others had fallen prey to Shreckengast and his goons.

Ryan looked around. "Where's Russell?"

Lance and Ryan went over to where they had left their friend by the front gate. Ryan spotted something on the ground and picked it up.

It was Russell's cast from his broken arm, still fully intact. The message from Shinbones – "See you soon" – was no longer scratched out. Ryan's eyes met Lance's and they needed no words. Ryan clutched the cast to his chest.

Out in the street, a crowd had gathered to watch the blaze. Nervous parents lined the sidewalk while police tried to keep the crowd at bay. Dane and Wade approached Ryan, along with Becky.

"Boy, I'm glad you made it out," Dane said. "Mom and Dad would have killed me if you didn't."

"Thanks for rescuing me," Becky said and hugged Ryan. That felt even better than when he had held her hand.

"Do you want a ride home or are you going to be okay if we leave?" Dane asked. "I need to go back to Kyler's house."

"Is Elsie okay?" Ryan saw the look Dane gave him and knew he didn't need an answer. "Go. We can walk home."

"Good job tonight," Dane said. "I'm proud of you. Curtis would be too." He and Wade left.

Becky looked over toward the burning house and spotted someone emerging from it.

"Oh my god!" She cried. "It's Kirby."

Ryan saw a firefighter assisting Kirby out to the street. Becky ran over to him and threw her arms around him. They held their embrace for a while and then the two of them walked away.

Lance started to laugh. Ryan shook his head.

"At least you still have me," Lance said and put his arm around Ryan's shoulder.

"Let's go home," Ryan said, exhausted. He clutched the cast as they walked down the street.

"Want to go to your house and catch a late-night horror movie?" Lance asked.

"No," Ryan said. "I've had enough frights for one Halloween."

As they walked away from the burning Wickstrom House, neither of them noticed the white rabbit that ran out across the lawn and into the night just as the clock from Town Hall struck twelve times.

ACKNOWLEDGMENTS

October has always been my favorite month of the year, and not just because my birthday falls in it, along with my daughter, Jenna's. It is a magical month, especially in New England when the foliage blooms into brilliant colors of red, yellow, and orange, and you can feel something special in the air. That magic lasts until the final day of the month and Halloween is celebrated in all its glory.

I've been drawn to the spooky season and the things it brings for as long as I can remember. The *Dark Shadows* television show was a part of that, as well as the Universal Monsters movies, and Creature Double Feature on Saturday afternoons. The authors I grew up with, Edgar Allan Poe, Bram Stoker, H.P. Lovecraft, Ray Bradbury, Robert Bloch, Richard Matheson, Stephen King, Peter Straub, and Ramsey Campbell, left me with an appetite for the macabre I could not satisfy.

This book is a big result of that. I want to thank all the team at Flame Tree Press, especially my editor, Don D'Auria, for championing this book and fine-tuning it along with copy editor Mike Valsted and all the rest. They truly have a magic all their own.

I also want to thank my wife, Rhonda, for her never-ending love and support without which I could not accomplish all of this.

The next time you carve a pumpkin, I hope you think of this book.

ABOUT THE AUTHOR

Gregory Bastianelli is the author of the novels *Shadow Flicker*, *Snowball*, *Loonies*, and *Jokers Club*. His novella *The Lair of the Mole People* appeared in the pulp anthology *Men & Women of Mystery Vol. II.*

Publisher's Weekly described *Shadow Flicker* as a 'dark disturbing treat'. *Booklist* stated: 'This is a gripping horror story from an author who deserves a wider audience.' *Publisher's Weekly* said of *Snowball*, that 'Readers will be riveted by this genuinely scary holiday phantasmagoria.' *Rue Morgue Magazine* said: 'If you want Halloween-infused Christmas terror tale … Bastianelli has got you covered … with several feet of blood soaked snow.' Horrornews.net has referred to Bastianelli as the 'messiah of macabre.'

Gregory graduated from the University of New Hampshire where he studied writing under instructors Mark Smith, Thomas Williams and Theodore Weesner. He worked for nearly two decades at a small daily newspaper. He became enchanted with the stories of Ray Bradbury as a young child, and his love of horror grew with the likes of Richard Matheson, Robert Bloch, Stephen King and Ramsey Campbell.

Gregory lives in Dover, NH. He is a member of the Horror Writers Association and the New England Horror Writers.

FLAME TREE PRESS
FICTION WITHOUT FRONTIERS
Award-Winning Authors & Original Voices

Flame Tree Press is the trade fiction imprint of Flame Tree Publishing, focusing on excellent writing in horror and the supernatural, crime and mystery, science fiction and fantasy. Our aim is to explore beyond the boundaries of the everyday, with tales from both award-winning authors and original voices.

•

Also by Gregory Bastianelli:
Shadow Flicker
Snowball

You may also enjoy:
Fellstones by Ramsey Campbell
The Lonely Lands by Ramsey Campbell
The Wise Friend by Ramsey Campbell
Somebody's Voice by Ramsey Campbell
The Queen of the Cicadas by V. Castro
Dark Observation by Catherine Cavendish
The After-Death of Caroline Rand by Catherine Cavendish
Voodoo Heart by John Everson
Ragman by JG Faherty
Sins of the Father by JG Faherty
Boy in the Box by Marc E. Fitch
Dead Ends by Marc E. Fitch
The Toy Thief by D.W. Gillespie
One By One by D.W. Gillespie
Land of the Dead by Steven Hopstaken & Melissa Prusi
Demon Dagger by Russell James
Portal by Russell James
The Dark Game by Jonathan Janz
Dragonfly Summer by J.H. Moncrieff
Those Who Came Before by J.H. Moncrieff
Tomb of Gods by Brian Moreland
August's Eyes by Glenn Rolfe
Creature by Hunter Shea
Lord of the Feast by Tim Waggoner

•